FOLLOW

YOUR

HEART

Theresa A. Bandaccari

FOLLOW YOUR HEART

Follow Your Heart is a work of fiction. Names, characters, places and incidents are products of the author's imagination or are used fictionally. Any resemblance to actual events, locales or persons living or dead is entirely coincidence.

2012. I Street Press All Rights Reserved.
828 I Street Sacramento, California 95814

Copyright c 2012 by Theresa A. Bandaccari
Second edition

Published in United States by I Street Press in Sacramento, California.

ISBN: 978-0-9889839-9-1

Printed in the United States of America

Library of Congress Control Number: 2012946296

ABOUT THE AUTHOR

Bandaccari lives with her Mom and their two cats in California. She graduated from California State University, Sacramento in the early 1990's but prior to that she graduated from Consumes River College in 1987. It was while she attended CSUS that she published in two poetry anthology books.

However, she has been writing for a number of years; those poems were the start of her publishing career. She worked a variety of different jobs which she brings into her stories. Writing has and will be her first love along with her family, her animals and her friends.

People need to be aware that they might appear in one of her stories as a character or experience. But she writes about places she knows firsthand since she's been there. The writing stems from issues that come to her, and she builds a story on a central idea.

DEDICATION

To Teddy Foster Martin- you're my new beginning. You've been teaching me to live again, but I won't forget the past of who touched had my life. But by adopting you was a good move I ever made because you're chosen to be in my home.

To Nadine- you were chosen by my aunt and uncle years ago to be a part of our family. So I knew the true meaning of being chosen because that's why I chose to adopt Teddy Foster Martin.

PROLOGUE

Jessica had everything that most people only envied. She had a sexy, thin figure that made every man stop, stare and fantasize about her body. She had intelligence as well, behind that blonde hair and blue as sapphires eyes. People thought she had everything she could ever want or need, or that's how they saw her, anyways. But it was far from the truth because people have to go back to the beginning or to the very beginning to understand her life now.

She was known as Jessie back then, but Jessica hadn't had the beauty people saw today. She was chubbier back then, and her hair wasn't a natural blonde either but a brunette like her father's. She had her mother's eyes. But she was determined to make her life different from the one in which she was raised.

They didn't have fancy meals like lobster, scallops and caviar every night or high entertaining social events. Sambos and Lyon's were treats to attend as a family. Otherwise, her mother made macaroni and cheese, homemade pizza, beef stew, Hamburger Helper, pasta and meatballs, and other things like that.

Jessie was an active child despite her heavy body. She rode her bike, ice skated, hiked and a lot of activity like that all her life. But food was her comfort when things went wrong in her life throughout her childhood. The pounds began to shed from her body when she hit sixteen. This was her ticket out of her middle class roots, because she was discovered by a talent agent two years later.

Now twelve years later she was in New York as a high priced model who had graced every magazine known to man. But there's a deep dark secret in Jessica's life no one really knew about. But now she was faced with it along with another secret since it kept her awake the last two years at night. She would be faced with both of them now.

But Jessica knew how to hide the dark circles under her eyes and put on a happy face. She wasn't just any model, but the right model for the layout or cover for those famous magazines. She had principles, since she never appeared in Playboy or trash like that.

1

"Jessica, I need you to hold that pose when she arrives," Brandon said, as he held a camera in his hand. "She'll need to know that you won't hurt her."

"What are you talking about?" Jessica asked, as she held an oversized brown teddy bear in her arms.

"Crap," he answered, as he stepped away the shoot. "Where's my damn cell?"

Jessica touched the softness of the bear with her narrow fingers and medium sized palms. She drifted back to another time in her life.

"Hey, Chubby Bear come over here," a boy called out to Jessie.

He had the same eyes and hair as hers. Nathan was her twin brother, but he was tall and lean like their parents. Most people said he was a chip off the old block when they saw him next to their Dad, Dillon. But Jessie was chubby ever since she could remember. Stephanie, their Mom, was a beauty, and most men stopped and stared at her often.

"What?" she asked him, as she popped the last bite of peanut butter cookie in her mouth.

"See, guys, it's all fat," he answered, as he lifted her t-shirt. "Pay up or shut up. She's our porky bear in the family."

The other boys tossed their bills on the ground and ran down the street. Nathan gathered up the money and held out a couple of bucks to her.

"Here go get some ice cream on them," Nathan

said back with a smudge smile.

She took it and headed off to the nearest grocery store for her ice cream.

"Jessica," Brandon yelled at her.

She blinked her eyes and stared back at him. He wasn't alone now. A little girl stood beside him. She had blue-green eyes and long brunette hair.

"Hi, Sweetie," Jessica replied calmly to her. "What's your name, Sweetie?"

"Sabrina," Sabrina answered in a low voice. "It's a pleasure."

"We need you both embracing that bear, one on each side of it," Brandon ordered, with a rushed tone in his voice. "Go with Jessica now, kid."

Jessica held out her hand to Sabrina. Her small hand was warm and sweaty in her average sized hand. They walked back to the oversized bear. But Jessica didn't remember walking away from it. She turned back to see that Brandon had picked up his camera again.

"He's soft," Sabrina said, as she petted the bear now.

Jessica turned back to her and smiled. They positioned themselves on opposite sides of the bear when the door swung open and banged against the wall hard. Jessica and Sabrina both jumped. Brandon looked back.

"Stop the shoot," the man dressed in a polo shirt and jeans said as he marched forward.

"What the hell!" Brandon exclaimed back. "This better be important, Travis. I'd like to get this done today."

"They dropped off the wrong kid," said Travis.

"We can make it work," pointed out Jessica.

"They wanted a two year old not a five year old. She's not…"

"Spit it out, Travis," Brandon yelled at him. "I can get some great shots with her since I have the best model on the planet here."

Travis's eyes bulged and jaw dropped. He noticed Jessica now.

"Becky, get him a chair and water," said Brandon. "Oh, shut up while I work with the models.

Brandon stared at Jessica and winked now. He knew her, and knew her well. She glanced over at Sabrina. She looked frightened.

"It's okay, Sweetie," she whispered to her. "It'll be fun. I promise."

For the next three hours, Sabrina smiled, laughed and giggled right along with Jessica, as they interacted with each other and the oversized teddy bear. Brandon smiled and didn't say anything more. He knew Jessica knew the camera and him for they'd been working together for the last twelve years now.

It was Brandon's photo that landed her the cover of Cosmo. It made her career early on and boosted his. They trusted each other. Brandon set the camera down and shut off the lights.

"That's a wrap, ladies," he said with a bright and cheerful smile, "Time for salad and pizza."

Sabrina glanced at Jessica and said, "I can't go. I have to go back to the home."

Jessica glanced over at Brandon. He nodded and walked over to Travis. He was on his cell still.

"We're taking the little one out to lunch. You're

not stopping us," he stated to Travis.

"Hold on, I'm responsible for her," Travis said, as he flipped his cell closed.

"Fine then come with us. We're going now, ladies. Are you ready?" he asked, as he turned back to them.

Jessica nodded and took Sabrina's little hand into hers. Sabrina looked frightened again, but Jessica smiled so she smiled back.

"Fine, but have her back at the home on Elm after lunch," snapped Travis. "You be good, Sabrina, and mind them. Do I make myself clear, young lady?"

Sabrina nodded. Travis got up and walked out.

"Jerk," Brandon said under his breath, "Our usual place, Jessica."

Jessica nodded. They walked out of the studio. Sabrina smiled brightly now, as they stepped into the sunny day. Brandon took her other hand, and they swung her between them. They walked four blocks and entered Mama's Pizza Shack.

"My baby," a woman said with a white apron around her waist.

"Mama," he said, as he kissed her on the cheek. "This is Sabrina from the..."

"Pizza and salad, and we can't forget the milk," Mama interrupted him. "Help yourselves to the salad bar. I'll get the milk and pizza going. Sit. Good to see you, Jessica."

"Good to see you, too, Wendy," Jessica replied back.

"I'll be back."

Wendy was off to the kitchen. Brandon was at the

salad bar with plates in hand. He held out one for each of them. Sabrina took hers and gazed at all what was there.

"Can I come back for more?" Sabrina asked him.

"Yes, but we also have a combo pizza coming, too," he answered back a small smile now, "little one."

Sabrina dished out a good looking salad with Honey dressing and a couple of bread sticks on the side. She walked over to a booth and sat down. Jessica followed her lead, and so did Brandon.

"So, do you think we got some good shots?" Jessica asked him.

"Yeah, you two acted like mother and daughter then a model and….," he answered, as he took a bite of his salad. "Sabrina, you're a natural just like Jessica."

"Thank you," Sabrina said, as she ate her salad.

Wendy placed three glasses of milk on the table and a pitcher of milk. Wendy smiled at them all.

"What, Mama?" he asked her.

"You look like a family," Wendy answered back.

"Mama, please," he said back.

"You're now thirty-two and don't date. How am I going to be a grandma if you don't date? Are you a monk or you know, what?"

"Mama, please," he repeated again, as his face turned a shade of pink now.

"Pizza is probably ready," Wendy said, as she headed off to the kitchen again.

"Is she your real Mommy?" Sabrina asked in a low voice.

"Uh…unfortunately, yes," he answered, as he chewed on his salad.

"You're lucky to have her," Sabrina said, as she sipped her milk. "Jessica, do you have a Mommy?"

"Yes and a Daddy and a twin brother," she answered honestly, as she glanced down at her salad. "I haven't seen them in over twelve years."

"Why?"

"My career takes me everywhere."

"But where's home?" asked Sabrina.

"Elk Grove, California."

"Pizza," Wendy said, as she placed it on the table. "You clean your plate and have at least one slice of pizza, and I'll hunt up some vanilla ice cream with chocolate syrup on it."

Wendy stared at Sabrina now. Sabrina's eyes sparkled with delight. Wendy winked at her and left. Sabrina finished her salad and reached for a slice of pizza. Jessica watched her, as she ate. Brandon kept up with her.

"You have cheese on your chin," Sabrina pointed out to him.

"Thank you," he said, as he dabbed it with his napkin.

"Why was Wendy talking about your birthday?" asked Jessica.

"No big deal," he answered back.

"She seems to think so," she pointed out calmly.

"When?" Sabrina asked, as she downed the first slice and reached for second piece.

"When what?" he asked her.

"Your birthday, when is it?"

"Today, but it's no big deal, kid."

"Today!" exclaimed Jessica.

"Happy birthday to you, happy birthday to you; happy birthday Brandon happy birthday," Wendy sang, as she walked to the table with two ice creams with chocolate syrup and another the same but with a single candle in the middle.

Wendy placed it in front of him. He stared at her. She dished out the other two then focused on him again.

"Make a wish, son," Wendy said with a big smile.

Brandon closed his eyes then opened them, as he blew out the candle. He looked up at her. "Thank you, Mama," he said, as he cleared his throat.

Wendy kissed him on the cheek, winked at Sabrina and Jessica and was gone. Sabrina finished her second slice quickly then ate her ice cream in silence.

"Sorry about that," Brandon said finally.

Jessica got up and walked to the ladies' room. There she stared at her reflection in the mirror.

"Why didn't you know? You've know him twelve years now," she replied at the mirror.

"Jessica," Wendy said, as she entered the room.

"Wendy, I didn't know," she replied back quickly.

"I know you didn't. You and Brandon have been friends and worked together for nearly twelve years now. You helped each other's careers but know nothing about your private lives," Wendy said calmly. "It's a big deal to him, but he won't admit it. So I had to let you know in my own way against his wishes."

"Against his wishes," Jessica repeated back a little confused.

"He doesn't seem to want anyone, especially you, to know about his private life," Wendy continued calmly.

"You two are a lot alike. You don't talk about your private life either. As matter of fact, today is the first time I ever heard you mention your family, and where you are from."

"I should get Brandon a present. What are his likes and dislikes?"

"Somehow, anything you give him, he'll love because it comes from you, my dear, Jessica."

"Mama, we need to get Sabrina back to the home. You know how Travis is," Brandon said, as he poked his head inside.

Sabrina walked in and headed for the stall next to the sink but didn't say anything. Wendy looked back at him.

"I didn't do anything to her. Honest, Mama," he said in his own defense.

"She doesn't want to go back, Brandon," Wendy pointed out to him. "This is probably the closest she has ever had been to having a real family. You should..."

"Mama, we really need to go," he interrupted her. "I'll wait for you two by the front door."

Brandon ducked out. Wendy stared at Jessica when the whoosh of water was heard. Sabrina emerged and approached the sink to wash and dry her hands in silence.

So Jessica and Wendy walked out ahead of her.

"I'm ready," Sabrina said to Jessica. "Thank you for everything, uh..."

"Call me, Grandma," Wendy said, as she knelt down to her level. "You're always welcome here, Sabrina."

"Thank you, Grandma," Sabrina said politely.

Wendy hugged her and carried her to the front door, as Jessica walked beside them. Brandon took her in his arms when Wendy hugged Jessica. They walked back outside while Sabrina rested her head on Brandon's shoulder, as they walked in silence. Jessica looked into the display windows as they walked.

"Somehow, anything you give him, he'll love because it comes from you," Wendy's voice echoed in her head now.

"That," Sabrina said, as she pointed in the window. "But..."

"I'll get it, and it's from us both," Jessica replied with a big smile.

She marched in and pointed to the family of bears in the window. The merchant nodded, as Jessica placed her credit card on the counter. Sabrina had three crystal bear key chains to add to the bill. Jessica smiled and nodded. Together they emerged with big smiles, as they held out the bag to Brandon.

"What's this, ladies?" he asked politely.

"Happy birthday," Sabrina answered back.

"Sorry we didn't wrap it," Jessica added, "A key chain for each of us to remember our day together."

Brandon opened the bag and took out keychain for each of them and smiled. He added his to his chain that was attached to his belt. Jessica noticed it had the Greek flag, and what looked like the islands on it. Brandon reached in the bag again to find the family of bears embracing each other.

"Thank you," he said politely, as he deposited them back into the bag.

Sabrina smiled warmly, as she gazed up at him. He bent down to hug her then he hugged Jessica. She took it along with Old Spice scent on his face. She gazed deeply into his eyes for the first time ever.

"Umm...you're welcome," she replied back in some awkwardly, as she stood that close to him. "We should head out now."

"I suppose," Brandon said, as his voice dropped.

They walked up the street in silence again. They reached a house that had a sign in front which read: Bell's Home for Children. They walked up the steps and were greeted by a woman dressed in a cotton plaid dress.

"It's about time, Sabrina," she barked at her now.

"I'm sorry. We had lunch and ...." Brandon stumbled to explain.

"Inside, girl, upstairs to your room," the woman barked at Sabrina again. "She knows the rules."

Sabrina hugged Jessica briefly then Brandon. She walked slowly by the woman when the woman slapped her butt. Sabrina looked back sadly now.

"Could we come see her again?" asked Jessica.

"Depends on," the woman answered back sharply.

"On what?" Brandon asked her.

"If she gets a new home or not, I'll be glad when she's gone from here."

"Why?" asked Jessica.

"This is an orphanage for last chance kids like her, dearie," the woman snapped back. "I don't have time to chat."

The woman walked back inside. Jessica stared at the closed door before Brandon led her back to the sidewalk. They looked upstairs to a window. Sabrina stood there with her hand holding up the key chain.

"That woman doesn't care about Sabrina," Jessica

replied painfully.

"Maybe not but maybe things will change with their new campaign. Sabrina will get adopted by a loving couple. She deserves that much at least," Brandon said sadly.

"You knew she was an orphan," Jessica stated, a little surprised by it.

"Why do you think I got so upset in my studio earlier? I thought you knew. That's why I agreed to do it. Didn't Beverly tell you?"

"That's why you were so upset," she answered back.

Brandon nodded. Jessica felt her cell vibrate in her pocket.

"Hello," she replied back sharply now.

"Oh, good I caught you, Jessica," said Beverly. "I have a shoot in Paris for Vanity Fair. They're thinking of branching out to travel and want to promote a new fragrance as well, so they want you to help promote them both."

"Aren't you going to ask about the Telly campaign?" she asked back.

"Oh, yeah, it probably went super since you're involved."

"Don't you care about what the campaign was for?"

"Easy, girlie, they paid us both handsomely for your time..."

"I spent the last three plus hours with a delightful five- year-old girl named Sabrina. She's an orphan. She's..."

Brandon grabbed the cell and flipped it closed.

Jessica stared at him now. "It won't help getting angry over it now. I've been there and done it for us both earlier. Now we can hope Sabrina will find a place to call home. She won't be forced out..." he said as he stopped himself. "Go do your next assignment, and I'll do everything I can to make sure Sabrina gets a home."

"But," she started to protest.

"I know she's a sweet and loving little girl, and yes, special to us both. But trust I'll do my best for her, Jessica."

She nodded, so he handed her cell back. They walked back to his studio in silence. Then she only waved back to him goodbye, as she left his studio where her small purse was. She headed out and didn't even really look into his face again.

2

Jessica sat on the plane near the first- class window. She left Brandon's studio without a word and regretted it now. She gazed out the colorful skyline and puffy white clouds now. Beverly booked a shoot in Paris for possible Travel World magazine, proposed with commercial and print ad, along with a perfume called Essence.

Essence was a sweet scent that filled her nostrils, as she got a twenty- ounce sample. She left it on the bathroom sink. She didn't bring it, or anything else that could possible spill or break. She dabbed a little of the fragrance behind her right ear and on her right wrist.

Her light tanned face was free of makeup. She had natural beauty without the makeup, but she was, and is a model, so makeup was part of the business. She thought of Sabrina's smile and got misty.

"Ms, can I get you anything?" the stewardess asked her.

"A bottle water, please," she answered, back politely.

"Of course, Ms," the stewardess said, as she offered her a bottle and a glass.

"Thank you," she replied softly.

"Hey, aren't you?" a heavy set man asked, as he pointed at Jessica.

Jessica smelled the whiskey on his breath. She only nodded and looked back out the window.

"Come on, buddy. She wants to be alone," the

stewardess said calmly.

"Wow!" Nathan exclaimed, as Jessie stepped out of her bedroom. "You look..."

"Different," she replied, with a big smile.

"Like a model," Nathan said, as he found his voice again. "Ryan is going to flip when he comes to pick you up for the prom."

"Do you think so?" she asked, with a shy smile now.

"I know so. I know he asked you because of all the other girls..."

"Stop right there, Nathan," Stephanie interrupted him. "Do you have a corsage and tux ready?"

"In my room, Mom," Nathan answered back, as he still stared at Jessie.

"Go change, Nathan. Ryan will be here soon. I have to finish your twin. Excuse us."

"She's fine the way she is, Mom. Leave it all like that," Nathan said, as he rushed into his room.

"Attention, passengers. Please pull your seats upright and fasten your seatbelts. We'll be arriving at Paris, France International Airport in about twenty minutes," the stewardess said over the speaker system.

Jessica closed her eyes and held onto the arms of her chair. She didn't have anyone beside her. Thank goodness. She didn't mind flying in the air, but the landing had been a different story. It goes back to years ago that she didn't want to go into now.

"We've landed, ladies and gentleman. Thank you for flying our airlines. Have a great time in Paris," the stewardess said over PA the system.

Jessica opened her eyes and grabbed her carry-on bag that was above her. She traveled lighter than most of the models. But she didn't want to be in the terminal too long to have a run-in with a man, like the one that happened earlier. A man stood in a dark suit and hat with a sign stated "J. Hudson" in bold letters. She walked up to him in her dark sunglasses now. She titled them down briefly.

"Hi, Stanley," she whispered to him.

"Hi, Jessica," Stanley said, as he gave a brief smile. "How was your flight?"

"Only one drunk, otherwise Ok," she answered, as they headed for his limo. "How are Bridget and the kids?"

"Great," he answered, as he held out his wallet.

She glanced at the recent photo of his family. She smiled back at him.

"You're a lucky man, Stanley."

"Well, I can't take full credit for Bridget and me hooking up. You had a hand in it. Remember?"

"I guess so, she wasn't cut out to be model and fell in love with Paris. But you know Paris since you have lived here all your life," she explained, as she slipped in the backseat.

"But I was born the USA," he said, as he closed her door.

He slipped behind the wheel and brought down the divider.

"I didn't know that. Where were you born?"

"A small town in Northern California, but you probably haven't seen or heard about it," he answered, as they headed for her hotel.

"Try me," she replied with interest.

"A hick town called Fiddletown," he said, with a small chuckle.

"What's so funny?"

"Mom was passing through when she went into labor. She said there was a big fiddle on one of the buildings."

"What did your Mom do for a living?"

"A modern miner and photographer, she can't believe she's a grandma in her early sixties. She was fifty-four when Amber was born. Then Amy and Duffy were born two years later. But she's going to be a grandma again."

"I'm jealous. I hope I'll get to see them before I leave here. When's the baby due?"

"We had an ultra-sound. It's a boy. Bridget already picked out his name David Jeffery. He's due any day now."

"Wow!"

"Here you go, Jessica. Beverly said your schedule is in the penthouse. I'll be back in an hour."

She nodded and slipped out of the limo. Jessica headed up to the front desk. The clerk looked up. She tilted her sunglasses down again.

"Hi, Mel," she whispered to him.

"Bear," Mel said back.

"I wish you wouldn't call me that. I need to freshen up before Stanley comes back in an hour. Let me know when he arrives."

"Of course, you have a message," he said, as he placed the pass key and paper on the counter in front of her. "It's from Brandon. He sounded tired and sad."

"Thank you."

She entered the private elevator and turned on her cell. It dinged. She had scrolled down and pressed her voice mail.

"Jessica, I'm sorry," Brandon said in her ear. "Please call me back. I'll miss you while you're away."

She stepped out of the elevator and walked up to the penthouse door. Beverly made sure she had the very best accommodations when she had a shoot. Jessica glanced at the paper.

"Jessica, I'm very sorry. B," she read out to herself.

She went to the bathroom to freshen up when a buzz on her hotel room phone got her attention. She picked it up.

"I have a call from the United States. Will you accept the call?" asked the operator.

"No," she answered back, as she placed the receiver down gently. It buzzed again. She picked it up again. "No if it's from the USA..." She started to reply back quickly.

"It's me, Mel, at the front desk. Stanley is down here," he interrupted her.

"Sorry. I'll be right down, and thank you."

She grabbed her small purse, pass key and cell as she headed out of the room. Her sunglasses were on the top of her head, so she slipped them on; as she walked back into the elevator to the main floor. Jessica spotted Stanley outside. He paced the ground, and this was odd for him. She walked up to him.

"Easy, Stanley," she replied calmly. "Just drop me off at the shoot, and go be Bridget."

Stanley stared at her and didn't smile.

"What's wrong?" she asked with concern now.

"She went into labor while I was at the airport. He had the cord around his little neck," he explained, as he moistened his lips now.

"Oh my!" she exclaimed back in shock.

"The doctor noticed it and reached in to remove it from his little neck. He's a special...."

"Get us to the hospital now."

"But..."

"I'll take call Beverly and tell her to postpone it a day or two. Let's move, Stanley."

"Are you..."

"Yes. Now let's get going."

Stanley stumbled, as she headed upfront with him. He closed the back door and headed for the front seat behind the wheel. Jessica scanned her cell then pressed Beverly.

"Hi, girlie," said Beverly.

"Hi, I have to postpone my shoot a couple of days," she replied back quickly.

"What's wrong, girlie?"

"An emergency came up. I need to be there for Bridget and Stanley," she answered back.

"Okay. But keep me informed. You're lucky he wants you and only you, doll. I don't know about the photographer, though. Well, don't worry about it. Give them my best, and don't worry about it, girlie. I got you covered."

"Thank you. Bye," Jessica replied, as she flipped her cell closed and smiled back at Stanley.

She noticed his knuckles were white as snow, as his hands clenched the wheel. He weaved in and out of traffic like a mad man. But he knew the road better than she did. She trusted his driving skills.

"All set, Stanley," she replied calmly. "Let's get to the hospital in one piece, my friend. Please."

Stanley pulled into the hospital and parked the limo. He got out, and Jessica rushed to catch up with him. He headed for elevator, and she barely got in when he pressed the button. Then the doors opened again, and he bolted down a hallway to a room next to the nursery.

He stopped and stared at small baby in a bubble. Jessica leaned on his arm now. Stanley took her hand and squeezed it hard. She felt his strength in hers now, as she felt moisture in the corners of her eyes behind her sunglasses.

"Are you family?" asked the nurse.

"He's the little guy's Dad," answered Jessica.

"This is his Aunt Jessica," Stanley said, as he found his voice again.

"Can we see and touch him?" Jessica asked the nurse.

"Yes. Please come in and know this is only precaution after..."

"We know," interrupted Jessica. "Let's go see your son, David Jeffery."

He nodded. She nudged him closer to his son. David looked red all over his body except where his diaper was, and pads and wires on his tiny chest. She slipped her free hand into one of the holes to go into a glove to touch him. He wiggled his hands and legs at her touch. Stanley stepped back.

"He has her fine light brown hair," she commented back to Stanley.

"And my hazel eyes," Stanley said, as he moved closer now.

"It's important to touch and talk to him. He has to know you, Bridget and his family, are here for him," Jessica informed him.

"Hi, Davey, I'm your Daddy. I love you, little guy," Stanley said, as he allowed the tears stream down his tanned face. "You have a Mom, a big brother and two sisters who love you so much, Davey. I can't forget your Grandma Helen, too. Your Auntie Jessica and godmother is here with me, little guy."

"What!" Jessica exclaimed surprised.

"We want you to be his godmother. We planned to ask you together, but he's a couple of weeks early. We thought we had time," Stanley said, as he turned to her with tears in his eyes. "We can't lose him, Jessica."

"Let's leave his care in God's hands," she replied calmly.

He nodded. The sound of someone clearing his or her throat was behind them now. They looked to the doorway to Brandon and Beverly standing there. Their faces were pale and with dark circles under their eyes. Beverly rushed up to hug Stanley as Jessica stepped back.

"How is he? How is Bridget?" Beverly asked him quickly.

"Jessica says we need to touch and talk to him," Stanley answered back. "I haven't seen her yet. We came straight here to be with him. I should..."

"One thing at a time, handsome, she's probably resting now," Beverly interrupted him. "Can he come in?"

Stanley nodded, so Brandon walked up closer. He stepped to the other side of Davey's bubble, his eyes fixed on him. Jessica walked up to him.

"Hi, I'm sorry, too," she whispered to him. "How did you know..."

"Helen is Beverly's adopted sister, and you know their other sister Wendy or Mama," Brandon interrupted her. "I flew my plane here when Beverly said you were in Paris. I was gassing up and setting my flight plan when she showed up. Mama wanted to come, but I was already in the air by then. You hung up while I was in the air. You didn't give me a chance to explain."

"Wendy will be here for you, Bridget, Helen and the kids after she gets someone to look after the business," Beverly said calmly to Stanley. "Jessica, the photographer bailed, so Brandon will do it. The client is okay with it and understood about a family matter coming up. He's nice to give you five days. You're lucky that he only wants you to do it."

She glanced over at Beverly and smiled, then nodded. Brandon reached in the bubble to touch Davey. He wiggled at Brandon's touch, too.

"Hi, little guy," Brandon said to him. "I'm Uncle or Cousin, Brandon. I get those things like that mixed up, little man. You'll discover that about me in the years to come."

"I didn't know you had a jet," she replied to him calmly. "I'm beginning to think there's a lot more I don't know about you."

"Probably."

"Beverly, you came," a woman cried out.

Helen stood in the doorway, and then rushed to Beverly and Stanley. Helen embraced them both, and then looked down at Davey. Helen had long, strawberry blonde hair and chocolate brown eyes to match her slender figure.

Jessica tried to understand that they were sisters, as she shook her head slightly.

"Hard to believe, right?" whispered Brandon.

She nodded, as she reached in to touch Davey, too. He wiggled for her again, too. She smiled at him.

"Hi, Davey again," she replied softly. "Your Daddy says I'm your godmother, so you have to grow up for me to spoil you so much."

"Babe," Bridget said in a weak voice from a wheelchair.

Stanley rushed to her and hugged her. Bridget was fair skinned and petite except the baby fat she developed in recent years due to giving birth to now four children. She was only two years younger than Jessica and was only five feet six inches compared to Stanley's six foot two stature. But they truly loved each other. They seemed to have a perfect life.

"Jess, you're here," Bridget said to her.

Jessica nodded but stayed at Davey's side. Brandon stayed with them, too. Stanley and Bridget moved in closer. She did look tired.

"It all came so fast then..." Bridget stumbled to explain.

"We all know. He'll make it. He's a fighter," Brandon said with a warm and friendly smile. "Mama will be out on the first flight available."

"Edna called my service," Stanley explained to Bridget.

"Edna told me that you were rushed to the hospital. She'll stay with the others until you get home. No additional charge," Brandon said, as he looked over at her. "She loves those kids, too."

"Brandon, come over here," Helen said to him.

He walked closer to her, and she hugged him. Then he leaned down to hug Bridget. Bridget embraced him back.

"Jess," Bridget said calmly. "We want you and Brandon to be David Jeffery's godparents. Will you?"

"Yes," she answered quickly. "But Stanley already mentioned it earlier."

"I was upset, baby," confessed Stanley.

"That's okay, babe. What about you, Brandon?" Bridget asked him with a smile.

"Yes," Brandon said with a return smile. "Jessica, can we talk privately?"

"Not business," stated Beverly.

"No, personal," he answered back, "please."

"Ooh...must be important to have please attached to it," said Beverly.

"Leave them alone," Helen snapped back. "Go, you two, and ignore her."

Jessica stepped towards the door, and Brandon joined her there. They entered the hallway together.

"You didn't know Helen and Beverly were related to me. I get it. You don't know a lot about my personal life because I've kept it a secret, from not just you, but all the models I work with," Brandon explained quickly.

"But you own your own plane," Jessica replied thoughtfully. "So Wendy is your Mom but also Helen and Beverly's sister?"

"Yes. Beverly was adopted and ….never mind. Wendy is Mama," he answered back.

"I thought you only had Wendy in your life these past nearly twelve years we've been friends. Why not tell me that you all were related?"

"I didn't want the models to know who I was, and who I was related to. I would like to think that I learned from that mistake years ago before you came into my life. We were twenty and eighteen back then and just starting our careers," he explained calmly.

"You said a mistake in your past. What was that?" Jessica asked boldly.

"I was sixteen and fell hard for a model. I told her that I was related to Beverly. Well, she or Rebecca became difficult for Aunt Beverly. She said she was involved with me and deserved better assignments," he answered, as he held out the door for her.

"What happened?" she asked with *interest now*.

"Beverly wouldn't get her better assignments because she wasn't that good. But Rebecca tried to get me to have sex with her. I didn't go that far, Jessica. I was only sixteen, and she was ten years older than I. Understand that fact I was still a virgin then, and she knew it. But Rebecca told Beverly that we had done the deed. It dissolved their contract right then and there," he answered sadly. "Then a tragedy followed after that, and I decided I wouldn't go there again with any model. It changed me, Jessica. And for the last twelve years plus, I wanted…"

"You said a tragedy. What happened?"

He sighed then carried on. "Rebecca stormed out of Beverly's office and found the first photographer she could find. Yes they had passionate sex on and off for the next couple days," he explained, as he stared off in the distance now. "It wouldn't have matter to Beverly if it was anyone but Jim. She had a huge crush on him, but she never crossed the line. During Rebecca's sex acts which she dialed and let Beverly hear over her cell phone as revenge on me and Beverly. Rebecca had become pregnant. Jim did the honorable thing and proposed to her. She said no, as they fought about the abortion that she planned to have the next day. She fell to her death on the roof two buildings from here."

"What happened to Jim?"

"No one knows, not even Auntie Beverly he had buried Rebecca and dropped out of sight. So you know why I don't celebrate my birthday," he answered sadly and sharply. "If that..."

"She died on your birthday!" Jessica exclaimed, in shock now.

He nodded. They stood there in silence for awhile before he spoke again.

"We better get inside," he said finally. "Please don't tell the other models."

"It stays with us. I promise. Sabrina would love Paris."

"You two seem so natural together," he said, as he held open the door for her again.

"We did. Didn't we?" she asked back with a big smile. "I've never met an orphan before."

"Uh…yeah, you did, two as matter of fact."

"There's my boy," Wendy said, as she met them in the hallway.

"Sorry Mama. I should have turned around the…"

"Hush. You found her and talked. That's all that matters now," Wendy interrupted him. "Now you know Helen and Beverly are my sisters." She stared at Jessica now. "My Mom and Helen's adopted Beverly at six weeks old. She thought it would keep us all together, but Dad left us anyway, for the other woman."

"I'm sorry."

"No big deal. We got Beverly, and it has been a wild ride for all of us."

"She knows Stanley was born in Fiddletown. She's from Elk Grove, Mama," said Brandon.

"I know Beverly told me years ago when she signed her, I believe," Wendy said with a bright smile. "You were born there, too, you know. Now let's go be with the family."

They all took turns being with David or Davey. Bridget and Stanley stayed the longest before she returned to her room. Jessica realized she was tired, too, so Brandon escorted her back to the hotel. They didn't talk anymore. But when Jessica was alone, she dreamed of Sabrina's smile, and it made her smile, too. She fell into a deep sleep now.

3

J essica gazed at her reflection in the mirror and thought of Sabrina. Then she thought of Beverly, and how she was adopted.

"It's possible to have a happy-ever after ending that is not just in Disney movies," she replied back to herself.

A knock on her door snapped her back to what she was doing. She tied the cloth robe around her waist and approached the door.

"Good morning, Jessica," Brandon said, as he held out bottled water and a brown bag to her, "Your favorites, my lady. Davey has improved a lot since yesterday."

He walked into the penthouse. He had his camera in his right shoulder and approached the balcony. "He's a fighter all right. Stanley told you that he was born in Fiddletown; so was I. I started to tell you yesterday," Brandon said as he turned back to her. "What?"

"Your Mom said that already. But you seem different today, and thank you," she answered, as she held up the water and brown bag.

"They liked the same ones I did of you and Sabrina. You knew you two hugging the bear, then you leaning on her, as she lay on top of the bear. She's a natural just like you are. Do you feel up to some test shots of this new adventure and perfume to boot?"

"You sound charged by it all," she answered back.

"It's a first ever launching a fragrance and a new magazine at the same time. Do you realize how this will affect our careers? It will be bigger than it ever has been before," he said with excitement in his voice now.

Another knock on the door, Brandon rushed to open it. Two women entered the room with a rack of clothes covered in plastic. He ushered them in and closed the door immediately after them.

"Casual look, ladies and very little makeup, I want her natural look," he said politely to them.

They nodded. He looked back at Jessica now.

"I want to see how you react to Paris as a first time tourist. Do you think you can manage a few test shots of that?"

She nodded. One of the ladies held out some clothes to her, so Jessica headed into the bathroom. She got the clothes on when a knock on the door startled her. Becky appeared at the open door now.

"Sorry. Brandon wants to know..." Becky started to say.

"I'm ready except for the perfume. I didn't pack any."

"I got it. You always carry as little as possible. You probably only have the one outfit that you came over in that's your own. But I stopped by your place to pick up some of your everyday clothes. You have wonderful taste for color and fashion," Becky said with a big smile. "Your neighbor let me in."

"Ladies, I want to capture some of this early morning light," Brandon called out.

"Coming," Jessica called out back. "Thank you, Becky."

Jessica stepped back into the penthouse. Brandon

stood on the balcony with his camera and light meter. She joined him there. He smiled at her.

"Great. Stand here and look at the view," he said quickly.

She stepped into where he stood. She glanced at the view then flashed her best smile at Brandon. She tossed her head back and let her hair fall naturally. She barely heard his shutter, but she knew he was close by. Jessica could smell his Old Spice aftershave. She leaned on the railing with one hand. She gave him a light laugh.

"That's my girl. Go with the mood. Feel the experience of seeing France for the first time," said Brandon. "Make people, especially lovers, want to come to the heart of romance."

Jessica laughed out loud. The sun streamed across her face and body now. She felt the warmth, as she smiled for him.

"Don't be so stiff," he said, as he lowered his camera for the third time in the last ten minutes or so. "Loosen up, Jessica. Relax your muscles. Think of something happy or romantic. Let yourself go."

"I don't..." she started to explain.

"I know you're nervous. I get that, so am I. But we can do it, Jessica. Now set this camera on fire with your natural beauty. A butterfly had emerged from the cocoon and taken its first solo flight, and its first taste of freedom," he said back confidently.

She flashed him a big smile. Jessica began to loosen up as she thought of Ryan. How he dropped his jaw and her corsage as she emerged from the stairs of her parents' home. Nathan nudged him to pick up her corsage.

"You're beautiful," Ryan whispered to her.

"Let's go downstairs, Jessica," Brandon said, as he brought her back to the present.

She nodded, and Becky was ahead of them. Becky was in the elevator and headed down with the equipment. Brandon stood before her now alone.

"You seemed a million miles away back there," he said in a calm voice.

"I was remembering our first photo shoot," she replied confidently. "It launched our careers."

"You set the camera on fire with those killer smiles of yours, and we've done a lot of shoots since then," he said back, as the doors opened, "After you, my lady."

"Thank you," she replied, as she stepped inside.

"I often wondered what made you smile like that. You seemed frightened at first, then I saw a confident woman emerge instantly, and I knew I had captured it all on film. I was lucky to be there, but I never asked."

"So you're asking now, almost twelve years later. I was remembering Ryan," she replied with a small smile.

"Who's Ryan?" he asked with interest, as he pressed the down button.

"Nathan's best friend and my prom date. He was my..."

"You probably had a lot of dates growing up," he interrupted her.

"Not really. Ryan was my first," she replied, as they stepped out of the elevator.

He stepped back and looked at her with disbelief.

"It's true. I didn't always look like this, Brandon. Believe it or not, I used to be fat."

"Not you. You look drop-dead gorgeous."

"The prom was my coming out party, as Mom called it. I think Dad was stunned, too, but didn't say anything for the next year or so."

"I'm sorry, Jessica," Brandon said, as they stepped out on the busy streets of Paris.

"About what?" she asked back.

They had minivan waiting for them. She slipped into the front seat while Brandon got behind the wheel. He slipped it into gear and focused on the road ahead.

"Later," he said, as they pulled away from the hotel a good distance behind. "Becky, did you bring extra memory cards?"

"Yes, and your other entire lens and other equipment you usually use," Becky answered from the backseat. "I had them all upstairs if you needed them. Do you want to use the diffuser at the Tower?"

"Yeah, and the 105 with the twenty-eight," he answered back quickly. "I have the fifty on it now."

"I'll change it," Becky said, as she reached for his camera between him and Jessica. "Hi again, Jessica, I can't..."

"Here," she replied, as she handed it back to her. It was still warm from his handling it. "You're a great assistant you know."

"Thank you," Becky said with a small amount of pink on her cheeks, as she took his camera. "It's my job to make the photographer's job easier."

Becky dove into a metal case next to her. She removed the current lens with another, and then she wiped it all down after she examined the back of the camera. Jessica watched her with interest now. Then Becky closed the metal case and placed the camera into a black bag at her feet.

"Yes?" Becky asked, as she looked at Jessica.

"Nothing, it's interesting to watch you work. I never paid much attention before."

"I don't know what I would do without her," commented Brandon. "We're here, Jessica. I'll need you to relax and act like you're a tourist in this most romantic city for the first time. Make people want to travel to the most romantic place in the world."

She nodded and headed for the Tower. Brandon had his camera again. He walked briskly beside, then ahead of her. She flashed him her awarding winning smiles that they both knew so well. She felt alive as the sun continued to warm her now. She stopped and placed her hands on her hips and tilted her head back, then flashed a big warm and friendly smile to Brandon.

"I like that," he said, with excitement in his voice now. "Yes. Yes. That's what I'm talking about, Jessica."

He felt alive, too. Jessica could hear it in his voice. They reached the Tower, and tourists were everywhere.

"That's Jessica!" exclaimed a woman. The woman grabbed a little blonde haired girl by the wrist. "You have to get her autograph, Honey."

"Mommy," the girl cried out.

Jessica stopped and so did Brandon. He glanced at them then at Jessica. He shrugged his shoulders back at her. She smiled at him. They approached her with excitement.

"You are Jessica, aren't you?" asked the woman.

"Yes. I'm here on assignment," she answered politely back. "Do you want my autograph, Sweetie?"

The little girl nodded and held out a piece of paper her mother had given her. Jessica took it and knelt down on one knee.

"To," Jessica replied in hesitation and stared at the little girl.

"Wilma," the little girl said back.

"To Wilma, love, Jessica," she replied, as she signed the paper.

"Thank you," Wilma said politely back.

Jessica grinned and replied back, "You're welcome, Sweetie."

"Jess…" Brandon started to say, as his cell rang loud bells in his pocket.

He stepped back and answered it. She glanced over at him, as Becky took his camera. He looked pale as a ghost now.

"Excuse me, Sweetie," she replied politely, as she headed in his direction.

She walked up closer to him. He didn't notice her and Becky at his side. He closed his cell when he noticed them finally. He glanced at Becky, and she held his camera firmly in her hands now.

"It's a wrap today," Becky said, as she slipped his camera into the bag on her shoulder now. "Are you leaving?"

He nodded and walked away. Jessica bolted after him as he slowly walked by the minivan. She grabbed his arm.

"Talk to me," she demanded, as she turned him to

face her now. "Please."

"I have to be with Davey. Mama said a doctor has flown in to see him. He has an assistant with him. You might know them both," Brandon said in a low voice.

"I don't understand," Jessica replied, a little confused.

"Didn't you say your first boyfriend was named Ryan, and your twin brother was Nathan?" he asked her, with pain in his voice.

"Yes. But what...." she stared to ask then it hit her. "They're the doctors."

"They're checking Davey's heart. It's not as strong as they want it to be," he explained painfully. "Are they good?
I want Davey to have the best."

"I haven't been in touch with Nathan in twelve years. I've had my career to deal with. Remember what I told Sabrina."

"Taxi," he called out. "Becky needs the van. Do you want to come with me?"

She nodded, as the taxi stopped near them. He opened the back door, and she slid in. He followed her. He gave the driver instructions, as they drove off.

"Nathan's a doctor," she mumbled to herself now.

"So you didn't know that he had gone into medicine," Brandon said calmly.

"No idea at all."

They sat in silence, as she thought of Sabrina. Her blue-green eyes sparkled with delight. Her small hand rested comfortably into Jessica's. It warmed her heart, as she thought of the child.

"Jessica, let's go," Brandon said from the outside of the taxi.

"Sorry."

They headed up to Davey's room. Beverly, Wendy and Stanley stood while Bridget sat in a wheelchair. Two men dressed in white lab coats had their backs to them. They stood the same height and build. Jessica held back, as Brandon approached them all.

"Brandon, did Jessica come, too?" asked Beverly.

A sandy-brown haired man with blue eyes stared back at her. Jessica stopped in her tracks. She could hear her heart in her ears now.

"Uh...Chubby Bear," the man said to her without thinking.

"No...Nathan," she managed to reply sharply finally. "It's been a long time."

"You know each other," Wendy said with a small smile.

"I'm her twin brother. Do you remember Ryan?" Nathan asked with a warm and friendly smile back.

"Jess, it's been years. I've seen you in magazines," Ryan said, as he hugged her. "I've followed your career while we were in med school."

"Why medicine?" she asked, as she stared at Nathan over Ryan's shoulder. "Mom and Dad couldn't afford it. Let alone any college. It's why..."

"Scholarships and grants, then I lived on Mac and cheese, hamburger helper and hot dogs just like we did at home, Chubby Bear."

"Uh...don't call me that," she snapped back.

"Yeah, Nat, she hasn't looked like that since she

was sixteen, almost seventeen before our prom," Ryan said, as he gazed at her body next to his. "I was the luckiest guy there. I had the most beautiful girl there."

"Stop and tell us what's wrong with Davey?" she asked him.

"As I explained to them, the cord cut his airway briefly and caused his heart to skip a beat or two before it was removed. It might strengthen in the days ahead, but we don't know for sure," Ryan explained calmly. "You look great. Do you think we can have a nice dinner somewhere?"

"I'm on assignment. Brandon and I have a deadline to meet despite Davey's problem," she answered back.

"But you do eat, Jessie."

"It's Jessica, not Jessie or Chubby Bear. Do you two get that?"

They both nodded.

"So, we'll be watching David for a few days to see if any and all developments arise," Ryan explained, as he turned back to everyone, "Any questions?"

"Yes," Brandon answered, as he stared at Nathan then Ryan. "What's the worst possibility?"

"He could stop breathing," Ryan answered back.

"Then die because we never worked on a baby this young before. Surgery is out of the question," added Nathan.

"No, not my baby," Bridget cried out with tears streaming down her face now. "Stan..."

"Yes. Let's go see our son," Stanley said, as he wheeled her into his room.

Beverly followed them in. Wendy stared at Brandon then at Nathan, Ryan and Jessica before her walking in.

"You wanted the truth," said Ryan.

"I know. Please excuse me, gentleman. Jessica, are you coming?"

"In a few minutes."

He nodded and followed his Mom. Nathan walked up to Jessica now.

"Mom and Dad wondered how you were doing through the years. It has been nearly twelve years," Nathan pointed out to her.

"You're no better," Ryan stated back. "You were in your second year before you told them about medical school."

"Shut up, Ryan!" Nathan exclaimed back in anger.

"Do you want to tell her why you went into medicine?"

"I said shut up, Ryan," Nathan snapped back again. "Do you want..."

"Fine, I'll check on our patient," Ryan said, as he headed for the room. "It's good to see you again, Jessica. I've never forgotten you after all these years. The guys in med school would have flipped if they knew what I know."

She nodded. Now she stood face to face with her twin brother. They stood together at the airport nearly twelve years ago when she had medium sized suitcase filled with two pantsuits and three dresses along ladies' personal things, including perfume. She was off to New York to be a fashion model. Beverly stood at the gate for her, she remembered briefly.

"I didn't want you to go, Sis," Nathan whispered in calm voice now. "But you had to see if you had what it took to make it back then, and you did it all on your own. Did you ever look back and think of the folks or even me?"

"Yes, more than once. You all haven't been far from my thoughts. More so now since I met Sabrina," she whispered back honestly.

"Who's Sabrina?" Nathan asked with interest now.

"An orphan I worked with a couple days ago," she explained calmly. "I've been thinking of her. She asked if I had a family. I said yes, but I never told anyone I worked with, up until that day."

"She changed you, Jessie."

"It was more like awakening something that was always there. Family and a deep....Brandon learned about you, Mom and Dad and yes, even Ryan that day.

"Jessie, I feel a change in you. You're holding back from me. I'm your twin. Remember."

"Yes, I know. Why did you go into medicine?"

"Not now, Jessie. Tell me about your life these last almost twelve years. I seemed to have lost that connection we once had as kids. Now I'm with you again, and I think I feel it again. But I also feel a wall which wasn't there before."

"Tend to Davey. He's my godchild. Maybe we will talk again, but not now."

"But Jess..."

She placed her finger to his lips, and then she turned to walk down the hallway alone. She felt his gaze on her back. She wiped away the tears on her cheeks now.

"Jessica, are you okay?" Becky asked, as she stepped out of the elevator.

"I'm fine. How did you know where to find us?"

"Brandon wrote down the name of the hospital last night in our room. He still loves those small motels despite the private plane and big mansion he has upstate New York," Becky answered back.

"Uh…"

"He's loaded. He's probably a billionaire now, but you can't tell it by his lifestyle and clothes. I think Wendy has kept him grounded all these years," Becky continued on. "I haven't told him that I know who his father was. I'm waiting for him to tell me. No one else seems to have a clue about his private life. I stumbled on it by accident. Well, except for you now. Gotta, go."

Jessica stood there, stunned, as Becky breezed by her. She shook her head and decided to take the stairs instead. By the time, she reached the ground floor and felt the sun on her body again that she could forget what Nathan and Becky had said now. She saw Sabrina at the window holding her teddy bear key chain in her hand. She felt hers in her pocket, so she pulled it out. It was a crystal clear teddy bear. It made her smile again.

"Jessie, I want to marry you someday," Ryan said, as they sat at a picnic table on campus. "Together we can travel the world and far away from here. We can have a whole new life together."

"But we're only seventeen, Ryan. You don't know what you want to do with your life outside of football and baseball," Jessie pointed out. "Your parents are banking on a full scholarship to a respectable college. I don't fit into their plans for you."

"But I love you, and I'll make them see that, Jessie," Ryan said eagerly. "Trust me, I won't leave you behind. Tell me that you love me, too."

"I can't."

"What do you mean, you can't?" Ryan asked, as he pulled back from her.

"I mean..." Jessie answered, as she bitten her lower lip slightly. "I'm not in love with you, Ryan. But I do love you."

"That makes no sense at all, Jessie," Ryan snapped back. "I haven't been with any girl since before I took you to the prom three months ago. I have to suit up for baseball practice. We'll talk more about this later, Jessie."

"No, we won't," she replied back.

Ryan shot a look back at her then turned to walk away. Jessica wiped the tears from her face now. She stood outside the hospital now.

"Jessica," a familiar voice called out to her.

She turned to see Brandon coming towards her. She shook her head and proceeded ahead when he grabbed her arm, hard now.

"What?" she asked coldly.

"You've been crying," he answered, as he gazed deep into her face. "Did Ryan upset you? I'll..."

"No just memories. It doesn't matter. Go be with your family."

"I want you to see what they accepted," he said, as he held out his phone. "They're exactly the ones I wanted them to use."

She glanced down at his cell to see the photos he told her about earlier. But she didn't say thing, as he had scrolled to the next photo and finished.

"That's nice," she replied back.

"I sent them to your cell. Do you know how to retrieve them?"

She shook her head no, so he held out his hand for hers. Reluctantly, she placed it in his hand. He glanced through it then handed it back. She noticed the first one he showed her was on her screen now.

"Thank you. I need to be alone," she replied in a low voice.

"Talk to me. I can tell something's wrong," he said back. "I'm sorry that I didn't tell you about my private life all these years. Go ahead and ask about anything. I'll tell you everything. But don't shut me out of your life now."

"I want to be alone. What part of that don't you understand, Brandon?" she asked in anger.

"Jess....."

She shot him a look that caused him to swallow his words. He nodded and headed back into the hospital. She found an open café and ordered three pastries. She ate them all in a matter of minutes of their arrival to her table. Then she went to the ladies' room to throw it all up. She felt weak when she returned to her table to pay her bill.

She felt cold and weak, as she walked the streets of Paris alone. She had her dark sunglasses on, so people wouldn't recognize her this time. Young and old couples in love walked the streets with her, as she thought of Sabrina staring out that upstairs window at the orphanage.

"Why not us, Sweetie?" she asked herself with a small sigh, "Why not us?"

"How's my Piggy Wiggy?" her dad asked, as he saw her at the front door.

Jessie stared at him, as she finished her second

cupcake in the last couple of minutes. She waited for him to come home from work.

"Do you want this?" he asked, as he held out a bag of turkey jerky.

Jessie's eyes lighted up, as she stared at the bag and nodded eagerly.

"Beg," he said to her.

Jessie brought her hands together and panted like a dog.

"That's my Piggy Wiggy," he said, as he held it closer to her face now.

She grabbed it and rushed off to her room. She could hear his roaring laugh in her room behind the closed the door. The walls were thin, so they could hear a lot of things they weren't supposed to. She stuffed a piece followed by another into her mouth and chewed fast.

"What did you give her this time, Dillon?" asked her Mom.

"Turkey jerky," he answered back; "A whole bag of it, Stephanie."

"She's only seven-years-old and already a hundred pounds. She needs to loose, not gain. Honestly, you and Nathan give her too much food," Stephanie said back.

Jessie could hear them through the thin walls. It wasn't the first time but many times as their bed creaked too at night. She chewed on a couple more pieces and felt the juice slid down her fat throat. Now tears streamed down Jessica's face, as she gazed up at the Tower. She shook her head and faced the road alone.

"Taxi," she called out.

4

J essica woke up to see Brandon staring at her. It startled her at first. So he stepped back and walked out of the room.

"She's awake," he said, as he entered the main part of the penthouse.

"That's a relief," said Beverly.

Jessica got up and walked into the room. Her arms clung tightly to her slender body. She felt cold and weak still.

"Jessica, you look like hell," Beverly said, as she stared at her over her tea cup.

"I feel like..."

She felt the room spin as a dark figure moved closer to her. She couldn't focus on who it was before everything went black.

Later she woke up in bed again and adjusted her eyes on Brandon's head on the edge of the bed next to her. She touched his hair lightly.

"Jessica," he said, as he sprang to life and stared at her now. "When's the last time you ate something?"

"Mama's Pizza Shack," she answered, as she brought her hand closer to her now.

"That was three days ago," he snapped back. "I'll get you something. Stay put."

He was gone. She closed her eyes and tried to feel the warmth of the blankets on her now. But she was still cold when he returned with a plate.

"Sausage and eggs," Brandon said, as he held it out to her. "Please, Jessica, it's all I have left out there, unless you..."

"Its fine, Brandon," she interrupted him. "I'm fine. How's Davey?"

"Getting stronger each hour that passes. Your brother knows his stuff," Brandon answered quickly. "What happened to you?"

"I forgot to eat with everything going on with Davey."

"You scared us all. Mama went back to the hospital with Aunt Beverly. I wanted to stay here with you," he continued on. "Do you know you talk in your sleep?"

She ate the eggs and sausage quietly. "No. What did I say?"

"Sabrina and you cried a lot. I couldn't wake you up. I asked Ryan and Nathan about it. They said you were probably dreaming and let it run its course. But you were thinking of Sabrina the orphan?"

She nodded.

"I said I would do anything for her. I meant it, Jessica. I know a couple who in Scottsdale, Arizona. They wanted to see her, so I arranged for her to spend some time with them. That reminds me, I have to call them. Excuse me. Finish all of it. I'll order you more."

"This enough," she replied back. "Thank you."

He shook his head, no, and left. She finished what was on the plate and left it on the table next to her.

"What the hell?" Brandon asked in a loud voice.

Jessica sat up straighter, as he walked back into the room. He had his cell next to his ear now.

"How could you lose a five year old? Didn't someone travel with her?" he asked rapidly. "What the hell!"

"What?" she asked with interest now.

"Fine, I'll take care of it now myself," Brandon snapped back. He hit the red button then scanned his cell again. He pressed another number. "It's me, Brandon. Sabrina and you'll find a picture of her in the Telly campaign. Find her. Thank you," he said, as he flipped his cell closed now.

"What's going on?" Jessica asked him.

"That idiot just drove Sabrina to the airport and brought a one way ticket and left her there alone in the airport. No one has seen or heard from Sabrina since," Brandon answered, as he paced the room.

"Who did you call just now?"

"A PI I know, and he owes me one. He better find her. That woman is going to pay big-time for this mistake. She crossed the wrong guy. Do you hear me, Jessica?"

She nodded and felt frightened by him now. She had seen him angry before, but this was beyond that anger. It felt and looked different this time, somehow. She couldn't figure it out, so it was the unknown that was scaring her most about Brandon now.

"Of all things that woman would do," Brandon said in a loud and angry voice, as he paced the penthouse still. "Sabrina doesn't even have a damn passport, much less an ID on her. We depend on adults to look after us, yet they fail us time and time again. They wonder why we grow up with trust issues. My god, Sabrina is only five-years-old!"

"Brandon, calm down. Let's get our business taken

care of here and make sure Davey is okay. Then we can search for Sabrina together," Jessica replied calmly.

She was on her feet and stared at him. He stopped at the balcony.

"Sabrina doesn't need a passport to go to Arizona," she continued to walk slowly to him. "Tell me why this has you like this, Brandon. We're friends. Aren't we?"

"Yes, but you don't understand," he answered back. He dove into his pocket for his cell. "Yes. What? I'm in Paris, you idiot. Do I need to find her myself? Go to..." He stared at Jessica. "Bye."

She turned quickly to the bathroom and started to close the door. But Brandon held it open with his hand and foot. They made eye contact again.

"I'm sorry. I don't mean to scare you. I wish I could explain this, but not now. Can you trust me, Jessica?" he asked with a pleading look in his eyes.

She nodded. So he smiled at her now.

"We'll go with the navy dress and handbag. You're right. We have work to do. Where's Becky?" he asked, himself as he walked back into main part of the penthouse.

There was a knock on the door, Jessica heard Brandon open it. She slipped into the outfit he suggested when Becky showed up. She had the perfume in her hand.

"Here or there?" Becky asked him.

"Here, Brandon was upset earlier. I got him to focus on this and Davey," she explained quickly.

"Ladies, I'm losing time here," Brandon called out.

"Coming," Becky called back. "Thanks for the warning. Let's go now."

They emerged from the bathroom together.

Brandon was on his cell again but hung up when he saw them. Becky grabbed the metal case and headed for the door. Jessica followed her, with Brandon closing the door behind him. They got into the elevator.

"So, how's David doing?" Becky asked him as they descended.

"Fine," he answered coldly.

He pulled out his cell again and scanned it. Becky stared Jessica.

"You look great in blue, but you always have. Doesn't this blue remind you of the Greek Islands, Brandon?" Becky asked him.

"The Greek Isles are a tad lighter blue," Brandon answered back, as he avoided making eye contact with her.

"Like South Lake Tahoe then?" Jessica asked back with a small smile.

"I guess; never been there. Never been wherever State it might be in," he answered coldly. "We'll be taking shots of the less-traveled-by-tourist stop, but don't worry, the Tower will be included. I want pre-sunset shots of you with it in the background. I need the sky filter and fifty and 105 again, Becky."

"Got it boss," Becky said back quickly.

He walked to the minivan again. Becky and Jessica held back as they stepped out of the elevator.

"What's this about the Greek Isles?" Jessica asked Becky. "We've never gone there for a shoot."

"He went there at eighteen with parents. I read about it because he hasn't said anything in years. Didn't you notice the chain attached to his belt. It has a crystal teddy bear on it now, too."

"Ladies, I want to get this done ASAP. I've got something else to tend to," Brandon said coldly.

They climbed into the minivan as he drove. They parked it and walked the streets. Jessica got a lot of stares from men and other tourists, but Brandon pushed on as though he didn't notice them at all. Becky carried the equipment without complaint, as usual. Jessica smiled so much that her muscles in her face ached. They seemed to be doing this for hours, since the sun was high in the clear, blue sky.

"That's a wrap for now. Let's do lunch at that café over there," Brandon said finally, as he swung his camera over his right shoulder.

Jessica glanced over at it. It was the same café in which she ate those pastries that she threw up. She gulped hard and stood there.

"Thank God!" Becky exclaimed back. "I'm really hungry."

"And what about you, Jessica?" Brandon asked her.

"What? A little; maybe a salad," she answered back. "Water, please, too."

"I need more than that," said Becky.

"Order whatever you want," Brandon snapped back, as he stared at her coldly; as they sat down, "A chicken salad with Honey mustard dressing on the side for me and this lady, and whatever she wants, on one bill."

"A double cheese burger with French fries, lots of them and a large ice tea," said Becky. "Didn't you want a bottle of water, Jessica?"

Jessica nodded. The waiter nodded and looked at Brandon.

"Me, too."

So the waiter left, and Becky tapped the table. Brandon held his cell again.

"Ladies' room," Jessica replied politely. "Becky, come with me. Please."

They got a little ways from the table, and she leaned toward Becky now. "How do you know about Brandon's private life?" she asked Becky.

"I read the society pages. Don't you?" Becky asked back.

"No," Jessica answered, as she stepped into a stall.

"Well, his Dad was related to that family they named 'something' Center. It's lighted every Christmas. He died over in Greece while on vacation with Brandon and his Mom," Becky explained in a calm voice.

Jessica flushed the toilet then headed for the sink to wash her hands. Becky was there and looked at her nails.

"Rockefeller Center," Jessica replied thoughtfully.

"Yes, that's it. Something about a boating accident," Becky said, as she looked up. "Brandon hasn't said anything about it in the fourteen years I've known him. I met up with him shortly after the accident and when he dropped out of college."

"Ladies, your lunch is ready," Brandon called out from behind the closed door.

"Coming, make sure I have the sauce for the fries," Becky called back to him.

"Barbecue," Brandon mumbled, as he seemed to have walked away now.

"What's that all about?" asked Jessica.

"Nothing, I'm starving," Becky answered, as she bolted for the door now.

Jessica threw away the paper that she dried her hands with and glanced back at the unused stall that she threw up in. She shook her head and headed out to join them at the table. Becky was chewing on something while Brandon played with his salad. His mind seemed far away now. She sat down and didn't disturb him. She ate half of her salad before she pushed it away.

"You're not going to finish it," stated Becky. "Are you okay?"

"No. I'm fine."

"Hand it over," Becky said, as she motioned with her hands.

"There goes our Piggy Wiggy," Brandon said in a low voice.

Jessica stared at him in disbelief, as she felt a chill down her spine. He stared back at her for a moment.

"Sorry, Jessica," he whispered to her.

She gave him a small nod when the waited had arrived.

"Yes," Brandon said to him.

"Anything else, sir?"

"She'll need a refill on her iced tea and your best dessert, too," he answered back, "Anything else, Jessica?"

"No, thank you," she answered uneasily.

"Ms. your voice sounds familiar. Weren't you in here a day or two ago?" asked the waiter.

"No," she answered uneasy.

"Sorry, Ms. I'll get a refill, and our best dessert Cream Alexander and the bill, sir."

Brandon nodded and the waiter left. Becky finished Jessica's salad and looked at Brandon's plate. He held it out to her, and she took it.

"Becky, I don't know where you put it all," he commented, as he stared at her.

"I burn a lot off calories working for you, my friend," Becky said, as she swallowed the last bite of his chicken.

"Enjoy, Ms," the waiter said, as he placed the dessert next to Becky and poured more ice tea into her glass beside her.

"Thank you," Becky said, as she stacked the plates for him. "I worked for his Mom at the Pizza Shack when I was in college."

Becky stared at Jessica then dove into her dessert. Brandon placed a card with the bill and shook his head. Becky had downed the tea and dessert before she looked at Brandon.

"Did I say something wrong?" Becky asked him. "I forgot. But aren't you two friends? I thought Jessica wasn't like all the other models because..."

"Ready to go?" he asked, as he got to his feet. "We have a deadline. We should have brought the tan outfit."

"It's in the van along with a small floral print dress. Everything will match," Becky answered, as she got to her feet, too. "She can change here or in the van, but it's her choice."

"Jessica," he said, as he stared at her now. "It's up to you."

"Ladies' room, please," she replied politely.

Becky bolted to the van. Brandon and Jessica stood

side by side now.

"Mama gave her a job when she lost her funding for college," explained Brandon. "I told her that whoever gets their career going first should offer the other a job. She stayed in college to graduate. I didn't. We were eighteen when we met at NYU. We've known each other for fourteen years."

"Does she know about Rebecca and your birthday?" Jessica asked him.

"No, on both accounts, she only knows Mama. However, I was surprised she showed up at the hospital. Did you tell her anything?"

"Nope, I promised."

"Which one, Brandon?" Becky asked, as she held out two dresses.

"Tan one."

Jessica took it and headed for the ladies' room. Becky was behind her. They walked in together. Becky leaned on the closed door. Jessica slipped out of her dress and into the new dress quickly.

"Aren't you two friends?" asked Becky.

"Yes, and no, I think we are only acquaintances. Well, I'm not sure really."

"Brush your hair back," Becky said, as she held out a brush.

Jessica brushed her hair back quickly. Becky picked up the navy blue dress and accessories before they left the ladies' room. They joined Brandon. He was on his cell again and flipped it shut at their arrival.

"I'll go ahead and put this one back in the van. Meet you two at Frenchy," Becky said to him.

He nodded, and Becky was off again. Jessica cleared her throat. He stared at her now.

"Davey is doing fine. No word on or about Sabrina yet," he said calmly. His cell rang. He flipped it open and listened. "Yes, let me know as soon as you know. Thanks. Bye."

Jessica stared at him.

"The PI said someone said she saw Sabrina with another lady at the airport," Brandon said calmly. "But airport security said Sabrina wasn't on their surveillance cameras or tapes. So how does a lady say she saw her in the airport?"

"Is someone jerking the PI's chain?" she asked thoughtfully back.

"What do you mean?"

"Telling him what he wants to hear in hopes there's a reward or something."

"I hadn't thought of that. Thanks Jessica," Brandon said, as he reached for his cell again. "What made you think of that?"

"Something Becky said," she answered honestly.

"It was brought to my attention. Did you mention who I was or a reward involved? Oh yeah, I get it. I had to check it all out. Yeah. Bye."

"Well?"

"No. What did Becky say? She doesn't know about my private life except Mama and NYU since we met there," he answered, as he stared at her now.

"She knows more than you think."

"Oh really," he said half seriously.

"You're related to Rockefeller, and your Dad died

on vacation over in Greece with you and your Mom. You're a billionaire and have a mansion upstate. She's been waiting fourteen years for you to say something about it all. Is that why you have that keychain of the Greek Isles on your belt?"

He stood there, stunned, but stared at her too. She could tell he how shocked he was by what she knew about him now.

"I didn't tell about Rebecca and don't plan to either. A promise is a promise, my friend," she replied back.

He shook his head and glanced at his watch. He started to walk quickly.

"What's wrong?"

"We need to get some shots of you with Frenchy. It's the statue of Romance, some people believe. It'll bring both ideas together. I want to get back to the Tower before sunset. You'll need to change into the floral print then," he answered quickly. "Are you up to walking three blocks that way?"

He pointed away from the café and the Tower. She nodded. So they headed out, as she could see the van in the far but not too far. Brandon had his camera on her now. They started to slow down. She flashed him her smiles as they arrived.

Becky stood near the statue and looked down at her hands. But she glanced up to them, so she moved away from the statue. When Brandon pulled his camera away from his face, Becky walked up to him.

"I need a new card," he informed her.

Becky held out something to him, and he handed

something back to her. She headed off to the minivan, and Brandon stared at Jessica now.

"Do what comes natural. We can only be here an hour at most. So make it all count, Jessica."

She nodded. Jessica posed and smiled for him. She thought of his facial features now, deep brown eyes, small sideburns to match his medium brown colored hair and narrow, dark eyebrows. He had strong jaw line, too and full lips. It made her sigh.

"That's a wrap for now," he called her back into the present again. "We can drive back to the Tower. You can change on the way over. Becky, come up front with me while she changes. Move it ladies, please."

Jessica changed in the backseat while Brandon drove back to the Tower. Becky had his laptop on her lap and was doing something there. When she straightened her new dress, they were back at the Tower, and Brandon had his camera again. He rushed ahead of Jessica now, so she smiled for him as she emerged from the van.

"Give me that 'I'm great at my job look'," Brandon called out to her.

Jessica smiled with a small giggle. Becky backed into her.

"What the hell!" Brandon exclaimed back.

"Sorry," Becky said back. "I've got the others on disk and the hard drive."

"Get the hell out of the shot," Brandon snapped at her.

Becky rushed by him and headed for the Tower. She was in tears now.

"That was rude, Brandon," replied Jessica. "Now go

apologize to her. She's working her ass off for you. You're being a jerk now."

"After the shoot," he said back.

Jessica placed her hands on her narrow hips and stared at him. She didn't smile for him.

"Jessica, come on, don't be difficult, not after all these years," he begged her, as he held his camera to his eye.

She continued to stare at him and didn't move.

"Jessica, let me get some shots then I'll apologize to her. Please. I promise."

She smiled again. They resumed their shooting up to the Tower now. He walked over to Becky who sat on a bench now. She was still upset. Brandon sat down next to her then they hugged. Jessica smiled.

"Okay. Let's wrap this up now, ladies," he said with a big grin. "Sunset is gorgeous for these last shots of the day. "

Jessica nodded so did Becky. They focused on the campaign, Essence and Travel World. Becky was in some of the shots as a fellow tourist. It added a lighter and happier tone to the assignment. Becky began to let go and smiled more. By the time the sun faded, they were tired but happy of what they accomplished as a team.

"I never saw you cut loose like that before," Jessica replied to Becky. "But it was fun to do it with you, my friend."

"I'm sorry," Becky said, as her face had a shade of pink to her cheeks now.

"You did great, both of you," Brandon said with excitement in his voice now.

He hugged them both and stood back to stare at the Tower. He placed his camera down next to Jessica before he walked closer to Tower. Jessica picked up his camera and held it.

"Do you know how to use it?" Becky asked in a low voice as they sat on the bench.

"Not really."

"Turn it on and do this," Becky explained, as she did it for her. "Now just center your subject and hit the silver button when you're ready to take the shot."

Jessica held the camera to her eye and saw a dark image of Brandon facing the Tower. His legs and arms were extended out, as she pressed the button. She heard it four times as she held the button down and camera steady. He moved slightly on each shot. Then he turned to face them now.

"What are you two up?" he asked them with a small grin.

"Nothing," Becky answered, as she held his camera now in her lap.

"Let's go look in on Davey then head home," Brandon said to them thoughtfully.

"Okay," Becky said, as she held out his camera. "I've got your bag. Jessica, are you coming?"

Jessica glanced up now and nodded. She got to her feet and glanced over at the Tower before she headed back to the van, too.

"Mommy, did you always want to have babies?" Jessie asked her as they made cookies.

"Yes. What about you, Sweetie?" asked Stephanie.

Jessie nodded, as she ate a handful of chocolate

chips.

"Not if you keep eating like you do. You really shouldn't eat like you do, Sweetie."

"But I'm hungry, Mommy."

"It's all in here," Stephanie said, as she tapped Jessie's head. "It controls everything we say or do."

"Jessica. Jessica," Brandon called out to her from the inside of the van.

She climbed in the back and let Becky sit up front with him.

"Jessica, are you okay?" Becky asked, as she focused on her now.

"I'm fine," Jessica answered, as she leaned back on the seat. "Let me know when we get there. I'm going to rest my eyes before that."

"Sure," Brandon said, as he started to emerge into traffic.

Jessica closed her eyes now. She saw Sabrina's face and felt wetness on her face now.

Why did this child tug so deeply within her heart and soul? Could she ever explain it to anyone? Would they understand?"

"Jessica, we're here," Brandon said, as he shook her now.

She opened her eyes and saw his face in hers again. He stepped back.

"Becky promised to never discuss my private life with anyone but you. She's upstairs now. She has my camera," he whispered to her.

Jessica got out and felt a chill in the air. He grabbed a flannel shirt off the floor and placed it over her shoulders now. She smelled his aftershave lotion, Old Spice, as she slipped her arms into the sleeves.

"You were thinking about Sabrina and something else back at the Tower?"

"It's not important. Do you think the PI can find Sabrina?"

"I dismissed him," he answered, as they walked inside.

"You should give him another chance, Brandon," she replied with a warm and friendly smile.

"Stop that! You know you can get me to do anything with that smile and stubbornness. You did it earlier. Remember."

She still smiled at him. He shook his head.

"Fine, I'll call him. He did mention a lead. I guess I'm being too impatient. I'll tell him that I'm doing it for you."

"That's kind of you, my friend," she replied, as they stepped out of the elevator and walked down the hallway together.

"He's improving," Wendy said, as she greeted them. "We're going to have his baptism here at the hospital. They're trying to locate a Catholic priest now. So many things to do in so little time before going back home, and I don't know if I can get them all done."

"Hi, Mama," Brandon said back calmly. "Excuse me. I have a call to make."

"Okay, Honey," said Wendy.

Brandon stepped away from them. Wendy led Jessica closer to Davey's room. Nathan stood there with Stanley, as they got closer. He stared at her.

"Nice look uh...Jessica," Nathan said with some hesitation.

"It's getting cold out there. It's..."

"My son's, I gave it to Brandon a couple Christmases ago," interrupted Wendy.

"Where's Becky?"

"Inside, showing your shoot at the Tower," answered Stanley. "So you'll be heading home now."

"After Davey's baptism," said Wendy. "He has to have his godparents be present."

Stanley nodded. Beverly emerged from the room with a big smile.

"We have some good shots there. I think the clients will love them for both. I like the dramatic shots of Brandon," Beverly said to Jessica.

"They're of my baby," cried out Wendy. "I didn't..."

"He doesn't know I took them either," interrupted Jessica. "We didn't tell him, but I think he knows something was up."

"Not much gets by him," added Wendy. "I've got things to do. So do you, Sis."

Beverly nodded and slipped by the men, then Jessica. Together Wendy and Beverly walked down the hallway. Brandon walked by them with a small smiled at them. Wendy stopped to touch his face. He joined Stanley, Jessica and Nathan at the entrance to Davey's room.

"All taken care of," he said to Jessica. "I'm going to look in on Davey."

"I'll join you," Jessica replied with a small smile.

"Jessica...I would like to speak to you privately," Nathan said in hesitation. "Please, it's a personal matter."

Reluctantly, she nodded while Brandon and Stanley walked into the room. She walked up to her twin. "What?"

"This isn't easy to say," Nathan answered, as he bit his lower lip slightly.

"Spit it out," she replied impatiently. "I'm tired and have things to do, as you well know."

"Dad and Mom aren't doing very well. Mom is in a care home, and I suspect any day now that I'll be putting Dad with her. That's if ..."

"What?"

"He doesn't give up first," Nathan answered back.

"You wondered why I went into medicine. I thought, I could find a cure for Dad's disease, but we're still far from it."

"What's wrong with him?" she asked with concern now.

"What Aunt Betty had years ago, Alzheimer's disease? He's slipping away from us faster than they thought."

"When?"

"A year ago and he refuses his meds. He pushed Mom down the stairs, and she fractured her hip. That's why I put her in a home because I can't take care of her on my own. I've needed your help but didn't know how to reach you."

"We can discuss this all later. I'll give you my number and address before I leave. I want to focus on something happy like this baptism."

"I took you to the airport. You owe me, Jessica," Nathan protested back.

She left him in the hallway without anymore words

on the subject.

5

Jessica and Brandon checked every gate in the airport when his PI friend showed up. He had Sabrina's photo in his hands and was in color. This was five-year- old girl missing for a week now, and she seemed to have vanished from the face of the earth. But it didn't stop Jessica and Brandon from trying to find her.

"Checked with the woman again," the man said, as he approached them. "She has gone onto change her original story. Something or someone frightened her since we first talked, man."

"You've got to be kidding, Ted. I flew heaven and earth to get here and to talk to that lady. Now she won't let me talk to her."

"She's says there's no point. She was mistaken," Ted said bluntly.

"Crap," Brandon snapped back, as he walked to the nearest window. He stared at the airplanes coming and going on the runway. "Is there anyone else?"

"No, but I brought these flyers in hopes that more people might have seen her."

"We have our own photo of her on our cells. No one seems to know anything. It can take days and maybe weeks to try and find someone who might have seen her," he said back. "But I'm not giving up, Jessica. I promise you that. Okay."

Jessica stared at Ted then at Brandon's back. She didn't know what to think at this point. She had been on a flight from

Paris and didn't sleep much. She kept seeing Sabrina's face, so she woke up. She wasn't alone in her thinking. Jessica saw how tired Brandon was, but he still pressed on.

Becky was ordered back to his studio upon their arrival. She downloaded his photos on disk and a laptop which she sent to the clients. Then she would have to get the dresses cleaned and returned to place from which they borrowed them from. She was tired, too but pressed on.

"What about the woman who dropped her off?" Jessica asked Ted. "Can we talk to her?"

"No dice there. The State fired her. They have a new couple running the home now. They can't release any information on her whereabouts," Ted answered back. "Sorry."

"Sorry doesn't cut it, Ted," Brandon snapped back, as he faced them again. "Do you realize how important it is for us to find Sabrina?"

"I got it, man, but I'm doing my best," answered Ted.

"Get out of here. Leave the flyers with Jessica. We'll find her on our own," Brandon said back. "She wanted me to give you another chance and I did. It's done, Jessica, we're on our own."

"Brandon, you still haven't explained why this upsets you so much," Jessica replied back calmly.

"I don't have time to explain it, maybe someday," Brandon said back. "You're still here."

"Fine; and good luck, man. You'll need it. Someone doesn't want you to find her," Ted said, as he handed Jessica the flyers. "Good luck with him."

"Thank you," she replied politely. "But I still would

like you to try and help us on the side."

"I'll think about it. You're one hot dame too bad he can't see that right now," Ted commented, as he headed back to his car.

Jessica watched him leave then turned back to Brandon. He held his cell out to a couple. They shook their heads, no. He let them walk away. He looked disappointed when someone approached her.

"Are are you looking for the girl in that flyer, Ms?" the woman asked her.

She was a stewardess. Jessica recognized the uniform. She had enough frequent flyer miles to go anywhere in the world free herself. She thought briefly.

"Yes," Jessica answered, as she felt her throat was dry as the Mojave Desert. "Have you seen her?"

She held out the flyer. The woman examined it closely. Brandon marched over.

"Yes, I have," the woman answered thoughtfully.

"When? Where?" asked Brandon.

"Last week, I think, it was here then a day ago when I was boarding my flight back here."

"Where was that?" he asked, as he stared her intently now. "Please, it's important."

"Austin, Texas," answered the woman back. "She kept her head down a lot."

"How do you know it was she?" asked Jessica.

"She saw a teddy bear, and her head shot up quickly. The man said something to her then she looked frightened. Her lower lip quivered."

"Can you describe him to a sketch artist?" asked Brandon.

"I'll try. My name is Amy Chambers. And yours?"

"Brandon and this is Jessica. We're Sabrina's friends?"

"You're that model I see in the magazines all the time," said Amy. "Aren't you?"

"Yes."

"Can you stay here for a little while?" Brandon asked politely.

Amy nodded. So Brandon was on his cell again. He stepped away from them.

"Let's sit," Jessica replied with a small smile.

"You're so beautiful in those magazines," Amy said, as they sat down. "Is Sabrina your daughter?"

"No, just a special friend."

"You look so tired. I hardly recognized you from a distance."

"We just got in from Paris."

"France?"

"Yes, we were on assignment. I want to thank you for your help. It means a lot to us both."

"Becky's on her way," he said to them. "She was an art major in college."

Jessica nodded. He went back to the window and looked out.

"Is he always like that?" Amy asked her.

"Not really. He's worried about Sabrina."

"He acts more like her father than her real father," said Amy. "He'll make a great Dad someday."

"Why do you say that?"

"In my business, I see a lot of different men, and he would be devoted to one woman and their children. I'm sure without a doubt, you'll find her."

"Becky, this is Amy. Amy, this is Becky," he introduced them to each other.

"Take a walk, Brandon. Jessica, could you calm this guy down?"

"How?"

"Go find a quiet place and make out. I don't care just get him out of here, so we can work."

"What!" Brandon exclaimed in shock.

"Let's go find some nachos," Jessica replied, as she stood up. "They need to be alone."

"Thanks, Jessica," Becky said with a small grin.

"Thank you, Amy," Jessica replied again, as she led Brandon off.

"How did you know I liked nachos?" Brandon asked her.

"I don't know. I said whatever popped into my head at the time."

"Back in Paris, I didn't mean to upset you. I realized it after I said it. Again, I'm so very sorry, Jessica. The café remember?"

"My Dad used to call me that, years ago. Then I lost weight, and he didn't say much to me after that."

"I'm sorry."

"Don't be. Things had to change. Nachos with lots hot peppers and two strawberry shakes, please," she replied sadly to the woman behind the counter. "You don't want to hear about my personal life."

"Yes, I do. When you told me, Becky knew more than I thought she knew. I realized how little you and I know each other. I was listening as Sabrina asked where home was. Now I've met your brother Nathan. What about your parents?"

"Stephanie and Dillon Hudson are still alive. Nathan is my twin brother. He told me that Mom is a home now. Dad has a disease that takes away the memory. Our Aunt Betty had it. She was Dad's only sibling," she answered sadly and honestly. "Food was my comfort until I turned sixteen the year before the prom. The pounds fell off, and I concealed my new body from everyone by wearing same overweight clothes. But when Ryan took me to our junior prom and people saw how good I looked, I didn't hide it anymore. I had been like that for nearly a year by then. I turned seventeen after our prom. It was the last time Dad and I spoke civilly to each other."

She stacked several hot peppers onto the chip with cheese. Then she popped it in her mouth and coughed. Brandon placed a twenty on the counter but stared at her. She stared down at the nachos.

"Jessica," he said, as he tilted her head up and towards him.

"We got into a big fight and haven't spoken to each other ever since. Are you going to help me eat these? I can get on a plane and go to Las Cruces, New Mexico to get a large pizza size. I..."

"Stop!" he exclaimed, as he touched her cheek now. "You don't need to go back to it. You've come so far, Jessica. Look at your career. Look at your body. I see how you turn heads of many men. I ..."

"We got a stretch of the man," Becky said, as she rushed up to them. "I let Amy go home. She looked beat like all of us."

Brandon turned to Becky and reached out for the drawing. He examined it.

"I had a time with his nose and mouth. They're still my weakness, but the eyes..."

"Um.....he looks familiar," Brandon interrupted her, as he thoughtfully looked at it.

"Nachos, can I have some?" Becky asked, as she stared at them.

"Here, I'm going to home to my own bed. We all can use a goodnight's sleep and feel refreshed after that," Jessica answered, as she slid the nachos over to Becky. "We're doing her no good by not sleeping. Do you hear me, Brandon?"

"Those eyes," Brandon answered in a low voice. "They remind me of someone I have known, but who?"

"Rest, maybe it'll come to you then," Jessica replied back.

Brandon continued to stare at the drawing. She walked away and left Becky with him. She got herself a taxi and headed home. She closed her eyes and saw Sabrina again. She jerked herself up then down again. She was parked in front of her apartment building soon enough. She paid the cabbie and headed up to her apartment.

Going by her phone, she noticed a flashing red light, so she pressed it. She smelled Brandon's after shave on the flannel shirt she still wore. She had forgotten to give it back to him after the baptism.

"Jessie, it's me, Nathan. God knows how much I missed you after all these years. I love you so damn much, Sis. It's nice to have the connection again. I'll let you know how Mom and Dad are doing. Call me anytime at (916)452-

7824. Bye," Nathan's voice said from the machine.

"Jessica, great job on all three accounts, they're pleased what Becky emailed them from Paris. They haven't seen the ones at the Tower yet," Beverly's voice said from the machine, "Sneaking those photos of Brandon. Bye."

"No more messages. Time remaining is eight minutes and ten seconds," the machine said before it went silent again.

Jessica flopped on her bed and was out like a light. She didn't have time to dream or think of Sabrina and Brandon now. But they were there deep in her mind and heart.

The next day Jessica hung the floral print dress on her bedroom door and slipped into a teal colored shorts and matching teal striped polo shirt. She was barefoot in her own apartment, and classical music played low on her stereo. She barely touched her croissant and green tea, as she paced the floor. A knock on the door made her to bolt for it full speed.

"Hi, Jessica," Becky said with a big smile now. "Do you have the dress?"

"In the bedroom on the door," she answered back. "Have you seen Brandon?"

"He's on his way up. Do you have a computer?" Becky asked, as she headed for Jessica's bedroom.

"No. Why?"

"I thought you might want to see our work this past week," Brandon answered, as he stood in the doorway.

"Uh...come in," she replied in hesitation.

"I don't think I've been here before," he said, as he

walked in.

"I have, but no, you haven't. I'm off to get this cleaned and returned. I dropped your every days on your bed, Jessica. See you guys later," Becky said, as she headed out the open door. "He knows. Bye."

Jessica gulped hard, as she stood face to face with Brandon now alone. He walked by her and glanced around the apartment.

"Classical music," he said thoughtfully. "I didn't picture you as the type."

"It calms me," she replied in her own defense.

"Easy Jessica, I'm not mad about the photos. Mama told me that she wanted copies. At first, I didn't know what she was talking about then I found them a little while ago," Brandon explained calmly. "I was separating the assignments and David's baptism out. That's when I spotted the four shots of a dark figure. Becky confessed that you took them of me at the Tower."

"I don't have a computer," she replied back. "I have water and green tea. Pick one."

"I see you didn't eat much breakfast," he said, as he still moved about the room. "Let's sit on the couch. I brought my laptop just in case."

"Jess...," a woman said, as she stood at the doorway next to her.

She wore a wire-framed glasses and reddish brown hair in a ponytail. Brandon and Jessica stared at her now.

"Jennifer, this is Brandon. Brandon, this is Jennifer, my neighbor," Jessica introduced them to each other. "Were you heading off to work?"

"You got it," Jennifer answered with a friendly

smile. "My black shirt and tan colored shorts give me away every time."

Jessica nodded and smiled back. She stepped away from the door and towards Brandon.

"What happened to your leg?" Brandon asked her.

"It's silly, really. I slipped on some tile at a friend's house. I'll have the boot off next week, hopefully," Jennifer answered confidently. "Do you need more tea, Jess?"

"Yes, but I need me to pay for it," Jessica answered back.

"I work at Starbucks," Jennifer said to Brandon. "I get it at an employee discount. " She turned away from him. "You know I drink it when I'm here for our movie night when it fits into your busy schedule." Now she stared at Jessica. "We're still on for this Friday. Aren't we?"

"Not sure. Brandon and I are trying to locate a friend of ours," Jessica answered honestly.

"Maybe we should see if Jennifer's seen Sabrina," Brandon said politely. "Do you have the flyers?"

"By the door on the table," Jessica answered back.

"I have more on CD, too, if you have a few minutes," Brandon said, as he sat down with his laptop.

"I've got time," Jennifer said, as she walked over to the couch.

Brandon turned on the laptop, as she sat down on his left; so Jessica sat on his right. He loaded the CD into the machine. Brandon opened the file and the images came alive on the screen.

"That's Sabrina. She's five-year-old and an orphan," he said, as he pointed to her on the screen. "Have you seen her?"

"That's you, Jess," answered Jennifer. "I never saw your raw work before. Oh gosh, you're the photographer."

Brandon nodded. Jessica scanned the screen to see her and Sabrina with the oversized teddy bear. Brandon pressed a button, and the images appeared larger and faded to another, like in a slide show. They all sat there in silence as they viewed them. Then it stopped.

"That's it, ladies."

"I'll take a flyer into work. We have a board for the community events and such. I'll post it there," Jennifer said with a smile. "I should go now, Jess."

Jessica got up as they both walked to her front door. Jennifer smiled back at her.

"If he wasn't your guy, I might have tried to get him to ask me out," Jennifer said to her. "Bye."

Jessica shook her head. She stared at Brandon from the open door. He seemed to be loading another CD in.

"Want to see it all?" he asked, as he stared at her.

She nodded and joined him. They viewed his next three CDs in silence. It was the first time he had been in her apartment. But somehow he fit right in with her simple taste and life. When he slipped the final CD out, he logged off his laptop and focused on her.

"Becky and I really talked in depth this morning. She told me about what she knew about my private life. She has spent several years trying to gather any and all information about me," he said, as he clasped his hand on top of the laptop. "I didn't offer her any new information about myself or what you shared about your private life."

"Did she ask?" Jessica asked with interest.

"Yes. But it's like you said, a promise is a promise,

so I'm not saying a word about your private life to anyone,"
he answered back. "But I'm sure Mama will have tons of
questions that I can't, or won't answer. I respect your
privacy like you have mine all these years. Whatever you
tell me; stays between us."

"I feel the same way," she replied back.

"But..." he said, as he got up to walk over to the
window.

"What?"

"I said it before, but I know so little about you," he
answered, as he glanced back at her. "I want to know you.
I've known Jessica the professional model, for twelve years
but learning about Jess or Jessie the private life. Nathan's
hair is brown and yours..."

"I dyed it for my seventeenth birthday present to
myself," she interrupted him. "When your Aunt Beverly
met me, I was only a blonde a short time, and I wanted a
different life than I had. I came from working class America
and wanted to put it all behind me. She offered me a
better and different life."

"Are you ashamed of your roots?"

"No. It was..." she answered in hesitation, as she
walked over to her stereo and felt his gaze. "I had to see if I
had what it took to be a model."

"You didn't want to be around people who knew
you before you lost all that weight," filled in Brandon. "I get
it perfectly."

She glanced quickly back at him. "You do?"

He bolted towards her and gazed deep into her
eyes now. "Yes, I do. You get so busy putting up this wall
that you forget to live. It's a wall around your heart

because you're afraid to follow your heart again. It might get hurt again or the pain is so intense; that it feels like its life is being sucked out of it."

He stepped back and gathered up his things. Jessica stood there and watched him, not knowing what to say or do.

"I called Ted again. I faxed him Becky's stretch. He agreed to help again. He's left for Austin, Texas already. I agreed to meet him there. Could you stay here and see if you can find any leads here?"

She nodded. He kissed her on the cheek and left. She didn't know how long she stood there, but she eventually put on her flip flops and headed out for Starbucks. She noticed Jennifer making drinks, as she walked in. She wore her dark sunglasses because she didn't want to deal with her fans. She needed a friend, and her only true friend outside of Becky and Brandon was Jennifer. She walked up to the register to an order.

"Can I help you, Ms?" an African American man asked her with a friendly smile.

"Venti, hot green tea, please," she answered in a calm voice.

"$2.95, Ms," he said back with a smile.

Jessica placed her Starbucks gift card down and glanced over at Jennifer now.

"Grande, passionate lemonade on the bar," Jennifer called out.

"Jennifer," Jessica replied in a low voice. She stepped closer to her. "Do you have a break soon?"

"Jess," Jennifer answered a little surprised. "Give me a second."

Jessica nodded and reached back for her card and tea before she sat down in comfy chair. She sipped her tea when Jennifer sat beside her now.

"What's up?" Jennifer asked with a warm friendly smile.

"He kissed me," Jessica answered still stunned. "Brandon kissed me on the cheek before he left for Austin, Texas."

"Really," Jennifer said, as she squirmed in her seat. "Awesome."

Jessica placed her tea down. "He has never done that before. We've been friends for over twelve years. Why did things change now?"

"Just go with it, Jess. Hey, I get off in a couple hours. I'll come by your place, and we can really talk about it. Okay?"

Jessica nodded. She noticed the flyer of Sabrina on the board now. Jennifer had gone back to work, so she hit the streets for leads on Sabrina. She didn't remove her sunglasses, as she talked to strangers about Sabrina. She wasn't getting anywhere with it and felt discouraged by it all as time passed. So she walked back to her place. Jennifer stood by her door and was still in her uniform.

"So let's go inside and talk about the dreamy man who kissed you," Jennifer said with a big smile, followed by a small laugh.

Jessica opened her door and walked in. She removed her sunglasses and placed the sunglasses on the table next to her door, along with remaining flyers. Jennifer walked in behind her.

"Jess, what's up?" Jennifer asked, as she sat down

on the couch. "OUCH! Yours?"

She stared at her then answered, "It must be Brandon's. Which one is it?"

"Baptism David Jeffery," Jennifer read out loud. "I don't recall seeing this one."

"It's our godchild's baptism," she answered, less confident than her usual self.

"Interesting," Jennifer said, as she put it aside. "So Brandon kissed you, and you didn't see it coming. Where's your head been these last seven years?"

"What do you mean?"

"You've got this glow around you these past seven years of your beauty, but there's something missing or longing in your life as well," Jennifer explained with a big smile now. "I've noticed it maybe he picked up on it, too. So where's dream boat now? You said something about Texas."

"Austin, Texas looking for Sabrina, it's where Amy had said she saw her there."

"Who's Amy?"

"The stewardess who gave us the lead and drawing of the man who was with Sabrina," she answered, as she walked back to the table by the door. "I think Brandon has Becky's stretch of the man. He might have given me a copy. Ah, here we are."

She walked up to Jennifer now. Jennifer stared, as her jaw dropped. A knock on the door startled them both. So Jessica walked back to the door to open it. Beverly stood there.

"So, were you going to tell me, girlie?" Beverly asked, as she walked into the room.

"What?"

"About Sabrina; Becky mentioned it in passing, but didn't go into great detail. Brandon headed off to Austin, Texas. Does it have to do with her, too?"

"Yes."

"Beverly, you need to look at this," Jennifer said, as she found her voice again; as she held out the drawing.

"Why, Jennifer?" Beverly asked, as she marched forward. "Why do...oh hell."

Beverly stared at Jennifer then at Jessica. She found a chair and sat down now. Her hands shook as Jennifer got there before Jessica.

"I know it was years ago. But could it be possible?" Jennifer asked her. "Time..."

"I didn't know," Beverly answered still in shock. "It's been seventeen years since..."

"I know."

"What's going on here?" Jessica asked in anger. "Tell me, one of you. I don't care which one of you does!"

"Jim, after all these years," Beverly answered, as she slowly got to her unsteady feet. "Not possible. Have you talked to my nephew yet?"

"About what? He knows about the sketch because Becky did it. He seems to be....tell me what's going on here?"

Jessica's cell rang to life. She glanced at it and flipped it open. Beverly and Jennifer stared at her now.

"Hello," she replied back calmly. "Brandon."

"Hi, I got to Austin, Texas. I thought you would like to know."

"Your Aunt Beverly is here," Jessica replied back, as

she stared at them. "She's looked at Becky's drawing of the man Amy said was with Sabrina. She said 'Jim'. You said he looked familiar to you. Does this help you any?"

"Oh, crap!" exclaimed Brandon.

"Does the name sound familiar?" she asked him.

"Yeah, it does Jessica. Remember Rebecca and me when I was sixteen?"

"Oh...oh, no," Jessica exclaimed back, "Not that Jim!"

"I thought he looked familiar around the eyes in spite her difficulty with them. That's why I had come here. Let her know I'll be back after Ted and I alert the authorities here. Let her know that for me. Okay. Bye, Jessica."

"Brandon," Jessica replied back into the phone, but too late. "He's going to alert the authorities there and come back here. How do you know about Jim?"

She stared at Jennifer now. Jennifer stared at her then at Beverly who had nodded.

"Beverly comes into Starbucks every March seventeenth for the last fifteen years to order his favorite drink," Jennifer explained calmly.

"Its, how I celebrate Jim's birthday," Beverly said to Jessica calmly. "I know it was hard for Brandon to be in Paris so shortly after his birthday. I try not to book him to be there around that time. I know it's painful for him, too. I knew it was affecting him the week we were all there. Didn't you notice? I had..." Beverly started to explain.

"I know, Brandon told me about Rebecca," she interrupted her.

"Dream boat is your nephew, but you never

introduced us," Jennifer said, with a slightly disappointment sound in her voice. "Beverly, are you going to be okay?"

Beverly nodded. She held the sketch steadier now. Silence filled the room now. The three women were there and didn't know what else to say. Jessica turned and stared out her window. She felt in the dark with three people she trusted in the world. She struggled to find the words. Was this another nightmare in her life? Could she weather this one out? Time would tell her this truth. But he had to block out her past. She had to focus on what was here and now.

"I think everything is out in the open now," Beverly said finally. "It could be him or not. It has been a lot of years since I saw him last. Does it matter if Brandon is my nephew?"

"Well, he was not bound to your contract between your workers. He wouldn't be crossing that invisible line that caused him a lot of pain, anyways," Jessica pointed out to her.

"You have some interest in Brandon," Beverly said, as she focused Jessica now.

"We're friends and have been for over twelve years," Jessica snapped back. "I understand why it was put in place. He told me that Rebecca committed suicide, and she hooked up with your photographer friend Jim. Was he more to you than you want to admit? I seem to think so, since you never mentioned him before."

"You and I have a professional relationship, not personal," snapped back Beverly.

"And now we have become personal after being in Paris with David. Let's face it that things have changed for all of us now."

"Jess," Jennifer said in surprise. "I haven't seen..."

"This side of me," Jessica interrupted her. "No you haven't. I don't expect you to tell anyone about what we discussed right now. Brandon wants to know about my personal life now. What should I tell him all, or part, or pieces of it?"

"I don't know," Beverly answered back.

"He wants to cross the line. So will you let us?" Jessica asked her.

"Stop this now!" exclaimed Jennifer.

Jessica stared at her now. She noticed the tears in Jennifer's eyes.

"For you and the sake of our friendship," she replied back. "Please leave now."

They both left in silence. How did a simple thing of talking about a kiss turn ugly? Jessica couldn't understand why this bothered her so much. She went back to her window and stared out it.

6

Jessica had another assignment that she was reluctant to accept, since she wanted to look for Sabrina and hadn't heard from Brandon in three days. Plus she wanted to keep her word to him about searching for Sabrina in New York. But she boarded the flight to Seattle, Washington and allowed her mind drift in and out of thoughts and images of Sabrina and Brandon.

She didn't want to be reminded of what happened back in apartment with herself, Jenny and Beverly. Both Sabrina and Brandon tugged at her heart and soul so deeply that she remembered what was missing in her life, love. But she tried not to think about it too much because it had a way of hurting too much. She knew about what love had done in her own past and Brandon's.

She stepped off the plane and slung her carry-on bag over her right shoulder. She glanced at the overcast sky and knew ninety percent of year how it rained here. The photographer could have done it in his New York studio, but it was here. He was now. It made her shake her head.

But she wore her long, tan London Fog coat and tanned suede boots that hit mid-calf. Her teal buttoned up blouse and tan mid-length skirt. She hadn't applied any make-up and perfume since the make-up artist always provided them for the models. They knew what the photographer wanted.

"Jessica, darling," a man said, as he approached her.

He was medium built, a brown mustache and hazel eyes that always made eye contact with everyone he met. He loved to kiss his models on their cheeks and pitched their butts, as he did it. But Jessica never let him do that early on in her career, so he always kept a safe distance between them.

"How was your flight, darling?" he asked, as he held out his hand for her bag.

"Fine," Jessica answered, as she glanced around. "Where's everyone else?"

"Just you, darling," he answered back. "You know how the others complain about the weather and their hair. Sure you've never been a problem since our first shoot. That's why I want you so often. I know I compete against Brandon for you because you're in so much demand these last what eleven years," he answered with a big smile.

"How long will this shoot last, Clifford?" she asked, as she took out her cell to turn it on. "I'm in the middle of something."

"Another assignment?" asked Clifford.

"No, a personal matter, how long?" she asked him, as she glanced at her cell for any possible voice mails.

"Depends on you, and how well you react to this project. Have you worked with stuffed animals before?" asked Clifford.

"Yes, my second to last shoot, with an oversized teddy bear," she answered back. "Why?"

"A coffee company wants to advertise their toy bear line. They want to increase their sales."

"I think I know who you're talking about now."

"Good. Let's get to work then."

Jessie nodded. They arrived near the set when her cell rang to life. She flipped it open quickly.

"Brandon," she replied quickly.

"Afraid not, Jessica," a female voice said back. "It's, Becky. Are you sitting down?"

Jessica glanced around and found a director's chair and sat down. "I am now. What's going on?"

"Brandon was in the hospital along with his friend. Oh, what's his name now?" Becky asked herself.

"Ted. What happened?" she asked quickly back.

"A car accident, they were run off the road and the car rolled a couple times before it stopped. The police said it was an accident, but Ted doesn't think so."

"Jessica, darling, we need to get this banked before Christmas," called out Clifford.

"You're on assignment with him," snapped Becky.

"Yes, it's for my favorite coffee house. Beverly talked me into it. I didn't have much luck in finding Sabrina while I was home."

"Jessica, darling, time is money, and we're getting good money for this," Clifford stated in a tone 'Let's get to work.'

"I'll be right there, Cliffy," Jessica replied back. "I'll call you later. Will you be at this number?"

"Yeah, but I'm going out to Austin with Wendy. She's pretty shaken by it."

"Okay. I'll call ASAP. Thanks."

"Sure."

"Darling, you need to slip into the shot now," Clifford said with a small smile. "And don't call me, Cliffy. You know how I hate that name."

"Fine," Jessica replied, as she tucked her cell into her coat and slipped it off.

"That's perfect for this shoot, darling. Let's get this done. A dab of blush, and we're set to go. Jaime. I need a little pink blush on her cheeks."

For the next two hours, Jessica smiled and posed with various bears in costumes from bunnies, flowers to Halloween and Christmas themes. She was tired when Clifford called it a wrap. She sat down in the chair again.

"Drinks for everyone including you, darling," Clifford said to her. "Maybe you'll have more than water."

She looked at him. Clifford leaned down at her.

"What's that supposed to mean?"

"You and I both are adults here. Let's get so drunk we can have so much sex that the heat will melt candles without even lighting them," Clifford answered, as he leaned deeper into her face. "I know we would be great together. Do you want me as much I want you?"

"Get away," she answered, as she shoved him away from her. "I'm not that kind of model, Cliffy."

Clifford frowned, as he crossed his arms in front of his chest now. "I said don't call me that or I'll..."

"What?" Jessica asked quickly. "I know, you screw all your models but not me. I've never crossed the line and won't do it now."

She gathered up her coat and carry-on bag when he grabbed her. She gasped.

"I can take you here and now and get you to give into your hidden wants and needs; but most importantly your deepest desires," Clifford said, as he stared deep into her eyes now. "But I would rather get you drunk and feel your hands lusting over every part of my body including him, as you slip him into you. It can be our heaven, darling. I want you in your drunken state to beg for more of his release in you, and I would gladly do it."

"I want my whiskey, Clifford," called out Jamie.

"Go screw her, and leave me hell alone," Jessica replied back boldly.

"I've done her so many times that I want someone new like you."

"Go to hell!"

"With you gladly, darling, but you'll want me someday, and we'll be ready," Clifford said confidently, "Coming. Give Beverly, a call in your hotel room."

He patted her cheek now then walked away. Jessica sank deeper into the chair again and began to shake. She dropped her coat and bag before she felt the wetness on her cheeks. She didn't know how long she sat there, but she slipped into her coat and stepped outside to a mist. She got a taxi and headed for her hotel. There she got settled in and stared at light rain outside her room window.

"So you're not chubby anymore," Dillon said, as he closed the door to her room.

Jessie looked up from her book and smiled at him.

"No, Daddy."

"Do you wear that bikini top in public, so all the men can see your breasts and narrow waist?" Dillon asked, as he licked his lips.

"Daddy, what's wrong?" she asked, as she sat up on her bed now and put the book aside.

He moved closer to her now. "Why not show me all

of it? I used to see you naked as a baby. Why, not now?"

"Daddy, I don't think so," she answered a little afraid of him now.

"I order you to undress in front of me now. I'm your father, and you will do what you're told to do, young lady."

He grabbed her top and gazed at her average breasts now. She covered herself with her hands and backed away. Dillon lunged for her. He pinned her under him now onto the bed. He gazed deep into her eyes.

"You're warm to the touch," Dillon said calmly. "Don't scream or move until we get inside."

She felt her shorts loosen then she felt something below. He continued to stare at her when she felt something hard pushed inside her. It hurt like hell, but she didn't cry out.

"That's, my girl. First, we do the finger then him, as you get used to the thrusts. Releasing in, you will be such a thrill for us, both. This will be our heaven, and you'll not tell anyone about what we do here. Do you understand?" Dillon asked her.

Reluctantly, she nodded.

"Good. I want to build up to it. I didn't want to have to rush it, but I do love your new sexy body, Jessie. I'll be your first before any boy gets you. You haven't done it. Have you? I know Ryan wants your body too, but I get you first."

"It's not like that with him, Daddy," she replied honestly.

"Good. We'll do this again on Friday. Your Mom is taking Nathan to the dentist. I want you under the covers naked as a new born baby or I'll make sure you are. Do you understand me?"

She stared at him. He pressed harder inside her. She squirmed a little now but didn't scream or cry.

"Do you understand me?"

She nodded. Jessica felt cold, as she stared out the window. She thought about her dad, and what happened before she was eighteen. She shook her head, as her cell rang to life again.

"Hello," she replied calmly.

"Chubby Bear....I mean Jessica," said Nathan. "Are you all right?"

"I'm fine. How did you get this number?" she asked him thoughtfully.

"Bridget," he answered back calmly.

"What's wrong?" she asked quickly.

"I just got a chill like when we were kids. Are you scared, Jessica?" Nathan answered back. "Talk to me, Sis."

"It's nothing. I'm in Seattle, and it's raining here. And it's cold here."

"Jess, it's me, your twin. You're scared about something. I felt it before we were eighteen. It feels like it did back then. I know you're hiding something from me, but I don't know what," he continued on. "I've been on your side. Remember? They weren't sure about you becoming a model. I st..."

"I made it. Didn't I? I have what it takes to make it in this business. Now let me; be. I have to go now like I said; I'm on assignment. I have to go. I don't want to want to be late."

"But..."

She flipped her cell shut and gazed out the window more instantly now. She wanted to forget the past and Clifford's advances. She glanced down at her cell and saw the image of Sabrina before it faded out. It made her smile now. She thought of her and Brandon, as she stretched out in her bed now. She closed her eyes and thought of the two people who tugged at her heart and soul now.

They managed to reawaken something she put aside, as she focused on her career. Had she given it all up, or put it on hold for her career? She didn't know the answers, as she fell into a deep sleep now.

Jessica woke the next morning to a light knock on her door. It was housekeeping, so she let her clean the room. She stepped out into the now drizzle of rain. She glanced up to see flashes of light across the dark sky. She heard a grumble, as she folded her arms closer to her chest.

"So Zeus said to Apollo give it back. But Zeus being Zeus said no way, man," Nathan said to Jessie.

"I can't believe that anymore. I did when we were little, but we're fourteen now," Jessie replied, as she ate her ice cream.

"It's the truth, Jessie," Nathan said back. "Dad told me so."

"You and I are taking science now and have a better understanding of it all now. It was easy to say or tell us that. He's not good at explaining things like God and science," Jessie snapped back, "We also older now, too."

"But they're Gods too, Jessie."

"Whatever," she replied, as she took her final bite of her ice cream.

He pushed her on the swing. She heard his grunt, as she moved closer towards the clear blue sky.

"You're packing it on, Jessie. What are you now one hundred plus now?"

"One fifty-five," she answered with a big smile.

"Why can't you be thin like Mom? She's beautiful and always thin, but I don't know about you. I worry about you dying young and never know love and have children," Nathan said seriously. "Do you hear me, Jessie? I love you, and I don't want you to die young and alone."

"Don't worry, I won't die young. I'll have a man I adore and half dozen kids to beat up their favorite uncle," she replied back with a big smile.

"Their only uncle if I survive this," he said back.

Jessica wiped away the tears, as she stared at the Space Needle. She walked the grounds of the old World's Fair alone with her own thoughts and memories. Her cell rang to life.

"Hello," she replied softly.

"Jessica, thank God, girlie," Beverly said on her end. "I got worried."

"I'm fine. What's wrong?"

"You didn't call me then Jamie called. I got really worried," answered Beverly.

"I was tired with the flight and shoot all in one day. Why did Jamie call you?"

"She said Clifford tied one on last night. She never seen him that drunk before," Beverly explained calmly. "She stayed with him longer than the rest of the crew. She said he was crazed with desire for you, Jessica. He went into detail how he wanted to feel every part of your body then you know what he wanted after that."

Jessica found a bench and sat down. She still had her cell to her ear and felt a shortness of breath.

"Jessica, Jessica. Are you still there?" Beverly asked a little panic to her voice now.

"Yes, I'm still here. Have you heard from your sister Wendy or Becky?"

"No. Why?"

"They were heading to Austin, Texas."

"Why?"

"Brandon and Ted got into a car accident. You didn't know."

"No. Jessica, come home. The assignment is done. Come back to New York. I'll hire you a bodyguard."

"Let it go, Beverly. I need to work it out on my own. Please."

"Jessica."

"I've got to go now," Jessica replied, as she glanced at a dark figure approach her now. "I'll be careful. I promise."

"Jess..."

The dark figure had become clearer. She smiled, as she flipped her cell closed. She got to her feet quickly and rushed to him.

"Brandon," she cried out in very loud voice.

She hugged him despite his arm being in a sling. He embraced her back the best he could. She stepped back to examine him. He had a bandage on the corner of his right eye, and his face seemed discolored a little. She combed back his bangs with her fingers gently.

"I was worried about you, but I had an assignment

to do," she replied, as she stared back at him. "I couldn't find anyone in New York…"

"I know," Brandon interrupted her. "Becky told me. I took the first flight out to meet you. I had to tell you this in person."

"What?" she asked with interest now.

"I think I got too close to who took Sabrina. I know him, Jessica, and if I'm right it's going to crush my Aunt Beverly," he explained carefully.

"Her Jim."

He nodded and lowered his head into his chest. She tilted his head up again.

"You said he looked familiar back in New York. You wanted to say it then, but you held back. Why?"

"I wanted to be wrong for my aunt's sake. I love and care about her. I know what it's like to be …," then he shook his head, "Never mind. Are you done with your assignment?"

She nodded.

"Jim was from Austin, Texas. He had been in New York long enough to lose his the Texas accent. I confirmed it when Ted and I arrived there. Jessica, they meaning, the police wouldn't help us. I'm an outsider so is Ted."

"So they wouldn't arrest him," Jessica replied, as she felt an uneasy feeling in her stomach now.

"He's not there anymore. He was one or two days ahead of us or always one step ahead of us. It's so damn frustrating," he said, as he pulled away from her. "As you can see, I can't fly my plane now let alone a car. I hate to…"

"There you guys are," Becky said, as she approached them. "Mama, I found them."

Wendy walked up with Ted. Ted looked banged up, too. Wendy hugged her.

"We'll find, Sabrina," Wendy whispered in her ear. "With all of us and your friend Jennifer, we can't lose. We will find her if it takes the rest of our lives."

Wendy smiled at Jessica now. Jessica smiled back. They held hands now.

"How did you get here, Jess?" asked Becky.

"Walked, why?"

"We have a rented minivan back that way," Becky answered, as she pointed behind her. "Can you use a lift back to your hotel?"

She nodded. So they walked back to the minivan. Brandon walked away from Jessica and Wendy. No one spoke on the way back to her hotel either. Becky drove the whole way, and Brandon stared out the window. Wendy held Jessica's hand in hers. Ted scanned the area in silence. They all followed her up to her room. She noticed Clifford at her door.

"Darling, Jessica," Clifford said, as he rushed up to her.

"Our assignment is done," she replied, as she stood taller now. "You said it was a wrap last night. I'm going home with them. Excuse me. I need to get my bag from my room since the maid is done."

Clifford stepped aside and followed her in. She glanced around the room for her bag.

"The maid left it with me," Clifford said calmly.

"Where is it, Clifford?" she asked anger.

"In my car downstairs," Clifford answered with a big grin. "Don't you want to come back to my place and you..."

"Go to hell," she snapped back. "Not in this lifetime or even in the next."

"What's going on here, Jessica?" Brandon asked, as he stood in the open door now.

Jessica saw him and everyone else behind him now. She felt a knot in her stomach now.

"Nothing," Jessica answered back, as she stared at Clifford. "Housekeeping gave you my bag by mistake. I guess she thought I wasn't coming back. I would like my bag back now."

Clifford glared at her then nodded. He marched by Brandon and shot her another cold stare. Jessica felt a chill down her spine now. But she followed him, as the rest of the group followed her. Becky caught up with her now.

"He didn't. Did he?" Becky asked in a low voice.

"No, and don't say anything to anyone. Do you hear me especially not Brandon?" she asked her back.

Becky nodded. They reached Clifford's car, and he held out her bag. She took it and placed it on his hood. She checked to see if everything was there. Clifford stepped up closer.

"I didn't take anything," Clifford whispered to her. "I would rather have your flesh be mine."

She shot him a quick glance. "I'll tell Beverly that I don't want to work with you ever again. Don't force me to explain it all to her. Now leave me alone. Goodbye, Cliffy."

Becky walked up and smiled. Jessica smiled back at her.

"Let's go," she replied back, as they started to walk away from Clifford. "How are we getting home since

Brandon can't fly his plane?"

"Ted. He surprised us all when he showed his pilot's license. I think Brandon is nervous letting anyone flying his plane," answered Becky. "Everything okay back there?"

"Fine," she answered, as they stood at the minivan. "Did you know Bridget gave Nathan my cell number?"

"Because I wouldn't give it to him," Becky answered, as she got in behind the wheel. "I know you gave him your home phone and address before we left France."

"He also wanted to know if you had a man in your life," Brandon said finally. "I said I didn't know. We worked together but didn't discuss our private lives."

Wendy leaned on Brandon's shoulder and closed her eyes. Ted scanned their surroundings, as Becky headed for the airport. Jessica heard her cell ring to life again. She flipped it open and put it to her ear.

"Hello," she replied, as she felt uneasy again.

"You haven't seen the last of me, darling. You'll pay for calling me that name. I'll come to you when you least expect it, and we'll have lots and lots of unprotected sex. That's how I like it so did Rebecca," Clifford said on his end.

Jessica glanced over at Brandon. He smiled at her, but she didn't smile back. She looked down at the phone. There was silence now. She closed it and focused on the image or Sabrina's face in her mind.

"Are you all right, Jessica?"Brandon asked her.

"I'm fine."

Jessica felt relief that they weren't sitting side by side now. Ted walked into the cot pit and closed the door.

Wendy settled into her seat and was fast asleep again. Becky sat down next to her now. Jessica took the window seat and looked out.

"Can I sit with you? Becky, can you excuse us?" he asked politely.

Becky got up and moved without a word. She marched over and sat next to Wendy.

"Please have a seat. Tell me about Texas," she answered, as she turned to smile at him.

"Not much to tell. He's a local, and the police protect their own from outsiders. Ted and I were the outsiders, and he seemed to know we were coming," he said, as he sat down beside her.

"How did the accident happen?"

"A big truck came out of nowhere and rammed us. The car flipped a of couple times, and that's all I remember. When I came to, I had been out like light for three days then they called Mama," he explained calmly. "She's on my emergency card that I carry in my wallet. They didn't check for it until I came to."

"Where were you and Ted going?"

"We got a lead to check out this old farm house. An old timer thought he saw a child there."

"Did you go back to see him after you got out of the hospital?"

"No one knew who I was talking about. So I've reached another dead end, how about you anything?"

"Nothing, Jennifer has one of the flyers up at her work. She talks to her customers about Sabrina, too. Maybe we'll get lucky soon. Didn't Becky tell you? I told her to tell you that I had nothing, too. I told her that before her and your Mom left to go see you."

"Maybe she forgot. Mama was a little upset when she saw me there lying in the hospital. She demanded my release and got me out of there in a hurry. I had never seen her that upset since..."

Becky walked up to them. Brandon looked over at her, so did Jessica. Jessica decided not to ask him why didn't tell her more. It was over with now.

"Your Mom is tired," Becky said to Brandon. "I'm going to the outhouse. She snores. Excuse me."

He nodded then looked back at Jessica. "You looked frightened back at Clifford's car. Is there something going on there?"

"No. I think I'll take a nap, too. Can you stay here with me?"

"Sure," he answered, as he took her hand into his free hand.

She felt its warmth and breathed in his Old Spice aftershave. She felt safe now. She rested her head on his shoulder and thought of Sabrina. A five-year old girl out there in the big uncertain world with a stranger she doesn't even know. Could it be Jim from Beverly and Brandon's past? What did Cliffy mean by Rebecca? Could he be in involved it, too?

She didn't want to entertain the idea that Cliffy could be involved in it. It could be coincidence that he mentioned Rebecca's name. She decided to not to mention it to Brandon. Jessica snuggled closer to Brandon now, as she fell into a deep safe sleep.

7

Jessica hadn't remembered leaving the plane, much less the ride to her apartment or even coming into her apartment. But she woke up to the sun rays streaming across her face, as she would lie on her bed under the covers. She stretched and got out of bed. Then she stepped into her small living room and found much to her surprise that Brandon was on her couch asleep.

But it made her smile naturally. She walked carefully to her small kitchen so not wake him. Jessica was almost there when her home phone rang to life. She had her hand on the receiver when Brandon popped up. They made eye contact now.

"Jess, it's me, Jennifer, call me at work. It's important," the machine said before falling silent again.

"I'm sorry. I need to call her," she replied, as she held the receiver to her ear now. "She said it was important."

"Is everything important to her?" he asked with a big smile.

"Only when she has me call her at work," she answered calmly.

"Maybe, if it's about news about Sabrina."

"Could be," she replied, as she pressed the number on the screen.

"Hello, Starbucks, Jennifer speaking. How can I help you today?" Jennifer asked on her end.

"Jenny, it's me," Jessica answered, as she watched Brandon sat up and patted the seat next to him.

"Jess, I think I have a lead on Sabrina. Can you come down?"

"Sure Brandon and I will be there ASAP."

"Great. See you, guys, soon."

Jessica returned the phone to cradle. Brandon stared at her now. She turned to face him.

"She thinks she has a lead on Sabrina. She wanted me to come down. I hope you don't mind coming along."

"It's, fine, Jessica. Are you all right?"

"Why?"

"You seemed upset or something was wrong yesterday. That's why I stayed the night. Did something happen in Seattle?" he asked with concern in his voice.

"Oh, I'm fine. Let's get going," she answered, as she got to her feet again.

"Don't you want to change first?"

She glanced at her now wrinkled clothes and nodded. She darted into her room to change. She grabbed her navy blue sweatpants and matching sweatshirt. She slipped into a pair of socks and tennis shoes when Brandon stood in the doorway.

"Casual look, I've never seen it before but like it."

"I don't want to call attention to myself and scare off who might have information about Sabrina," she replied, as she glanced up at him.

"Good idea. Ready?"

She nodded and headed out by him. She felt his hand graze her ribs, as she headed for the front door. She picked up her sunglasses and keys. Brandon was behind her then beside her. They walked down the hallway together. He took her hand into his. She didn't pull away. He was one man she always felt safe with.

She enjoyed the early morning walk with Brandon at her side and couldn't be happier having him there but also longed to see and be with Sabrina, too. They stepped into the coffee shop and spotted Jennifer at the bar making drinks.

"Hi, guys, I'll be there in second," Jennifer called out to them.

Jessica nodded. Brandon released her hand.

"Hot green tea, but what size?" he asked her.

"Grande, and thank you," she answered politely back.

She watched him join the short line of customers, as she found an open table. A teenage boy sat a table next to her with his head down. He had a skateboard at his feet. His jeans had big holes in them and were dirty. But he also wore a dirty oversized Harvard sweatshirt. His hands cupped his drink.

"Are you looking for the little girl in that flyer on the wall?" the boy asked her in a low voice.

Jessica stared at him completely now. "Yes."

"Jess, this is Taylor," Jennifer said, as Brandon and her walked up. "Eat this slowly, Taylor."

Jennifer sat at his table and handing him a sandwich. Taylor unwrapped and took a bite. He chewed it before he put it aside.

"Thank you," Taylor said politely. "I saw the drawing after I noticed the flyer. I remember the girl a while back. She was happy." He looked up at Brandon. "It was you and a woman, but you didn't notice the man watching you."

"I was with them," Jessica replied, as she lifted up her sunglasses.

"Yes. But the man was watching him more than you. No offense Ms because you're beautiful; but he was more focused on your friend here."

"It's okay. Tell us what you know."

Taylor took another bite and chewed it. Jennifer touched his hand gently. He nodded.

"The man didn't notice that he was being watched. I tend to watch people more closely now. I've been on the streets for the last ten years not including the two years I lived with Mom. I've gotten to read people pretty well," Taylor explained in a low but calm voice.

"How old are you?" asked Brandon.

"Sixteen. Yeah, I know on the streets since I went back to them at the age of six. I had two years with Mom. But Mom had a choice me or the new boyfriend. Guess who she chose. I've been beaten up and raped by unknown attackers when I was younger. I've stayed away from the drug scene," Taylor continued on quickly. "This man had a real hate in his eyes for you, mister. I thought his eyes glowed passion red, but I could have been mistaken. Then you entered Mama's Pizza Shack. He got a call and raised his voice to the other person on the phone. He stormed down the street."

"Which way?" Brandon asked, as he focused on Taylor.

"The same way you guys went after Mama's Pizza Shack," answered Taylor. "I saw you guys leave, and I headed up the other way. He followed you from your building. I followed him in hopes to get some money for some food. I held back in caution. I can't tell you anymore than that. I'm sorry."

"It's okay," Jennifer said, as she touched his hand.

"Why?" Brandon asked him. "Why are you sorry?"

"Outside of Jennifer here, I didn't...." Taylor tried to explain.

"It's okay. Your life is starting to change," Jessica replied, as she touched his hand, too. "We want to change Sabrina's, too."

"God closes a door and opens a window somewhere else," Taylor said with a small smile. "My Mom said it to me before she left me at the Subway's ladies' room door. I was scared and didn't realize that she must slipped by me. I knew about her and boyfriend's argument over what do with me. I tried to ignore it. But I would never see her again."

"Good deeds deserve rewards," Brandon said with a smile now.

"That man is bad news, mister. You better find Sabrina fast before he hurts her like me or worse."

"Thanks, Taylor," Brandon said, as he held out his hand.

"Here's a key to my place go and crash there as long as you like and help yourself to the food in the refrigerator, too."

They shook hands. Jessica hugged him. Then she hugged Jennifer before Brandon and she left the coffee shop.

"That was nice of you."

"I've got a spare hidden, and I'll get in later. I need

to tell Becky."

Jessica nodded. He picked up his cell out of the sling and struggled to open it. So she flipped it open and scanned his directory then hit the green button; before she handed it back to him.

"Thank you," he said before he placed it to his ear.

She nodded again. She smiled, as she glanced at him on the phone. He smiled back at her.

"Mommy, where do babies come from?" Jessie asked her Mom.

Stephanie looked up from the sewing she was doing. She stared at her for a time. Jessie waited patiently.

"Well, a Mommy and Daddy get...uh. You won't have to worry about it, Sweetie," Stephanie answered her finally.

"Why not, Mommy?" Jessie asked with interest.

"You might not be able to because of all that weight. You need to stop eating so much. I'm worried about you, Sweetie," Stephanie answered with concern in her voice. "Are you upset about something?"

"I'm fine, Mommy," Jessie answered with a small smile.

"You know you can tell me anything."

"I'm fine, Mommy."

"Jessica. Oh, Jessica," Brandon called out to her. "We're here."

Jessica stared at him then where they were. She realized they were where they last seen Sabrina.

"Why here?" she asked him. "Ted said they weren't able to give out any information on the lady before them."

"But we're going act like a couple or young couple seeking a child like Sabrina, and we had already talked to the lady before them about adopting Sabrina," he answered back. "Maybe if we fake trying to remember her name, they'll..."

"Tell us her name," filled in Jessica. "Then Ted can see what he can find out about her."

"Exactly," he said with a bigger smile now.

"Do you think they'll believe us?" she asked with interest.

"Yeah, hold out your ring finger," he said, as he reached into his sling again. "Help me put this on."

She helped with the sapphire diamond gold ring followed by a gold wedding band onto her finger. He had a plain gold band a little larger, too. She had not much time to react much less think at this point.

"Now slip this one on my ring finger," he said, as she stared at it. "We have to make it believable, Jessica."

"What if they ask about your bruises and arm?"

"It was a photo shoot that had gone bad in Europe. Let's go," he answered, as he motioned her to the steps.

They walked up, and he rang doorbell. A woman about their age answered the door. She wore jeans and t-shirt that seemed new. She smiled at them.

"Yes, can I help you?" she asked them politely.

"Yes, you can or at least I hope you can," Brandon answered with a big grin. "My lovely wife and I want to adopt a child."

"Oh, please, come in," she said, as she allowed them in. "My name is Buffy. Yeah, I was named after Jimmy Buffet the musician. My parents were crazy about the guy."

"I'm Dillon and my lovely wife Stephanie," Brandon said calmly.

"Pleasure to meet you both," Buffy said, as she closed the door. "Its story time, so my husband is with the remaining children now. Come this way."

They followed her to the living room. There were a least dozen children on the floor listening to a man in a cowboy custom. He glanced their way with a brief smile. But the children still focused on him. Buffy walked into another room, so they followed her there.

"Peter's great with the kids. Our youngest is six to the oldest being twelve," Buffy explained, as she sat behind a simple desk.

"You're new here. We talked to an older woman before. What was her name, Honey?" asked Brandon thoughtfully.

"Uh..." Jessica answered in hesitation.

"You must be talking about Jill Claymore. The State fired her a couple weeks ago," Buffy said with a serious look on her face now.

"Why?" Jessica asked back.

"There was an incident with one of the State's charges, as you know we or this place is some children's last place before they enter the general public. Well, she..."

"What?" Brandon asked acting surprised.

"She left a little girl at the airport to catch a flight to see another young couple like you thinking of adopting her," Buffy continued on calmly.

"Oh, my not the one we were interested in," Jessica replied back, as she glanced at Brandon. "Not, our dear sweet little Sabrina. She is only five."

"Afraid so," stated Buffy.

"What's the State going to do?" asked Brandon.

"What do you mean? Oh, in trying to find her, nothing. They say they don't have any resources or time to find her," Buffy answered back. "I think their wrong in doing that to a five-year-old child especially a little girl. I wish I knew how to reach the PI who had by shortly after her disappearance was. He seemed to want to help but…"

"But what?" asked Jessica?

"I or we didn't know at the time when we talked to him that the State wasn't going to do anything about Sabrina. I think about her at night. How can a child just disappear like that?"

Jessica began to cry openly now. She could see Sabrina clearly upstairs in that room above them. It made her cry even harder. Brandon placed his arm around her, and she buried her head into his sling and chest.

"She's gone, but not forgotten," he whispered to her.

Jessica looked up and removed her sunglasses. She wiped away the wetness on her cheeks. He tilted her head up to his.

"You're not faking this. You really feel for Sabrina," he whispered to her.

"Yes. Don't you?" she asked in a low voice back.

"Uh…yes. Why else would I be looking for her and getting banged up in the process," he answered back in a low voice, too. "Buffy, could you leave us for a few minutes?"

"Sure," Buffy answered, as she left the room.

"Can we leave now?"

"Just a second," he answered, as he moved to a file cabinet and opened a drawer.

He pulled out a file and stuffed it in his sling. Jessica couldn't believe it. He walked back to her side.

"I'm sorry, Stephanie, maybe we can find another little ..." Buffy said, as she re-entered the room.

"I don't think so," Brandon interrupted her. "I think we need to go home and rethink this. Thank you. Have a good day. Honey, let's go."

Jessica slipped her sunglasses back on and took Brandon's free hand. They walked back to the front door with Buffy close behind them.

"I really am sorry, Stephanie. Peter and I aren't irresponsible like that," said Buffy. "We love children, despite we can't have any of our own."

"You don't seem the kind," Jessica snapped back honestly. "Can we go, dear?"

Brandon nodded, as he struggled to open the door. They stepped outside and walked a good distance before she stopped suddenly.

"I took Sabrina's and Claymore's personal files. We could find more leads, I hope," he said back to her. "I've got to get a hold of Ted to tell him what I got."

"Let's go to Mama's," she replied finally.

He nodded, so they walked to Mama's Pizza Shack again. She didn't know what else to say to him. This was side of Brandon that she never knew before. Then the names he used were of her parents. She couldn't recall ever saying their first names. She shook her head and walked on with him.

8

They were in Jessica's apartment instead now. Ted examined Jill's personal file while Brandon looked through Sabrina's. Jessica sat in her room alone. She and Brandon had a disagreement about the files over an hour ago. They had left Mama's Pizza Shack, too. So she marched off to her room when Ted arrived. Someone must have told him where to find them.

"Come in, Jennifer," Brandon said politely and loudly. "She's in her..."

"I'm in here, Jennifer," Jessica replied, as she stood in her bedroom doorway. "What's wrong?"

"I need to talk to you privately," Jennifer answered without her usual smile.

"In here then," she replied sharply. "I don't want the thief to hear us."

Brandon closed the front door and walked back to the couch. Jennifer joined her on her bed now. Jessica stared at her.

"I found these," Jennifer said, as she placed the bag next to Jessica.

Jessica looked inside and saw photos. She took them out and examined them carefully. She couldn't believe her eyes.

"Where did you find them?" she asked still shocked.

"Actually, I didn't find them. He didn't want me to say it was him that found them," Jennifer answered in a hint of hesitation in her voice. "Taylor found them."

"When? How?"

"He went back to where he saw the man standing outside Brandon's studio after he left the coffee shop. The man had been watching you and Brandon for awhile," Jennifer explained calmly.

"Apparently," she replied, as she re-examined the photos. "These seem to have…"

"A professional look about them," Jennifer filled in. "I thought about it, too."

"Jessica…" Brandon said, as he stood in the doorway. "What do you got there?"

He walked over and grabbed the photos out of her hands. He examined them quickly then he leaned against her dresser. His face had gone pale as snow now.

"Brandon, I think I have an idea…" Ted said, as he entered the room. "Brandon, you look like you've seen a ghost."

Brandon held out the photos to him. Ted examined them, too quickly before he looked at Brandon again.

"He has been watching you for awhile now."

"Those were taken in the last month or so," Brandon said in a weak voice. "It was before I went to Paris, Monte Carlo and Martha's Vineyard. The main focus is me and Jessica. The other models aren't as clear. He knows how to use a camera."

"Everyone knows how to use a camera," said Ted.

"I mean, he knows how to use a camera, man. Don't you get it?"

Ted's eyes popped open then he nodded. They stared at each other.

"So what does this mean?" asked Jennifer.

"Man, this is not random and is definitely our guy. We were right about going to Austin, Texas. It's Jim. Now the hard part is to locate him without us getting banged up again and telling Beverly," explained Ted, "Any ideas how to tell her?"

"Not a clue," Brandon answered, as he shook his head. "But we'll table it for now. Did you find anything useful in Claymore's personal file?"

"Yeah, I would like to check it out. I need to see how these two are connected," Ted answered thoughtfully, "Anything in Sabrina's?"

"She was dropped off at the orphanage at the age of one. She had burns on her arms and legs which healed in time. Oh, she had bruises on her ribs, too," Brandon explained calmly. "She had a typed note around her neck with her; and birth date along with shots she was given."

"Where's the note?" Ted asked with interest.

"In her file, it's enclosed in a plastic bag. Why?"

Ted bolted towards the living room. Everyone followed him, as he searched the open file.

"Possible can get fingerprints off who left her and be able to get a clue of her past. These all have to be linked somehow. I don't think he did this randomly, now. My gut tells me how they're all linked."

"Maybe, they all know each other. Jessica is a high priced model after all," pointed out Jennifer.

"That's too easy. It has to be something deeper," Ted snapped back. "I've got to go now. See you later."

"Keep me informed. I can't work like this," Brandon said, as he lifted up his sling.

"It's tricky, but you can use tripod," Jennifer

informed him.

Brandon shot her a look. She stepped back towards Jessica's room.

"Sorry."

"It's okay. You said the photos seemed professional," Jessica replied calmly. "How did you know that?"

"A friend of mine is a professional photographer. You know her, Jessica; Wendy of Mama's Pizza Shack," Jennifer answered cheerfully now.

"How did..." Brandon started to ask, "Never mind."

Ted left, and silence filled the apartment now. Brandon stared out the window. Jennifer sat on the couch with Sabrina's file in front of her. Jessica watched them both and didn't know what to say or do now. She walked into her small kitchen and decided to make some green tea.

"Um...Jess," Jennifer said in hesitation.

She glanced back. "Do you want a cup?"

"That would be nice. Thank you," Jennifer answered back politely. "I take it that you and Brandon didn't know that Wendy was a professional photographer. I assumed that's why you and he hung out there so often. She was giving him the benefits of her experience."

"She's my Mama," Brandon said, as he stood behind Jennifer. "Not many people know that fact."

"But you didn't know her career as a professional photographer slash geologist," Jennifer stated back. "How much do you know about her private life?"

"Jenny, don't go there," Jessica warned quickly to his defense.

"It's okay, Jessica. I know she was into geology and photography when she went into labor with me. But outside of that not much," Brandon answered in a low and sad voice. "I have never thought to ask after, he or Dad..."

He turned back to the living room. Jessica rushed to his side. She could see the pain now in his eyes. Brandon pulled away from her and stared out her window.

"I'm sorry, Brandon," Jennifer said, as she walked back into the room.

He nodded but didn't look at either one of them. Jessica walked back into the kitchen to finish making up the tea. She heard laughter in the other room, and so it eased her a little. But she pictured Sabrina in her mind.

"Do you want me to kiss it and make it all better, Heidi?" Jess asked a little girl with long, red hair in braids.

"That's okay. Just one of your bear hugs will do," Heidi answered with a bright friendly smile.

Jess hugged Heidi close to her body despite how big she was. Heidi hugged her back.

"We need to at least clean it up some," Jess replied with a warm smile back.

"I suppose, but it's a real pain," Heidi said, as she got to her feet and brushed off the loose dirt off her clothes.

"Having two parents being doctors," Heidi answered back. "They fuss over the littlest things."

"It's nice to have someone or people who care for you so much. It's something that you shouldn't take for granted."

"You got to be kidding, Jess. They won't let me live my life. Heck, I'm surprised how they let me come outside at all," Heidi said seriously.

"You're only five but very out spoken for your age."

"As opposed to you, a quiet church mouse who allows her twin brother show her stomach to prove it's fat not anything else," snapped Heidi.

"Ouch!" Jessica exclaimed, as she felt the sting of hot water touch her flesh now.

"Jessica," Brandon said, as he was at her side in an instant.

"I'm fine," she replied back. "Do you want honey or lemon in your green tea?"

"However, you fix; it is fine," he answered, as he stared deep into her eyes. "Jennifer can pretty goofy at times. Can't she?"

"I did my goofy walk. It works every time. Oh, sorry," Jennifer answered back. "Phone, I'll get it."

"Let it go..." Jessica started to reply but couldn't keep her eyes off Brandon.

"Excuse me, Jess. It's a guy claiming to be your brother on the phone," Jennifer interrupted them.

"What?" she asked, as she glanced over at Jennifer.

"Nathan's on the phone," Jennifer answered, as she held the cordless phone.

"Nathan," Jessica replied, as she reached nervously for the phone.

Jennifer nodded. Jessica took it into her living room then to her bedroom.

"Hello," she replied finally. "What's wrong, Nathan?"

"This little girl Sabrina," Nathan answered with some hesitation in his voice. "Is she yours?"

"How did..." Jessica started to ask with some confusion in her voice. "No, but uh..."

"I got a feeling something was up then the letter came a little while ago. I had to call you to find out what's going on, Chubby Bear."

"What letter?" Jessica asked, as she stood up off her bed now, "Nathan, what letter?"

"Calm down, Chubby Bear," Nathan answered calmly. "I have the letter here. It didn't say much, but it makes reference to you. So I had to call, Sis."

"Read it to me," she replied, as she entered the living room. "I'm going to put you on speaker phone. I want some other people to hear it, too."

"Okay. Here goes: Stop searching for Sabrina or Jessica and the child will meet the same fate," Nathan read over the phone.

Brandon stared at her, so did Jennifer. Jessica gulped down some air, as she saw their reactions.

"Anything else?" she asked him. "Like a stamp."

"No dice and no return address. It looks like it was just placed in my mailbox," Nathan answered calmly.

"Crap," snapped Brandon.

"Is that Brandon with you?"

"Yes. Are you sure there's nothing else?" Brandon asked, as he stood by the cradle.

"I'm sure. What's going on?" Nathan asked with concern now in his voice. "Tell me. Is my sister in some kind of danger?"

"Slow down, Nat, I'm right here and safe," Jessica answered quickly, as she stared at Brandon. "Do you hear me?"

"Yeah, I hear you, but I feel you're frightened, Chubby Bear," Nathan answered back.

"It's…" Jessica started to reply.

"Sabrina is a little girl I photographed with your sister prior to our shoot in Paris. She's missing, and we're now getting some pieces of who might have taken her," explained Brandon. "We need to keep the line clear for my PI, so we got to go now. Thanks for the call. Bye."

"But…" Nathan's voice trailed off now.

Jessica stared at Brandon's face now. He averted his eyes from her graze and walked over to the window again.

"What did Nathan mean by a feeling?" asked Jennifer.

"He's my twin brother. For years, we always knew or had a connection to each other then one day it stopped," Jessica answered, as she glanced over at the back of Brandon. "We didn't feel anything for years until recently."

"In Paris when you two met up again," filled in Jennifer.

"How long?" Brandon asked, as he faced them now.

"What?" Jessica asked him.

"How long have you not had the connection with Nathan?"

"Oh, maybe twelve or thirteen years, why?"

"They say twins are connected in every way possible unless or until one dies or one has gone through something traumatic in their life."

"Who are they?"

"Scientists or researchers," Brandon answered back sharply. "Don't you read? Oh, forget it. I need to find Ted and tell him what Nathan has. Excuse me."

Brandon bolted toward the door and out before Jessica could say another word. She felt Jennifer's gaze, so she turned to her.

"Are you going to leave, too?" she asked her.

"Why? I want to know all about your twin brother Nathan," Jennifer answered with a big smile. "Come let's talk."

"Nathan is five minutes older than me," Jessica replied, as they sat down on the couch together. She looked back at the closed door. "We haven't had contact with each other since I came to New York."

"You have some feelings for Brandon, don't you?" Jennifer asked her.

"We're friends. I worry after what happened in Texas, that's all," she answered, as she focused on Jennifer. "Nathan is a doctor now or least that's why I met up with him in Paris. Bridget's new born son had some kind of problem, so Nathan and Ryan came to Paris to check out the little guy."

"David Jeffery, yours and Brandon's godchild, right?"

Jessica nodded and breathed in and out slowly before she continued on. "I never knew he was into medicine the whole time we were growing up."

"Who's Ryan?"

"I guess his partner and best friend," she answered thoughtfully, as she looked back at the closed door again. "He was my first love and only love. We got really close."

"How close? Did you two have sex?"

"Heaven's no! But he did want to marry me though. I told him that we were too young to think about that kind of thing. It got too serious, so I broke up with him within months prior me coming to New York."

"I knew you had a past. A past you never talked about not that I wanted to know all of it. I did, but it had to be when you were ready to share. Maybe Brandon was right."

"About what?"

"Something traumatic happened, so you lost your connection with Nathan. Therefore, you left your past behind and focused on your life and career here in New York. What happened, Jess?"

"Uh...nothing," she answered in hesitation.

"Jess, I wo..."

The phone rang to life. She hit the speaker button. "Hello, Jessica, girlie."

"Beverly, what's going on?"

"I have another assignment. Are you up to it? I know Brandon isn't able to, so I got..."

"Not Clifford. Anyone but him," she replied sharply.

"He already agreed to it. In fact, he was eager to work with you again. Is there a problem I should know about here?"

"No. Fine, what am I doing this time, and where?" she asked coldly.

"Sports Illustrated swimsuit issue and in his studio here in New York."

"Why there?"

"He said something about better control of lighting and conditions for the shots."

"When?"

"Tomorrow morning at eight, is that okay?" asked Beverly.

"Fine, I'll be there. Bye," she answered, as she pressed the speaker button again.

"Doesn't sound like you, Jess," Jennifer said to her.

"What do you mean?" she asked quickly.

"You don't like this guy, Clifford. Didn't you two just do a shoot in Seattle recently?"

Jessica nodded, as she got up and walked over to her window. She crossed her arms across her chest now.

"Beverly likes to keep me busy. I'm her best model. I rack in some good money for us both, you know."

"Jess, tell me, what's up with this guy," Jennifer said with a concern tone in her voice. "Please talk to me, Jess. I've known you ever since you moved in here."

"I'm tired. You're probably tired, too. You can see yourself out. Please," she replied, as she headed for her room.

She kept her back to her. She didn't want to make eye contact. She didn't want to have to explain what Clifford had pulled in Seattle. It still unsettled her now.

"Jess, I..."

Jessica closed the door to her room and leaned against it. She waited for Jennifer to leave then flopped on her bed. She shook her head. It had been a long day, and she never had her tea. But it was late now, and she had to be at his studio by eight. It made her stomach uneasy. Nathan's call made her uneasy, too.

The kidnappers knew about her brother. How? She thought to herself, as she leaned on her pillow. It was hard for her understand it all. She moved her ring finger and noticed she still had the rings that Brandon had her help put there. She smiled at them before she tucked her hand under her pillow.

She knew she should remove them prior to the shoot tomorrow. But she wanted to have something close to her tonight that was a part of Brandon. She couldn't believe how Buffy revealed everything so easily to them without much effort on their part. It was another side of Brandon she didn't know about.

She smiled at it though despite everything. She was no longer mad at him for stealing Sabrina's and Jill Claymore's personal files. But she had another problem on her hands. The letter Nathan had received. What did it mean? She fell into a very deep sleep now and tried not to think about it all too much now.

9

It was dark outside when Jessica woke from her much needed sleep. She had clung to herself tightly since she had no one to cling to. She felt sweat escape her body. Then a knock startled her, and she slowly edged towards her front door. Jessica peeked through the little hole in the door.

"Wendy," she replied, as she opened the door. "What brings you here?"

"This," Wendy answered, as she held up an oversized black case.

Wendy walked deeper into the apartment, as Jessica closed the door. She didn't know what else to say.

"I need more light," Wendy said, as she sat down. "Did you hear me, Jessica?"

"Yes, of course," she answered, as she turned on more lights.

"Now, come sit next to me," Wendy said with a small smile. "It has been brought to my attention that you didn't know my career as a photographer."

Jessica sat down next to her and folded her arms close to her body again. Wendy opened the oversized black case onto her lap. There was a photograph before them of a waterfall in color.

"This is Yosemite after winter's thaw," explained Wendy. "This is Yellowstone in the heart of winter just after sunrise."

Jessica looked at each photograph, as Wendy

explained them. She could hear excitement in Wendy's voice, as she explained them. Then they had gone through about a dozen photos when they reached a familiar place to her. She placed her shaky hand on it.

"The Mother Lode and the mining camps," she replied in a soft voice.

"Yes. It's where I met Brad," Wendy said, as she moved Jessica's hand aside to reveal a new photo. "He was a handsome, fella. I had no idea who he was or who he was related to. I didn't really care."

Wendy took Jessica's hand into hers and stared into her eyes. Jessica glanced up then down again.

"I fell head over heels in love with him. I couldn't believe how fortunate I was to have a man as handsome as Brad look my way," Wendy whispered softly. "But I had two the most wonderful weeks of my life with him. He seemed to be from working class just like me."

"Why was he there?" Jessica asked, as she gazed deeper into the photo of Brad.

"He said, the company he worked for was thinking of what to do with those old mines up there," Wendy explained, as she tilted Jessica's head back into hers. "You see, Brad wasn't honest with me in the beginning. The first three days were hard on him, so he told me on the fourth day the truth. But it didn't matter to me by then that he was running away from his family; but they found him eleven days later. He was forced back to New York. I followed him like a long lost puppy dog. I loved him that much. Brad felt the same way about me, too."

"So you married into wealth," Jessica replied back.

"And I left it all behind when he died," Wendy said

sadly. "Brandon did it too out of guilt or loyalty to me. I don't know which for sure now. We don't talk about that time in our lives. But I can tell you this for sure that Brad loved Brandon and me with all his heart and soul, and we loved him that much as well. I still love and miss him."

"What happened in Greece?"

"I leave it to Brandon to explain."

"When's the time is right?"

"You'll know it and so will he but for now give him time and space," Wendy said, as she closed everything up and walked to the door.

Jessica followed her there. They stood in the doorway.

"You won't find Brandon in Brad's photo. He's not there that I can tell you, my sweet Jessica," Wendy said, as she touched her cheek before she left.

Jessica closed the door and dragged her comfy chair to sit in front of her window. She didn't know what time it was or how long she sat there. But she watched a golden sunrise warm her petite body. She had to change for a shoot that she dreaded now.

She never wanted to see Clifford again, but she couldn't tell Beverly what happened in Seattle, not yet anyway. She removed the rings from her finger and left them on her dresser despite how she wanted to keep them on.

An hour passed, and she stood at the door of Clifford's New York studio. She could hear voices on the other side of the door. She drew in a cleansing breath and exhaled, as she turned the door knob. She could see fake mountains and ocean backdrops at the far end of the studio. She didn't see Clifford right away. He stood by what appeared to be sand. He had his back to her, as she walked up.

"Jessica, darling," Clifford said with a big smile. "Had to have one thing real besides you, darling."

"Jessica, your clothes are in here," a blonde haired woman called out to her.

"Excuse me while I go change," she replied politely to him.

He grabbed her arm hard. She gasped. He leaned toward her right ear.

"I wouldn't mind us doing it there after everyone is gone. It's so sexy and less clothes to peel off that knock out body of yours," he whispered calmly.

She pulled herself free of his hold. She headed for the dressing room. She prepared herself for this assignment with some calmness and professionalism. She emerged out of the dressing room ready to work and bolt as soon, as he called it a wrap.

Jessica tried to ignore Clifford's face, as he licked his lips. He blew her kisses behind his camera. She kept her composure with each snap of the shutter.

"That's it people," Clifford said finally. "Good work, people. Jessica, can I speak to you after everyone leaves?"

"Uh sure, but it has to be quick. I'm meeting someone," she answered in hesitation.

"Just about fifteen minutes of your time, darling," he said back with a big smile.

Jessica slipped into the dressing room and expected to find her clothes where she left them. But her clothes and shoes disappeared from the chair. She kept the bikini and robe on, as she stepped out into studio. It was very quiet. She felt uneasy, as she walked deeper into the studio.

She felt something hit her hard against the sand. She adjusted her eyes to see Clifford on her. His eyes had desire in them, but she couldn't move. His body was on hers and had her hands pinned into the sand.

"I'll have drunk or sober now. You're mine, darling. No one's here, so you can scream all you want. But the studio is sound proof unless the front door isn't closed tight. It doesn't matter anyway," Clifford said, as he dove for her mouth.

"Get the hell off her," a voice yelled at Clifford.

She was free of him, and a dark figure was beating the crap out of him. But Clifford managed to get in a few shots, but clearly the dark figure was better of the two. The figure had hit Clifford so hard that now he didn't fight back. Jessica stumbled to her feet, as the figure stepped into the light.

"Taylor," Jessica replied in surprise.

"I didn't trust that man," he said to her. "Are you all right?"

She nodded. He reached for something in the darkness of the studio. Then Taylor held it out to her in the light. It was her clothes and shoes.

"Change quickly. I don't know how long he'll be out," Taylor said, as he spit out some blood.

"You're hurt," she replied back.

"Go change. We need to get out of here. Please."

She ducked behind the fake scenery to change quickly. She re-emerged dressed and spotted him dragging

Clifford to the sand. Clifford had a split lip and black eye starting to form. His face was red and badly bruised. Taylor tied his hands to his feet then he looked at her.

"Are you ready?"

She nodded, so he guided her to the front door. They stepped out into the bright sun. Taylor glanced at her watch and started to walk away. She took a hold of his arm. Taylor stared at her now.

"Thank you doesn't seem to be enough," Jessica replied, as she found her voice again. "Please let me buy you something to eat and clean your wounds. I owe you that and so much more. Please, Taylor."

Taylor nodded this time. Together they walked up the streets without a word to Mama's Pizza Shack. He held the door open for her, and she walked in. Wendy emerged from the kitchen. She rushed to them.

"What happened, Taylor?" Wendy asked with concern in her eyes.

"A fight with jerk, Mama," Taylor answered back. "She convinced me to get cleaned up and buy me some food."

"I'll get washcloth and pizza going," Wendy said back. "Slip into that booth, and I'll get you a glass of cold milk." She smiled at Jessica. "Thank you for bringing Taylor here."

"Uh..."

Wendy touched her cheek and left. Jessica noticed Taylor held his side now, as he slipped into the booth. She slipped in across from him.

"You didn't say Clifford's name," she pointed out to him.

"And I won't either. If I hadn't come in when I did, you and I know what that jerk would have done because I've seen a lot of men like him on the streets. No woman or girl deserves it not even you," Taylor whispered to her.

"Here, Sweetie," Wendy said, as she placed the milk before him. "Let me see the damage. Is the girl or lady okay?"

He nodded, as Wendy cleaned his face with the washcloth. Wendy hummed a soft an unrecognizable tune, as she tended to his wounds. Taylor stared at her then at Jessica.

"So how do you two know each other?" Wendy asked, as she finished up.

"Jennifer," they answered together.

"Oh my, what small world," Wendy said with a small smile. "I'll see if the pizza is ready."

She was gone, and he reached for the milk. He tried to drink but pulled back. His split lip hurt him obviously.

"I know Brandon gave you place to stay. But what can I do for you? Name it, Taylor."

"Stay away from that jerk. He'll rape you and have no remorse about it. He won't stop with one time but continually. I know I've seen and know his kind. It won't matter if he or the woman he's screwing is drunk or sober. He takes pride in his own personal pleasure," Taylor whispered to her. "That's what you can do for me. I can't guarantee that I'll be around next time."

"I'm model, and he's a photographer," she replied in a low voice. "I have to work with him now since Brandon is in no condition to work."

"Then you make sure you're never alone with that jerk for a second. He's proud of those private jewels down there and seems to be on a mission when it comes to you. He might go as far as getting you pregnant then still screw you during the pregnancy and after. He's that dangerous."

"Here you are, Sweetie," Wendy said, as she placed the combo in front of them. "Did the police take her to the hospital and arrest the perk?"

Taylor nodded and reached for a slice. His knuckles were raw and red. He took a bite and smiled at Wendy. Wendy kissed his forehead and left. They were alone again.

"You're wise beyond your years, Taylor," she replied back.

"I've been on the streets for a long time, but you don't want to hear it all. You're too much of a lady to hear it," Taylor said, as he chewed slowly. "Have a piece. Mama's is the best
I've tasted around in the city. I always come back here."

Jessica took a slice and chewed on it. She didn't know what to say. But she didn't stare at him either.

"Jessica," said Taylor.

"Yes," she replied calmly and made eye contact with him.

"I was given up for adoption at birth. My records were closed of who my parents were, but you wonder why I know your need to find Sabrina," he said, as he brought his hands together in front of him. "I was bounced around the various orphanages until I arrived at where Sabrina was. I was four then."

"But people like to adopt babies," replied Jessica. "And you said a different story when we first met."

"It's hard to deal with the truth sometimes. But not me, I was different than most babies," he said sadly. "I'm sorry that I lied to you at our first meeting."

"You look healthy and normal. But why did you lie?"

He shook his head, no. He reached for his shirt and lifted it up. There in the middle of his young chest was a long line leading to up to his right shoulder to his left waist. Then he pulled his shirt back down.

"It was very noticeable when I was little. No explanation as to why it was there, so people didn't want to take a chance. I arrived at the same place Sabrina was, and the same lady was in charge back then," Taylor explained, as he clasped his hands together in front of him again. "She treated me differently, so I ran away from there shortly after my arrival. I've seen her on the streets from time to time, but she doesn't recognize me anymore."

"Why do you say that?"

"Two things, I'm older now, and my hair is lighter then back then. She didn't know who I was about a week ago when I approached her for some spare change."

"You saw her," she replied a little shocked.

"She was coming out of the bank in Manhattan," he said calmly. "She had a lot of cash in her hands and in purse."

"Do you know where she went?"

"Fashion district, why?"

"Hold on," Jessica answered, as she reached for her cell, "Last week, right?"

He nodded. She scanned her contacts and pressed Brandon's number. It rang a couple times, as she tapped her fingers on the table.

"Hi, Jessica," said Brandon.

"Has Ted found Jill yet?"

"He got a lead. But it didn't pan out. He's got a lead on Sabrina, and I'm waiting for him to get back to me on it. Why?"

"I'm here at Mama's with Taylor He told me that he saw Jill coming out of a bank in Manhattan with a lot of money last week."

"That's interesting."

"I thought so, too."

"I've got another call. I'll get back to you, and I'll let Ted know what you told me about Claymore, got to run. Bye."

She flipped her cell closed and placed it on the table. Taylor stared at it.

"She had one of those too in her purse," added Taylor. "Do you want to know what I think?"

"Of course."

"I think she was paid good money to leave Sabrina at the airport. The man who took Sabrina had connections and didn't stop there. It took a lot of planning on his part to be several steps ahead of you. Oh, someone is leaking him information."

"But only a few of us know about Sabrina's disappearance," she replied thoughtfully. We haven't even gone to the police with any of it. We kept it all in house sort of speak."

"It's just a thought," he said, as he looked down at his hands. "I'm not stupid, Jessica."

"I never said you were," she replied back. "You're

what my dad called street smart like him. You know how to survive on the streets where most people don't."

"I was too trusting in the beginning, but I wised up. You don't want to hear it like I said before."

"Tell me about it. Please."

"It was horrible that first night on the streets, Jessica. I had a pair of oversized boots on, holes in my socks, cords and an oversized sweatshirt," Taylor said, as he glanced into her face briefly. "Are you sure you want to know?"

"Yes," she answered, as she touched his hands.

He pulled his hands back, and she took a hold of them again. She felt them slightly shake in hers. She wanted to be encouraging for what he was about to reveal.

"It's okay. I can handle it," she replied calmly.

"I ...I didn't have money or food," he said in hesitation. "One man said he would give me some food if he could feel my body." Taylor stared off in the distance now. "I let him because I was really, really truly hungry. We did it in an alley. It was cold as he undressed me. Then I felt a sharp pain. When I woke up, another man stood over me and said I was fine fuck, and the first man nodded next to him. I felt the sharp pain again." Taylor had tears in his eyes that glided down his face now. "They were molesting me, and I didn't know it. I didn't know how to stop them either. I passed out every time they entered something up there."

"How did you find out?" Jessica asked before she thought it through.

"Two nights of it after they passed me onto a woman on the streets, and she wore a lot of make-up. She asked if I was still a virgin. They said take him and find out yourself," Taylor answered painfully. "They got money for me, and she took me up to a warm room. She fed me then ordered me to lie down on her bed after taking a hot shower. I was naked. She said this is what pleases a woman as she held my tiny penis. I felt it being moved around then she whispered in my ear pee little man this makes Mommy happy."

Jessica continued to hold his hands in her despite she felt sick to her stomach. She had to focus on him and nothing else. No outside thoughts.

"You need to make he's safely inside before you pee. This pleases Mommy to no end. I guess I did it more than once because she said it was each time. I would get food each time. I don't know how long I stayed with her, but I was tied to the bed and gagged. She had me do it a lot, but one day she untied me and let me go. I think two years had passed by then. I was back on the streets with some money and a backpack full of food."

"Then what happened?" she asked, as she felt her throat was really dry.

"I've had sex with women and men when I needed food until I met Jennifer and Mama here. They gave me free food and clothes without expecting anything from me," he answered back. "I told you that you are a lady. You didn't deserve to hear this story of my life."

"Does Jennifer and Wendy or Mama know about this?"

"No. They only know I'm a homeless kid who lives on the streets," Taylor answered sadly. "They don't deserve to hear it either. Please don't tell them."

"I won't. But I have to ask you one thing that has been bothering me though," Jessica replied thoughtfully.

Taylor stared at her seriously for a time. He seemed to be thinking it over now.

"Okay. What's been bothering you, Jessica?"

"The way you talk. It's not like a..."

"A four- year-old but more mature," he interrupted her.

She nodded.

"Mama or Wendy taught me how to read and write when I had been on the streets three years. I read discarded books, magazines and newspapers that people left behind in garbage cans, dumpsters and waste paper baskets. What I don't understand is why I have this," Taylor said, as he reached into his backpack for a dictionary. "Jennifer gave it to me like I said they give me food, clothing and on occasion things like this. But they don't expect anything in return."

"They're givers," she replied with a smile.

"So are you and Brandon," he said with a small grin. "But you have a secret that's so buried deep inside you that you don't think a living soul will understand. But I'm going to tell you here and now that you'll share it with the right person. You will know when it feels right to you. Then you will truly heal. I won't tell anyone about that photographer. It's not my place to tell. It's your second secret, and you will reveal that one too when the time is right."

"Thank you, and thank you for coming to my rescue," she replied, as she touched his hands.

"No problem," he said, as he slipped the dictionary

back into his backpack. "Wendy or Mama, I've got to go now. Business you know."

Wendy walked over to their booth. She hugged Taylor, as he stood up. He waved bye to Jessica and left. Wendy sat down and stared at Jessica now.

"So how do you know Taylor?" Wendy asked with interest.

"He spotted the man watching Brandon, Sabrina and I before she disappeared," Jessica answered calmly. "I wonder something."

She felt her cell vibrate in her pocket. She must have slipped it into her pocket without even thinking about it.

"Hello," she replied, as she flipped it open.

"Hi, Jessica, it's Ted," he said on his end.

"Hi," she replied, as she looked at Wendy a little confused as to why he was calling her.

"I had a false lead on Sabrina. So I still need to look into something on Jill Claymore, but Brandon wanted me to update you," said Ted. "Have you talked to him recently?"

"Yes. Why?"

"Nothing, I got to go, but he wanted me to keep you informed," Ted answered quickly.

"But he didn't tell you about the latest I found out from Taylor. He saw Claymore coming out of a bank in Manhattan with a lot of cash."

"No he hasn't been...." Ted started to say. "I got to go. Bye."

She flipped her cell closed and shook her head. Wendy leaned in closer.

"Everything, okay?"

"Yes. I need to go. The pizza was great. Thanks for cleaning Taylor up. I wanted to do that myself. How much for the pizza we barely touched?"

"On the house you know that, Jessica. I'm glad you brought Taylor in despite those minor scrapes on his face," Wendy said with a small smile now.

"Why?"

"I worry about him on the streets alone. He's only sixteen, and it hasn't been easy for him I'm sure," Wendy answered sadly.

"Why do you say that?"

"He was too young to be thrown out on the streets at four-years old," Wendy answered thoughtfully. "He needs a home and a family to care and love him. He's a smart kid and doesn't belong out there alone."

"I agree," Jessica replied with a big smile. "Maybe things will change for him someday for the better."

"Maybe."

Wendy walked back into her kitchen. So Jessica decided to go, too. But she thought of what Taylor told her, and what Wendy said about him. She told him that she wouldn't tell anyone what he has been through. She knew firsthand what it was like to keep a secret, but how did he knew she had one. She shook her head and headed back to her apartment.

She saw no blinking light on her machine. She decided to stretch out on her bed and not think of anything. Jessica knew what he said about something painful down there. She dismissed it quickly, as it had come up. She wanted to keep it buried forever.

10

Jessica couldn't reach Brandon by phone for three days. Ted called her on the second day to ask if she knew where he was. He seemed to forget about what she mentioned before about Jill Claymore and the bank. But she didn't bring it up again. She didn't answer Beverly's calls on her cell or machine. She didn't want to talk about what happened between her and Clifford either. However, Jessica was grateful Taylor arrived when he did.

She paced her apartment often now. A knock on her door caused her to sprint toward the door quickly. She flung it open but was disappointed. She walked back into her living room.

"Well, hi, to you, too," Jennifer said, as she walked in. "Still no word from Brandon."

"No, and I'm really getting worried now. Ted called the day before yesterday to find out if I know where he is."

"Does Becky?"

"No one has heard or seen him in awhile. It's like he disappeared just like Sabrina. I'm afraid something might have happened to them both now."

"Easy, girl, I've never seen you like this before. You really care about them both," said Jennifer.

"Why shouldn't I? I've know Brandon for twelve plus years now, and I've...never mind. Then Sabrina is only five. Five years old, Jennifer. Do you remember what you were like at her age? I do. I was a fat and struggled with my weight until I was sixteen almost seventeen. Then things changed forever. There was no going back. Innocence was lost forever, too," Jessica rambled on.

"Slow down, Jess. That's a lot of process my friend," Jennifer said calmly.

Her phone rang, and she glanced at the caller ID. She let it go to the machine.

"Leave a message." Beep.

"Jessica, what's going on? It's me, Beverly. Wendy said you were in with Taylor a few days ago. Clifford got beat up the day of the shoot. Do you know what happened? Call me back."

"Why didn't you pick up?" Jennifer asked her. "She said Clifford got beat up."

"My focus is on Brandon and Sabrina. Do you want to help me find Sabrina?" she asked her point blank.

"Sure. I've got some vacation time due me. Let me call my boss to see how much. Can I use your phone?"

Jessica nodded. She walked back into her bedroom to grab her wallet and keys. She noticed crystal teddy bear dangling from her keys now in her hand.

"I'll find you, Sweetie, even if it takes me forever. I promise you that, Sabrina," she whispered to the bear.

"I've got three weeks. I told her that it was a family emergency, so it goes into effect today. I'll have to work through the Christmas season, but it's worth it. I'm here for you, Jess," Jennifer said, as she stood in the doorway.

"Thanks. Do you have a car?"

Jennifer nodded, so they headed out of the apartment. They stopped by her apartment to pick up her car keys. Then they headed downstairs to an underground parking garage that Jessica didn't know existed. But she followed her friend to royal blue Cobalt car and slipped into the passenger side without a word.

"Do you have your cell charged and with you?"

She nodded. They headed out on the busy streets of New York. She closed her eyes after rolling down her window.

"Where do we go to now, my friend?" Jennifer asked her.

"Not sure. We tried the airport with not much luck. I don't know," Jessica answered, as she fought back the tears.

"Sabrina has really gotten to you," Jennifer said with a concern. "I've known you awhile now, but this little girl has gotten to you, Jess."

"I'm afraid for her. What do we know about the man who took her? Why? Why does he look so familiar to Brandon? I have so many questions but no concrete answers. Damn it."

"Relax. We'll do our best to find her. You said Ted has been looking for Jill Claymore as well as Sabrina. What has he come up with on her?" Jennifer asked calmly.

"I never asked or don't recall," she answered thoughtfully.

"It's okay. Let's go somewhere quiet and call him. I got just the place," Jennifer said with a small, friendly smile. "Close your eyes and listen to the music."

"But..."

"No, buts Jess."

Jessica closed her eyes and listened to the unfamiliar music. She felt her body relax despite it being music she didn't know. She saw Brandon's smile then Sabrina's.

"Class. Class, I need your attention please," a woman said, as she stood in front of the classroom. "Jessica Hudson, can you come up here?"

Jessie got out of her seat and walked up to the front of the room. Her eyes focused on the woman when she stumbled to the front. She stopped herself quickly. Jessica glanced at Mark and noticed his leg out.

"Jessica," the woman said to her.

Mark grinned at her, as she walked up to the front. She stood face to face with a woman with a salt and pepper hair in tight bun, bifocals and plain clothes. She appeared to be in her early or late fifties.

"Yes, Mrs. Hanagan," Jessie replied politely.

"How old are you, Jessica?" Mrs. Hanagan asked her.

"Twelve almost thirteen," she answered back.

"Tell the class what you want to be when you grow up," said Mrs. Hanagan.

"A fat bear," called out Mark.

"No, a model that will make you wish you hadn't treated me like this. Why? Because I wouldn't give you the time of day," Jessie snapped at him, as she faced the class.

Her eyes narrowed, as she scanned the room. She spotted Nathan in his chair with a big smile on his face. He winked at her now. She stood taller now.

"That's a joke. Right, Chubby Bear," said Mark.

"No joke. You'll see. You, all, will see. Someday I'll be a high priced model, and I won't give you any the time of day except the ones who are good to me now."

"Like me and your brother," said Ryan.

Her eyes shifted to Ryan now. He sat in front of Nathan. She nodded and bolted out of the room. Jessica rushed into the girl's bathroom and began to shake now.

"Jess," Jennifer said, as she shook her hard on the shoulder.

"What?" Jessica asked a little startled.

"You seemed so far away right now. You were shaking. Are you okay?" Jennifer asked with concern in her voice.

"I was. Where are we?" she asked, as she glanced around the open area.

"Rich people live here, but I love the fall foliage up here. It's so peaceful here and away from the big City," Jennifer answered, as she got out of the car. "There's a mansion over there that reminds me of the Deep South back to Civil War maybe later."

"Oh," she replied, as she got out of the car. "It's nice here."

"I think so," Jennifer said with a big smile. "I don't see any life in that house in all the times I've been here. But I love fall foliage around it and grounds. I can imagine children and parties there long ago."

"I'll call, Ted," she replied, as she leaned against the car now.

"Okay. I'll be over there," Jennifer said, as she pointed off to Jessica's left.

She nodded and scanned her cell. She found Ted's number on her incoming calls and pressed it.

"Hello," said Ted. "Jessica, have you heard from Brandon?"

"Uh, no," she said a little surprised by his bluntness. "Have you got any leads on Sabrina and Jill Claymore?"

"I thought I had one on Sabrina. It didn't pan out, too old. Then I traced Jill to that bank Taylor said he saw her come out of," answered Ted.

"Oh really," she replied, as she stood taller now. "What did you find out?"

"She had an apartment on the upper eastside of town. She paid rent there for about six years then stopped," Ted answered thoughtfully.

"When did she stop?"

"About a month ago, so I talked to the landlord. He said she packed what little was in apartment and left. He asked her for an address to forward her deposit. She said she wasn't that hard up anymore to give it to someone in need."

"So you have another dead-end."

"I thought so, but I found a piece of paper in her apartment."

"What did it say?" Jessica asked with interest.

"Austin, Texas and Mother Lode," he answered back. "We, Brandon and I, had gone to Texas. Brandon was too quiet while we were there. He was thinking about something real hard, but he wouldn't share it. Now he has disappeared. I have no idea what Mother Lode means."

"California has a Mother Lode where Marshall discovered gold. Could it be that?"

"I don't know. I don't have the money to fly there to find out. It might be another false lead, got to go."

"Okay," she replied, but it was too late.

Jessica scanned the area and spotted Jennifer. She walked in that direction. She smiled at the landscape of fall starting to make its way here. She didn't see much fall foliage in the City.

"A plane crashed into the South Tower," a voice said from Jennifer's headphones around her neck. "I say again a plane hit the South Tower of the Twin Towers."

Jennifer held a 35 mm camera in her hands, as she turned to look at Jessica. Jessica walked up closer.

"Do you remember where you were, and who you were with?" Jennifer asked her calmly.

"Uh..."

"I do. Right here and alone. Our lives changed a lot that day. I wanted to catch the early morning light on that mansion I told you about. It's hard to believe it was ten years ago. It had life prior to that day, and I was eighteen back then," explained Jennifer.

"I was twenty and can't remember much about September eleventh," Jessica replied back. "Sorry. Did you live in New York all your life?"

"Brooklyn, my relatives always drove out of the city every summer. That's how I found this place. I know I said it didn't have any life to it, but it did prior to 9/11. The first time I saw the mansion at the age of ten. When I noticed it empty now fourteen years later, it's sad to see a house like that empty. It was better to say no life in it then the uneasiness or sadness surrounding the place. Don't you feel it?"

Jessica felt a sudden chill consume her body. She nodded and rubbed her arms.

"Death, but it doesn't show signs of

abandonment," she replied in a low voice.

"I know. There seems to be a staff to keep the grounds and house up but no homeowners present."

Jessica stared at the house and grounds. She walked up to the Iron Gate winding up to mansion and touched the gates. She saw an image of Wendy, a dark haired man and a small boy. She pulled back her hand and began to shake.

"Jess, what the heck..." Jennifer said quickly.

Jessica stared back at her. She mouthed words but didn't hear anything from her mouth.

"Jess."

She rushed back to the car. She could hear Jennifer not far behind her when they reached the car at the same time.

"You look like you saw a ghost," Jennifer said, as she looked into Jessica's face.

"Wendy," Jessica replied, as she found her voice again. "We need to get Becky to help us find Sabrina since no one seems to know where Brandon is."

"Do you have her number?"

Jessica nodded and scanned her cell. She pressed Becky's number.

"Where are you?"

"Uh...not in the City. Why?"

"Taylor and I want to help find Sabrina. Ted said no one has been able to reach Brandon. I'm worried. It's not like him to be out of touch. I have Taylor with me now," Becky rambled on.

"Fine, we're coming back into the city," Jessica replied back. "Me and Jennifer, I think more people looking for her. The better our chances are in finding her."

"You know, Brandon does care about her. You do know that, Jess."

"Yeah, it's like a personal quest all his own that he won't reveal to anyone."

"Not even you," Becky said as little surprised.

"Nope, he doesn't tell me everything, you know."

"Well get back here. Beverly wants to meet us all at Mama's Pizza Shack in a couple hours."

"Why?"

"Don't know. See you guys soon," Becky said, as the line went silent again.

Jessica flipped her cell closed. Jennifer was behind the wheel and ready to go. So Jessica slipped into the car. They headed back into the city in silence.

"Where?"

"Mama's," Jessica answered, as they entered the city limits.

"You bet."

Jessica shook her head, as she thought of the images back at the Iron Gate. She tried to focus on it again but couldn't' get it back.

"We're home," Jennifer said, as she tapped Jessica's window.

"Thank you."

They walked in, and Jessica scanned the place.

"Over here, girlie," Beverly called out.

They walked closer to the booth. Becky nursed a large soda while Beverly only stared at them. Taylor wasn't there and Wendy, too. They slid in across them. Beverly glanced over at Becky.

"Don't you need to do something," Beverly said coldly Becky.

Becky picked up her soda and walked to the kitchen. She didn't look back.

"I don't know why you didn't' want to do a photo shoot with Clifford. But someone gave him a black-eye and split lip, so the fashion industry is hurting a little now with the two top photographers being beat up," Beverly said calmly. "I wanted to talk to you about thing personal."

"Should I leave, too?" asked Jennifer.

"You can stay. My sister, Taylor and nephew trust you."

"You don't trust, Becky," she replied with a surprise tone in her voice.

"Not with this. I've never told a living soul about it," Beverly said softly. "It's difficult since Brandon made his mistake with Rebecca years ago." She glanced around the room then stared at them again. "How can I be angry with Brandon when I was no better? I was in love with Jim, but I crossed the line. It's why I put it in place, so it wouldn't happen again. I know Brandon thought I did it because of Rebecca. But it was me who made a mistake seventeen years ago and regretted ever since. I wanted to tell Brandon all these years but I can't."

Beverly wiped the tears from her face. Jennifer reached out to touch her hand. Beverly stared at her then at Jessica.

"I've kept you and Brandon apart all these years because of my mistake. He's in love with you, Jessica. I can see it in his eyes, but he won't cross the line again. I've made him feel guilty for years," Beverly said sadly. "I...I had

a one night stand with Jim seventeen years ago." Tears
poured down her cheeks, as Jessica and Jennifer looked on.

Jessica folded her hands in front of her and waited
for more. "The family doesn't know."

"What?" Jennifer asked in a low voice, "About the
one night stand."

"About the child that was conceived out of that
one night stand," Beverly said quickly. "I didn't know until I
was four months along. I've been on the heavy side, so
then I disappeared from the family for six months. I had
given my baby up at the hospital and took a month for my
body, mind and spirit to heal. I never told Jim about our
child."

"That's why it hurt when Rebecca went to him,"
Jessica replied calmly.

Beverly nodded.

"Was it a boy or girl?" Jennifer asked with interest.

"I didn't want to know. The doctor did say it was
healthy though despite...never mind," Beverly answered in
hesitation.

"So you have a son or daughter out in the world,
and he or she doesn't know you're its mother," Jessica
replied calmly.

"Yes, and I've seen how Brandon looks at you at
times," Beverly said calmly, "It was how I looked at Jim
when I was in love with him. I told Brandon about the line,
and he would back down. Now he's thirty-two, and my
sister is dying to be a grandma. I'm sorry."

"We got to find Sabrina," Jessica replied coldly.

"Do you feel the same way about Brandon?" asked
Beverly. "If you do, I'll tell him about my mistake and

release him of crossing the line, Jessica."

"I know he wants to tell me something, but it hurts him a lot. Then he shifts into overdrive to find Sabrina, and I don't understand it. I want to find Sabrina, too," admitted Jessica. "I always thought he was my age until his birthday. He seems to have some secrets."

"Just like you, Jess," Jennifer said with a grin.

"Can I stay now?" Becky asked, as she stood at the table now.

"Yes. I'm sorry. Let's put our heads together and try to find Sabrina," Beverly answered with a friendly smile now.

"Where's Taylor?" asked Jennifer.

"Oh he went back to Brandon's studio to see if there was any clues of where Brandon might have gone," Becky answered back. "Here he is now. Any luck?"

Taylor shook his head. He slid in next to Beverly. Jessica stared at them both then shook her head.

"Sorry, no luck at the studio and airport," Beverly said calmly, as she wrote on a napkin.

"No luck at the orphanage and Jill Claymore's apartment," added Jessica, "Ted told me on the phone. He did find a piece of paper with Austin, Texas and the Mother Lode."

"California's Mother Lode," Taylor said with interest.

"That's what I thought too, but he says he doesn't have money to go check it out."

"We can check it out," Taylor said, as he sat up straighter. "I've never been out of New York. Have you, Jessica?"

She nodded with a small smile. "I'm from California. I haven't been there in over twelve years now."

"Why?" Taylor asked back.

"Busy I suppose."

"Or running away from your past, well, I'm up to a road trip there or anywhere out of New York," Taylor informed everyone. "I'm tired of this city. I was six when those two towers came down. It's time for somewhere new. Maybe I'll go looking for my parents after we find Sabrina. It's time to find out why they gave me up. You made me realize I need to find them, Jessica. Thank you."

"What did I do?" she asked him a little confused.

"People like you care. Why shouldn't my parents?"

"Uh..."

"Don't put her on the spotlight like that Taylor," Jennifer said back. "Anyone who cares about another person is normal. I helped you, too."

"I know. It means a whole lot to me, too. That's why I want to help. You've all become like a family to me. But you're not my biological family. Does it make any sense?"

"Of course, it does Taylor," Jessica answered back with a small smile, "You need to know those questions most kids wonder. Did they love me? Why did they give me up? Who do I look like him or her or someone in the family close or distant relative? Will I be like him or her in a career? But what's most important question of all. What's my medical history that I should know about? Will he a..."

Jessica stopped to notice everyone stared at her now. She didn't continue on.

"So we hit the streets again and maybe the airport

again," Beverly said confidently. "Let's divide up into the upper and lower part of town and go in..."

"I'll take the lower side alone. I know a lot of people there. You all would be a fish out of water there, so stay focused here. They'll talk to me if there's anything out there," interrupted Taylor.

"Jess and I will cover the upper part while you and Becky cover the airport again," filled in Jennifer. "And be careful out there. We don't know who beat up Clifford and why. It could be related, but we don't know for sure."

"Sounds like a good plan to me," Beverly said calmly.

"What about Wendy and Ted?" asked Becky.

"We'll touch base here with them as a development comes up. After we think we have a solid lead that's when we unite back here," answered Taylor.

"Reunite?" Becky asked back.

"We need to decide how to get Sabrina back safely."

"What if Brandon shows up?"

"Uh...we'll deal with it later. Let's go. We're losing time which Sabrina might not have," Taylor answered with a sense of urgency in his voice.

Everyone started to head out when Jessica held back. So did Taylor. He stared at her briefly.

"You still..."

He nodded. She was surprised no one asked Taylor about his split lip since Beverly mentioned about Clifford's attack. But they walked out of Mama's Pizza Shack together. Becky and Beverly headed for the airport. So it was Jessica and Jennifer who had the upper part of town.

Then Taylor seemed to head for the lower part of town. But she worried about him knowing what happened to him years ago. But he seemed confident that he could handle himself, so she had to trust him on it. So she tried to place her worry in the back of her mind with Sabrina and Brandon, too.

Then Jessica was amazed how Taylor took charge of everything now. He reminded her of someone she knew. But who, and this did bother her a little as her and Jennifer got into Jenny's car again.

"That's some kid," Jennifer commented, as she started her car again. "He's changing, you know."

"What?"

"I said Taylor is changing," Jennifer repeated again. "He's beginning to trust and want to be around people more."

"You never said how you and Taylor met."

"He was looking through our dumpster at work. He tried to tell me that he dropped something in there, but I knew better, Jess."

"Are you saying he lied to you?"

"Not really," Jennifer explained with a smile. "He did have wall up when I first met him. It took me giving him food, clothes and few blankets here and there that he trusted me. I guess he knew where to get food and drink. He chose Starbucks out of the various coffee shops in New York."

"Yes, I suppose. He thinks Wendy has the best pizza in town."

"He would. Did you see that split lip? I meant to ask him about it but didn't get around to it. Do you know?"

"He got attacked too, but he doesn't want to make a big deal of it. I brought him to Wendy. She cleaned him up, and he'll heal from it."

"You seem to know about it. Were you there?"

"Sort of," she answered honestly as possible. "Let's focus on Sabrina. I hope Brandon shows up soon."

"You miss him."

"Uh...yes he's my friend like you. You can move this faster than this. Can't you?"

"I did it before."

"Fine let's roll now."

"Whatever you say, Jess. I think you and Brandon would make an awesome couple."

"You heard about the line."

"I also heard she regrets putting it there and let it come between you and Brandon."

"Can we not discuss this?"

"I get your message loud and clear."

"Good. Let's listen to your music again."

"Awesome, isn't it?"

"Yeah," Jessica answered with a big smile now.

11

Jessica and Jennifer knocked on a lot of doors trying to find Sabrina but the two days into their search when they all rushed back to Mamma's Pizza Shack. Jessica had remembered what Brandon told about Jim, and how he debated on telling the group still. She also remembered he said he loved and care about his Auntie Beverly. She thought about it, as she walked in.

"There she is," Wendy called out. "She's here."

Taylor was in a booth and put down his slice of pizza. Becky was with him. Beverly emerged from the kitchen with a large pizza in her hands.

"Ted's on his way over," Beverly said, as she walked to table next to the booth. "Help yourselves."

"What's up?" Jennifer asked no one in particular.

"Beverly," Taylor answered, as he wiped his chin. "Got something addressed to you, Jessica."

"Me. Why?" she asked surprised.

"You and Brandon actually, but we haven't seen or heard from him still. So we're relying on you now. It's all we have. Ted wants to check it out before you open it," answered Taylor.

"I'm here," Ted said, as he rushed in. "She hasn't touched it yet."

"No," Beverly snapped back. "I placed it in plastic and touched it a little as possible."

"Where is it?" Ted asked her.

"In my briefcase," Beverly answered back.

"Your office," he called out to Wendy.

She nodded, and he headed that way. Jessica decided to head that way, too. Ted grabbed the briefcase off the floor and placed it on the desk. He pulled out some stuff from his pocket and went to work. Jessica stepped closer to the desk and Ted.

"Dusting for prints," Ted explained, as he examined the envelope. "Ah, some prints might be the captors or Beverly's. I'll have to get hers to compare."

Jessica turned to the door. Beverly stood there and seemed worried. She noticed the wrinkle lines on her face.

"You're worried about Brandon," she replied calmly to her.

Beverly nodded and stepped closer.

"I'll need to finger print you," Ted said, as he stared at the envelope with gloves on.

"Beverly, I know you care and love your nephew. We'll hear from him soon. He's got to be okay."

"Come closer," Ted said to Beverly. "I only need these two fingers since they're ones I lifted off the envelope."

"That's where I touched it," said Beverly.

"I see. It matches, so this person or captor is smart. They wore gloves and typed it," Ted said thoughtfully. "Jessica put on some gloves, as you take out its contents out. Lay it flat on the desk."

Jessica noticed a second pair of gloves, so she put them on. She took the envelope from Ted and nervously opened it. She unfolded it and laid it flat on the desk pre Ted's instructions.

"I have the girl Sabrina. I want a million dollars for her safe return. I will know when you got it. I will give three days to get the unmarked bills ready. I will be in touch and don't try anything Brandon, or I will kill Sabrina. I know why she means so much to you. I know who you are," Jessica read out loud.

"Okay," said Beverly.

"What? Do you know what it means?" Ted asked quickly.

"No," Beverly answered quickly. "He or she would kill her. She's only five."

"There's more," Jessica replied calmly. "PS Brandon, I know you have the money to pay for her return."

"Holy crap," Ted snapped back. "I was right about the guy being smart."

He dusted it and nothing appeared. So there were no other fingerprints on it except for Beverly's. Ted didn't look happy at all. Beverly found a chair and sank deep into it.

"I'll tell the others," Jessica offered calmly.

"Yeah, fine. I need to talk to Wendy privately. Could you send her in?" Ted asked her.

"Of course," Jessica answered, as she headed out of the room. "Are you okay?"

"I've been so careful. How did the captors know Brandon was related to me, or who he is?"

"I don't know. But it didn't say anything about you," Jessica answered thoughtfully.

"But it was delivered to her place, Jessica," pointed out Ted.

Jessica nodded and walked out. She saw the faces of Wendy, Taylor, Becky and Jennifer focused on her.

Wendy walked up to her now.

"The guy wants a million dollars unmarked and knows Brandon has money," Jessica replied in a calm voice. "Ted wants to speak to you, Wendy."

Wendy nodded and walked back to her office. Jessica walked over to the booth and slid in next to Taylor. He stared at her still.

"He knows about us all being connected. He must have been planning this for awhile now," said Taylor.

"But we only got the assignment about over a month ago," replied Jessica. "So how could he know about Sabrina?"

"Maybe he planned on someone else but ditched it upon seeing Sabrina," answered Taylor.

"It's possible, Jess. Anything is possible. What did the ransom note say?" Jennifer asked with interest.

"He's giving us three days to collect the unmarked bills then will contact us again. He doesn't know Brandon isn't around," explained Jessica.

"How in the world did he know? We left that world behind us fourteen years ago," Wendy said, as Ted walked up beside her. "I or Brandon and I decided to put it all behind us and forget. Who was I kidding? Look at what I shared with you, Jessica! Did you tell anyone? But, how about you, Jennifer?"

"Just, Jess," answered Jennifer. "I'm sorry."

"No one," replied Jessica.

"Fine, I'll get the million unmarked bills. I'm sure Brandon would want to fork over the ransom," Wendy said to no one in particular. "People are so greedy these days. Ted, come with me. I'm not comfortable carrying around that much money."

He nodded, and they walked out the front door. Beverly entered the room still shocked. Jennifer walked over to her. Jessica turned to Becky.

"Did you tell anyone?" she asked her in a low voice.

"No. I promised Brandon back in Paris," Becky answered back in a low voice.

Taylor chewed on a slice of pizza. Jessica knew he didn't talk to many people. She could talk freely in front of him. She trusted him like only a few men she has in her life. Taylor was stranger that knew things beyond his years.

"Fine, I guess we don't have to comb the streets and airports anymore," Jessica replied back.

"It would good to find out where he has her, so the ransom doesn't have to be delivered," Taylor said in a low voice.

"Do you think he won't release her?"

Taylor nodded.

"Why?" she asked him.

"She can identify him, and it's personal to him," Taylor answered calmly.

"What makes you believe it's personal?" Beverly asked him, as she walked closer to the booth.

"He delivered it to your home not your place of business. He addressed it to Brandon and Jessica making sure Brandon's name was first."

"But how..." Beverly stumbled to ask.

"Just a guy feeling since he wanted a million unmarked bills. He didn't specify small or large or combination of the two when getting the money. It's not relevant to him," Taylor continued on. "He's out to hurt Brandon and possible you, Beverly and Wendy. One or all of you wronged him, and Sabrina will suffer from it."

"That's not fair!" exclaimed Beverly.

"Who said life is fair? I've been on the streets for twelve years now not knowing why my Mom gave me up at birth. Not knowing who she is or my dad for that matter, Beverly? You didn't give a rat's ass about me on the streets. Yes, I walked by you more than once these past twelve years. You couldn't even spare a penny, but your sister Wendy could. It amazes me that you two are sisters. Yes, you can be so different."

"You don't understand, young man," Beverly snapped back.

"Enlighten me, Ms," he said, as he glared back at her.

"Stop!" exclaimed Jessica.

"I was adopted as a baby," Beverly snapped back.

"You were lucky. I wasn't. I was considered unadoptable by the time I was four. I ran away from the same place Sabrina was at, and I never looked back once or until now."

"Why weren't you unadoptable?" Beverly asked in a calm voice now. "Why now!"

"Sabrina. She deserves a home and not live like I do or to die too young and not know why. Never mind why I wasn't adoptable. You're not my Mom, so I don't have to explain myself to you. Besides I have a burning question she can only answer."

"Why did she give you up?" asked Jennifer.

"No, something very personal," Taylor answered,

as he stared at his slice of pizza. "I'm out of here. Please, excuse me, Jessica."

She slid out, and let him grab his backpack and walked out. She slid back in and began to shake.

"You know what he wants to ask his Mom. Don't you, Jessica?" asked Beverly.

"Yes, but it's between them. If he wanted anyone to know, he would have shared it but he didn't. I have to respect his silence."

"Damn that kid drives me crazy," snapped Beverly. "He's so stubborn like..."

"Who?" Becky asked.

"Never mind... we need to focus on Sabrina and getting her back safe."

"We have to wait on Wendy then for contact again," pointed out Jessica.

"I can't stand not doing anything. Does anyone have any idea where my nephew is?" Beverly asked, as she glanced at everyone.

"If there was any clue, it walked out with Taylor since he went back to the studio," stated Jennifer.

"Damn kid," said Beverly.

"Let's eat and wait for Wendy and Ted's return," said Becky.

"Fine, but Wendy said you all like combination the best. I'll make a hot one."

"The one over there is fine," Becky said, as she pointed to the table.

"It's only warm not hot."

"It's okay. Let's eat and relax until they get back," said Becky.

"She'll eat anything," Jessica commented with a warm, friendly, small smile.

"That's me all right," Becky said with a return smile. "Remember Paris and the café."

She nodded, and Becky laughed. Soon everyone laughed when Becky told them what happened at the café. The tension was gone briefly, but she thought of what Taylor said and didn't say. She thought about his scar that he showed her and understood. It was personal between him and his Mom.

"Your birthmark is behind your left ear," Dillon said, as he zipped up his pants. "I like licking it before you know."

"Dad, this isn't right," Jessie replied, as she was stretched out on her bed naked.

"Yes it is. Don't you know Daddy knows best," Dillon said with a gleam in his eyes now.

"No, Dad not again, we already did it more than once," Jessie pleaded with him.

He was on her again. She couldn't fight back. He bound her hands and feet like the last two times they did it. She refused to undress for him, so he punished her this way. Dillon had his tongue in her mouth now. She felt his bare chest on her flesh. She felt the thrust. He was in her again. His hands cupped her face when he dove for her left ear.

"Not again, no not again, isn't four enough for one day?" she asked him.

He moaned, as she felt his release. She gulped hard, as he made his way to her face and mouth again. He reached for one her breasts, as he placed his tongue in. He squeezed hard, as she squirmed. Then he looked into her eyes.

"It's good we have protected sex, little girl. Otherwise, you might have a little brother or sister on the way," Dillon said with a big smile. "This made number seven. My lucky number don't you know. It took seven times that night to create you, little girl. I didn't want unprotected sex that night."

"Nathan, too," she snapped back.

"I didn't know I created twins that night almost nineteen years ago. I like young virgin girls like you were in the beginning better. I love doing you often. It makes me feel young again and horny as hell. Your Mom doesn't satisfy this hunger like you do. I'm going love continuing it on into my old age with you. You excite me, pussy cat," he said back.

"Jess, Jess," Jennifer said to her.

"What?" she asked, as she was brought back into the present.

"Hi, Jessica," Nathan said, as he stood by Jennifer now. "You seemed a million miles away right now."

"How...uh...why," she stumble with the words.

"We need to talk about Mom and Dad. I was sent a ticket before I even thought of calling to get one," Nathan said with a small smile. "Did you know I wanted to talk to you about them? You know the connection. It's funny that I sensed fear in you as I came up. What's wrong?"

"Brandon is missing, and there's a ransom now for Sabrina," answered Jennifer. "You two look like twins."

"They are," said Beverly.

"Oh, I didn't know," Jennifer said shyly.

"I didn't..." she replied, as she stared at him now.

"I got a two way ticket and a typed note where you would be plus cab fare," Nathan said now worried. "If you didn't send all this... What's going on, Chubby Bear?"

"Stop calling me that," she snapped back at him.

She bolted for the bathroom. She leaned against the closed door, as she slid down to the tile floor. She clung tightly to her body. A knock on the door startled her.

"Occupied," she called out.

"Jess, it's me, Jenny," Jennifer said in a low voice. "Let me in. Please."

Jessica got to her feet and opened the door. Jennifer squeezed in and closed the door behind her. They stared at each other.

"You're not thinking this was planned. Do you?" Jennifer asked her finally after few minutes of silence.

"Strange things have happened. Look at all who rallied around to find Sabrina. What are the odds? What other possible answer could there be?" she asked her thoughtfully. "Look at the evidence. It's all around us?"

Jennifer walked over to the sinks. Then she turned back to face Jessica.

"Yeah, you're right now that you mention it. Makes you wonder what will happen next," Jennifer answered thoughtfully. "Jess, Becky said something changed in Paris but didn't say what. Was she referring to Nathan? Then you got this blank look on your face after Taylor left. You know what he wants to ask his Mom. Can you tell me?"

She shook her head no then looked away. Jennifer walked back over to hug her. Jessica pulled away.

"All right, something is really bothering you. Now

spill it, Jessica," Jennifer said, as she placed her hand on her hips. "Is it Brandon or what? Tell me now."

Knock. Knock.

"Occupied," they echoed together.

"Bridget and Stanley are on the phone in the office. Come quick," Becky said from behind the door. "They want us all there. Please."

Jessica pulled the door open and headed for the office. There Beverly and Nathan stood by the desk and phone. Nathan stared at her.

"You look and feel like hell, Sis," he commented back.

"Thanks. Bridget, Stanley, I'm here. What's going on?" she asked them.

"Are you and Brandon all right?" Bridget asked with concern in her voice.

"I'm fine. But I don't know about Brandon since he hasn't been in touch with anyone in awhile now," she answered confidently and honestly. "Why?"

"We got a phone call to check on your friends in New York," Stanley answered with a concern in his voice, too.

"Did you recognize the voice?" Jessica asked him.

"No, and the number was blocked. But it was a deep voice though."

"Like an electronic device?" she asked thoughtfully.

"I guess. What's going on, Jessica?" asked Stanley.

"Sabrina was kidnapped, and Brandon has disappeared," she answered honestly.

"Not the little girl from the Telly campaign," said Bridget.

"One and the same," Jessica replied back.

"Beverly, are you still there?" Bridget asked with concern in her voice now.

"Yes I am," Beverly answered calmly.

"Will you lose the account on account of the little girl being kidnapped?" Bridget asked her.

"I don't think so. Why?"

"I was just thinking Sabrina worked with her, Brandon and Jessica last that they might hold you responsible for her kidnapping."

"That's stupid...."

"No, she might have something there," Jessica interrupted her. "Look almost everyone involved with my last two assignments in this room and after here. Think about what Taylor said. It was like being planned out."

"You're right, Jess. We're all involved somehow. Look me and Taylor joined after Paris, and Beverly, Becky, Brandon and Jess were before Paris. Then over there Stanley, Bridget and Nathan entered it. Then me and Taylor."

"Excuse us," Nathan said, as he grabbed Jessica's arm.

She gulped hard, as he pulled her out of the office. He shoved her into the nearest opening which happened to be the ladies' room. His eyes blazed with wonder and confused.

"What the hell is going on here, Sis?" Nathan asked in anger now. "If you didn't send me the ticket, and everything else, then who the hell did?"

"I don't know," she snapped back in anger, too. "I don't know what the hell is going. I don't have all the pieces yet."

"Pieces to what?" Nathan asked her.

"To what's going on," she answered back. "And don't look at me like that way either."

"What way?"

"Like him."

"Who?"

"Our dear old Dad, I don't give a rat's ass about him, but Mom I do love and care about just like you, Nathan," she yelled back at him.

"But I need you to come back to California. I need your help with them both. I can see Dad is some sore spot in your heart and soul, and I don't know why. It was there twelve years ago, too, but I defended you against him, not thinking you could make it as a model. Then I went behind his back and drove you to the airport. I never told him or Mom that I drove you out there. I've kept your secret all these years," Nathan rambled on. "I love you, Jessica, and would do anything for you if I could. Haven't I proven that? Can't you tell me why you ran away from home, and what's going on here? I feel your fear now and won't let it go."

"Let the past be. I have to find Sabrina before the ransom is delivered. Taylor was right about her being able to identify him. He won't let her go scot free. Excuse me, Nathan," she replied, as she kissed him on the cheek. "You're in the ladies' room dear, brother."

She walked out and back into the office. She saw all eyes on her now, as Nathan rushed in behind her. She sighed and moved closer to the desk.

"Bridget, Stanley, take care of your family. I'll handle things here with or without Brandon. Give David a hug and kiss from his godmother. Bye," she replied, as she disconnected the speaker. "So we have to figure out where the man could have taken her."

"Becky says, you have a drawing of the man who possible took Sabrina," Beverly said to her. "Can I see it?"

"Uh...I don't have a copy on me now," Jessica answered in hesitation.

"I can draw another. I remember what Amy said," Becky said with a small smile.

"No, I mean we don't have the time. Let's close Mama's and all hit the streets. Maybe we'll get lucky. Let's Go, people. I'll leave my cell number with Wendy for anyone who doesn't have it and on."

"We all should," Jennifer said confidently.

They all added their information to the paper Jessica started with hers. Then they spread out through New York. Jennifer took Nathan since he didn't know New York that well. Jessica watched her twin walk away with Jennifer. She didn't answer his question why she ran away from home.

If she knew one thing about her twin, he wouldn't be letting this go because of their past history. So she knew she wasn't out of the woods yet with Nathan. But she couldn't dwell on it now. Her focus was on Sabrina despite Brandon not being around. She knew he would want her to continue.

"So what direction are you going in?" Becky asked her.

"I suppose that way," she answered, as she pointed towards the orphanage.

"Fine and good luck," Becky said, as she and

Wendy headed another way but not towards Brandon's studio.

Jessica nodded and walked away. She thought of how Brandon and she held Sabrina's hands in theirs, as they walked this way. It seemed so long ago, and she sighed. How can a little girl answer what was causing her past couple years lack of restful sleep? She couldn't explain it to anyone much less herself. She shook her head.

She glanced at the clear blue sky above her and walked in slow motion. She stopped at the store where she brought the key chains and teddy bears holding each other. The merchant had a broom in his hand and smiled at her.

"Coming back for more?" he asked her.

"No. I'm trying to locate that little girl who was with me that day," she answered back. "Do you remember her?"

"Yes, but I haven't seen her. I saw her picture at Starbucks on their community board. She's a cute kid."

"Please, keep a look out for her. She might be with a man that she doesn't know."

"I can do that for you."

"Thank you. Have a good day."

12

Two days more passed Jessica sat across Nathan at Mama's Pizza Shack. No one seemed to notice Sabrina on the streets. It frustrated Jessica to no end after the first day, so she suggested Wendy go open her restaurant again. By the second day frustration set in her entire body now.

"You wanted to come here," Nathan said to her. "We've looked everywhere. Stop playing with your food."

She glanced up at him. "How's Mom?"

"Healing, but you judge for yourself," Nathan answered, as he brought a photo of her on his cell. "This was taken last week. Most people have their kids and animals on their cells. I have our parents on mine, but none of my twin sister through the years since she left before I got one. Do you want to see Dad?"

She shook her head, no, but took his cell. Stephanie had crow's feet around the eyes and a harsh look on her face and through the eyes now. She wasn't the radiant beauty she saw as a child. She looked more defeated or skeleton of what she used to be. Jessica moistened her lips and noticed a faint black eye.

"It was really black for awhile there. She's gaining strength each day," Nathan said calmly. "She's starting to get white hairs and hates it."

"Uh...." She replied in hesitation. She turned quickly to bells on the front door. "Brandon."

She rushed to him. His hair was longer than usual and a mess. He didn't have the sling anymore. His flannel shirt was hanging out of his pants and torn. His jeans had dirt everywhere. But Jessica didn't care about all that she hugged him and discovered a bad odor.

"Where have you been?" she asked, as she looked at his dirty face.

"Brandon," cried out Wendy.

Wendy rushed to him, as she emerged from the kitchen. She hugged him then pulled back too. She placed both hands on his face and stared at him.

"Go change and clean up, too," Wendy said in soft but loving voice.

"Yes, Mama," he said back. "Excuse me."

He walked away. Nathan walked up to them.

"Wasn't that, Brandon?" he asked Jessica.

Jessica nodded and so did Wendy. Jessica stepped away from them briefly.

"So how's your pizza, Nathan?" Wendy asked him.

"Great best ever, my twin here hasn't touched much of her salad though," Nathan answered with a big smile

"She's been worried about Sabrina and Brandon. It's good to have him back. I wish, we heard from that damn kidnapper," Wendy rambled on. "I should go tell him the latest. Oh...."

"We'll let everyone know he's back," offered Nathan.

"Thank you," Wendy said, as she danced toward the stairs that led to her place above the restaurant.

It made Jessica smile now. She glanced over at Nathan who looked at her now.

"What?" she asked him.

"You have feelings for him, and it's more than friendship. You weren't in love with Ryan years ago when he said he wanted to marry you. I..."

"You knew," she interrupted him. "Ryan wanted to marry me."

"Yes. He ran it by me before he approached you and Dad about it."

"He asked Dad!" exclaimed Jessica.

"He asked you first, but you turned him down. So he never approached Dad about it. You broke Ryan's heart back then. I'm surprised he talked to you at all now. Then you got into all out fight with Dad about becoming a model. I came to your defense and drove you to the airport shortly after our eighteenth birthday. Twelve years pass, and no word from you. I saw you on the cover of a magazine two months after you left," Nathan said with anger in his voice. "I lied to them, Jessica. And I paid the ultimate price."

"What?"

"He went wild after you left. Mom got slap here and there until this last time. I couldn't shield her from him," he answered painfully.

"What are..."

"I got black eyes, split lips, and cracked ribs but that was nothing compared to this," he interrupted her, as he revealed his back to her.

She ran a faint impression on his back of an iron. She started to touch it when he showed her his chest to see faint scars there, too. Nathan had tears in his eyes now.

"Ryan wanted me to tell you why I went to medical school. This is why Jessica. He used his belt at first than a whip and finally Mom's iron. I couldn't take it anymore," he explained to her. "He pinned me down on the kitchen floor. I didn't realize how strong he was all these years until that moment. You know how disgusting it is as your flesh burns. It hurt like hell, Jessica. Mom called the police. I had passed out from the intense pain and odor."

"I'm so very sorry, Nathan," she replied with tears in her eyes, too, now. "I do love you."

"You owe me, Jessica. Tell me why you hate Dad so much. He adored you. He never hurt you like this. It's only recently that discovered Dad suffers from uncontrolled rage."

"Is there a cure? Is that why you went into medicine to find out what was wrong with Dad?"

"Jessica, you're avoiding what I want to know," he said, as he stared at him.

"I can't, Nat. Please. I'm sorry Dad hurt you. I didn't know he would flip out like that."

"Jessica," Brandon said, as he walked up to them now. "Mama told me everything."

"You look better," she replied to him.

"I'll call Jenny and the others," Nathan said to them. "Please excuse me."

"Ted has been worried about you," replied Jessica. "You could have called."

"No, I couldn't. You see...let's sit down," he said, as he pointed to her booth.

She slid in and so did Brandon. He took bites of her salad quickly down.

"I was heading here after checking out something when everything went black," he started to explain. "When

I came to, my cell was smashed next to me, and I was in a place that was extremely hot. I think I walked for miles before I found a building. The guy asked why I was out in the Mojave Desert without any food and water. I was shocked. I had to get food and water in me before anything else. Nothing made sense to me, as I searched for my wallet. Nothing, I only had SIM card from my broken phone. No keys either or ID. It was hard to speak with a big knot on the back of my head. It took awhile to regain my voice and make my way back here. This is the first place I came hoping to find you, Jessica."

"And you did," Jessica replied back. "I was worried but had to keep looking for Sabrina. Where were you last?"

"Garment district," Brandon answered, as he drank some water that was on the table. "I told you that the drawing looked familiar. Ted and I went to Texas on that hunch of mine. I told you about Jim or my Auntie Beverly's Jim." He paused to catch his breath. "I believe Jim is behind Sabrina's disappearance."

"But why in the gourmet district?" She asked with real interest.

"That's where his old studio was years ago. I told you after Rebecca died and was buried then he dropped out of sight," Brandon explained quickly. "I expected to find out it all boarded up for lack of use."

"But it wasn't. Was it?" she asked back.

"Exactly," he answered, as he shook his head and pressed on. "It was clean like someone was living there. Then I found this on the floor."

He held it up for her to see.

"An SD card," she replied a little surprised.

"Whoever knocked you out didn't get it?"

"No. I had put it in my secret case on my leg. I haven't seen what's on it yet. I haven't told Mama about it. I wanted to share it all with you first. You're important to me and so is Sabrina."

"I called everyone but the kid," Nathan said, as he stood at the booth. I even called Stanley and Bridget. She wants to talk to you when you have the time."

Nathan started to walk away when Jessica took hold of his arm. He stared at her.

"Thank you. Look maybe after we find Sabrina we can really talk, Nat. We can work out things like Mom and ...."

"The old man," Nathan filled in coldly. "I've had to deal with them alone for twelve damn years. Now you walk back into my life and put me off again. I'm history. Goodbye for good this time."

He stormed out the front door with the bell clanging. He had side stepped Beverly and Jennifer.

"Nathan," Jennifer called out.

Jessica began to shack then cry openly. Brandon was at her side holding her. She leaned into his chest. He rubbed her back gently.

"Easy, Jessica," he said calmly.

"Brandon," cried out Beverly.

"Brandon," Jennifer and Becky said at the same time.

Jessica pulled away from him. She let everyone hug him. She slid back into the booth and picked up the SD card. She placed it in her wallet when Ted walked up.

"So you're back, man," Ted said to him. "Where

have you been and not answering any of my calls?"

"Following up on another hunch and couldn't call with it like this," Brandon answered, as he held out his damaged cell from his pocket. "I can only hope the SIM card still works."

"Well, fill us in," said Ted.

Jessica pulled out her cell and found Nathan's name. She stared at it.

"Where do I begin my dear twin?" she asked sadly to his name. "I didn't know he would hurt you. But I had to go. I couldn't..."

"Hi, Jess," Jennifer said brightly. "What's up with Nathan?"

She stared at Jennifer. She gulped hard before she spoke.

"It's personal," she answered in a low voice.

"I can see that, my friend. You're in tears, and Nathan stormed out of here like someone set his pants on fire. He would ask what your life was like here. When I said, he would have to ask you then he asked about me personally," Jennifer said back. "He seemed really interested in me and what I had to say. I haven't been a center of a man's world in sixteen years. I was fourteen. I went to work at Starbucks at fifteen. I got an early work permit back then. But your brother asked if I ever planned to go to college or have a family someday just out of the blue. It surprised me."

"It's nice having Brandon back," Jessica replied, as she closed her cell.

"Your brother loves and cares about you, Jess."

"I know he does. I've always known it all our lives;

believe it, or not, we used hang out a lot until we turned seventeen," she replied sadly.

"What happened?"

"Things changed for us, both," she answered, as she stared out the window, "To be young and innocent again."

"It's, okay, Honey," Jessie replied, as she knelt near a little girl who was crying. "What's your name?"

"Annie French," she answered back.

"Why are you so upset, Annie?" Jessica asked calmly.

"I can't find my Mommy. She was right here a second ago, but I can't seem to find her now."

"I'll help you find her. My name is Jessie. Take my hand, and we will look for your Mommy together. Okay," Jessie replied with a confident smile.

"I'm scared, Jessie. What if we don't find her?" Annie asked sadly.

Jessie hugged her then combed back Annie's bangs from her chocolate brown eyes. She took Annie's hand into her.

"Positive thinking," she replied to her.

Annie smiled a smile, and they walked hand and hand. Jessie smiled as they walked. She noticed a blonde woman ahead with another woman.

"I turned around, and she was gone. Beverly, I don't know where Annie is," the first woman said panicked.

"We'll find her, Tina," Beverly said calmly.

"Excuse me, ladies," Jessie replied politely. They looked at her then Tina looked down.

"Annie!" Tina exclaimed out loud.

"Mommy!" Annie exclaimed back, as she rushed to her Mom's open arms.

They hugged each other tightly. Beverly and Jessie looked on and smiled.

"Thank you so much," Tina said with tear in her eyes. "How can I ever repay you?"

"Just be her Mom and love her for who she is and wants to be," Jessie answered thoughtfully.

"Have you ever thought of becoming a model?" Beverly asked her.

"Uh...no," Jessie answered honestly, as she stared at Beverly now.

"You're beautiful. You can make a lot of money as a model," Beverly said back. "We owe you for returning Annie to us."

"I love you, Annie," Tina said, as she held her in her loving arms.

"I love you, too, Mommy," Annie said back. "Thank you, Jessie."

"You're welcome, Annie," Jessie replied, with a small smile and wiped the mist from her own eyes.

"Here's my card. Call me if you want to be rich and famous," Beverly said, as she held out her card. "Your name is Jessie."

"Jessica Hudson," Jessie replied, as she took the card.

Annie hugged her legs now. So Jessie bent down and hugged Annie again.

"Stay close to your Mommy now."

"I will. I promise."

"Jess, Jess," Jennifer said, as she brought her back

into the present.

"Uh… what?" she asked in hesitation now.

"Taylor's here," Jennifer said quickly.

"Leave me alone I tell you, all," Taylor snapped at anyone who approached him.

"Easy, Taylor, you're with friends," Brandon pointed out calmly.

"Yeah, right, go to hell, man. I have no friends. No one gives a damn about me. People only want they want from my body," shouted Taylor.

"What?" asked Wendy?

Taylor bolted for the men's room. Brandon and Ted bolted after him. But they met a closed door instead. Jessica got to her feet and walked slowly to them.

"Go. Let me talk to him," she replied back.

"But…" Ted started to say back.

"Let's go," Brandon said, as he winked at her. "I'll take care of Mama. You'll explain it all later."

Jessica hesitated then nodded. They walked away, so she knocked on the door.

"Go away. I'm off limits," Taylor yelled from behind the closed door.

"Taylor, it's me, Jessica. I'm alone. Please open the door," she replied calmly.

He opened it a crack. His eyes danced with mixed emotion. She shoved it wider with her body, so she could step in. Then she closed the door behind her quickly.

"It's, okay, Taylor. We're alone now. Talk to me," she replied quickly and calmly. "They don't understand, but I do."

He stared at her, as he stood by the sinks now. He

moved quickly from when she managed to get in. She kept eye contact with him, as his eyes slowly returned to normal now.

"I know what it's like first hand," she replied, as she moistened her lips and felt her throat very dry now.

"How? When?" Taylor asked calmly.

"Just know I've been there," Jessica answered back calmly. "It's hard to put it behind you and move on. But you have to before it destroys you inside and out. I know the streets are rough. I understand. But you have real friends who really care and love you out there, Taylor. They are worried about you now."

He slid down the floor and began to cry. She rushed over to him and pulled him close to her chest. She cried with him. They sat down on the floor with his arms wrapped around her.

"Jessica, is everything all right?" Brandon asked, as he opened the door.

Jessica opened her eyes and stared at him. Then she nodded.

"You've been in here over an hour now."

"We'll be out soon," she whispered back.

Brandon nodded and closed the door again. They were alone again. Taylor looked at her face now. His face was puffy now, but he had stopped crying now.

"You understand where no one else will," he said in a hoarse voice.

"Yes. I haven't told anyone just like you in years."

"So we have what Clifford tried to do to you and this. They're our secrets."

"Yes, I suppose. Do you want to go out there and

see everyone now?"

He nodded. Together they walked out of the men's bathroom. Wendy was the first to hug him then Jennifer and Becky. Ted shook his hand firmly, and Brandon started a handshake but hugged him instead at the last minute. Beverly flipped her cell closed and walked up to Taylor.

She combed back his hair and smiled. Then she hugged him and stepped back. Taylor smiled at them all now

"You need a haircut," Beverly said with a small smile.

"Don't give him a Beatle haircut, Auntie," Brandon said with a small grin.

She stared back at him. Brandon laughed so did Wendy then Beverly. Taylor, Becky, Jennifer, Ted and Jessica were clueless. Brandon stopped laughing and looked at them all.

"The first time Auntie Beverly took me to get a haircut was something to say in the least different," he explained with a smile now. "I'll take Taylor to get his haircut, Auntie."

"What I thought you looked adorable in that Beatles haircut," Beverly said defensively.

"You didn't have to deal with the teasing and smart ass remarks like I did in school," said Brandon.

"You looked cute," Wendy said with a smile, "As it began to grow out."

"You would, Mama. I'm taking him, and that's final."

"Do you have a picture?" Jennifer asked with interest to Wendy.

"I think so," answered Wendy.

"Don't you dare, Mama," warned Brandon. "Is everything okay now, Taylor?"

"Yes. I'm sorry, everyone," he apologized, as he glanced at everyone.

"What happened?" asked Jennifer.

"It's weird. A voice said you've met your mother, but she won't want you because of what you do on the streets," he answered, as he shook his head.

"You said a voice. What did it sound like? Where did you hear it?" Ted asked with interest.

"Distorted somehow that's why I couldn't figure out where it came from. It was in your place above your studio and in the studio. It kept repeating it until I ran out of there. I stopped to set the alarm and lock it up. You didn't give the access code."

"Uh..." Brandon said in hesitation.

"I gave it to him," said Becky.

"6169," Taylor blurted out. "Sorry."

Jessica stepped back and side stepped everyone. She walked over and slid back into the booth. Jennifer walked up.

"What's up?"

"It's the month and day of..." Jessica answered back.

"I know," Brandon said back. "How can I forget the first time we met? Did you pick it up?"

She nodded. She held it out to him.

"Sweetie," Wendy said, as she wrapped her arm around Brandon's waist. "You need to get a new phone. Did you lose all your contacts?"

"Not if the SIM card was damaged," he answered with a small smile.

"Doesn't your mobile company have it on your account on the internet?" Jennifer asked him.

"I don't know, but I'll check into it. Jessica, can you come with me?"

"Sure," she answered back. "But…"

"I'll stay around for Nathan to come back. He can't go very far. He doesn't know the city like we do," Jennifer interrupted her.

"Thanks, Jenny," Jessica replied, as she slid out and hugged her.

"Taylor is in safe hands. Ted is some PI. I better go rescue Taylor. Excuse me," said Wendy.

"Tell him that I'll be back later to get his haircut," Brandon said to her.

"I will. Now you two, be very careful out there. I'll call you on Jessica's phone if he wants the ransom delivered," Wendy said, as she kissed Brandon on the cheek.

"We will," Brandon said, as he kissed her back.

Wendy hugged Jessica, and Brandon and Jessica walked out. They walked a little ways in silence before Brandon stopped.

"What?"

"I saw your face as I walked in that desert. The thought of never seeing you again sent me forward. I had to get back to you, Jessica. I promised to get Sabrina back. You…"

"It's okay. You're back, and we'll get Sabrina back. Do you still think Jim is involved somehow?"

"It's possible. Have you said anything to anyone?"

"No. You're hoping that memory card might confirm your hunch."

He nodded.

"Let's get you a replacement phone then see what's on the memory card," she replied with a smile.

Brandon smiled back and took her hand into his. He brought it to his lips to kiss it. Jessica felt warmth on her face.

"I think you're blushing, Ms Jessica Hudson. What will your daddy, think of that?"

She pulled her hand free from his. She marched down the streets until he caught up with her. They looked deep into each other's eyes when he caught up with her. They looked deep and long into each other's eyes and caught their breath.

"I'm sorry," they said together.

They both laughed and walked down the street hand and hand. They got him a new smart phone and loaded his old SIM card in it. It was undamaged. Jennifer was right about companies having account access on the web. So they downloaded his photos onto his new cell. Then they picked up his laptop and sat in Central park. Jessica looked at the ducks while Brandon downloaded the memory card. She was anxious and nervous, too.

"Here we are," Brandon said to her.

She leaned in, as he opened it. Photos of a mansion stared back at them. She sat up straighter now.

"What?" he asked her.

"I've seen it before. Jenny took me out there not too long ago."

"It's my family estate," he said back. "I left it behind."

"What! You lived there."

"Yeah until I was eighteen, wait a second," he said thoughtfully.

"What?" she asked with interest.

"Not many people know about the estate's location. Dad didn't want people to know where it was. It was limited to family."

"Did Beverly tell Jim?"

"She could have, I guess. Interesting," Brandon said, as he scanned the images. "They're of places and things that matter to me."

He stared at an image. Jessica looked at the image of a painting or portrait of a man.

"Your dad," she replied, as she moved it to the next image.

"Enough!" he exclaimed, as she closed it down.

"What was...."

He stared at her, and she saw pain in Brandon's eyes now.

"You're right. Let's call it a day. Walk me home. Please, Love."

Brandon got to his feet and offered his hand out to her. Together, they walked back to her apartment in silence. He walked her to her door, and she stood in the doorway.

"I'm glad; you're back. I really did miss you."

He nodded and kissed her on the cheek. He walked down the hall. She went inside and stretched out on her bed. She closed her eyes and saw Brandon's face, as she fell asleep.

13

"You have issues. I know, but she's your sister and twin," Jennifer said at Jessica's closed door. "Both of you are good at shutting down or running away. It doesn't resolve anything."

A knock startled Jessica. She walked away from her stereo and over to her front door.

"Good morning, Jess," Jennifer said, as Jessica opened the door. "Come on in, Nathan."

Nathan was shoved towards the opening and into Jessica. They stared at each other then she stepped aside. Nathan was pushed farther into the apartment by Jennifer. She grabbed Jessica's hand, too.

"I won't stand by and watch two people I care about and love to be at odds," Jennifer said coldly.

"Jenny," replied Jessica.

"Talk. Talk both of you to each other, not me," Jennifer said coldly. "I'll be outside the door, however, long it takes."

Jennifer walked back to the open door and closed it behind her. Jessica shook her head and looked at Nathan.

"So, this is your apartment," he said, as he looked around, "Not anything flashy just the basics."

"I'm not here a lot with my assignments and all," she replied back. "You said Mom is a care home."

"Yes, and finally healing. Dad's is a separate area since he has uncontrolled rage. They keep with those kinds of issues away from the mainstream of people living there.

His retirement pays for it," explained Nathan.

"He's not old enough to retire," she replied back.

"I meant to say his disability. He lost control of a forklift after you left while he was on the road. He got injured on the job. So they listened to him complain about his leg endlessly until they put him out on a permeate disability. He was only forty then. That's when I found out he was twenty-one, and Mom was eighteen. They married young."

"They never showed us a wedding photo all our lives," Jessica replied thoughtfully. "I wonder why."

"I thought it was odd, too. I saw other people have photos of their wedding but not our parents."

"So what brings you here?"

"Outside the ticket and all," he answered back. "The place is upping their costs, and I tried to make up the difference. But I …"

"Why can't their income pay for it?" she asked, as she interrupted him.

"Mom didn't work outside the home. I've been paying hers, and now they want another two thousand a month. I'm stretched to the limit. I need to live, too," Nathan said painfully.

"Is that each?" she asked calmly.

"No, for both," he answered, as he stared out her window. "Sure is a busy place. I didn't see a whole lot of it when I went to medical school."

"You were here," Jessica replied a little surprised.

"Briefly then I transferred to UC Davis. They had a study on Alzheimer's. I wanted to see what they were all about it. It was there that I found my answer about Dad."

"So you stayed."

He nodded, as she walked up to him. He turned to look at her.

"I'll pay his and half of Mom's. I'll have my bank send it to them before you leave," she replied calmly. "I'm really, truly sorry that he hurt you and Mom."

"I'm sorry, too, Jessica," Nathan said with a small smile. "You know how much I love you."

"I know," she replied, as she kissed him on the cheek. "Now there's a woman outside my door who said she cares and loves us. Yes, us the dysfunction kids of Stephanie and Dillon Hudson."

They both laughed then hugged. They heard the door open now. Jennifer stood there.

"Come over here," Jessica replied with a big smile.

Jennifer walked over. Nathan grabbed her into a big hug with Jessica again. Jennifer laughed and smiled, too. Jennifer leaned into Nathan's chest and rubbed his chest affectionately.

"You must have small amount of hairs or a bare chest, but either way doesn't matter to me," Jennifer said to him.

Nathan stared at Jessica in horror. Jessica picked up on it.

"You're acting like those things really matter. Nathan's a highly paid doctor," she replied confidently.

"They don't. It's the heart what matters to me," Jennifer said with a big smile. "I'm surprised that no girl has captured your heart yet."

Nathan's face turned a shade of pink which Jessica hadn't seen before. Jennifer looked up at him and smiled.

"I only marry for love, not money. My parents had struggle their whole short lives despite they how hard they tried to keep a roof over our heads, clothes on our backs and food more than a day at time. But they still died too young. I was raised by relatives because of going to work too soon," Jennifer explained sadly. "That's why I went to work earlier than most kids. It didn't help that much in the beginning and a little late for them."

"How old are you?" Nathan asked her.

"Twenty-eight almost twenty-nine," Jennifer answered thoughtfully.

"Jenny, where's Mom and Dad?" Jessica asked with interest.

"In heaven, I hope with their parents," Jennifer answered, as she stepped away from Nathan. "Do you remember that drive by shooting three years ago, Jess?"

"I think, Wendy mentioned it when I came back from Spain. No, it wasn't..." Jessica answered, as it hit her.

"Afraid so, the City paid for their funerals since they caught the perks two days later. I hadn't seen them much since my relatives dragged me away from them. They got the court to believe that they had done child endangerment despite my parents' denials. They loved me, and I never doubted it for a second. The court ruled in my relatives favor, and I didn't see my parents for years," Jennifer said, as she walked the apartment. "Mom was sixteen when she had me. Dad was seventeen. But if you saw them on the streets, you would think that they were in their sixties, but they were in their early forties. I had just seen them only two days before the shooting. I barely recognized them."

"So you don't have any family," Nathan said a little surprised.

"Yes, since I was upset with my relatives when I realized what they had done to my parents and accused them of. So I walked away from them at eighteen and tried to find my parents. But they found me instead and a lot of years had come between us. It's why I care about Taylor. He's the little brother I always wanted Mom and Dad have. We met days after nine eleven. Did you know he's only sixteen?"

"He told me," answered Jessica. "He's wise beyond his years."

"That's true."

"Jenny, are going to be okay?"

"I'm fine," Jennifer answered with a brief smile.

"I thought, you went to college," Jessica replied thoughtfully.

"I would sit in on some classes that interested me, but no, I never enrolled," Jennifer said sadly. "College wasn't in my future like I said with my parents struggling and relatives who really didn't care what I wanted out of life. They just wanted to get me away from my parents."

"There are grants and scholarships," pointed out Nathan.

"No," Jennifer said, as she shook her head.

"I went medical school on grants. Our parents struggled, too. They were not much older than yours were. You can still go to college if you want it bad enough," Nathan said with excitement. "I can help you."

"I would like that, but no, thank you."

"Why not?"

"My manager is sending me to management school for Starbucks in the spring," Jennifer answered calmly.

"Jenny, when did you plan on telling me this? When did it come about?"

"Last week, I don't want to talk about it. I'm glad you two patched things up. I really do care and love you, guys," Jennifer answered, as she stood at the window. "Don't we have a little girl named Sabrina to find?"

"Yes, we do," Jessica replied with a smile. "But I'm treating you to a fancy dinner tonight with no arguments."

Jennifer started to protest then nodded. A knock on the door got all of them to turn around. Brandon stood in the open doorway. Jessica felt her heart flutter at his presence. They locked eyes without a word for a minute or two when Jennifer blocked Jessica's view.

"You two have strong feelings for each other," Jennifer whispered to her. "It's more than friendship, my friend."

"We can't cross Beverly's line," Jessica pointed out in a whisper back.

"Did you hear Clifford was arrested?" Brandon asked them.

"No. Why?" Jennifer answered back.

"Rape," Brandon answered, as he side stepped Jennifer. "Mama is gathering up the family. I came to get you three."

"Why?" asked Jessica.

"We haven't heard from the kidnapper, and we started to comb the streets of possible places they might be. I've printed out that memory card. We can discuss it with everyone."

"Memory card?" asked Jennifer.

"I'll explain when we're all together. Nathan, you're enlisted in the search,"

Brandon answered, as he placed his right hand on his shoulder. "Let's roll everyone. Mama wants us there ASAP."

They nodded. Nathan took Jennifer's hand, as she walked by him. She didn't refuse it. Brandon took Jessica's, as they walked out of the apartment. They stepped out onto the streets of New York and smiled at each other.

"We'll find her. She has too many people who love and care about her," Brandon whispered to her with a wink.

She smiled back. They all arrived at Mama's Pizza Shack. She scanned the room, as she had let go of Brandon's hand now.

"I don't believe it," she replied, as she stood at the door.

"It's us, all of us," Bridget said, as she walked up. "We are all here to help get Sabrina back safely. Your godson's here, too. Beverly is holding him now."

Jessica hugged Bridget then she hugged Stanley and their other children, as she made her way to David. There Beverly held him ever so gently in her arms. She had tears in her eyes.

"You missed that with your own child," Jessica whispered to her.

Beverly nodded. She placed David in Jessica's arms. David stared at her. Jessica glanced up at Beverly.

"Maybe, we'll find your child someday, and we can explain."

"It's too late, Jessica," said Beverly.

"It's never too late. Love never died only grows stronger each and every day."

"But I gave it up at birth."

"It doesn't matter. The child will know you did love it. Otherwise, you wouldn't have carried it full term. It knows your touch because it's like…"

"Coming home," filled in Taylor.

"Exactly," Jessica replied back. "Where did you come from?"

"The kitchen, I wanted to learn how to make raviolis', and Wendy is letting me try in her kitchen," Taylor answered back with a smile. "He's going to capture a lot of women's hearts as he grows up."

"You're pretty good looking yourself, Taylor. I love the haircut by the way," Beverly said with a small smile.

She combed back his short bangs. Taylor smiled at her and didn't move or say anything. Jessica noticed how they looked at each other. It seemed familiar, as she stood there.

"Beverly, did you hear about Clifford?" Brandon asked, as he walked up.

"No. What?"

"He was arrested for rape," Brandon answered quickly.

"Finally there justice in this crazy world," cried out Becky.

"What!" Brandon exclaimed back.

All eyes focused on Becky now. She looked around the room.

"I've heard how he pursued models in the past. It

was a model who pressed charges. Wasn't it, Brandon?"

"Yes," Brandon answered with a small gulp. "But..."

"Never said anything because they had to stop him, not me," Becky interrupted him. "I don't run their lives. I mean, you can't even see that I've been in love with you all these years. Why else would I not tell you what I've known about your personal life all these years? When it comes to matter of the heart, you have no clue Brandon, but you're an excellent photographer. I'll give you credit for that but not love, my dear."

"You got to be kidding," Brandon said in shock.

Becky realized what she revealed and bolted out of the restaurant. The only noise was David, as he fused a little. He felt wet in Jessica's arms.

"Uh...Bridget, your son needs to be changed," she replied with a little hesitation.

"Oh," Bridget said, as she glanced around the spacious room. "Where's the diaper bag?"

"Here, Mommy," a boy answered, as he stepped towards her.

"Thanks, Sweetie," Bridget said, as she touched his cheek and took the bag. "We'll be right back."

She took David from Jessica's arms and rushed into the ladies' room. Beverly watched her and turned back to Jessica.

"Did Clifford..." Beverly started to ask.

"Brandon has some photos to share. Don't you, Brandon?" Jessica asked quickly.

"Oh, yeah, I do. Everyone gather around and look at them. They may look familiar to some of you and not to others," he explained, as he laid them out on two tables.

"How did you get them?" asked Ted.

"On my hunch, I found the memory card, and I placed it in my special place. So whoever knocked me out didn't know about it," Brandon answered with a deep sigh.

"Oh goodness," Wendy said, as he held the photo of the mansion.

"I know. Does this remind you of something?" he asked, as he held another one in his hand.

Wendy stared at it then tears formed, as she sat down. She shook her head. Brandon rushed to her side now.

"It can't be. Why?" Wendy asked him.

"I don't know, Mama, but it's someone we all know. I'm sure of that fact."

"Why do you have the Clayton Mine in California?" asked Nathan.

"What!" Jessica exclaimed, as she made her way to her twin's side.

"Don't you remember it, Jess? It was a place you, me and Ryan explored a lot in our teenage years before we had turned ..." Nathan said, as he stared at her now. "Seventeen, you changed on me or us that summer."

"That's my summer cottage in Maine," Beverly said out loud.

"I didn't know you had a place in Maine," said Helen.

"About seven years ago, I brought it," Beverly said thoughtfully.

"Where I work," Jennifer said, as she held a photo.

"The alley I stayed in after nine eleven," Taylor said, as he held another photo. "I approached you for money for some food."

"Yes, I remember. We were only miles away from Ground Zero, but we could feel and smell the impact still," added Jennifer. "You didn't live in Manhattan back then. Did you?"

"No."

"You found these on a memory card that you attached to your leg," said Ted.

"Yes. I had a friend print out all fifty photos for me while I waited for Vera to finish Taylor's haircut," said Brandon. "This person or persons have been watching us all for some time now. They know these places matter to each of us in ways I don't fully understand."

"Look at this way," Ted said, as he divided out his photo from the group. "Bring what means something close to you. Everyone do it."

They scanned the photos and did what he told them to do.

"It's like I thought," Ted said thoughtfully.

"What's that?" Brandon asked, as he walked back to stand beside Ted. "Oh, I see."

"What?" asked Jennifer?

"There's a pattern here," Ted explained carefully. "We're pieces to this big puzzle, and Brandon, Jessica and Beverly are at the core or heart of it all."

"Why us?" asked Jessica.

"I haven't figured it all out yet, but it's a start in finding Sabrina. I know that for sure."

"So this is our first solid lead then," stated Brandon brightly.

"I'll need to check out all these places for possible

clues. However, it will take time and…"

"Take the plane. I'll come if you want."

"No, you wait with Jessica in case a call comes in."

"Okay. But on one condition," Brandon said thoughtfully.

"Tell you everything. You got it, man," Ted said with a smile.

"What do you want to the rest of us to do?" asked Helen.

"Life as usual except continue to figure out where Sabrina is," Ted answered confidently.

"Do you think she's still in New York?" asked Taylor.

"It's possible, son."

"I'm nobody's son, sir," snapped Taylor.

"Taylor, let it go," Jessica replied back calmly.

"For you, I will."

Wendy sat at the table away from the photos. Brandon and Jessica walked up to her. She had tears streaming down her face now.

"You know, Brandon," Wendy said to him.

"I know. This hurts you, Mama," he said, as he held her close to him. "I can't forget it after all these years. How can you ever forgive me?"

"It was an accident. You were only a boy," Wendy answered back.

"No, I was a young adult, Mama," he said back.

"Let it go, please."

"It'll always be there Mama on that day. It haunts me," Brandon confessed sadly. "Sorry. Please excuse me."

Brandon walked out of the restaurant. Jessica

stared at Wendy now. "It's guilt. Isn't it?"

"Yes, but he has to tell you when he's ready just like you're running away from your own secret or secrets."

14

"**N**o, ransom to drop off yet," Brandon said, as he walked into Mamma's Pizza Shack.

"Not yet, I'm getting a little nervous with all that back there," Wendy said with a small smile.

"Geez and Ted's tracking all those photos for a possible more leads to where to find Sabrina," he said, as he hugged her.

"This was taped to the front door," Taylor said, as he walked in. "I didn't touch it much."

Jessica rushed over to them. Brandon opened it carefully while they all looked on.

"Brandon and Jessica see you survived the desert," Brandon read out loud. "You got the money now in your Mom's upstairs home. Now you and Jessica need to drive to the mansion with the money. You place it in the Oak tree on the out edge of the property. The one you hit with the Classic at sixteen. Then wait for more instructions."

Jessica looked up at Brandon's face. He didn't look happy. She touched his arm.

"I...I...." he stumbled to say.

"Taylor, help me with the money," Wendy said to him.

Taylor nodded and followed her. Now Brandon and Jessica were alone.

"The person or persons who kidnapped Sabrina knows about your private life," Jessica replied calmly. "Do you still think its Jim?"

"All clues come back to him including this one.

Auntie Beverly and Jim were the only ones who knew about the Classic," he answered back. "I wanted to impress Rebecca. I was young and foolish."

"So what happened?"

"I'll explain on our way to the mansion," he answered calmly. "Here's the money."

"Is there any word about Clifford?" Wendy asked him.

Jessica tightened up and stared at her.

"Not really. I shut my phone off when we went to the Carlton last night. I didn't want to spoil Jennifer's celebration. I'm glad that you invited me," he answered with a friendly smile.

"What's this?" Wendy asked with interest.

"Jenny is going to manager school in the spring. She'll be a manager of a Starbucks," explained Jessica.

"Oh, that's wonderful! She's such a good friend," Wendy said in delight. "I need to do something special for her."

"Mama, we'll see you later," Brandon said, as he kissed her on the cheek.

"Bye," Jessica replied with a small smile.

"Be careful, kids," Wendy called out to them.

Brandon nodded and tossed the duffel bag into a small pickup outside the restaurant. She didn't notice it before, but he held her door open. So she slid in, and they headed out of the City.

"Do you know what bugs me the most about Sabrina's kidnapping?" he asked her.

"No. What?"

"He's always one step or two ahead of me."

"I'm sorry."

"Hey, it's not your fault, Jessica."

"So what happened to the Classic?" she asked him.

"The story is a short and quick one. As I said before, I wanted to impress Rebecca and taking Dad's prize car out without his permission was my downfall. I thought, I could handle that power under the hood," Brandon explained thoughtfully.

"Piece of cake," Brandon said to himself confidently. "Rebecca will be so excited to see me behind the wheel of this."

He hummed along the long driveway. When a gray squirrel darted out in front of him, he swerved to avoid hitting it and met the Oak tree. Smoke escaped the engine now.

"Damn it," he said to himself.

"Brandon, what happened? Are you okay?" Beverly asked, as she rushed up beside him.

"What? Who's that?" he asked her, as he pointed to the man.

"Jim. He's a fashion photographer," she answered back, "Your Dad's prize car."

"I know I'll never hear the end of it for the rest of my life."

"I can have a friend fix it back to its original condition," Jim said calmly.

"You can," Brandon said with excitement in his voice.

"Sure, kid," Jim said with a friendly smile. "I'll call him now. It'll be our little secret just the three of us."

"Thanks, man. I owe you one," said Brandon.

"I was young once, too," Jim said back. "No problem, kid."

"I told you that it was brief," Brandon said, as they could see the estate now.

"Did your Dad ever find out?"

"Yeah, two years later and all hell broke loose. We're at the spot," Brandon answered, as he parked the truck.

She got out and so did Brandon. He carried the duffel bag to the Oak tree. He placed it in the center of the tree and touched its base. He seemed to be in deep thought. She glanced at the house and the grounds then started to walk. She was lost in her own thoughts, too.

"Mom, do you like your life?" Jessie asked Stephanie.

"What do you mean, dear?" Stephanie asked back, as she looked up from the garden.

"Being married to Dad and having me and Nathan," she answered back. "Didn't you want something else in your life?"

"I love you, Dad and you, kids very much. Sure we've struggled to make ends meet at times. I can't say; I'm super happy with my life, but I'm happy no less."

"You're so beautiful, Mom. Why didn't you become a model or an actress or something to show; you're real natural beauty?"

"It wasn't in the cards, dear. So I'm dealing with the hand I'm dealt."

"Because Dad knocked you up with us, and you never got a chance to explore your own possibilities or dreams."

"Jessica Marie Hudson, I will not hear you say that again," Stephanie snapped sharply at her.

"I'm sorry, Mom. Please forgive me."

"I do. I know we can't afford to send you and Nathan to college, but you can get some good jobs right here. Right, dear?"

"Of course, Mom, I'm going to be eighteen in a couple weeks," Jessie answered with a small smile.

"Jessica," Brandon said, as he lightly touched her arm.

She stared at him. He smiled at her.

"You seemed so far away right now."

"It's nothing important. It must have been great living in a house like this," she replied thoughtfully.

"We should get going," he said, as he took hand into his. "Jessica, I...never mind let's go."

They walked back to the truck. They drove back into the City in silence. He dropped her off at her apartment and started to leave when his cell rang.

"Hello," he said calmly. "Nothing disturbed. Okay. How about...I see. No, we'll check it out ourselves. It's her home State. She'll know where or how to get there. Yeah, all the other places including the Greek Isle especially Krete. Thanks, man. Bye."

"Ted," Jessica replied, as she turned on her stereo.

"Uh... yes, I thought you and I could check out California in a day or two. I need to tie up some things here first."

"Like the ransom."

"That's my first priority to see if we really to see if we need to go or not. Will you come with me if I have to? I know you're from there and know the area."

"Of course."

"I know it probably has changed in twelve years, but like Mama says: follow your heart," he said with a small smile. "Let's go to Mama's."

"Fine, she's a very wise woman you know, Brandon."

"I know. Are you ever going to tell me anything about your private life? I'm still interested, Jessica."

"Well, you know Nathan is my twin."

"And nothing more than that, come on, Jessica. I hardly know you outside your professional life," he begged her.

"But I can say the same about you, Brandon."

"Okay. You got me. Maybe we both need to share more."

She nodded and smiled. He smiled again. They walked into Mama's Pizza Shack and slipped into a booth. Wendy walked up to them with Taylor who held something hot. His eyes danced with excitement.

"Here try them," Taylor said, as he placed the plate on their table.

"He's been working hard to get the dough right. I think, he's mastering it now," Wendy said proudly.

Jessica took a fork and cut into a ravioli into two pieces then scooped up some white sauce. She bite into it and chewed slowly.

"I love it," she replied, as she finished it.

Brandon dove in for a taste. He had a much bigger piece then she did. His eyes lighted up, too.

"Mama, you need to add this to your menu. It's

light and very different. What's in it?"

"Fresh black pepper, parsley, crab-diced up fine and a white Alfredo sauce with fresh Parmesan cheese on top," answered Taylor. "You're not just saying it. Are you?"

"No, this is really good, Taylor," Jessica answered, as she kissed him on the cheek.

Taylor turned a shade of pink in his face. He stepped back from the table and her.

"I would order it," said Brandon. "Do you have more?"

Taylor nodded and rushed back to the kitchen. Brandon glanced at Wendy.

"Did you make the drop?"

"Yeah, Mama, so now we wait," he answered calmly.

Taylor returned with a bigger helping of raviolis' on a plate. He placed it in front of Brandon. Jessica took the first plate and began to eat.

"Thanks, man," Brandon said with a smile.

"They're not too big. Are they?" Taylor asked them.

"Perfect size. Everything is great, so relax," Brandon answered back. "$8.95, Mama and four of it go to creator."

"What!" Taylor exclaimed.

"Sounds good to me," Wendy said with a returned smile. "Let's go type it out on the computer, so we can have it on our specials of the week."

"You're kidding me, right?" asked Taylor.

"No. Now come into my office," Wendy answered, as she nudged him towards her office.

"That's nice of you and Wendy," Jessica replied, as

she pushed her empty plate away.

"Maybe it'll get him off the streets. He's good kid. Do you know he cleaned my apartment and studio? I never had it that clean before."

"No. He's had a rough life since he has been on the streets at the tender age of four," she answered thoughtfully. "He was in the same orphanage Sabrina is from."

"Oh, really, you seem to know how to reach him," said Brandon.

"We talked while you were away. I don't know how much he shared with your Mom and Jenny. I have to respect what he told me as private unless he reveals it."

"So it's like a secret about his life," Brandon said, as he ate. "I get it. You and I have our secrets like anyone else in the world. But you have to follow your heart when you want someone to know the real you."

She nodded as he finished eating his. He placed a twenty on the table. His cell rang to life again.

"Hello," he said calmly. "Yes, I get it. I can do it tomorrow at eight in my studio. Don't be late. Yes. Thank you."

"Who was that?" she asked with interest.

"A photo shoot, the swim suit issue. Clifford was working on it when he was arrested," he answered, as he glanced down at his cell. "They want me to shoot it now."

A dark, short haired woman walked in. She looked to be in her mid-fifties and marched over to their booth. She removed her dark sunglasses. Jessica knew her from somewhere, but where.

"Are you, Jessica Hudson?" she asked her.

"Yes."

"The model."

"Yes."

"Have you worked with Clifford Reins in the last month or so?"

"Excuse me. Who are you?" Brandon asked her politely.

"Sorry, assistant DA Danni Reynolds," she answered back politely.

"We worked on a swim suit issue recently," Jessica answered thoughtfully.

"I'll need you to come down to my office. I have to ask you some questions privately then. Be there at eight tomorrow morning," Danni said, as she held out her business card, "And don't be late."

Danni left the restaurant. Brandon and Jessica made eye contact now. Wendy and Taylor re-emerged with big smiles.

"You guys looked confused," said Wendy.

"Assistant DA wants to talk to Jessica about Clifford," said Brandon.

"Oh. Is it good or bad news?" asked Wendy.

"I don't know," Jessica answered honestly.

"What's this, Honey?" Wendy asked, as she held up the twenty.

"For the food, Mama, Jessica and I are paying customers. No more freebees. I don't need your accountant on my case again. Besides you have to pay him something," Brandon answered, as he looked at Taylor.

"Then it's his," Wendy said, as she stuffed it into Taylor's pocket of his flannel shirt. "Your first honest job money, and enjoy it."

Taylor took it out of his pocket and looked at it. Tears streamed down his face as he glanced at each of them. Then he hugged Wendy, and she hugged him back.

"Thank you," he said to her.

"You're welcome, Taylor," she said, as she held his face into hers. "You're worth it, and you're loved. Okay. Understand me, I love you, Taylor. Believe it in your heart and follow your heart always. It knows what it wants and needs."

"I...I ..." Taylor struggled to say.

"It's okay," Wendy said, as she touched his chest at his heart.

Jessica wiped away the tears, as she looked on. She glanced at Brandon. He was misty eyed, too. He stared at her and took her hand firmly into his. It was warm and loving but most of all made her feel secure. She hadn't felt that way in years. What Wendy was saying was true, and she knew it in her own heart. She felt his thumb rub her finger, as he held her hand.

"Jessica," he whispered softly. "I wish..."

"I've got to go. I'm sure Beverly will have assignments for me booked well into the New Year," Jessica replied, as she slowly pulled away from his hold. "How are you going to deal with Becky?"

"That's right. She admitted; she's in love with me," he answered thoughtfully. "It will be a little awkward, I guess."

"Talk to her carefully. It's like Mama said about the heart knows what wants and needs."

"I heard her," Brandon said with a small smile.

"I owe you lunch or something."

"No. It was a great dinner with Jennifer, and I owed you. But I would..."

"No, fancy dinner like that again," she interrupted him. "I have a figure to keep because it pays the bills."

She slipped out of the booth. Then she hugged Taylor and Wendy and was off. She didn't want to look back.

"Too intense," she told herself. Then she heard her cell ring, so she flipped it open. "Hello....hello."

"How could you?" asked the female voice on the other end.

"Becky," she answered back.

"Yeah, I know, I told you to go make out when I did that sketch for Brandon. I wanted you both out of my hair, as I focused on what Amy had to tell me. Now you're stealing him from me. I thought we are friend, Jessica. I bet you loved it when Clifford was all over you," Becky snapped back in anger.

"Stop! Brandon and I are just friends. You and I are friends, too," Jessica snapped back in her own defense.

"Oh hell, you can get any man with that body of yours. Your lover boy is on the line," Becky snapped back again. "Bye."

"Jessica," Beverly said, as she rushed up to her. "I'm so glad that I caught up with you, girlie."

"What's wrong?"

"Brandon is doing the swim suit issue, so you have to reshoot with him," Beverly answered back. "Is that a problem? I know he's recovering from his ordeal, but he said he's up to it."

"No, unless you call Becky flying off, the handle."

"What do you mean, girlie?"

"Remember how she admitted her true feelings for your nephew. Or has that slipped your mind? I just got a call from her."

"Oh, I better call and talk to her."

"She said Brandon was on the other line."

"Then she's at his studio," Beverly said quickly.

"I guess."

"I got to get there fast. Excuse me," Beverly said, as she rushed by Jessica now. "Come on pick up, Becky. It's me, Beverly."

"You two get in now," Brandon yelled from the truck, as he pulled up. "It's faster."

Beverly and Jessica got into the truck. Brandon punched the accelerator hard. They reached his studio in no time, and Brandon rushed inside. Jessica and Beverly weren't too far behind him.

"Put it down, Becky," Brandon said calmly. "Please, Becky."

Becky had Brandon's camera in her hands. She was in full of rage. Lights were shattered, as Brandon stepped on the broken glass. Crunch followed by another crunch and another.

"Becky, you're threatening your career here," Brandon said calmly to her.

"Why does she get you? Why not me? I've known you longer and knew who you are all these years," Becky yelled back at him. "Why, Brandon?"

"Becky, please," he begged her. "Stop, I love you like a special friend and sister."

"Go to hell," Becky yelled back still in anger.

He grabbed her and his camera quickly. Jessica stepped forward and took his camera. Then she stepped back, as he held onto Becky. Becky cried hard in his arms. He rubbed her back now.

"I love you, Brandon," Becky said in between sobs.

"The heart knows what it wants and needs, but I can't love you like you want me to. It would be a lie, Becky. I don't think I know how to love someone like that," he said, as he looked her in the eye. "I loved someone a long time ago, and she took her own life and the baby she was carrying, too."

"Was it yours?" Becky asked him.

"No. But I was young and very foolish back then. I'm not ready and may never be ready to go down that road again," he answered honestly. "I'm truly sorry, Becky."

"What about Jessica?"

"What about her?"

"Don't you have feelings for her," Becky said with interest.

"Let it go, Becky."

Becky wiped away her tears now. She looked back at Jessica and Beverly now. She cleared her throat.

"I'm sorry, Jess. I'll clean it all up now," Becky said sadly. "I'll pay for what I broke out of my paycheck."

"Don't worry about it. Call Ralph and tell him to put it on my tab of what you broke. We'll need it all new by tomorrow morning. We have a shoot to do," he said calmly back.

"Fine, whatever; excuse me," Becky said, as she

walked away.

"Thanks for taking it," Brandon said to Jessica.

"You're welcome," she replied, as she held out his camera.

"Rebecca?" Beverly asked to him.

"Yes, Auntie, I've thought of her a lot recently. I was in love with her, but now I'm not so sure. It's in the past," he said thoughtfully. "Jessica, I'd like you for my last shoot. It'll give you time with the assistant DA. I'll be here when you're ready. Excuse me."

He walked away, too. Beverly stared at Jessica. Jessica stared back.

"Yes, I know about Rebecca and the tree. He told me, as we made the drop. You and Jim knew about it. Was there anyone else?"

"Just the guy who fixed the car," Beverly answered thoughtfully. "Why?"

"The person knows a lot about Brandon's private life. We saw it with the photos. It's hitting home too close to home for my liking," Jessica answered thoughtfully, too. "I want a break until we get Sabrina back."

"But Jessica..." Beverly started to protest.

"Enough. I need a break. I've barely have time for me these last twelve years."

"Seeing your brother has made you this way. Hasn't it?" Beverly asked, as she snapped at her.

"In some ways yes, but some other things, too. I need a break after the swim suit shoot. I'll let you know when I'm ready to work again."

"You may not have a career to come back to if you're gone too long," warned Beverly. "Is it worth the risk?"

"Yes. It's like your big sister says the heart knows what it wants and needs and to follow your heart," answered Jessica. "You were in love once, so you should understand Becky. Plus you heard your nephew just now. It makes me wonder my own feelings about love and life."

"I don't like my best model out of the spotlight, but I have to respect your wishes. What's this with assistant DA?"

"I'm to be in her office about Clifford. I'll be fine."

"I had to be there earlier. Be careful. Clifford is innocent of those charges."

"Don't count on it, Beverly, and I don't feel like talking about this now. Excuse me."

She walked over to Becky. Becky swept up the glass while Brandon took the broken lights out of the building. Becky didn't look up.

"Becky," she whispered to her. "Can you stop and look at me? Please."

Becky leaned on the broom handle and looked up. Jessica cleared her throat.

"I didn't always look like this. Believe it or not until I was sixteen things changed for me. My Mom was the beauty of the family and probably still is. She had poise, confidence and the looks that made every man turn their head. It got to my dad sometimes when I was young."

"Then men had eyes for you. How did he take that?"

"Not very well, I'm afraid," she admitted honestly. "He wanted me all to himself."

"Jessica!" Becky exclaimed out loud.

"Hush, no one knows why I left California behind except maybe you. I haven't told anyone the truth or whole truth. But it's our secret, and that tells you what I think of how important our friendship is," Jessica replied in a low calm voice.

"Brandon doesn't know," Becky whispered back.

"Nope, not even my twin. You're the only one who knows."

"Why but me?" Becky asked with interest.

"You told me what you knew about Brandon's private life. So I felt I owed you something personal about my life. Okay."

Becky nodded and gave a small smile. Jessica hugged her.

"Good. Are we friends again? Did you make the call?" Brandon asked with a smile.

"Not yet, but I will," Becky answered back. "Again, I'm sorry, Brandon."

"It's okay. You'll find someone to return your love," he said, as he took the final light out.

"I'll keep your secret, Jess. I'm sorry for what I said earlier."

"All is forgiven."

"So you're on the trail of the kidnapper or kidnappers," Brandon said in his phone. "So there are clues leading you to another clue, man. Keep me informed. Yeah, day or night. No, we made the drop, but no word yet. Okay. Bye."

"Ted?" they asked him.

"Whoa! Ladies, not all at once," he said with a smile. "Does a seashell mean anything to you, Auntie?"

"A seashell," Beverly answered confused.

"Ted found one on your front porch of your Maine house which a magazine open to a photo of Michigan. He's on his way there now," Brandon explained, as he put his cell in his pocket.

"The State of Michigan," stated Becky, "Where exactly in Michigan?"

"He didn't say. Why?"

"I was born and raised there before going away to college."

"I always assumed..."

"I lived here. Mom loved the Broadway shows here, so Dad sent us into the City to enjoy that," interrupted Becky.

Jessica walked away. She thought of all the photos, and who they connected with. She shook her head when Brandon approached her.

"You're thinking about something, Jessica."

"I should go back to my apartment to lie down. I think I have a headache coming on."

"Lie down upstairs. We can talk later."

"Are you sure?"

"Positive. Go."

She headed upstairs and found his bed. She stretched out and fell into a deep sleep within minutes of hitting one of his pillows.

15

"**Y**ou're saying three models have come forward to accuse Clifford of rape," Jessica replied, as she sat in a comfortable chair in Danni's office.

"Afraid so, and someone said you might be a victim, too," Danni said, as she sat on the edge of her desk. "That's why I contacted you and wanted you to come in."

"What?" she asked quickly, "Who?"

"I got this is email," Danni answered, as she handed her the paper.

Jessica took it and read, "Contact Jessica Hudson for possible rape victim. Do you know who sent it?"

"No. Why?"

"Can you track down who sent it?"

"Uh...there's something you're not telling me," Danni answered in hesitation. "But you need to tell me."

"A little girl I worked with was kidnapped. We're trying to track her down. It sounds like the kidnapper. Now can you please track down who sent it?"

"Calm down. You're saying we had a kidnapping, and I don't know about," answered Danni.

"Yes. I and Brandon and everyone else close to us have been searching for her. We suspect we know who it is but can't seem to locate his whereabouts. Please," Jessica pleaded with her.

"Give me a second," Danni said, as she stepped out of her office.

A young man walked up to her, and she handed him the paper. He took off, and Danni returned to Jessica.

"Okay, I'll help you if you help me. Did Clifford Reins rape you?"

"No. Taylor stopped him in time. He's my hero, but it's only between us," Jessica answered honestly.

"When did it happen?"

"Sometime back not sure exactly," Jessica answered thoughtfully. "I would say maybe a week or two ago. It was the day of our shoot at Clifford's New York studio."

"We got a search warrant for evidence at his studio and gathered up his appointment book to back up the women's statements of their attacks. You will be listed in there, too. I'm sure," Danni said thoughtfully back. "Anything else you need to tell me about Clifford? Now is a good time come forward with it all instead of later?"

"Brandon's assistant Becky might know more than me," she replied back.

"Why?"

"She seemed to know him uh..."

"I'll check into it. Thanks. Now I take it the police aren't involved in the kidnapping, right?"

She nodded.

"I have connections off the grid that maybe able to assist you in your search. I'll call you if anything comes up. Is there anything else?"

"Do you know anyone who can help with adoption procedures?"

"My friend Susan, I'll contact her and have her contact you. She's a lawyer in adoption or legal ones anyway. Are you thinking of adopting the little girl after she's found?"

"Yes," Jessica answered confidently.

"Good for you. Thanks for everything. I'll be in touch on that personal matter," Danni said with a small smile.

"Thank you so much," Jessica replied with a big smile, as she walked out of Danni's office.

She walked into the elevator and leaned on the back of it, as the doors closed. Then she bolted up straighter.

"What are doing, Jessica?" she asked herself out loud. "Are you seriously considering adopting Sabrina? Look at your life. What kind of life can you offer her? You're a model with assignments all the time."

She felt her cell vibrate in her pocket. She flipped it open, as she stepped out of the elevator.

"Sis," she heard, as she held it up to her ear.

"Nathan."

"Yeah," he said back. "I need you here. Can you get the first flight out?"

"Uh.....sure. But what's going on? Is it, Mom?"

"No, Dad. Now before you take it back. Listen to me first. Mom needs us both to deal with him. They're trying to increase or change his meds," explained Nathan.

"But he's not making it easy."

"Exactly, you got it."

"I said would help, and I'll be there as soon as I can. I have to tie up a few loose ends here before I come out. I'll call first," she replied calmly.

"Thanks, Chubby Bear," he said back. "I love you."

"Me too, see you soon," she replied, as she ended the call. She saw Sabrina's photo appear, "Soon, Sweetie, soon."

She looked for Brandon's number.

"Brandon's cell leave name and message," Brandon's voice said in her ear.

"Damn. Brandon, I need to go out of town. An emergency back...home," Jessica replied back. "I'll be in touch soon."

She flipped it shut and stepped out in the morning sun. It was warm with a touch of crisp, bite in the air to remind her that it was fall now. She scanned the area and was about to flag down a taxi.

"Jess," Jennifer called out to her, as she rushed up to her. She tried to catch her breath. "Wait."

"Jennifer, what oh, that's right your store isn't too far from here. What's wrong?"

"Nathan," Jennifer answered, as she bent over and placed her hands on her knees.

"We just talked. I'm going out to see him."

"Good. Give him, my love," Jennifer said, as she stood tall again.

"I didn't know that he had left."

"He made good time giving the circumstances. I miss him already. He left after you took us out to dinner. He got the call when we were in my apartment. But where's home?"

"Elk Grove, California," Jessica answered, as she felt uneasy about those words now.

Why she didn't know yet? Her cell vibrated in her hand. She looked at it.

"I have to take this," she replied to Jennifer.

Jennifer nodded.

"Hi, Brandon," she replied on her end.

"I'm going with you. We're booked for the next flight out. Be ready when I swing by your place," Brandon said quickly.

"I thought you were going to wait to hear from you know who."

"There's no activity at the drop off site. I got everyone photographed except you," Brandon informed her. "There must be a reason you haven't gone home in over twelve years. I won't let you face it alone, Jessica."

"How did you know?"

"I could hear a slight change in your voice. I'm coming. No arguments," answered Brandon.

"Fine, I'm heading back to my place now."

"Good. Bye."

She flipped her cell closed again. Jennifer stared at her.

"He's picking you up and going with you," Jennifer said with a small smile. "He has feelings for you, and it's more than friendship, Jess. I think you have feelings for him, too."

"So what if we do. We have a contract with Beverly to never cross that line."

"That's stupid! What line?"

"It makes things less complicate. I have to go. Bye."

"Bye."

Jessica flagged for a taxi and hugged Jennifer before she got in. She waved to her then glanced down at her cell. Sabrina and her with the oversized teddy bear stared back at her. She shook her head.

"Ms," the driver said to her.

"Sorry," she replied, as she got out.

"Keep the change, buddy," Brandon said, as he appeared at the front passenger side seat.

"We'll need one to the airport," she replied back.

"No, Taylor is taking us in the truck."

"Does he know how to drive?"

"Don't know and don't care. Pack light like always."

She nodded and headed upstairs to her apartment. She tossed a pair of sweats and dress pants into a small bag. Brandon was at her door. She tossed a sweatshirt and nice blouse in, too then zipped it closed. He took it from her. Together, they walked hand in hand downstairs. Taylor was behind the wheel.

"Hi, Jessica," Taylor said with a big smile.

"Hi, Taylor, you look happy," she replied, as she slid next to him.

"Wendy says people love my raviolis'. It's a real hit. I've never had so much money in my life at one time," Taylor said with excitement. "I want to learn how to make my own sauce next."

"Maybe you should enroll in a cooking school," suggested Jessica.

"No time," Taylor said, as he merged into traffic. "I have so many ideas of different things that I'm up most of the night trying to write them all down."

"So that's what's in the black notebook," Brandon said thoughtfully.

"Yeah, your Mama wants me to write them all down. My spelling isn't very good on some words, but I'm the only one reading it."

"Don't count on it."

"What do you mean?"

"Mama is probably reading them when you're working. I know if a book is open then she'll look," Brandon answered with a chuckle and big smile. "That's who she is."

"Here we are," Taylor said back. "Call us when you land. I wish I could go though."

"Maybe another time," Jessica replied, as she kissed him on the cheek.

"Yeah maybe for the wedding," Brandon said with a smile.

"Okay," Taylor said back.

Brandon hustled her up to a ticket counter. Jessica looked at him puzzled. He had their tickets in his hand.

"Who's wedding?" she asked finally.

"Don't worry, Jessica. It's not, us, but romance is in the air. Spring-time could be ideal for a wedding," he answered, as he grinned back. "Let's go."

She boarded their flight, and she sat by the window. She gazed out at New York. She thought of the Twin Towers that weren't there anymore. She wiped the wetness from her face.

"Jessica," Brandon said, as he sat beside her. "Are you all right?"

"Uh...fine."

"Mom, Dad and I were happy during those early years. Dad was a smart man and second cousin to the famous Rockefeller family. But he made his fortune on his own on his own terms," Brandon said in a low voice.

"Are you telling me your personal life?" she asked, as she sat up straighter.

"Yes. I want you to know the whole me not just the professional photographer. I hope you will do the same."

"We'll see. How did your Dad make his money if not from the family name? Clearly he didn't have their last name."

"Publishing industry specifically Bantam Books and its subsidiaries like where Jackie Kennedy was an editor. Then he made tons of investments that paid out good money. As a kid, I never went without again then I turned thirteen. I picked up my first camera. I wanted to see what I could do with it." He had paused for some time before he spoke again. "Dad and I started to drift apart by the time Rebecca came along. Jim was showing me different aspects of Fashion photography. I didn't want to be with Dad anymore. He wanted me to go to college and follow him into his business ventures. He tried to get me over Rebecca, too. I kept telling him that he didn't understand and get the hell out of my life."

Brandon looked towards the center aisle now. Jessica turned his face to face hers. He had tears in his eyes. She wiped them gently away.

"I shouldn't have told him that, Jessica. He ...never mind."

"He loved you, Brandon, and you loved him. Loves sucks sometimes, too," she whispered back.

"Jessica, I want you to know everything. Now we're going back to your private life that I know so little about," he said calmly now.

She had bitten her lower lip and took her hand away when he took it into his. She glanced away from him now. He turned her head to face his now.

"I see how it's painful for you to go back there. That's why I wanted to come. You're not alone on this trip to your past."

She shook her head. "I left there the day after my eighteenth birthday with your Aunt Beverly. I left Nathan in the airport and never looked back."

"I have to go, Nat. I have to see if I can make it on my own," Jessie replied to Nathan. "I can't stay here. I don't need you to fight my battles either but grateful you're on my side about this."

"Chubby Bear, Dad doesn't want you to be a model, and I don't know why. You're beautiful since you lost all that weight. It's your body, and what you want to do with your life. But New York is so far away, Chubby Bear," whined Nathan.

"I have to go now," she replied, as she hugged him quickly. "I love you."

"I love you too, Chubby Bear," Nathan said, as he held her tight in his arms. "Don't forget that important fact most of all."

"I won't," she replied, as she pulled away from him.

She rushed to Beverly, and they boarded the plane together. Jessica was in the present again with Brandon who stared at her now.

"So Nathan drove you to the airport," he said calmly.

"Yes. I boarded that plane and didn't look back at him or the scenery. I didn't want to remember any of it."

"That's kind of harsh, but I sense California is painful for you."

"Not all of it," she replied defensively. "Tahoe and The Coast are so...peaceful."

"And what about Elk Grove? That's where the pain lies, right?"

"Ladies and gentleman, we're making our final approach to Sacramento Metro Airport. Welcome to California. Please return your seats to the upright position and fasten your seatbelts. Thank you for traveling United Airlines. Enjoy your visit," the stewardess said over the PA system.

"I'm here for you, Jessica," he said, as he squeezed her hand lightly.

She smiled briefly and glanced out the window. She shook her head.

"Back here to hell," she replied to herself.

"Excuse me."

"Nothing, Brandon, nothing."

They exited the plane, and Jessica flipped her cell to open to turn it on. Brandon held their bags now. She walked through the airport terminal as her cell rang.

"Hello," a male said on the other end.

"Nat, I'm here with Brandon. We're at the airport," she replied back.

"Ryan's there already," Nathan said back.

"How..."

"Someone texted about your flight, so Ryan volunteered to pick you guys up."

"Jessie," Ryan called out to her.

"I see him," she replied back. "See you soon."

"Okay, Sis."

She flipped her cell closed when Ryan hugged her. She patted his back. Then he shook hands with Brandon.

"How did you..." Brandon started to ask.

"Nathan said someone texted him about our flight plans," she interrupted him. "We'll discuss it later."

He nodded. Ryan took Jessica's bag from Brandon and headed out. They followed him.

"Did you have a good flight, Jessie?" Ryan asked, as he smiled back at her.

"Fine, how long..."

"Half hour to an hour at the most," Ryan interrupted her. "You'll be staying at your folks' house. It's where Nathan and I live now. We share expanses. But he wants to meet you at their new home, so I'm taking you guys there first. Is that okay?"

"Fine," Jessica answered coldly.

"Did you bring a bathing suit?" Brandon asked, as they got into a car.

"Everything is the way you left it twelve years ago. No one touched a thing in your room except to clean it of dust," Ryan said from behind the wheel. "Your Mom wanted it that way. You never told me that you were leaving back then."

"It all came about quickly," she replied back, as she turned to Brandon now, "But why a bathing suit?"

"I thought Tahoe or the coast would be an opportunity to wrap-up the swimsuit issue. You said they're so peaceful. I brought my camera just in case," Brandon answered back.

"I'll think about it, but you saw what I packed," Jessica replied back. "Does Mom know I'm here, Ryan?"

"I'm sure Nathan's telling her and your Dad now. He sure has a temper like before the meds," Ryan answered, as he shook his head.

"What?" Jessica asked him.

"He was really crazed when you left twelve years ago. Didn't Nathan tell you why he went into medicine?"

"We talked in New York. I saw what the bastard did to him. But Nat never told the bastard how he took me to the airport, and where I had gone either."

"Nope even being burned by the iron more than once, Nathan never told him. Your Dad discovered men looking at you on the cover of Cosmo. They were lusting over you and wondered what would be like to screw a woman like that," Ryan explained back. "He looked at the picture and went off. He slapped Mom around, and it got worse. This last time was the worst because Nathan wasn't there to stop him."

"What did the bastard do?"

"She was pushed against the wall several times to bust some ribs. Then if that wasn't enough from him, he pushed her downstairs where he kicked her in the ribs and head. Nathan walked in, as he held her head in his bloody hands. She begged him to stop. Well, your Dad gave her a black eye before he charged at Nathan," Ryan answered sadly. "Nathan had a needle ready as he charged. I don't know how Nathan got it into him. But it calmed him, and he fell asleep. So Nathan was able to get Mom medical attention she desperately needed."

"He didn't tell me all this," replied Jessica.

"It wasn't his proudest moments, Jessie. He had just come off a grueling sixteen hour shift and if the needle had gone south. Well, your Dad would be dead. It was that close to his heart. Your brother didn't realize how close it was until after they were in the hospital. I had to tell someone, Jessie, just as I'm telling you now."

"I understand," she replied, as she glanced out the window.

"Honey, are you all right?" Brandon asked her.

She jerked back at him with tears in her eyes. He touched her face and looked deep into her eyes. He pulled her close to his chest. She took in his embrace.

"We're here," Ryan said calmly. "Jessie, I'm sorry."

She pulled herself together and slipped out of the backseat. Brandon took her hand, as they let Ryan lead the way.

"Jess," Nathan said, as he rushed up to them.

"I'm so damn sorry," she replied, as she gazed long and deep into her twin's eyes. "Can you ever forgive me?"

"For what?" he asked back.

"She knows in detail what your Dad did to Mom, and what you did," answered Ryan.

"Damn it, Ryan!" Nathan exclaimed at him.

"Where's the bastard?" she asked coldly.

"Barricaded in his room, we can't get him to try the new meds. They're supposed to act quicker," Nathan answered back. "Jessica, I ...."

"Give them to me," she replied, as she held out her hand steady.

"No, Jessica..." snapped Brandon.

She glanced at him. "I have to. No one else can reach him."

"He'll hurt you," protested Brandon.

"No, he won't. He's hurt me already but not anymore," she replied coldly, "His meds, Nathan. Please. I owe you and Mom this."

Nathan placed orange and purple pills in her open palm. She closed her hands. He led her down the hallway to his room.

"Dad, it's me, Piggy Wiggy. I'm back. I need to talk to you," she called out to him. "Dad, do you hear me?"

The door opened after the sound of something scraping the floor. Dillon had white hair now and a white beard to match. He had aged these last twelve years. Jessica walked closer to the door.

"Piggy Wiggy," Dillon said to her.

"Yes, Daddy," she replied, as she felt knots in her stomach now. "Let me in. We need to talk."

He opened the door wider. She stood face to face with him now. She stepped in, and he rushed a chair against the door again. Dillon faced her, as she faced him. She held the meds tightly in her hand now.

"You've come home," Dillon said, as he approached her. "I've missed our times together. Can we do it now? I still remember how good you feel being inside and touching those..." Dillon licked his lips now.

"We can, but you have to do something for me first," she interrupted him.

"Anything," he said with excitement in his voice.

"Take these for me. They'll help your sexual performance and give me real pleasure," she replied calmly.

"Of course, Piggy Wiggy," he said, as he took them from her, "Anything for you."

He swallowed the pills and started to unzip his zipper to reveal his penis. She felt her stomach flip.

"We've missed you awful lot," he said, as he

backed her to his bed.

He grabbed her with his free hand. He unbuttoned her blouse and had his hand on her right breast. He squeezed it hard, but Jessica only stared at him. His eyes were glossy with a deep desire which she remembered from years before. Then they changed quickly, and he released her breast. Thud.

He was on his side and snoring now. She zipped up his pants after she placed his penis inside. Then she redressed herself and marched over to the door to remove the chair.

"He's out," she called out from the open door.

"What the hell!" Nathan exclaimed in shock.

"I want to see Mom now. Please," she replied calmly.

She wanted to settle her stomach by seeing her Mom and get away from him.

"Men strap him to the bed," ordered Nathan,

"How?"

"Never mind; you're right about them being acting fast," she answered back.

"I'll take her to see our Mom," Nathan said to Ryan.

Ryan nodded. Brandon took Jessica's hand, as she walked beside Nathan. She leaned on Brandon's shoulder.

"You're shaking," he whispered to her. "Are you all right?"

"Fine, now."

"Honey, Sweetie," Stephanie said with a big smile now.

"I brought you a visitor, Mom," Nathan said calmly.

Stephanie glanced at Jessica and brought her hand to her lips. She had tears in her eyes now. "Jessie."

"Hi, Mom, it's been a long time," Jessica replied, as she approached the bed.

"Twelve plus years," Stephanie said, as she reached out to her.

They hugged each other. Jessica was careful how she held her since she knew what the bastard did to her.

"I know what he did to you. It's why you left," Stephanie whispered into her ear.

Jessica pulled back to examine her Mom's face. She had aged too since she was gone. But she also knew what happened between her dad and her. She wanted to ask how and when, but they weren't alone.

"Who's this good looking man?" Stephanie asked, as she glanced over at Brandon.

"My friend Brandon, and he's a professional photographer, Mom," Jessica answered with a big smile.

"Not the one who put my daughter on the cover of Cosmo over twelve years ago," stated Stephanie.

"The one and only, Mrs. Hudson," Brandon said with a bigger smile now. "I see where Jessica gets her natural beauty. It was that cover launched both of our careers, Mrs. Hudson."

"Come closer and call me, Stephanie," she said to him. "Or Mom like Ryan calls me that you know."

"He has a Mom," Nathan pointed out to her, as he retreated to the doorway. "Remember I told you about her and others especially Sabrina."

Jessica shot a glance at her twin. He smiled back at her.

"What? She means something to you. You didn't say it was a secret. Why else would you be looking for her?"

"Now we talked about it years ago," Stephanie started to say.

"I was heavier than Mom and time and things change. Like Nathan meeting Jennifer," she replied, as she still stared at him.

"Who's Jennifer?" Stephanie asked with interest now.

"A girlfriend of mine," she answered back. "She sends her love by the way."

Nathan lifted an eyebrow. He folded his arms across his chest. She laughed a light laugh.

"What?" Nathan asked back.

"Some things never change, dear sweet brother."

"Your room is still the same way you left it, too," said Stephanie.

"I know Ryan told me on the way out. Are you going to leave here soon?"

"No, I'm afraid not. I would be lucky if I ever walk again after my last fall down those stairs," Stephanie said calmly. "I'm tired now. Please come again soon. We'll talk more. You had a long flight. Nathan, take them home."

"Yes, Mom, do you want your meds?"

"No, Honey. Take them home," Stephanie answered calmly.

"It was a pleasure to meet you, Mrs. Hudson," Brandon said politely.

"Same here; now scram."

Jessica leaned in to kiss her Mom on the cheek

when Stephanie slapped her away. So Jessica got up and headed for the door. Nathan walked in and kissed their Mom's on the same cheek. She accepted it.

Jessica walked into the hallway when Brandon took her hand into his. She stared at him with tears in her eyes. She brushed them aside.

"Some homecoming," she replied back bravely.

"You can sleep in your old room."

"No, Nat, I'll sleep in the study. No buts. Please."

They walked out to Ryan's car. Nathan slid behind the wheel and drove back to a gray house with white trim. The old two story house stared back at her, as she gazed at it.

"Is it like you remembered?"

"Yes," she answered, as she took his hand. "I want you to stay in my old room since you want to know about my personal life."

"Jess...I," he said in hesitation.

"Sixteen years I lived here then headed for New York to become a model. What some people would say as a rags to riches kind of story or from working class America. Neither one of them has a college degree, but he worked hard for us. Mac and cheese, homemade pizza and simple things in life not rich like you with a silver spoon in my mouth," Jessica replied, as she looked at Brandon now. "Do I disappoint you the more you see the real me?"

"Uh no, just a woman hurting from her past, and I don't know all of it as to why. But I'll tell you about my personal life and maybe you'll feel safe to share your pain but not all of it at once. Please."

"Fine," she replied, as they headed inside.

She walked him to her old bedroom and opened the door. It was exactly as she left it. A couple dolls on the bed and a big teddy bear in a rocking chair. She shook her head.

"Goodnight, Brandon," she replied, as she started to leave.

Brandon kissed her on the lips and stepped inside. "Goodnight, Jessica."

She walked away with tears in her eyes and down her face now.

16

Jessica sat on the couch of the study and glanced around the room. Then she walked over to the desk and ran her hand along the glossy redwood finish. She noticed a framed cover of Cosmo, so she picked it up. She was eighteen back then. She put it down and noticed a smaller framed photo. She picked it up and examined it closely.

"It's a photo of Mom and Dad," Nathan said, as he stood in the doorway. "I found it buried in Mom's night stand."

Jessica glanced over at him. "Our desk has held up all these years."

She put the framed photo down. Nathan walked up to her.

"She was his high school sweetheart. Mom told me when I brought it to her. We know so little of their life before us," he said calmly. "Did you know?"

"No, Mom and I didn't talk much but you know that. I helped her prepare food which I consumed often and lots of it," she answered thoughtfully.

"Knock knock," Brandon said, as he entered the room.

Nathan and Jessica turned to face him. He walked up closer. He ran his hand along the surface of the desk.

"Nice," he said with a smile.

"Thank you," Nathan and Jessica replied together.

"Uh..."

"We built it for Dad for Father's Day," Nathan said with a smile. "I think we were ten back then. My sister designed the cabinet doors."

"Oh really," Brandon said, as he stepped around other side, "Grapes and vines that's interesting."

"There's a fishing boat on the other side," Nathan pointed out with a big smile.

Jessica shoved him hard. Nathan stared back at her. A phone rang, and they reached for their cells.

"I have to take this," Nathan said politely. "Please excuse me."

He walked out of the room. Jessica stared back at Brandon now that they were alone again.

"How did you sleep?" she asked him.

"All right, now I can say honestly that I slept in a girl's room without the girl beside me," he answered thoughtfully.

Jessica felt warm and walked away from the desk. She looked out the window to the backyard.

"Tell me what happened at eighteen?" she replied with her back to him.

"First, tell me what's going on in that pretty head of yours?" Brandon asked, as he walked over to her.

"I'm not a true blonde. I dyed it before I met your Aunt Beverly. I was a brunette like Dad and her sapphire blue eyes. He always had some kind of food for me when he walked through the front door. I could hear them through the thin walls," she replied thoughtfully. "We moved into this house when Nathan and I were about two.

He was starting to make some good money then, but it called him away from home on and off for next years ahead. But he would sneak away to give me food then fight with Mom briefly before returning to work if he wasn't on the road. I don't know what he really did for a living. I'm not sure if they noticed him gone, but the food and lifestyle was the same right up to when I left. The only thing changed was we lived in this house. But we were still working class America, and college was out of our reach for all of us."

"Is that why you became a model, or was it something else?" Brandon asked her.

"I guess both. Going to the prom with Ryan changed things for me. I was sixteen and lost a lot of weight. I turned seventeen that June and was thinking about a career. So the following year turning eighteen was a world of change. If he had a surplus of money, he didn't shower it on his wife and children. He told us not even think or plan on going to college unless we paid our own way. But he said it was really a waste of good money," she answered thoughtfully.

"Dad having the same disease our Aunt Betty had and it was in medical school I learned of his uncontrolled rage. Mom said he would fly off the handle then go away for awhile. When he came back, he was sweet as could be. I guess he learned to control it because I can't remember him being out of control until after you left. Can you? I'm still so sorry Nathan," Jessica replied with tears in her eyes still.

"It's okay, Sis. No one knew about his uncontrolled rage. We didn't see it until you and he had been fighting about college," said Nathan.

"I didn't see college as a waste of time and money.

He had to have some money to pay for this house. He didn't want me to leave because I...never mind," she replied, as she stopped herself.

"Mom wants to see you alone, Jessie. She told me last night," Nathan said in a low voice. "I had to check on Dad and his new meds. I still don't understand how you got him to take them."

"Are you using your car?" she asked him.

"Yeah, I'm heading into the hospital, but I'll check on them later," he answered back.

"We can get a rental," said Brandon.

"Take the Blazer," Ryan said, as he entered the room. "No one is using it right now."

"Are you sure?" asked Jessica.

"Yeah, I'm sure. It's not like we're all going up to explore those abandon mines up in the Mother Lode anytime soon," answered Ryan.

"Mother Lode," Brandon said with interest.

Jessica's eyes went wide. She stared at Brandon now. "Do you think..." she asked in mid-thought.

"Go see your Mom. We'll talk later," Brandon said calmly.

"Thank you, Ryan," she replied, as she walked over to him.

Ryan held out the keys, and she kissed him on the cheek.

"Sis," Nathan said, as he cleared his throat.

She looked back at him and Brandon stood side by side now. She smiled. "Yes."

"Mom wanted that black book on the desk. Could you give it to her?"

"Sure. What's in it?" she asked him.

"Not sure really, but she told me where to find it, and that's about it," Nathan explained with a slight shrug of his shoulders. "And oh bring it to her."

She picked it up and headed out of the room. She reached the front door when a man's hand was on the knob. She glanced to her side.

"I'd like to come but can wait outside while you and your Mom talk," Brandon whispered to her.

"Fine," she replied, as she stepped through the open door.

She walked out in the early morning light. She shielded her eyes from the fall morning sun. She glanced over to see the Blazer in the driveway, so she walked in that direction. Brandon slid into the passenger side while Jessica got behind the wheel. She flipped down the visor then quickly back up.

"What?" he asked her.

"My sunglasses and purse are in the house," she answered back.

"I'll get them," he said, as he headed back inside.

Jessica flipped the visor down again. It was a photo of her and Ryan at the prom. She shook her head, as she flipped it up again quickly. Another photo landed on her lap. It was one of her tied to her bed naked.

"Your lover needs a picture of you to get him through those days and nights on the road," Dillon said, as he leaned over her now with a Polaroid camera.

Jessie squirmed, as she had the gag in her mouth. A picture popped out. She felt his hand between her legs. She fought back the tears as she felt something pushing inside her. Another picture was taken.

"Be still. It won't hurt as much," Dillon said, as he laid on top of her now. "Here it comes, my love. You're so ripe down there, my love."

Dillon's hands were on her face. Jessie felt a big push inside her. He lunged for her neck. She felt his bites on her neck. Then he stopped and stared at her.

"That felt good my love. Remember this is our secret. Go take a shower and jump around a little in there. We don't want unexpected pregnancy," he said, as he untied her.

She sat up and saw him zip up his pants. He grinned at her. It sent shock waves through her seventeen year-old body.

"Want more?" he asked her with a grin. "I think I can get him to perform again."

"No. I'm going," she answered, as she grabbed her clothes off the floor.

"Jessica," Brandon called out to her.

"Uh...oh, thank you," she replied, as she reached for her purse and sunglasses.

"You're welcome," he said, as he got back in.

She placed the photo in the door pocket and started the Blazer.

"You seemed so far away right now. Do you want to talk about it?"

"No, not right, now. Maybe someday but I don't know for sure. Can you give me time?"

Brandon nodded. They drove in silence. She pulled into the care home and got out. Brandon rushed up to take her free hand into his. She glanced at him and forced a smile.

"I'm sorry."

"I get it, Jessica. Memories run wild in our minds when we're near something that triggers them. Remember the Oak tree."

She nodded, and they headed inside. They walked down to her Mom's room where Jessica hugged him before she walked in alone.

"Hi, Mom," Jessica replied, as she stood at the doorway.

"Jessie," Stephanie said with a warm smile. "Come sit on the bed."

"Nat wanted me to bring you this," she replied, as she held up the black book.

"Oh good, come sit."

Jessica sat on the bed and held out the book. Stephanie took it and struggled with it at first. Then she held it out to Jessica.

"Read this, Sweetie," Stephanie said calmly.

Jessica took it and glanced at the page. It was her Mom's handwriting. She glanced back at her Mom. Her eyes were filled with excitement now. Jessica cleared her throat and stared back the open book again.

"My angel," Jessica began to read out loud. "I know I would love her for the rest of my life. She has my eyes sapphire but her daddy's brunette hair." She glanced at her Mom then the page again.

"Her hands and feet are so tiny compared to her twin brother's.

Would she need me as she grows up?

She's my world now.

I have so many hopes and dreams for her.

I hope I won't dash them for her.
What lessons will I teach you, my angel?
Will you listen to my wisdom with an open mind
and heart?
Or will you put up a wall like I did with your
Grandma Sara?
Gosh, I have so many things racing through my
mind right now as I look at you.
But the most important thing is I love you, my
angel.
I want you to know that always.
You will stand on your own in world, and I hope
and pray you won't be alone.
I love you, my sweet angel, Jessica Marie."

Jessica brushed aside the tears from her face, as she closed the book. She glanced over at her Mom. She had tears in her eyes, too. Jessica placed the book closer to her Mom now.

"I wrote that the day you and Nathan were born," Stephanie whispered to her. "I failed you, Jessie in so many ways. You talked about children..."

"But Mom..." she interrupted her.

"Let me finish, Sweetie."

Jessica nodded.

"You talked about a family, and I replayed it over and over in my head since that day you told me. I had dashed your dream. I had no right doing that to you, Sweetie. I'm sorry. You were telling me what you wanted in life. How could I take that away from you? I had no damn right. He had no right to take away your innocence either," Stephanie explained slowly. "I blame myself for it."

"Why?" Jessica asked with tears flowing heavily down her face now.

"You struggled with your weight then you lost it without even telling me. How did I not notice?"

"Stuffed pillows, Mom, I grew tired of them and the fat suits. But how did you..." Jessica replied in hesitation.

"This last beating, he said I wasn't as good as our daughter. I was shocked at first then horrified, as he went into great detail of how he seduced you in your own bed. He said you liked every bit of it."

"I didn't, Mom. I had to undress before him and felt uneasy about it. I wouldn't agree to it, but I felt dizzy, as he held me close. Then I woke up tied to my bed and with a gag in my mouth. It's uh..." she replied, as she buried her hands into her face now.

"You left and haven't come back until now," Stephanie said, as she touched Jessica's head. "You didn't think you could tell me the truth. I didn't talk to you like this when you were growing up. Rehearing the poem, I know how much I failed you,
Jessie. But I want to start over. Will you let me?"

"A wise woman said: the heart knows what it wants and needs," she answered, as she pulled her hands away from her face.

"Yes, she is a wise woman."

"For last two years, I have this aching in my heart, I didn't know why until now. Sabrina tugs at my heart and soul so deeply that I know she's meant to be a much deeper part of my life than I can ever realize. Then there's Brandon. I see him differently now, too," Jessica explained thoughtfully. "It was his Mom who said that about the heart. Oh Mom, I do love you. I always have even when you kept me at a distance. I want us to be close maybe close like Mom and daughter should be."

"Thank you, Jessie," Stephanie said, as she held out her arms.

Jessica moved closer and leaned in. She felt her Mom kiss her on the cheek. Jessica didn't know how long they stayed in that embrace, but it felt good to her. She walked out of her Mom's room with a big smile on her face. She noticed Brandon playing chess with an elderly man. She walked up closer.

"You look in better spirits," he said with a big smile back.

She reached down and hugged him. Then she gazed deep into his eyes before she kissed him on the lips then stepped back.

"I like that greeting, young man," the man said with a grin. "I knew a girl a long time ago who did it that to every time she saw me."

"Jessica Hudson," a nurse said, as she walked up. "Your Dad wants to speak to you."

She had bitten her lower lip slightly. She drew in a big breath and exhaled slowly. "Later," she replied finally.

"But," the nurse said back.

"She said later," pointed out Brandon.

The nurse nodded and walked away.

"Can I have a hug, little lady?" asked the elderly man.

"Of course," Jessica replied, as she walked over to hug him, too.

"I love hugs from pretty ladies," the elderly man said with excitement in his voice.

"Now, Arnold," warned Brandon.

"My, Honey, has been gone a good year now," Arnold said back. "That was nice, little lady. Thank you."

"You're welcome, Arnold," she replied with a big smile.

"It's good to see you smile again. I take it went well with your Mom," said Brandon.

"Yes. She had me read a poem that she wrote when Nat and I were born," she replied back.

"So she writes poetry for her daughter, and I take it you didn't know."

"Nope, I don't think Nathan knows either."

"Jess, thank ...God. You're still here," Ryan said, as he bent at his waist to catch his breath.

"What's wrong?" she asked, as she rushed over to him.

He reached inside his back pocket and held out an envelope. She stared at him.

"It was on my car. It wasn't there when I came home. Then he showed up," Ryan answered, as he looked back.

Ted walked in. Brandon walked towards them now. Ted stopped at Ryan and Jessica.

"What brings you here?" Brandon asked him.

"All clues lead to here," Ted answered him. "I think that's the final clue."

Jessica held the envelope now. She opened it and a photo slipped out. It sat on the floor. They all stared at it.

"Oh my..." Jessica replied, as she gulped hard.

"Holy crap!" exclaimed Ryan.

"Okay guys, one of you needs to talk to us,"

demanded Brandon.

"I know the place. It's an abandon mine like the one we saw in the collection of photos from the SD card," she replied thoughtfully. She glanced at Ryan. "We explored those mines as teenagers."

"And before that," Ryan added back.

She picked it up and examined it closer. Ryan stepped closer to her.

"I think it's Jameson mine up in the Mother Lode," Jessica replied thoughtfully. "What do you think, Ryan?"

Ryan examined it then pointed out something. Ted and Brandon stepped closer.

"Do you remember that?" Ryan asked her.

She looked at the board above the mine. She glanced at him. "Yours, Nat's and my initials, we put them on every mine we explored years ago."

"We were fifteen," said Ryan.

"So you know how to get there," Brandon said eagerly.

She nodded so did Ryan.

"Let's go then," Brandon said, as he took her free hand into his.

"Bye, kids," Arnold called out to them.

"Bye, Arnold. We'll be back soon," Brandon called back to him. "I promise."

"I'll hold you to it, sonny boy," Arnold called out back with a smile.

"He's sweet," replied Jessica.

"He's lonely," Brandon said to her. "He has middle stages of what your Dad and your aunt had. The nurse told me, and it's been five years since his wife died."

"Oh that's sad. I'll drive," she replied back sadly.

Brandon nodded. She slid behind the wheel before Brandon, Ryan and Ted got in. She headed for the Mother Lode now and Jameson mine. Brandon sat up front with her but stared out the window. Something ran through his mind again, but she had no clue of what.

"We're close, Brandon. I can feel it," she whispered to him.

"I know, Jessica. I can feel it, too," he said sadly. "Ted, you said all clues led you here."

"I traveled all over including the Greek Isles and a photograph was at each of them," explained Ted. "I stopped by New York again and walked up to that orphanage you two went with Sabrina. I was drawn to her old room that she shared with three other girls. I found this."

"Oh crap!" Brandon exclaimed, as he reached for the something in the backseat.

Jessica glanced out of the corner of her. Brandon brought it forward. She stopped quickly. He held up the crystal teddy bear keychain.

"Wendy said you guys were in California. I checked your flight plans which led me here," continued Ted. "I remember you had one of them, Brandon."

"Yeah, I do. Jessica and Sabrina gave me one for my birthday," Brandon said, as he stared at it.

"Let's roll," she replied confidently. "This has gone on way too long and too far now. It has to end now." She punched the accelerator hard. They tore down the road and soon arrived at their destination. She pulled onto the grounds of Jameson estate. She marched towards the abandon mine. She could hear the crunch of gravel and dry needles at her feet and behind her.

She reached the entrance and stopped. It was dark in there. She needed light. Jessica heard footsteps behind her. Brandon, Ted and Ryan were there. They had flashlights.

"Why didn't I think of that?" she asked herself.

"Jess, let us go in first," Ryan said to her.

"No. You follow me," she replied, as she took Brandon's flashlight. "This is personal now."

"But Jess…" Ryan started to protest.

Brandon was at Jessica's side. He took her hand now, as they walked deeper into the mine. She gulped hard and looked at the fork in the road.

"Which way?" he asked her.

"Left, Sabrina, we're coming," she answered, as she called out in loud voice.

"Jessica," a hoarse voice called back.

Jessica sprinted to the voice. There she was tied to the old mine's cart. Sabrina had past food wrappings littered around her. Jessica began to untie her little hands while Brandon untied her feet.

"Let's get her out of here," Ryan said calmly. "I'll examine her outside."

They nodded. Brandon carried Sabrina into the light. He shielded her eyes from the brightness of the sun. He sat her down on a rock. Ryan began to check her out. Jessica looked on with worry and wondered how long she had been there alone. Brandon had gone back into the mine to find Ted. They reappeared outside a few minutes later.

"She's fine, Jess. Dirty and maybe a little scared otherwise fine," Ryan said with a smile.

"I think this belongs to you, little one," Brandon said, as he held out the keychain to Sabrina.

"Thank you," Sabrina said politely.

He nodded and flipped his cell open. He stepped away from them now. Jessica hugged and held Sabrina for awhile. She didn't fight back her tears of joy of seeing her again. She didn't care how Sabrina looked, but she was safe now and in her loving arms. That's all that matter to Jessica now.

"Her kidnapper or kidnappers aren't here," Ted said coldly. "They haven't been here in days, but they made sure she had everything food, water and access to a bathroom."

"We can discuss this back in New York," replied Jessica. "Let's get you cleaned up, Sweetie."

Sabrina smiled and hugged Jessica again with dirt all over her, but Jessica didn't seem to mind it. Brandon stood by the Blazer now. Jessica carried her over to the Blazer. Ted and Ryan followed close behind her.

"I told Mama. She's spreading the word as we speak."

"Good," she replied, as she lowered Sabrina in the backseat in the middle.

"I'll drive," Ryan said to her. "You stay close to her."

Jessica nodded and slipped in beside her. Brandon slipped on the other side. Ted rode up front with Ryan. Sabrina leaned on Jessica's body. She cradled her close and smiled at Brandon.

"You're good with her," he whispered to her.

"I suppose," she whispered back with a smile.

He smiled back. The next twenty-four hours had become a blur to Jessica to some extent, but before they headed back to the New York. Brandon spent some time with Arnold while Jessica and Sabrina visited her Mom and were introduced to each other.

Then they flew back to New York in Brandon's private plane. Ted offered to pilot it home, so Brandon could be with Jessica and Sabrina. Brandon stared out the window when Jessica returned to her seat next to him.

"You seem to be in deep thought again," she whispered to him.

"Is she asleep again?"

"Yes. I noticed it before we rescued her. What's wrong, my friend?" she asked, as she touched his arm.

"I need to tell you what happened in Greece," he whispered back. "It's time."

"Not now. Wait until we get home, and we can be completely alone," she whispered back.

"But Jess..." he started to protest to her.

"Not until, we are alone," she replied, as she kissed him on the cheek. "Let's just enjoy the moment we found Sabrina. She's safe and sound."

He nodded and kissed her on the lips instead of the cheek. She didn't care at this point. She was going to enjoy the moment being at his side for however long it would last. She knew her Mom was happy to meet Sabrina.

17

Jessica walked into Mama's Pizza Shack to cheers. Brandon held Sabrina in his arms since she still was unsteady at times on her feet. It made Sabrina smile and cry at the same time, as Brandon sat her in their private booth by the window. Beverly and Jennifer showered her with lots and lots of attention. Sabrina took it all in.

Bridget, Stanley and their children gathered around Brandon and Ted. Jessica found a quiet corner away from everyone. Wendy and Taylor emerged from the kitchen with raviolis' and two hot combination pizzas for everyone. No one noticed she slipped away. Becky walked in and joined the big celebration. Jessica's cell vibrated. She stared at it.

"Hi, Nathan," Jessica whispered calmly.

"Hi, Sis, you guys got back safely. That's good," he said to her.

"What's wrong?" she asked him.

"You didn't talk to Dad before you left. I understand you're upset that he hurt me, Sis. But we have to forgive and let it go. It's in the past. He can't hurt me anymore or Mom."

"Forgive. Forgive the bastard! I don't think so, dear brother. How can I forgive what…" she started to ask, as she saw people stared at her now. "Do you want to talk to Jennifer? She's here, you know."

"Jessie, I want to talk to you and what's going on here," answered Nathan.

Jessica handed her cell to Jennifer. "It's, Nathan."

Jennifer took it and walked away with it. Beverly had brushed Sabrina's hair. Sabrina had her teddy bear keychain in her hands.

"Are you happy to be home?" she asked Sabrina.

"Back here in New York, yes, but I don't have a home," Sabrina answered sadly. "Remember, I'm an orphan."

"Jessica," Danni said, as she walked in another woman. "Is this her?"

"Excuse us," Jessica replied back politely. "Outside please."

Danni nodded, and they followed Jessica outside. They stood in the crisp midmorning air.

"This is my friend Susan," Danni introduced her.

"Pleasure," Jessica replied with a nod. "I haven't talked to her about the adoption yet. She's still recovering from being in an abandon mine shaft in California."

"Slow down, Jessica," Susan said calmly. "You found her, not the police."

"Yes. There was a ransom but never picked up at Brandon's family estate upstate. Ted followed clues we got from a memory card Brandon found. The kidnappers or kidnapper knew how we were all connected," Jessica explained, as she caught her breath. "Ted found all clues led to California. Where Brandon and I were there on personal business, a photo of the mine shaft was left in envelope that led us to Sabrina. We brought her back yesterday. But we thought it was best that she get more rest before facing all who tried to find her."

"Wow!" exclaimed Danni.

"Yes, wow," Susan said back. "But any sign of the kidnappers?"

"Nope, they took good care of her though. She had food, water and bathroom access and warm blankets. She wasn't physically harmed but emotionally that's hard."

"What do you mean?" asked Susan.

"I held her all night close to me on my bed while Brandon slept on the couch all night," explained Jessica.

"Oh dear, do you still want to proceed in adopting her?" Susan asked with concern in her voice. "She may need long term therapy and may never adjust to the world around her the same way again. Then the costs for the adoption process, my fees, court costs and unforeseen problems."

"Like who kidnapped her and why?" Jessica asked back.

"Exactly, however, I'll waive my fees since it's clear to me how much you love and care about Sabrina. But it will be difficult since you being her only parent and your profession," Susan explained thoughtfully.

"What's wrong with my job?" she asked sharply back. "I've done it for more than twelve years of my life."

"Slow down, Jessica, hear me out," Susan said, as she held her hand up. "The court will look into your past and make sure nothing bad is there or potently harm to Sabrina's life with you. Should I know anything like that? I can disclose it now as client confidentially between you and me as your lawyer."

"Do you have to tell the court the nature of it?" Jessica asked painfully.

"No," answered Susan. "Danni, can you excuse

us?"

Danni nodded and headed inside. Susan looked back at Jessica now.

Jessica had bitten her lower lip before she spoke again. "I used to be my dad's Piggy Wiggy then I lost a lot weight about seventy pounds on or around sixteen almost seventeen." She swallowed hard and looked out at the street. "He had me undress before him, or he would do it himself. I don't know how he got me tied to my bed with my legs and arms apart and a gag in my mouth. That's still fuzzy to me to this day." She wiped away the tears. "I lost my innocence and virginity to the bastard. It started with his finger then you know what followed."

"All this while you were tied up?" Susan asked calmly.

"Yes. He would bite my neck until his release. He did it more than once each time then I had to jump around before I took a shower," Jessica explained, as she stared at Susan. "He didn't want an unexpected pregnancy. He planned to do it into our later years for of our lives. I couldn't let it happen, so I took Beverly's offer."

"So you became a model and never went back home until now. Was he the personal business in California?" Susan asked seriously.

"Yes. He had beaten Mom so bad that she's in a care home now. Nathan has scars on his body that I caused," she answered painfully.

"What you've disclosed here stays with us. But we have to track down the woman who left Sabrina in the airport. Plus we have to arrest her kidnappers before we proceed with the adoption. Is there anything else?"

"Danni had me in to see if Clifford Reins raped me. I think he would have if Taylor hadn't arrived when he did. Otherwise, I have nothing else to hide in my past or present," she answered confidently.

"Good. It'll make the process maybe a little faster. But you're not married that could cause some minor problems. I'll work on it," Susan said with a confident smile. "Here's my card call me, anytime. Let's enjoy this one of two celebrations to come."

Jessica nodded, as they walked inside. Danni had approached them with a big plate of raviolis'.

"These are great, Susan. You need to try them," Danni said with a big smile.

"Taylor made them," replied Jessica.

"The one who...." Susan started to say but stopped.

Jessica nodded. Danni looked back at Taylor. He was with Sabrina in the booth. Taylor made her laugh out loud.

"That's a good sign," Susan said to them.

"He has been very protective over her since Brandon put her there," Danni said to them.

"I'm going to get some, too," Susan said politely. "Please excuse me."

Danni swallowed what she had in her mouth then looked back at Jessica. "Sabrina's lucky to have people who cared about her disappearance and went searching for her.

The State discovered Clifford was getting women drunk. I mean really drunk that they didn't know what he was doing to them. It was his version of a date rape drug. He had unprotected intercourse with at least a dozen women. He transmitted a disease to all of them. He wanted you, Jessica. Thank God, Taylor came to your rescue that day."

Jessica gulped hard and stared at her. "What about Jamie is his assistant?"

"She was one of the first to come forward. She told us about you. She's dying from two diseases since they didn't catch it in time. Plus no cure for one right now either," Danni explained thoughtfully. "She was the one he used most often when the others said no to his advances. She got his latest victim to come forward with her. Clifford has no remorse of what he's done. He has jeopardized the modeling industry now. But he doesn't care because he still wants you, Jessica. He's crazed over having you in his bed and screwing you to no end."

"Like the bastard has been after twelve plus years," Jessica replied thoughtfully to herself.

"Who?"

"Never mind, but enjoy them and put Clifford away for good," she answered painfully. "Please excuse me."

She walked up to the booth when Jennifer held out her cell. She took it and slid on the opposite side of Taylor and Sabrina.

"Where's Beverly?" she asked them.

"She got a call. She walked into Wendy's office," Taylor answered back.

"Nathan is upset with you," Jennifer said to her. "I love talking to him, but you had him really upset. What's up?"

"I couldn't deal with what we were talking about. Now let's drop it. Please."

"For now, but we'll talk more, later."

"Fine."

"Jessica, I'm tired," Sabrina said a soft spoken voice.

"Do you want to lay down?" asked Taylor.

Sabrina nodded. He slid out and picked her up. She wrapped her arms around his neck.

"We'll be upstairs. I have a room up there now," he said to Jessica.

"You'll be safe here, Honey," she replied back to her. "But I'll be here if you need me. Okay?"

Sabrina nodded and leaned in for a kiss. Jessica kissed her, and Taylor took her upstairs. Jennifer slid in across from her.

"I've never seen you like that before," said Jennifer.

"She's been through a lot," she snapped back.

"Now we can talk," said Jennifer.

"Excuse me, Jennifer. I need to speak to Jessica alone," Brandon said politely.

"I can't believe this!" Jennifer exclaimed, as she threw up her hands. "Later Jess, without interruptions just me and you got it."

She nodded, as Jenny stormed off.

"She's pissed off," said Brandon.

"I suppose, what's wrong?" she asked, as she focused on him now.

"I want to tell you what happened in Greece fourteen years ago," he answered back.

"Okay but not here. Let's take a walk," she replied, as she got to her feet again.

"Don't you want to be nearby if Sabrina calls out?"

he asked her.

"I really should," she answered thoughtfully.

"Mama," Brandon called out to her.

"Yes," Wendy said back.

"Could Jessica and I have a private place to talk?"

"My room and tell Taylor that we need more sauce," Wendy answered with a big smile.

"Thanks, Mama," Brandon said back, as he blew her a kiss. "I'll tell him."

Brandon guided Jessica upstairs. He looked in the open door. Taylor had Sabrina asleep with a teddy bear in her arms. Taylor glanced over at them then kissed her before he walked over.

"Yes, she's asleep now," Taylor whispered to them.

"Mama says, she needs more sauce," Brandon whispered back to him.

Taylor nodded. Jessica touched his arm. "You're getting..." she started to reply.

"Protective over her," Taylor interrupted her. "Yes, she's been through the worst kind of hell. She only knows of one person; she saw day in and out. It was a man who looked a lot like your drawing. He didn't hurt her physically but emotionally she might be scared for life. You two care about her a great deal, and she loves you both very much. Now please excuse me."

Taylor headed downstairs. Brandon and Jessica stood side by side as they stared at Sabrina sleeping peacefully on Taylor's bed. Then he led her to another room. He pointed to the bed as he closed the door. Then he noticed a photo on the chest and picked it up since he wanted to lean against the chest.

"I didn't want to go," he said, as he put the photo back on the chest. "But I did it for Mama." He rubbed his hand on his legs and didn't look at her. "Dad and I had been at odds ever since I was a teenager. I didn't want to go to college, but he wanted that for me. I did feel guilty of messing up the car which I still hadn't told him about until you. But I wanted to confess then everything went crazy. By the time I was eighteen we fought more than talked. That's why Greece was important to Mama."

"Take your time, Brandon. I'm not going anywhere," she replied calmly.

Brandon picked up the photo again. He held it out to her. She recognized Wendy and Brandon right away then another man stood between them. He smiled, as he wrapped his arms around them both.

"We actually got along until he mentioned Rebecca," Brandon continued, as he sat next to her now. "It felt a knife entered my heart and soul again. But it was pulling it out quickly and leaving me to bleed out. The last week of us talking and laughing like we used to was suddenly gone." He wiped away the tears now. She put the photo aside and took his hands into hers. "It happened so quickly, Jessica. It was a blur for awhile then it became clear later."

"What?"

"We all went on the boat. Mama was upset that Dad and I were fighting again. She begged us to stop. I shoved him back." Brandon paused for a moment or two. "I guess I shoved him too hard. He went over the side of the boat. By the time, I reached for him, and I saw his body float downward. He didn't know how to swim. I dove in and brought his lifeless body back up to the surface." He paused again and moistened his lips. "The skipper helped me bring his body up on the boat. Mama was screaming to no end. I had blackout after that when I awoke in a hospital with Mama at my side instead of being with him. Then she said Dad was dead, and it was ruled as an accident. Dad hit his head on the side as he lost his balance before going over."

Brandon cried in her arms now. She held him close to her chest. She rubbed his lower back, as he cried. Jessica didn't remember how long they sat there, but he stopped and glanced up at her.

"I killed him, Jessica. I can't live in that house knowing that fact. He was the love of Mama's life," he whispered to her.

"It was an accident, Brandon," Wendy said, as she stood in the doorway. "No, two men loved each other more than you two did. But he pushed people's buttons that was his downfall. I've told you to let it go, son."

"But you left the mansion, too," stated Brandon.

"It wasn't because of you or him. I didn't want to walk around a big house with a half dozen servants waiting on me alone. I didn't come from those kinds of roots," she explained to him. "It was what your Dad's roots not mine. Sabrina is asking for you, Jessica."

"Oh, thank you."

"Go to her," Brandon said, as he stared at her. "She needs you now."

Jessica grinned and hugged him briefly. She got to her feet and headed for Taylor's room. Sabrina held a teddy bear then she reached out for her. So Jessica held her close to her body.

"You're safe now, Sweetie," she whispered to her.

"Don't leave me," Sabrina said, as she held onto her ever so tightly.

"She's a natural," Wendy said, as she stood in the doorway.

Jessica noticed Brandon and Wendy stood there. He smiled at her then winked.

"It's like you say Mama about the heart knows what it wants and needs," he said back.

"Well put, son," Wendy said, as she smiled at him.

Jessica rocked Sabrina back to sleep then accompanied them downstairs. It was quiet in the restaurant, and half dozen patrons were eating now. Everyone had seemed to go their own way now. When she glanced around the room, Wendy headed back into the kitchen. Brandon walked towards the office.

So Jessica headed for the front door. There she stood face to face with Jenny. She pointed to the booth, so they walked over and sat down. Jennifer stared at her with her hands clasped in front of her.

"So are you going to explain yourself now?" Jennifer asked coldly.

Jessica cupped her upper teeth over her lower lip then let out a little sigh. She stared back at Jennifer. "I'm sorry. I behaved badly to you and Nathan. I couldn't deal with what we were talking about the scars run long and very deep. You and Nat don't understand," she explained carefully.

"Try me, Jess. We've been friends for awhile now. Then you can apologize to him. I know and have seen what your Dad did to your Mom. He showed me what he did to her despite how painful it was for him. The injuries she had within an hour after they occurred. But it still doesn't explain why you left California in such a hurry and didn't go back until twelve plus years later. Did your Dad hit you like that, too?"

"Good God, No! What Nat and Mom went through was a result of my leaving. He hurt them the worst possible way. They paid the price with their bones and flesh because I left," she answered with tears in her eyes now.

"What are you saying, Jess? Was Nathan hurt, too?" Jennifer asked, as she leaned forward.

Jessica nodded. Jennifer took her hands into hers. "I sensed there was more than what he told me. But I didn't push it. What did your Dad do to him?"

"A hot iron on his flesh," she blurted out. "He wasn't like that prior to my leaving. If I had known, he was capable of that kind of violence..."

"You blame yourself for their pain. You said you didn't know of his rage. Wasn't there signs of it growing up?"

She shook her head no, now.

"It's okay. I'm sure Nathan will understand."

"He wants me to let it go and forgive the bastard. But how can I knowing I caused it all? I shouldn't have only thought of me. There would be consequences that could have been prevented."

"Jess, stop it!" exclaimed Jennifer.

Patrons stared at them now. Jessica bolted upstairs to Taylor's room. But she stopped and looked in. Brandon was there with Sabrina and Taylor now. She leaned back against the wall, so they wouldn't see her there. But she could listen to them talk.

"How can you stand or sit here and tell us that you understand us?" asked Taylor. "You don't know what it's like on the streets or being an orphan."

"Let him explain, Taylor," Sabrina said calmly. "We owe him that much. Didn't he give you a place to live and all this?"

"I guess," answered Taylor.

"Guys, I know what it's like because I'm an orphan, too," said Brandon.

"What!" Taylor exclaimed in shock.

"Let me explain. I was a year old when Mama found me," Brandon started to explain. "The residence of Fiddletown took care of me in a mine ever since my real Mom left me there to die, I guess. They named me: Brandon Foster."

"Why didn't anyone take you into their home?" asked Sabrina.

"I don't know. I never got around asking because we never came back. She brought me back here to New York. But I had trouble adjusting so she said because being alone in the mine but eventually settled in. I've considered Mama as my real Mom."

"But you never lived in an actual orphanage," pointed out Taylor.

"No, but I do know loneness, Taylor. I found it difficult to be in that mine when we were there to rescue Sabrina. Maybe because I lived in one and remember the coldness and darkness of the mine I was in. I had forgotten about that life until we were in there," he continued on.

"Jessica was more driven to go into that mine then me, but I couldn't show her, my fear."

"You held me tight until we got out. You placed me on that big rock and stepped away," Sabrina said thoughtfully.

"Yes, I know. I didn't want anyone but most importantly Jessica to how it affected me that day being in there."

"She doesn't know about your past," said Taylor.

"No. We're only beginning to explore our personal lives now. You started the interest, little lady."

"How so?"

"Asking where she was from and about her family. I realized I didn't know her private life either."

"Oh that day, it was your birthday, too. We had pizza and ice cream."

"Yes. Now you need to get some sleep."

"I'll stay with her," said Taylor. "But I don't think we'll get much more business tonight."

"I'll check on her now. Goodnight, kids," Brandon said to them.

"Goodnight, Brandon," they echoed back to him.

Jessica headed towards the stairs and doubled back to appear she on her way up when she heard him at the door. He smiled at her.

"Hi, I was going to check on Sabrina. Is she still asleep?' she asked him back politely.

"No, but I'm sure Taylor will get her back to sleep. You and Jennifer were in a deep discussion downstairs, so I came up. She's okay now. Let's go downstairs."

Jessica nodded, as he followed behind her. She

debated in her mind whether to discuss with him of what she just heard or not. She shook it off. Jennifer was nowhere in sight to Jessica's relief. Brandon headed for the kitchen, so Jessica followed him.

"Good job today," Wendy said, as she wiped her brow now. "Beverly logged in the daily receipts before she left despite our celebration. But her mind was elsewhere."

"Maybe it was the phone call that she got earlier," suggested Brandon.

"I didn't know. She'll talk when she's ready. That's one you have to understand about some orphans," Wendy said thoughtfully.

"What do you mean?" Jessica asked with interest now.

"Some are real chatter boxes, but others seem to shut down inside afraid to reveal they were orphans once."

"Why?" Jessica asked with interest.

"A trust issue, I guess and not knowing why their Mom gave them up. But I really think it's mostly about love. They don't know if they're worthily of someone's love on an intimate level," answered Wendy.

"But he or she should know the people who adopted him or she was chosen out of those kids to pick from."

"You're right, Jessica, in some ways. But I still think once he or she gets beyond those intimate issues he or she will blossom. Love can prevail and he or she will be totally committed to the relationship."

"All comes back to your saying, Mama," Brandon added with a big smile.

"Exactly, now you two go home. I'll take care of

Sabrina tonight. She'll be fine with me and Taylor. You two need a relief from being up with her all last night. You look beat still. Let me close up shop, now."

They nodded. She followed them out to the front door. They stepped outside, and she locked the door behind them. So Brandon drove her home and walked her to her door. He seemed like he wanted to say something to her but also seemed to hold back. She kissed him on the cheek and stepped into her apartment.

She watched him walk back down the hallway alone. She thought of what Wendy said about orphans and to find out he was one, too. It was a shock to her, but she had to keep in mind what Wendy said. What did he think of her silence about her past? Was he thinking she was an orphan, too? She had a twin brother Nathan, but they both could have been orphans. But Brandon said she looked like her mother.

She leaned against the door now and shook her head. Did this change her view of Brandon? She shook her head, no and walked into her bedroom. He was still Brandon. He was there for her. She had him as her friend. But she kissed him, and he kissed her. He was the only male friend that she let be close to her over these past twelve plus years. Why was that?

Did it go back to the bastard, and what he did with her? She shook her head again, as she dressed for bed. She turned out the light and faint scent of Sabrina's freshly shampooed hair was on the pillow. She had forgotten how she helped Sabrina clean up thoroughly after her ordeal in the mine. Sabrina washed her hair twice since the rescue in two days.

18

It was seven days later, and Jessica stood at the steps of the courthouse. The State granted her temporary custody of Sabrina. There was a manhunt for her kidnappers and Jill Claymore. It had become local and national news now. But this wasn't why she was at the courthouse this day.

"Jessica," Danni called out from the top of the steps.

Jessica glanced up and headed up to her. She straightened her beige skirt for unknown the countless time. She didn't want to bring Sabrina down to the courthouse with her. So Wendy and Taylor kept her occupied at Mama's Pizza Shack.

"Thanks for coming," Danni said with a small smile. "Are you okay?"

"I'm tired. Sabrina screams out in the night sometimes, but I rock her back to sleep. Otherwise, I'm fine. What's wrong?"

"I have to call you to the stand," Danni answered with a slight hesitation in her voice. "Now before you explode let me tell you why."

Jessica nodded.

"Clifford states how you made advances towards him for years. Then he decided to act on it, and you pulled away. So then you had someone beat the crap out of him," Danni explained calmly and carefully. "Now I know we discussed in my office sometime ago. We talked before this trial started what happened at his New York studio and in

Seattle. But I'll need you and Taylor on the stand for the New York incident. However, you're on your own when comes to Seattle."

"What about Jamie?"

"She didn't hear you and Clifford talking. She saw him leaning towards you but nothing more."

"But she's been involved with him in the past."

"Not relevant. Are you ready to tell the court about it?"

"I suppose. Do I need talk about events today?"

"Probably, I've subpoena Taylor, too, Jessica. This isn't going to be easy despite the mount of evidence against him. He wants to get off at all cost which he doesn't care what it does to you and your reputation. But it could hurt your chances of adopting Sabrina if we lose. I don't plan on losing but the possibility is there."

Jessica felt weak in the knees. She started to fall, but someone had her from behind. He carried her to a bench and sat her down there. Danni stared at her with concern.

"What...are..." she tried to ask him.

"Mama told me. Taylor needed a ride," Brandon answered back.

"He can't stay, she replied to Dannie. "Make him leave, Danni. Please."

"Thank you for bringing, Taylor, but I'll have to ask you to leave, Brandon," Danni said, as she stared at him now. "Let's not let the press, make more out of this then it should be. If you care about your friends and the people involved in this case then walk away now."

"Jessica."

"Please," she begged him.

"Okay for you. Have Taylor call me when you two are done then."

"I promise."

"Jessica," Taylor cried out, as he went in front of her. "Are you okay?"

"Fine," she answered, as she got to her feet. "I'll be okay."

Taylor helped her. Danni stared at Brandon, so he walked away. They headed into the courthouse. Taylor walked beside Jessica. His hair was combed, wore dress navy blue slacks and an emerald polo shirt with white sneakers. It made Jessica laugh. Danni and Taylor looked at her.

"Sneakers," she replied, as she pointed to them.

They laughed, too. Then Danni took Taylor aside to tell him why he was there.

"Put me on first," Taylor said in a low voice. "I can explain my actions. Jessica didn't see it coming. I've lived on the streets. I know men and women like him. Believe me, I know firsthand."

"Easy, Taylor," Danni said calmly. "You two wait here until you're called. Talk to no one. Jessica, put on your sunglasses."

Danni headed down the hall to the mob of press. She led them into courtroom, and silence filled the hallway now. Taylor sat beside her now. He bounced his knees up and down, so Jessica took his hand into hers. He stared at her.

"The truth is on our side," she replied calmly. "Just tell the court what you saw and did. You rescued me that day, and I'll be forever grateful, Taylor. I wish I knew how to bring your parents back into your life again. You're a great kid despite what you've been through."

Taylor's face turned a shade of pink. She kissed him on the cheek. He gave her a small shyly grin.

"Taylor Rivers," the bailiff called out.

"That's me," he said back, "Mama's maiden name. We did it, so I could get a social security card in my name. How cool is that!"

Taylor walked towards the bailiff with a big smile now. Jessica shook her head but also smiled. She felt something familiar about him but still couldn't put her finger on it.

"Time will reveal it," she whispered to herself.

A couple hours later, the press rushed out of the courtroom. Jessica heard loud noises but still kept her sunglasses on. Danni and Taylor walked side by side now towards her.

"It's up to you now, Jessica," Taylor said calmly. "I told the court the whole truth and nothing but the truth. Your testimony should bury the bastard."

"The judge granted a recess for the day. His testimony really shook up the defense team. They didn't know how to redirect," Danni said with a big smile. "He sat there calmly and explained everything. Clifford sat there stunned then outraged. That's how we got a break for the rest of the day, but you'll be on the stand tomorrow morning, Jessica. Sleep well. I'm sure; they'll want to attack you full force."

Jessica nodded and held out her cell to Taylor. He took it and searched. Taylor stepped away from them.

Danni watched Taylor then turned back to Jessica.

"Taylor seemed to notice things that most of us don't. How old was he when he entered the streets?" Danni asked her.

"Four," Jessica answered calmly. "What do you plan to ask me on the stand?"

"Your account of that day, and what happened in Seattle," Danni answered back. "Do you think you can handle it?"

"Yes. But what do you think they'll ask me?"

"Your sexual history since he states you've tempted him with your body for the last twelve years. So he responded to it then had Taylor attacked him."

Jessica shook her head.

"What?"

"Why does it have to involve that?" she asked painfully.

"They have these other women accusing him of rape. So you're the only one he didn't get, and that's makes you the prime target," answered Danni. "You and Brandon aren't involved. Are..."

"Heavens no," she interrupted her. "We're just friends and work together. I have a contract with Beverly that I won't cross that line. I don't want to lose her as my agent."

Danni stepped back and stared at her. "I know, Susan is helping you with the adoption of Sabrina, and you and Susan have client lawyer confidentiality between you. But..."

"I'm not a virgin," Jessica blurted out.

"Brandon's on his way," Taylor said, as he held out

her phone. "I'm sorry. I'll wait outside."

"No, we're done here," she replied, as she got to her feet. "I'll try and get some sleep, but it depends on Sabrina. She's my main priority now."

"Jessica, we need to talk about it before tomorrow. We need to be prepared," said Danni.

"Not now. Bye," she replied back.

Taylor and Jessica walked out of the courthouse. She smiled at him. Taylor smiled back. She leaned on his arm.

"Jessica," Taylor said shyly.

"Yes."

"I know I said sometime back that you were running away from something. I sense it more since you came back from California," Taylor said calmly. "Someone hurt you, too, and you left it there in California. But then you had to go back and get Sabrina and stood face to face with the man who hurt you; the man who scared you for the rest of your life." He stood at the bottom of the steps and had her face him. "If there's one thing I've learned since you walked into my life, I can dwell on what happened to me on the streets with those men and women, or I could choose the high road. I can be a victim and not let people in, and my heart and soul can be cold and unattached to the world. When you guys brought Sabrina into Mama's Pizza Shack, it was clear to me what choice I had to make."

"Taylor," she started to say.

"I decided to embrace people around me. Look at me. I'm not homeless anymore. I have a place to live, clothes that fit me, plus shoes, and I have hard earned money in my pocket that I didn't have to beg for. I'm not that four year old anymore but sixteen and want to go to college. So Brandon agreed to help me get a GED. But I won't forget my early roots because it shaped me or formed me into the young man I've become. You let people in when it's necessary because of what that man did to you years ago. You let him define your personal life, and now it has effects on your professional life."

"What are asking me to do, Taylor?" she asked him directly.

"Reveal it to someone who really truly cares about you. Let the healing begin. It's time now. You helped me see that in the bathroom. Remember."

She nodded. A honk startled them both. They turned to see Brandon in the truck. Taylor opened the door for her.

"If not me maybe him," Taylor whispered to her as he got in.

"How did it go?" asked Brandon.

"We have to be back tomorrow," answered Taylor.

Jessica glanced at the top of steps to the courthouse. Danni stood there with her briefcase and files. Danni looked worried, but Jessica waved to her with a smile.

"Can you discuss the case?" Brandon asked them.

"Nope, not until it's over," she answered back.

"I still don't understand why you two were called."

"Shed light or cast a bad light on all the models that sleep around with their photographers," Jessica snapped back. "How's Sabrina?"

"She's fine. Mama has kept her busy. Did you hire a

therapist for her?" he asked as he drove.

"Yes. Susan thought it would help her with the ordeal she has been through. But I think the State will take over the cost in time."

"That's it. I never understood why the State gave you temporary custody of her," Brandon said thoughtfully.

"She's clung to me pretty much or ever since..."

"But she has clung to me, too."

"But you're a man, Brandon. Girls tend to feel safe with other girls," Taylor said confidently. "It's important she heal from her ordeal while they try to locate her kidnappers and bring them to justice."

"Mama was right about you. You're pretty smart. Do you still want to go to college or cooking school?" asked Brandon.

"Maybe both, but we'll see. When do we start studying for the GED?"

"As soon as you like, I brought the books over. Mama put them in your room."

"Sounds great," Taylor said with a big smile.

They walked into the restaurant. Sabrina rushed up to them with a drawing.

"For you, Jessica," Sabrina said, as she held it out to her.

"Are you sure?" she asked, as she got down to her level.

Sabrina nodded.

"Thank you," she replied, as she glanced at each piece of it. "A sun, a house, a woman and a little girl in then in a far corner is a man with a camera around his neck. It's beautiful. We'll put on the fridge when we get back to our place. Thank you Sabrina."

Jessica hugged her, and Sabrina went back to the booth. A woman approached them. Jessica stood up. Taylor headed for the kitchen.

"How's she doing?" Jessica asked her.

"That's progress. Her first drawings were black and so dark then she gazed out the window a little while ago. She seemed so deep in thought then she drew that one," answered the woman. "I'm Sophia, by the way. The State is paying my bill now. They may or may not pay you back for our first session. I need to talk to Susan."

Jessica nodded. Sophia smiled and waved to Sabrina.

"She's adorable. Why would people kidnap an orphan?" Sophia asked, as she headed out the door. "Bye."

"Bye," Brandon said back. "That's the million dollar question."

"Do you think Jim is still involved in it?" she asked him.

"Yes, but I have something on my mind right now," he answered, as they walked towards Sabrina now. "It has been bothering me ever since we came back from California. You..."

"Hi, everyone," Nathan said, as he walked in with a big smile on his face.

"Nat, what's wrong?" she asked him quickly.

"I'm in love, Sis. I owe it all to you," Nathan answered, as he kissed her on the cheek.

"What!" she exclaimed in confusion.

"You told Jenny what I found difficult to explain. I didn't think she would accept me. But she has, and I owe it all to you, Sis," he answered with excitement.

"So you're in love. I'm so happy for you. Does..."

"Mom knows and is happy for me, but he's not happy about it. But I don't care," Nathan interrupted her.

"Excuse me," Jennifer said, as she walked in behind them now.

"There's, my lady," Nathan said, as he smiled at her. "Will you marry me, Jennifer?"

"What?" Jennifer asked stunned back.

Nathan was one knee now and held a box out to her. Jessica stepped back so did Brandon. Jennifer stared at Nathan, as tears glided down her face.

"Yes," Jennifer answered back.

Nathan placed the ring on her ring finger then got to his feet to kiss her. Wendy and Taylor emerged from the kitchen.

"Put it there, man," Brandon said, as he held out his hand to Nathan.

Jessica stepped farther back as Wendy, Taylor and Sabrina approached the happy couple. Her eyes met Taylor's, as he hugged Jennifer. Jennifer had a bounce in her step, as she approached her now.

"Will you be my maid of honor, Jess?"

"Of course, I would be honored. Will it be here or ...."

"Haven't discussed it yet, I just got engaged now," interrupted Jennifer. "Isn't it gorgeous? A perfect emerald surrounded by tiny sapphires. I've never seen anything like it my whole life."

Jessica glanced down at the ring then looked at Nathan. He nodded. She smiled at him then at Jennifer.

"Let me guess you have," said Jennifer.

Nathan stood next to Jennifer now. He wrapped his arm over her shoulders and smiled.

"A long time ago, we explored a mine, and I found some rare sapphires near the entrance," Nathan began to explain slowly.

"And I found the raw stone which was a good size emerald. I nearly tripped over it," added Jessica. "I gave it to, Nat."

"We talked about having the emerald cut into two pieces and have the sapphires divided up between us and put into settings of some kind after they were cut and polished, but we didn't have the money to do it," Nathan continued on. "About a year ago, I found them in a box tucked in the back of my sock drawer. I had my half set in a ring and yours into a pedant, Sis. You always loved necklaces when we were kids. I hoped to give the ring to the woman I would marry and wore a size five. Mom's rings are five, so I figured it on that thought." He held out the pedant to her. "I hope you approve. It connects us all together forever."

"Oh, Nat," Jessica cried out. She hugged him tight. "Yes, I do, but you forgot the most important thing, dear bro."

"What's that?"

"It was the same mine we found Sabrina in."

"Oh, crap!" exclaimed Brandon. "Now what are the odds in that?"

He stared at them all now. He bolted out of the front door. Wendy stared at the closed door and glanced a looked over to Jessica. Jessica didn't understand it. They wanted to celebrate. She had Nathan put her half around her neck.

"That's it let go of the past," Taylor whispered to her. "Or take the high road like you've done in the past."

Jessica walked to the closed door and looked back.

"Go to him," Wendy said to her. "We'll watch her."

So she walked to Brandon's studio. The door was open, so she walked in cautiously. Brandon sat in the middle of his studio and held his camera. She walked slowly towards him, but he didn't look up at her. She noticed several SD cards in cases on the floor beside him.

"Brandon," she replied in a low voice.

"I think, I know why you didn't want to return to California," he said in hoarse voice.

She sat down on the floor with him. He still didn't make eye contact with her. She placed her hands in her lap.

"Something happened between you and your Dad. I started to suspect it when you didn't want to see him again. Then I remember what Arnold who I played chess with. Do you remember him?"

He looked up at her now. She nodded.

"He had some clarity at one point there as we played chess. He remembered you and Nathan as teenagers. He talked how all men lusted after your body. But he also remembered you turned seventeen and was considered jail bait," Brandon continued on.

She felt tightness in her body but tried to remain calm and composed. She focused on his face which now looked at his camera again.

"He went onto to say your Dad was no exception. I

didn't want to hear this. I wanted to focus on our chess game in front of us, but he had his moment of clarity and hasn't going to let it go. He was your Dad's best friend and was your Mom's first boyfriend. But you see your Mom and Arnold had a fall out years ago. But it didn't keep him from keeping track of your parents." Brandon paused for a moment and picked up another memory card. "Your Dad got your Mom pregnant on purpose, Jessica. He didn't want any man including his best friend to have her that way. Planting a seed in her assured him of having her all to himself, but I side step it now."

Jessica tried to hold back the tears now. Brandon slipped another card in his camera. He seemed to be examining it.

"Your father raped you, Jessica. I'm not sure when or even why, but I know he lusted your body in a way man should but not your Dad. He should have known better, and I don't hold it against you," he said, as he looked up at her. "You have never let me or anyone knows about your personal life because of this secret. You felt responsibility for it. Well, I'm here to tell you, no. He was the one who did wrong, not you. He probably would have continued if you hadn't left when you did. But you had no idea what he would do to your Mom and Nathan. Now you're torn because you have the mother you always wanted as a child. Nathan is back in your life too, but they're your guilt. You can't be truly happy despite us finding Sabrina. I know and understand it, Jessica. I told you what happened in Greece because I can't handle the guilt anymore. I had to let it go. You helped me with it as you held me. Mama's words rang true to me after fourteen years. Now will you let me help you?"

"I can't believe what I'm hearing from you. You sit there telling me all this, but you forget an important thing in your life," Jessica answered in anger.

Brandon looked up at her confused.

"Were you ever going to tell me?" she asked him. "I overheard you talking to Taylor and Sabrina. You're an orphan too just like them. Was this why you helped Taylor and had to find Sabrina? You wanted to throw it in their young faces that you had a home, and they didn't."

She got to her feet quickly and marched toward the door. He grabbed her arm. She gasped. He turned her to face him now.

"Yes, I did in time plan to tell you, and no, I didn't plan to throw it in their faces I was adopted. I didn't go through legal adoption channels, Jessica. I was abandoned by my own Mom as a new born, and I lived alone in a mine for a whole year," he answered with pain in his eyes. "Mama took me back here after a dummy birth certificate was made. She was prospecting and photographing when she came across me in that same mine Sabrina was in. You guys explored it years earlier. I felt it, as I walked into the mine with you. I had come home, and it scared the crap out of me. Mama said she found me in a mine in California. Frankly, I didn't remember it." Brandon released his hold. "The people let Mama take me back here because they didn't want the responsibility for a year old. I didn't lie to you and Becky when I said I never seen Lake Tahoe because I wasn't there long enough to remember it if I had. But I was drawn back there several times as a boy but didn't go. It was like Greece, but I didn't refuse, Mama. She gave me a home after my real Mom left me to die in that damn mine."

They stood there in silence now. Jessica tried to understand everything that both of them revealed. Each of them revealed secrets. What was going to happen now with their relationship? Jessica shook her head.

"Jess...ica," Brandon said in hesitation.

"I need to take Sabrina back to my place. Wendy has probably fed her already. I've got to be in court tomorrow morning," she replied thoughtfully. "I think, we've said enough for one day or maybe a lifetime. Please excuse me, Brandon."

She walked out, and he didn't come with her. She picked up Sabrina at Mama's

Pizza Shack and headed back to her place. She didn't know what to say to Wendy. But she promised Nathan and Jennifer a nice dinner in a day or two. She also said she wasn't feeling too good right now.

It wasn't a lie entirely because she needed to time to absorb all her and Brandon told each other in his studio. She fell asleep with Sabrina snuggled close to her body. She hoped she would sleep through the night without any screaming. She didn't think she could handle it this night of all nights. But her mind did wonder how he put it all together. Did she miss a step in her cover up of her past? But she ignored that thought, as she fell asleep.

Her eyes popped open shortly after Sabrina drifted off into a deep sleep. Yes, it was what Taylor said to her that came to mind. He knew things more than most people. Danni told her that to some extant earlier in the day. How could she have missed that comment? She shook her head slightly and drifted off to sleep.

19

"**S**o you're saying my client was going to take you right there in his studio," Howard Laws said to Jessica.

"Yes," she replied calmly. "It wasn't his first advancement towards me."

"Oh, really, how come this fact hasn't come out until now, my dear? Maybe because you're lying," Howard Laws snapped at her quickly.

"No, I'm not," she answered, as she remained composed. "It happened as we were wrapping up in Seattle after the Starbucks account. But he had been going after me for years before that."

"I see."

"Your honor, I must remind the court, Ms. Hudson is not on trial here," Danni said, as she stood up from behind her table now.

"Mr. Laws, do I need to remind you that, too," said Judge Jones.

"No further questions, your honor," said Laws.

He sat down. Clifford stared at him and pointed to Jessica. Danni approached the witness stand.

"Good morning again, Ms. Hudson," Danni said confidently with a smile.

"Good morning," Jessica replied back with a small smile.

"What happened in Seattle, Washington, Ms. Hudson? Did anyone know of his intentions?"

"At the wrap of the assignment, most of the crew headed out since Clifford said he was buying drinks for everyone. I don't drink liquor, so I planned to go to my hotel room. I was tired when he approached me. We exchanged words to the effect what he intended to do with me," Jessica explained carefully and calmly.

"And what was that?"

"To get me drunk, so we could have lots and lots of unprotected sex. He had been coming on and off me for the last twelve plus years now. I turned him down every time, but this time he was more aggressive. I think he would have done it if Jamie hadn't called out to him when she did."

"Who is Jamie?" asked Danni.

"His assistant, she called Beverly later that night and told her about the state of mind Clifford was in. Beverly talked to me the next morning and told me. But Becky told me to keep a watch out for Clifford. She knew stuff. Models talk to her about personal stuff like she's a true friend."

"Now we all know Jamie was the one along with another model who brought charges of rape against of Clifford Reins the defendant. She has VD but also AIDS, and she has only had one sexual partner for the last fourteen years which is the defendant. Did you know these facts?"

"No not, until he mentioned she was his sexual partner at times in passing that day. But he never said anything about VD and/or AIDS. But he also mentioned another woman too," Jessica answered calmly.

"Who was that?" Dannie asked with interest now.

"Rebecca. He didn't say her last name, but I think

she was connected to another photographer's past. He told me of a model with the same name."

"I see, and this Rebecca you mentioned. Why do you think she's connected with this other photographer?"

"She had unprotected sex with another photographer which resulted in an unwanted pregnancy. She fought with the baby's father, and one said she committed suicide and other said she fell to her death. It's unclear what her state of mind was."

"She didn't love him. She was out to destroy Beverly Rivers. Brandon was just a boy. He didn't know how to fuck a woman like Rebecca. She was an easy screw," Clifford said, as he stood up and licked his lips, "Just like you would be, darling. How about we does it right here in this courtroom? I'll..."

"Mr. Laws, control your client," snapped Judge Jones.

"I want her so bad. He's ready for her now," Clifford said out loud.

"Enough. I think we've heard enough from your client. Take him away," ordered Judge Jones.

"Can't you see why I fucked them all because I really wanted him in you, darling," Clifford said, as he was led away.

"I'll dismiss the jury now to come up with a verdict. But it's clear what has been said here, but I await your verdict ladies and gentlemen of the jury," said Judge Jones.

Jessica didn't remember much after that. She sat in Danni's office and shook for longest time. She was speechless ever since Clifford left the courtroom. She didn't even remember coming back to Danni's office.

Taylor walked in with Brandon at his side. Danni looked up from her papers. It made Jessica turn around and face them. She didn't know what to say. But Brandon opened his arms to her, and she rushed into them to feel his warm but gentle embrace again.

"Let's leave them alone, Taylor," Danni said, as she got up and escorted him back out of her office.

With the door closed, Jessica cried in Brandon's chest. They were alone, and she felt safe in his arms now.

"It's okay, Jessica," he whispered to her. "I'm here and won't let anyone ever hurt you again. I promise you that with my very life."

She gazed up at him and touched his face. Then she looked deep into his eyes, as he stared back at her, too.

"Taylor told me what happened in court. You couldn't tell me in Seattle and here what Clifford wanted from you because of your past. But hear me now, my love. None of this is your fault. They wanted and took advantage of you when you got used to the new beautiful you," he whispered in a calm voice. "Your Dad took away your innocence and maybe even your trust in all men including me. So Clifford scared you into silence and made you withdraw more into yourself. They're jerks, my love. Now let's move on together."

"We can't. I have a contract with your Aunt Bev…"

He kissed her on the mouth. She felt his lips touch her cheek then her neck. She wanted to get lost in it, but she pulled away from him. Brandon stared at her confused. A knock then the door opened.

"The jury's reached a verdict," Danni said at the open door. "Are you two coming ?"

"You bet," Brandon answered quickly. "I want to see him put away for good."

He held out his hand, and she took it. They all headed for the courtroom. Taylor walked with Danni. Wendy held Sabrina's hand, as they joined them. Beverly walked up to Jessica and Brandon. They must have all come down for moral support for Jessica.

"We need to talk, kids," Beverly said to them, as they walked into the courtroom now.

"Later, Auntie," Brandon said politely back.

They took their seats, and Sabrina made her way to Jessica. She stood in front of her.

"Yes, Sweetie," she whispered to her.

"All rise," called out the bailiff. "Court is now in session the honorable Judge Joseph Jones presiding."

"Please be seated," Judge Jones said to everyone.

"Can I sit on your lap?"

Jessica nodded, and Sabrina climbed into her lap. Jessica held her close, as she watched the jury file in. They didn't look at anyone in the courtroom.

"Mr. Forman has the jury reached a verdict?" asked Judge Jones.

"Yes, your honor," answered the foreman.

"Will the defendant rise?" Judge Jones asked Clifford to stand.

His attorney helped him stand since he was unsteady now on his feet. He faced Judge Jones without a word.

"Mr. Foreman read your verdict," said Judge Jones.

"In the case of Clifford R. Reins vs. the State of New York, we the jury of said above case find the defendant guilty of twelve counts of rape of twelve different women and one attempted rape," read the foreman. "We sentence him to the State of New York's Correctional Facility for life without the possibility of parole due the defendant transmitted AIDS and VD unknowingly to his victims."

"Mr. Clifford Reins, you have heard the verdict of your peers. I sentence you to life in prison based on the information provided. The Jury is dismissed. This case is over," Judge Jones said, as his gavel hit the desk.

Clifford was escorted out by a couple guards. He didn't look back. The press bolted for the doors now. Danni packed up her file and briefcase then shook hands with the defense lawyers.

"Where's Becky?" Jessica asked, as they stepped outside the courtroom again.

"Tending to the restaurant with Jennifer and Nathan," Wendy answered back.

"This was no place for her, Mama," Brandon said, as he glanced at Sabrina.

"She wanted to come," Wendy said with a smile. "She doesn't understand but wants to be Taylor and Jessica and you."

"The case is over, Mommy," Sabrina said, as she looked up at her.

Jessica hesitated then replied, "Yes, Sweetie, we can go now."

"I need to talk to you, kids," Beverly said to them again.

"I said later, Auntie. Maybe at the restaurant," Brandon said back.

Jessica took Sabrina's little hand into hers. Brandon

took Jessica's other hand, as they walked outside. Wendy was beside him and Taylor. Beverly and Danni were behind them.

"A beautiful day to be alive," Brandon said to them.

A large van pulled up, and he led everyone to get in. A man wore a baseball cap and t-shirt, but he looked familiar to her. Sabrina patted the seat next to her, so Jessica slid in next to her.

"Mama's Pizza Shack, we have a celebration to get underway," Brandon said, as he sat up front with the driver.

"Yes, sir, my friend," the man said with a big smile.

"Oh My, Gosh!" exclaimed Jessica.

"We took the first flight out. Your brother is engaged to a wonderful, girl," said Stanley.

Jessica reached up and hugged him briefly then she sat back down, as everyone fastened their seatbelts. Stanley drove to the pizza shack. It was packed with customers. Bridget had severed plates and pizza to a family at a table when they all walked in.

"Help, please," she begged them.

Brandon, Taylor and Stanley headed for the kitchen. Brandon re-emerged with an apron and tub to collect the dirty dishes. Wendy went to her customers and wrote down their orders. Becky was washed dishes in the kitchen. Jessica took Sabrina's hand into hers firmly and started to restock the salad bar with stuff and plates and forks and knives.

It was a couple hours when things died down. The last customers left, and Beverly stood at the register next to Wendy. Helen emerged from the kitchen and scanned the room. Sabrina and Jessica wiped down the last dirty table.

"You need to tell them," Helen said to Beverly.

"I've tried at the courthouse, but our..."

"No excuses. Do it now before we get hit again. They need to know," interrupted Helen. "Brandon, Jessica, could you come over here for a second?"

Jessica looked back at Brandon. So they approached the register together.

"Yes, Auntie Helen," he answered with a big smile.

"Your Aunt Beverly has something to say to you both," said Helen.

He shifted his attention to her now. Beverly stared at them both then cleared her throat.

"It has become clear or brought to my attention that you two have become close," Beverly started to say.

"We're friends, Auntie."

"Out with it," said Wendy.

"Be patient," Beverly snapped back.

"What our sister is trying to say is. It's more than friendship you two share. Her contract between you and her about crossing the line Jessica is void. So if you two want to explore your feelings for each other, Beverly isn't going to stand in the way of your happiness, Jessica. She won't fire you and will still represent you as your agent," explained Helen.

"We see the attraction," added Wendy. "So we got our sister here to..."

"Strong armed me to release you from it, Jessica," interrupted Beverly.

"It didn't take too much," Wendy said with a big smile.

"No, it didn't. I guess I was beginning to see it, too," said Beverly. "You told her about Rebecca that's when I saw the error of my ways. I may have lost the love of my life, but I can't stand in the way of your happiness. I love you both so very much to do that to you."

Jessica hugged her. Brandon hugged them both when the bell on the door dinged. They looked back at the door.

"No," Sabrina yelled in a loud voice.

Sabrina stared at the tall man with a beard and white hair sprinkled in it and his hair. He wore a plaid flannel shirt, jeans and cowboy boots. Beverly blinked her eyes twice, as she stepped back.

"I see you found her," the man said, as he stared at Beverly. "It has been a long time, baby, maybe too long."

"James," Beverly said in shock.

"Excuse me," Jim said, as he bolted out the door.

Brandon hopped the counter and headed out the door. Screech of wheels sped off and sound of a runner. Jessica stepped outside to see Brandon in the distance. He walked slowly towards her breathing hard now. Sabrina clung to her legs.

"He won't get you again, Sweetie," she replied, as she knelt to her level. "I promise you."

"So do I Sabrina," Brandon said, as he reached them now.

Sabrina hugged Jessica, as they stood up. Brandon touched Sabrina's back. She stared at him. Taylor walked outside, and Jessica watched him as he walked. She shook her head again.

"What is it, Jessica?" Brandon asked her.

"I'm not sure, but I'll tell you after I figure it out. Shouldn't you call Ted and tell him we've seen Jim here?"

"That's a good idea," Brandon answered back. "I'll be there a second."

"Sabrina," Taylor said in a low voice.

Sabrina smiled at him. He had something behind his back

"I got something for you," he said to with a smile.

"What?" she asked with excitement.

Taylor held out a small black and white kitten. Sabrina rushed towards them, and she petted it. Then she smiled back at Jessica.

"Do you like it?" he asked her.

"Yes."

"It's yours," he said, as he placed the kitten into her hands. "It's about six weeks old, I think. I kept hearing cries in the kitchen, and I was able to locate it earlier. It's okay. Isn't it, Jessica?"

"Of course," she answered, as she walked over to pet it too."We need to find a vet to examine it. Tell us its sex, so we can name it properly. Plus get food, milk and a bed for it."

"Don't forget a litter box and collar with tags," added Taylor.

Sabrina brought it close to her face. It meowed and pawed at her face. Sabrina laughed. Brandon walked up.

"What do we have here?" he asked, as he petted it, too. "Nice fur ball."

"Teddy is its name, not fur ball," answered Sabrina.

"But we don't know its sex yet," pointed out Jessica.

"It's okay. It can be a boy or girl depends how you spell it," said Brandon.

"It's better than fur ball," Sabrina reminded them.

"Yes it is," Brandon said with a smile. "You're right about that, little one."

"Let's go inside and show everyone," Taylor said to Sabrina.

She nodded. Jessica stepped back with Brandon. He smiled at her, and she smiled back.

"Auntie released you from that contract. So where do we stand now?" asked Brandon.

"I don't know. We've had a tough couple days. Jim is out there, and Sabrina confirmed he was and is her kidnapper. Do you think we'll catch him and find out why?"

"I have my theories on that but nothing solid yet. But I'll tell you first, my love," he answered, as he looked into her eyes. "Did anyone tell you that your eyes sparkle like sapphires? That's why I chose that ring back at the orphanage."

"Uh...those rings are probably still on my dresser. I should give them back. I took them off for the swimsuit issue and didn't feel..."

"Anyone, tell you how you talk too much," he interrupted her.

He pulled her close to his chest and kissed her. Jessica found herself kissing him back. They were lost in each other when someone cleared his or her throat. They looked it that direction.

"It's about time," Jennifer said with a big smile.

"Maybe we can have a double ceremony."

"Babe, don't push it," Nathan said to her. "I'm just getting my twin back and don't want to rush her into anything."

"Nat, I have to explain something to you. It's about my relationship with him, and why I had to leave," Jessica started to explain.

"Not today, Sis. You and Brandon can treat us to one of those fancy dinners and celebrate our engagement like you promised. Let's make up for lost years, Sis before addressing that thing I want to let go forever," said Nathan.

"Sounds good, Nat," she replied, as she hugged him.

They walked into Mama's Pizza Shack. Brandon made reservations for everyone to a fancy restaurant and called for the family limo. They shut down the shack and partied well into the next morning. They danced on the dance floor, too. Jessica was tired but happy. Brandon carried Sabrina to Jessica's bed. Jessica held Teddy and placed him or her beside her.

"I think these belong to you," she whispered to him.

He shook his head and walked out of her room. She followed him to her door.

"Brandon," she whispered back calmly.

"Listen I know you had to take them off then you helped me with them and this," he whispered back, as he held out his hand. She noticed he still wore the gold wedding band. "It makes me feel closer to you, and that's a big deal for me."

"I felt the same way, but it changed when I

removed them," she replied honestly.

"Then wear them again," he said back.

"I...I..." she stumbled to say.

"At least wear this," he said, as he took the sapphire ring and placed it on her ring finger. "You have a promise I won't leave your side ever. You know what you have to do now. Don't you?"

"Confront the bastard. But why?" she asked him painfully.

"So you can heal within, my love. You helped me with Brad and Rebecca. Now let me be there for you, as you face him. Will you let me help?"

She nodded. He took the gold wedding band and slipped it into his jacket pocket. He kissed her on the lips then headed down the hallway. She noticed Nathan and Jennifer at her door making out. Brandon tapped Nathan on the shoulder, as he passed them.

Jessica smiled and waved to them all before she closed her door. She walked back into her room. Sabrina was sound asleep on her. But Teddy stared at her.

"Hi, Teddy, go to sleep, baby," she whispered to him.

Teddy snuggled down next to Sabrina and closed his eyes. She could hear his faint, little purr pick up speed, as his body stayed there.

"Why not, Mommy?" Jessie asked her Mom for what seemed to the millionth time in the last two weeks.

"I've already told you, Jessie. Daddy breaks out in hives, so a dog or puppy is out of the question."

"Why not a kitten, Mommy?" she asked her.

"Jessie, enough," Stephanie snapped back. "The

subject is closed. Now go finish your homework before dinner."

"Fine," Jessie replied, as she marched off towards her bedroom.

"And don't slam the door," called out Stephanie. "Or you'll be grounded for a week."

Jessie grabbed a couple cupcakes off the counter and walked into her room. Tears streamed down her face now. Her phone came to life, so she wiped away the new tears.

"Hello," she replied, as she cleared her throat.

"Is this Jessica Hudson's residence?" asked a woman.

"Yes it is, Jessica speaking. Who is this?"

"Marie Southern from the Southwest Care Home," Marie answered back. "I'm afraid; I don't know the time difference, but I've been trying to get a hold of Nathan Hudson. It keeps going to his voice mail."

"What's wrong?" she asked calmly.

"Your D..." Marie started to explain but paused.

"Jessie. Jessie, open up," Nathan's voice said, as he pounded on her door.

"Marie, hold on my brother's at my door," she replied, as she opened it. "Marie's on the phone."

Nathan rushed passed her and took the phone. Jennifer and Brandon were at the door, too. She motioned them in. Then she closed the door and noticed Sabrina was awake now.

"I got it," Brandon said to her. "Let's get you and Teddy back to bed, little one."

"Holy shit!" exclaimed Nathan.

Jennifer went to his side, and they all looked at him. Jenny clung to his arm, as he turned to the window. Brandon guided Sabrina to the bedroom.

"Thank you. I'll tell her. Again thank you, Marie," Nathan said calmly.

Jessica started to walk to him when Brandon emerged from the bedroom. He took her hand, as they walked up to them. Nathan had tears in his eyes when he stared at Jessica.

"No!" Jessica exclaimed out loud. "Not now. Please it isn't so. I was just..."

Brandon pulled her to his chest. Jessica started to cry, too. She snuggled closer to him and stared at her twin. Jenny held Nathan close, too.

"What happened?" Brandon asked calmly.

"Mom's gone, Sis," Nathan answered, as he stared at her. "I know you and her found each other again. Mom was looking forward to making up for lost time, Sis. She was happy after your visit. She wanted to come to New York and see your life here. I was going to make plans for all of us to be here at Christmas. You know how she loved the holiday best of all. She loved you, Jessica."

"I know," Jessica replied, as she walked up to him. "I loved her and you all my life. Please tell me what happened. I need to know."

"They thought Dad took his new meds, but he fooled them," Nathan started to explain. "Maybe we should sit down, Sis."

"No, tell me."

"They're not sure how he got the knife, but he cut through his restraints. They didn't know he knew where she was," Nathan explained slowly. "But he did. By the time, they discovered him missing from his room. She was an afterthought, but it was too late. He was on top of her with his pants off, and it was exposed. She didn't have her covers on her body. He stabbed her repeatedly in the chest. But she had fresh bruises on her face, too."

Jessica felt weak in the knees now, and Brandon guided her to the couch. Nathan knelt in front of her with Jenny at his side. Brandon brought Jessica close to him.

"They suspect he had sex with her by force then he killed her. It was still erect. Sis, it was all quick, maybe very painful for Mom."

"She didn't deserve it, Nat," Jessica replied, as she stared at him. "I was going to have the mother I always longed for as a child."

"I know she confirmed what I suspected why you left for New York. I'm sorry, Jessie. When did it happen?"

"It's not important now," she answered back. "We need to go back and give her a proper burial, Nat. I don't want the bastard there. Do you hear me?"

"Yes, Sis," Nathan answered, as he hugged Jessica again. "We both loved her."

"I'll fly you guys back personally. I'll do the flight plan now, and you can bring anyone with you if you want to," Brandon said calmly.

He took out his cell and walked away from them. Jessica held her brother and cried. She didn't remember much of anything else, but Brandon wasn't too far from her.

She had brought Sabrina a navy blue dress and black shoes then she had to get permission to take Sabrina out of State for the funeral. So her first call was to Susan, as she had brought Sabrina's dress. Then she packed their clothes in her carryon bag. When she boarded Brandon's plane, she stood at the top of the steps and looked back at New York.

"You're coming back," Jenny whispered to her. "You belong here, Jess."

Jessica nodded and took Jenny's hand into hers. They walked into plane. There she saw her friends Wendy playing with Sabrina and Teddy. Beverly stared out the window. Becky was listening to Taylor explain something on his lap.

Then she stared at her twin Nathan. He was sad and dark circles under his eyes. Jennifer walked over and sat beside him. She took his hand in hers. He stared at Jessica now and tried to smile. He felt lost just like she did.

"Excuse me," Ted said, as he rushed by to the cockpit.

So Jessica took her seat and gazed out the window, too. She shook her head and closed her eyes. She let out a small sigh when she felt warmth on her hand. She opened her eyes to see Brandon was beside her now.

"Ted agreed to fly. I wanted to be with you, my love. Remember I said I would always be here for you."

She nodded. Then she snuggled close to his shoulder and closed her eyes again. She felt safe with him. It was nice having his hand holding hers. She could face it and know what was back in California awaiting her. She had to bury her Mom but wasn't alone in that. She had Nathan but also Brandon. He kept his word about being at her side through anything she would face.

He started to hum a tune that she recognized from Wendy had done before. Jessica still didn't recognize it, but she felt her eyelids heavier now. She felt herself snuggling tighter to him. He didn't flinch by her closeness. He was strong and supportive, and she needed it now more than she ever realized.

20

Jessica nodded, as Nathan made all their Mom's funeral arrangements. She felt numb now being back in California within a short time had made her this way. She gazed at the front doors of the Southwest Care Home now with Taylor at her side. Brandon had left her a message to meet him there.

"Jessica, are ready for this?" Taylor asked for about the sixth time since they left the funeral home.

"Yes," she answered, as she took his hand into hers. "This is the place she was before the bastard killed her. He lives here, too."

They walked into the place hand in hand. She glanced around and spotted Brandon, so they headed that way. He wasn't alone.

"Hi, Arnold," she replied, as she kissed him on the cheek.

Arnold looked up at her with tears streaming down his cheeks. He knew.

"I loved your Mom so much. I wouldn't have done that to her," Arnold rambled on sadly.

"I know, they'll have her buried in a couple days and a closed casket," she replied, as she knelt before him. "We thought it was best that way and remember how she looked in our minds."

"You look so much like her now," Arnold said, as he touched her cheek. "I asked him to have you come here. I know, it's hard for you, Princess, but you deserve this."

His shaky hand held out a photo. She glanced at it

FOLLOW YOUR HEART

and saw a chubby girl that looked like her. She looked up at him quickly.

"Your Mom, she was eight then, and it was the year we met," Arnold said in a soft voice. "She sent my heart thumping and racing all at once. I wanted to marry her right there and then. But she didn't want to. We dated years later then we had a fight. A fight I regret now. It gave your Dad an opportunity to step in." Arnold paused for a moment and moistened his lips. "I heard of Your Dad's plans despite him being my best friend and tried to warn your Mom. I was your Mom's ex-boyfriend, and she didn't want to listen to me."

"To what?" she asked him.

"To take away what women only have once in their lives," answered Arnold. "She said I was wrong. I should have pushed harder for her to stay with me, but she told me I was wrong. It was what I wanted not Dillon. I gave up on her and left." He paused again. "I passed him on the street later that day. He had a pleased look on his face. I should have rushed back to her and pleaded with her harder. But I didn't. Stephanie made her choice, and I moved on. When I came back from college, I saw you and Nathan as babies but not real small babies. I knew he succeeded. He had taken your Mom's virginity from her that day I saw him on the street."

"Please come to her funeral," Jessica replied, as she let the tears stream down her face. "Did she see you again?"

Arnold nodded. "You were a teenager and chubby like she was. We talked about you, and how you two were so much alike. She told me that you two weren't close. I asked why. She didn't answer me but walked away. Then I saw her again when she came here. We talked again. She was happy to be a part of your life now. She wanted to make up for those years she kept you at a distance. But she asked me to share with you this, so take the photo now. I know in time I won't remember her. I did love her long ago and still do."

Arnold touched her cheek again. Jessica kissed him on the cheek again and hugged him, too. The nurse took him away, and Jessica held out the photo for Brandon and Taylor to see.

"That's Mom," she replied with tears flowing down her face. "We both were fat. I don't know when she changed, but we both had a weight problem. She never got a chance to tell me this and so much more. So much more I need to know about her."

Brandon pulled her close to his chest. Taylor stared back at where the nurse took Arnold.

"No, I don't want to see him, Taylor," she replied softly.

Taylor looked back at her. "You'll have to someday soon. You don't have much time."

"Can we go now?" Jessica asked Brandon.

He nodded. They left the care home together. Taylor didn't say anymore, and she was glad about that fact. But they arrived at the house, and she held back. Nathan held a box as he emerged from the front door. Jenny was behind him with another box.

Taylor approached her and took hers from her. He followed Nathan to a U-haul trailer. Jessica didn't notice it at first. She walked up to Nathan.

"Hi, Sis," Nathan said calmly. "What's wrong?"

She held out the photo to him. He placed his box into the trailer. Then he wiped his hands before he took it from her.

"Where did you get the picture of you?" Nathan asked her.

Jennifer looked at it, too. "I never saw a photo of you when you were younger, Jess."

"It's not me," she answered finally. "It's Mom, Nat. She was eight in that picture."

"What!" Nathan exclaimed in a loud voice, "Mom. How? Where?"

"Arnold gave it to me. He felt I should have it now that she's gone. He was her boyfriend before the bastard. Arnold is at the care home Mom was," Jessica explained quickly. "He's losing his memory, but he and Mom talked about me."

"Awesome," Jennifer said with excitement. "He loved your Mom all these years."

"Taylor, can you help her with more boxes?" Nathan asked him.

"Sure. I'll draft Brandon, too," Taylor answered with a big smile.

"Be back," Jennifer said with a smile.

They walked up to the house. Nathan stared at the photo again.

"So this is Mom. You two looked a lot alike," he said thoughtfully. "Does Arnold know..."

"Yes. That's why he wanted to talk to me. Mom and Arnold talked about me. I guess he knows how Mom treated me growing up. She had Arnold as a backup plan in case she never had to chance to explain," Jessica continued thoughtfully. "Mom was the bastard's conquest."

"Chubby Bear, you're talking about Dad. How can you be so mean and cold towards him?" Nathan asked her.

"He's why I left. What's with the boxes?"

"I'm moving out," Nathan answered back. "Ryan is moving to New York, so we're moving our client basis there. I plan to sell this after Dad's gone. Jenny and I and Jenny decided to pack up my personal stuff, and we played with the idea of renting it until..."

"That's fine. What about Mom's stuff?"

"We're packing it, too and going to put it in storage, but we have to see what her will says. We can bring your stuff, too. Dad's will be in storage here since he's still alive," Nathan answered thoughtfully.

"My dresser, chest and bed burn them. The rest of my clothes give to charities, and whatever is left I guess bring it to New York. I'll find a place for it in my apartment," she replied coldly. "Can I have the photo back?"

"Jessie, will you talk to me? You said you know Dad abused me. Did Dad hurt you somehow or someway I didn't know? You seem on the verge of telling me then stop in your tracks. You get angry and put up a wall that I can't break down?"

"Drop it," she replied, as she took the photo back and headed up the driveway.

"Hi, my love," Brandon said with a smile. "What's wrong?"

"I'll wait in the Blazer. Keep Nat away from me now. He doesn't understand, and I'm in no mood to explain what the bastard did to me and Mom."

"My love, there's a photo in the door. I think it was your Dad's. It's you naked on a bed."

She glared at Brandon now. Then she sprinted for the backyard, and she ran into the backyard to cry. She wiped away the tears and sat on the air conditioning unit when Brandon stood before her.

"I put it in my pocket before anyone else saw it. You dropped your Mom's," he said calmly. "Let's go somewhere away from here. You take me wherever you want to go, my love."

She looked up at him and a smile formed on her face now, as she got to her feet and tucked her Mom's photo in his pocket of his shirt. He smiled back and held out the keys. Then she kissed him on the lips.

"Thank you," she replied, as she took his hands into hers despite the keys being there, too. "Let me take you to the place that I started to shed those pounds years ago."

"Sounds good, my love."

They walked out of the backyard, and she tossed the keys on the Blazer's driver's seat. Brandon stared at her.

"It's within walking distance. It's about five miles from here given or take. Are you up to it?"

"I'll follow you anywhere, my love," he answered, as he took her hand into his.

They left the house and people behind, as they headed up the street. Jessica felt confident again, as she walked with his hand in hers. It was an open area with lots of green grass but a playground in the distance. It was exactly how she remembered it. She noticed Brandon looked around.

"Come on," she replied, as she ran towards the playground.

Brandon chased after her. She was a little ahead of him when they reached the playground; both of them had red in their cheeks. They both laughed.

"This was my gym," she replied, as she extended her hands out. "It took a lot of work and discipline then to hide it from the world."

"But it all paid off," he said, as he wrapped his arms around her waist. "But I don't think it would have matter to me what you looked like."

She looked back at him. "Why?"

"I look in the heart of a woman now. After Rebecca, I had to reevaluate what I was looking for in a woman. Beauty comes and goes but not the heart."

"Comes back to what Wendy said about the heart knows what it wants and needs."

"Exactly," he said with a big smile.

He rocked her in his arms, and Jessica took it in and the warm sun on her face. Things had changed between them now. Would her Mom be happy for her? She started to cry at the question. Brandon held her tighter and didn't say anything. It was different feeling then what she had with Ryan.

"Jessica," he whispered in her left ear.

"Um," she managed to reply back.

"I'm glad; we're sharing our personal lives now," he whispered back. "I remember a shy but determined, young model. I didn't know what drove you to excel, but now I do. You weren't just doing it to prove something to him."

"No. I wanted to find out who I was. I struggled with it too until that point in my life. I wasn't good at lot things because of my weight," she admitted honestly.

"You were smart in school. Weren't you?"

"Average and sometimes above if the subject interested me. I wanted to go to college, but the bastard wasn't going to pay for it. He thought it would be waste of time and good money. That's why I was surprised about Nat..."

"He went to college and became a doctor," Brandon interrupted her. "You know, I dropped out, but you can go. I'll stand by you all the way. Did you hope it would help you find what you were good at?"

She nodded. "But I can't. I'm thirty years old and have a busy modeling career and plan...never mind."

"What?" he asked, as he turned her to face him. "Tell me."

"Do you remember Susan?"

He searched his mind then smiled, "The attorney with Danni."

"Yes. She's helping me with getting permanent custody of Sabrina. Now before you say anything; I haven't said anything to her yet. I want her to feel safe and settled before I tell her."

"That's great!" he exclaimed back. "Now we just need to get Jim arrested, so she will know he's not coming back for her."

"And why he took her in the first place," added Jessica. "I think it's connected with you and your Aunt

Beverly."

"I'm beginning to think so, too since he showed up at the restaurant."

"I wish Mom hadn't been killed," she replied, as she walked over to the swings. "Nathan used to push me on these. He didn't want me to die too young. I was heavy then. I told him it wasn't going to happen since I planned to marry a man I adore and have half dozen kids. So they could beat him up since he's their only uncle. But it's a dream that has slipped away from me now. Did you know Mom never wanted to talk to me about where babies came from?"

She stared at him with tears in her eyes then focused on the swings again.

"Get on. I'll push you, and you can reach for the sky," Brandon answered back.

She smiled, and let him push her higher and higher with each push. She let out a musical laugh that she hadn't done in years. Then they walked back to the house hand and hand. Brandon didn't say anything about her revelation. So she concluded that he didn't want the same things she did long ago. Maybe Rebecca scared him of ever thinking of that kind of life.

Jessica walked into the house. It had lots of boxes everywhere now. Everyone arrived to help which surprised her. She walked into the family study and noticed Brandon was behind her. She glanced at the bookcases and noticed all the books the family had collected over the years.

"You're not alone, my love," he said to her. "You seem to be thinking about something or someone."

"Mom was beautiful when I was a kid. She had the

makings of a model, too. I guess, I thought about it one day when I was younger or I was fat. Then your Aunt Beverly brought it back to me when I brought Annie back to her and Tina. But Mom would be upset with him about my being overweight, but she never discussed with him or me that she was fat once, too," she replied thoughtfully.

"Maybe she would have if we had more time. He took her away from me just like..."

"I'm here," he said, as he pulled her close to him.

"It's so unfair," she replied, as she cried into his chest.

"It's okay to cry, my love. You loved and cared about her despite everything said and not said between you, too."

She didn't remember the rest of the day or even the days later. Now she was back in New York. Nathan traveled back by way of his U-haul truck now. They buried Mom, and Jessica focused on the task at hand which was adopting Sabrina.

Now Susan sat in Jessica's apartment. Sabrina was at her therapy session. Jessica brought two cups of hot green tea into her small living room.

"Where's does Sabrina sleep?" Susan asked her, "Oh hi, kitty."

"That's Teddy. He's Sabrina's kitten. They sleep in my bed with me," she answered back. "Taylor gave him to her."

"He's so sweet," Susan said, as she petted him. "He loves to be petted."

"Sabrina gives him a lot of her attention. I think he eases some of her nightmares."

"How so?" Susan asked, as she took a cup. "Thank you."

Jessica sat in her comfy armchair and had her tea, too. Teddy climbed up and snuggled in her lap. He looked back at Susan and purred.

"He's like this when she's not around. Her nightmares aren't as intense, as they were those first few nights. I spent an hour here and there up with her. Now it's three hours before she screams then she touches Teddy and me then goes back to sleep."

"Sounds sweet," commented Susan.

"What's sweet is this little guy puts his tiny paw in her hand after she touches my face. He begins to purr and puts us all back to sleep."

"That's adorable," Susan said with a smile.

"Yeah, Jennifer thought so, too when we got back from...."

"Jessica, I'm sorry to hear about your Mom. How's Nathan holding up with her being gone now?"

"We packed a trailer and van of his stuff and theirs. We put the bastard's in storage, and Nathan and Ryan are driving the van with his stuff and mine here. Nathan's moving here, so is Ryan."

"What about..."

"The bastard is staying where he is. I think Nathan and I need distance from him to heal. He abused Nat after I left. He has scars on his body," she explained, as she sipped her tea.

"That's good. Sorry, Nathan was abused by him, too."

"Me, too."

"Any word on who kidnapped Sabrina?"

"Not since Jim poked his head into Mama's Pizza Shack."

Brandon walked in. His camera dangled from his neck and held it back from swinging too much. He smiled at her and kissed her on the cheek.

"Hi," he said to Susan. "How's it going?"

"Uh…" Susan answered in hesitation.

"He knows about my plans for adopting Sabrina. We have no more secrets between us now," Jessica filled in with a big smile.

"You need a character reference for her. I'm so there for her," offered Brandon.

"Good to know, and thank you."

"Water, my love?" he asked Jessica.

"You know, where it is."

"Thanks," Brandon said, as he headed into her kitchen.

"Brandon is trying to flush out Sabrina's kidnapper. Jim is from his past, so Brandon has made himself more visible every day since we got back."

"But wasn't it only a few days ago?"

"Yes, Ted and he thought it was a good idea when they about it back in…"

"No need to explain. I'll let you know more, as I find out. He's good looking."

"Sabrina's adores him."

"And you're falling head over heels in love with him," Susan said with a big smile.

"Think so."

"I know so like me and my Thomas."

"Are we done here?" Jessica asked politely.

"Yes. But walk me out," Susan answered with a smile.

Brandon emerged with a bottle of water. "I hope you're not leaving on my account."

"No. We're just wrapping up," Susan said with her briefcase in hand. "Be careful out there."

"I'll be back," Jessica replied, as she placed Teddy in the chair.

He stretched and yawned, as he looked up at her. Meow.

"He doesn't want you to go," said Brandon.

"Then you keep him company then," she replied with a small laugh and followed Susan out.

They walked down the hallway. Jennifer's door opened, so Jessica stopped at the door.

"Hi, Jenny," Jessica replied cheerfully.

"Hi, I'm off to work. Excuse me," Jennifer said, as she closed her door and side stepped them.

"Just a second, Susan," she replied to Susan. "Jenny, what's wrong?"

Jennifer stared at her for a moment. "I miss, Nathan. That's all. Now excuse me."

"Can we talk later?"

"Sure fine," Jennifer answered, as she walked out ahead of them.

"She's upset. It's more than, Nat. But I think she won't say it in front of you since she doesn't know you."

"Love can be confusing and hard sometimes," said Susan.

"But also exciting, too," Jessica added.

"That's true. I wanted to know if Brandon feels the same way you do about him."

"I know he enjoys being with me, listening and holding me, too. He's even kissed me more than once, but no, I don't know the depths of his feelings for me yet. We're stepping away from our professional relationship to a more personal one now." Jessica laughed a small laugh. "We've known each other more than a decade and just getting to know each other in that way."

"Go slow. Everything you went through with your Dad and don't let Brandon pressure you into anything you're not ready for," warned Susan.

"You mean sex. He found a Polaroid the bastard took of me. We haven't discussed it. I'm sure we will someday," Jessica replied honestly and thoughtfully. "I placed it and Mom's photo in his pocket and haven't seen them since."

"A photo of your Mom?" Susan asked with interest.

"Yes, Arnold gave it to me. Mom was fat like me. I was shocked at first, but now I understand. The poem she wrote when I was born how she shared it with me before her..."

"Treasure the good, Jessica," interrupted Susan.

"You sound like you understand what I went..."

"Yes. I was a victim, too, but Thomas was my rock. He stood by me to this day, as I get caught in a moment. His love gets me through it. I faced my father as an adult with Thomas at my side."

"That's why you wondered about Brandon."

"Yes."

Jessica nodded. They stood at Susan's car in the

parking lot of her apartment building. They hugged then Susan slipped into her car.

"Are you going to pick up Sabrina?" Susan asked her.

"Yes, then a family dinner at Mama's," she answered with a smile.

"Jessica, it's time," Brandon said, as he stood by his truck now.

She glanced over at him with a smile then back to Susan.

"Let me know if you need anything else," she replied to Susan.

"I will. But you, both be careful with that guy on the loose," warned Susan.

"We will. Thank you."

Susan started her car and pulled away. So Jessica walked up to him. He smiled at her.

"He's in the truck. Let's go get her," Brandon said, as he opened her door.

She slid in and placed Teddy on her lap. She watched Brandon slid behind the wheel. He started to head for the therapist office.

"Brandon, uh...I know we never really talked about the Polaroid of..."

"Jessica, I don't hold it against you. I saw how he treated you. No wonder you were so closed off," Brandon interrupted her. "Then Sabrina broke through the wall. I haven't talked about it because I know you have to go back and face him."

"What! Are you out of your mind?"

"Hear me out, my love. I suspect you got him to

take his new meds because he wanted one thing in return. But he didn't know how strong the new meds were. Otherwise, he would have waited until after," he answered quickly. "Am I wrong?"

She shook her head, no, and looked down at Teddy.

"It's not your fault, Jessica. He's a sick bastard just like Jim for kidnapping Sabrina. Here she is. She needs you to be happy now."

"Hi, Sweetie," Jessica replied, as she slipped out of the truck. "I really missed you so did Teddy."

They hugged. Sophia, her therapist, stood there with a smile.

"How's it going?" she asked Sophia.

"Good. Hey, Brandon," answered Sophia.

"Hi, we have Teddy in the truck and dinner at Mama's with the family," said Brandon.

"Define family, Jessica?" asked Sophia.

"Let's see people who love each other and care about each other's happiness. Why?"

"Sounds solid. So I'll see you in a couple days, Sabrina."

"Yes," Sabrina said, as she climbed into the truck, "See Teddy."

Meow. Sabrina buried her face into his small body. Jessica slid in next to them. They were at Mama's Pizza Shack in no time. Jessica glanced around the room and noticed it was packed except for their booth marked reserved.

Beverly and Wendy were already there. Taylor emerged from the kitchen with a bowl of something that he placed on a table near the bathrooms. Sabrina joined them with Teddy. Brandon nodded at Taylor and pointed to the booth. Jessica sat next to Sabrina and Teddy.

The bell rang above the door again. Brandon stood by the booth and stared. Jessica looked that way, too. Wendy brought Teddy and Sabrina closer to her. Beverly glanced back in that direction now, too.

"What..." Beverly managed to say.

Jim stood there. He stared at them all then stayed fixed on Beverly.

"Yes, it's me after all these years, Beverly. I kidnapped that little girl next to your big sister there," Jim said calmly. "But I looked into those eyes and had second thoughts about taking her life. So I thought of a ransom, but I didn't want the dirty money either. It's still there where you put it Brandon untouched."

"I was so much in love with you back then," Beverly blurted out. "I would have done anything for you. I loved you that much."

Jim nodded. Jessica noticed behind Jim a figure of someone. But it wasn't clear at first but then she realized it was Ted. He had something in his hand. But she couldn't make it out clearly. Jim still stared at Beverly.

Sabrina snuggled closer to Wendy. Jessica touched her little body with her hand. Jessica took a quick glance at Sabrina. Sabrina feared him. Jessica could see it in her eyes, so she turned back to Jim, too. Brandon stood there without any sudden moment.

"Have you ever thought of our night together? I have; that's why I left you clues where to find the little girl. How can I forget the passion we shared that one and only night?" Jim asked painfully.

A long silence now filled the restaurant, as patrons looked at what was going on. They were aware of feeling in the room now. They were a part of it. Jessica didn't know what Brandon and Ted were thinking right now since the place was full of people.

21

"Yes, I have," Beverly answered, as she stood outside the booth now and faced him. "So much so that I've kept my beloved nephew apart from a woman who could possibly love him again. It hurt like hell when Rebecca went to you. Didn't you see it wasn't just a one night stand for me? My God James, I was so much in love with you that it changed me forever."

"You're under arrest for kidnapping of a minor child, endangerment to child and asking for a ransom," Ted said from behind him.

Jim turned to him with a serious look on his face now. "So you're the law now. Yes, I remember you and Brandon being in Texas. I see you have healed, too."

Jim held out his hands. Ted cuffed him, and he didn't seem to resist them. He stared back at Beverly who had Taylor now at her side.

"Before you take him away, I have one more thing to say to him," Beverly said, as she stood taller now. "We had a child out of that one night stand. I didn't know its sex because I gave it up. It would be..."

"I know," Jim interrupted her, "Sixteen-years-old now. You better add murder to my charges if I survive this." He turned briefly to Ted then back to Beverly before he spoke again a sigh escaped him. "Our child is standing beside you like he should have been at his birth. I did and still do love you, Beverly. That's why I couldn't kill Sabrina. I saw you when I looked into her eyes. Then I remembered our son deserves to know who his Mom is. Sorry to drive you crazy in Brandon's studio, son. I killed Jill Claymore yesterday, after she confirmed what I suspected; she was holding back from me. Ted, take me out of here, now."

Ted opened the door, and Jim stepped through it and left. Ted walked out behind him. Patrons resumed eating, and some got up to pay their bills. They left money at their tables and walked out. Beverly found the edge of the booth to sit down. She glanced up at Taylor who now stared down at her.

"That's what was so familiar," Jessica whispered to herself, "The final piece of the puzzle."

"Is Uncle Ted coming back?" Sabrina asked no one in particular.

"I don't know, Honey," Wendy answered honestly.

Beverly glanced up deeper at Taylor now. He stared down at her intently. Jessica noticed he was built like Jim but had Beverly's face. Beverly was able suggest a haircut, and Taylor didn't protest it. Somewhere deep inside they connected despite his outburst of her not being his Mom.

Somewhere deep they were Mom and son or son and Mom. Jessica shook her head and glanced over at Brandon. Brandon still stood outside the booth beside her. He was in shock of the news and discovered he had a cousin which stood near him. Did he notice Taylor on the street prior to Jennifer introducing them to each other? If they hadn't met up in the search for Sabrina, would they have found out about each other? Jessica thought about Jennifer.

"Excuse me. I have to go see someone," she replied

back. "Get some dinner, and I'll be back as soon as I can, Sabrina. Love you, Sweetie."

Jessica slid out of the booth and side stepped Brandon. She waved to Sabrina and Wendy. They waved back. She kissed Brandon on his cheek with no response from him. She headed for Starbucks. She walked into a very quiet store. No patrons anywhere. She noticed Jennifer at the register, so she walked up.

"Hi, Jennifer, I've got some good and bad news for you," she replied with an upbeat tone in her voice.

"Fine, tell me the bad news first then," Jennifer said, as she readjusted her glasses.

"We or he turned himself in. Jim didn't resist arrest. He admitted to everything including murder."

"Who's Jim?"

"Beverly's Jim," Jessica answered calmly. "She told us about him and their one night stand. Remember?"

"Vaguely," Jennifer answered sadly. "All right enough is enough. You're going to tell me what's wrong now!"

"I told you that if you weren't feeling well that you could go home," an African American man said to Jennifer. "It's slow, and you've done all the prep work for us pretty much on your own. You're a great assistant manager who gets things done. Now go on home and be with your friend, Jennie."

Jennifer stared at him, and he smiled back.

"Maybe Moe, let me talk to my friend here, but on a condition," she told him.

"What's that, my friend?" asked Moe.

"I'm going on my half and will stay and close, but

you go home to your girlfriend. Isn't today her birthday?"

"Oh my, gosh I forgot. She's going...."

"Don't worry. I picked up the scarf that she was drooling over a couple days ago. It's wrapped and in your duffel bag," Jennifer interrupted him.

"You're the best, Jennie," Moe said, as he hugged her. "Do you want me to stay until your half is done?"

"Now, go."

Moe smiled and whistled, as he stepped into the back. Jessica stared at her now.

"What's up?"

"You, Ms Downer, who manages to remember a co-worker's girlfriend's birthday despite how she feels personally," replied Jessica.

"I believe in love. I love your twin brother Nathan with all my heart," Jennifer said calmly. "So tell me the good news."

"Beverly and Jim had a child, and she never told Jim. She never told anyone about the baby until she told us. Remember?"

"Okay. So?"

"Excuse me, I have package for a Jennifer Owen," a man said dressed in a brown uniform and baseball cap which shadowed his face.

"Bye, Jennie. Thanks a lot," Moe said, as he headed out the front door.

"That's me," said Jennifer.

"Then this for you," he said, as he kissed her on the lips.

Jennifer pulled back. "Nathan Paul Hudson if I didn't love you so much."

Jessica laughed out loud. Jennifer and Nathan laughed, too. He tossed the hat aside and walked around the counter to kiss her again.

"I love you, too, babe," Nathan said, as he stared into her eyes. "Brandon hired some people to take care of rest of the house, so Ryan and I applied to practice medicine here earlier today. I don't want to spend any more time away from you, Jennifer. How could I forget this day?"

Nathan held out a small box. Jennifer took and opened it. Her eyes widened, as she stared at it.

"You can wear it on our wedding day," Nathan said to her. "You didn't take what Mom left you, Sis."

He held out a box and a book to her. Jessica stepped closer. Jessica's hands began to shake, as she took them. The book had red spots on it, and the box was black, too.

"Mom wanted you to have them. They were Grandma Sara's which Mom never wore on her wedding day. She also wanted you to have the black book that you brought her before..."

"I know. It's her blood," she interrupted him.

"I should have washed it off, Jess. I'm sorry."

"It's okay, Nat. I'm going back to Mama's. I need to get Sabrina home. And thank you," she replied, as she kissed him before she left.

She walked slowly back to Mama's Pizza Shack. The restaurant was empty except for Taylor, Beverly, Brandon, Sabrina, Teddy and Wendy. They sat and ate in silence when she walked in. She sank deep into a chair not far from the booth and placed the box and book on the table.

"Mommy, what are those?" Jessie asked her Mom.

"They're sapphire earrings. They were your Grandma Sara's," Stephanie answered back.

"Do you think I could ever wear them, Mommy?"

"I suppose maybe," Stephanie answered sadly.

"Mommy, why are you so sad?"

"It's nothing important."

"But, Mommy."

"Fine, Grandma Sara's wanted me to wear them on my wedding day, but I didn't do it. Okay. Now take your cupcake and leave me alone."

"Jessica, are you all right?" Brandon asked her, as he sat next to her. "What's in the box?"

"Nathan's back. He's with Jenny now," she answered back calmly. "It's the black book I brought to Mom. It has her blood on it, so it was with her when..."She looked up at him. "The box might have the sapphire earrings that were my Grandma's Sara's. Mom didn't wear them on her wedding day. Sabrina, let's go home. Please excuse me."

"I'll drive you two, home," Brandon said to her.

"Fine," she replied, as she got up again. She scooped them back up and led Sabrina and Teddy outside, "Good night, everyone."

Brandon drove them home and carried Sabrina into Jessica's apartment. Jessica held Teddy, as she opened her door. Brandon took Sabrina to the bed while Jessica turned on more lights and placed Teddy on the floor. She knew he would climb onto the bed to be with Sabrina.

So she left her keys, book and box by the front door and sat down on her couch. Soft classical music filled the apartment now. Brandon knelt in front of her. He took her hands into his.

"You had a memory on your way back to the restaurant," he said calmly. "Didn't you?"

She nodded.

"Was it a good or bad one?"

"Mixed," she answered, as she looked down at their hands. "Do you remember the book that I brought to Mom? You said I looked really happy."

"Yes," he whispered back. "It's that one."

"She wrote a poem the day Nat and I was born. It was for me. I was so moved and happy that day. I had my Mom, and I thought…" Jessica replied in hesitation then started to cry again.

Brandon moved to sit beside her now. He held her close. She buried her head into his chest.

"Let the music calm you, my love," he said in a low calm voice.

She smelled his Old Spice aftershave. She felt the warmth of his firm chest against her right cheek, as his hand lightly touched or stroked her blonde hair. His heart was beating slow but steady. She closed her eyes, as the sobs eased.

"Mommy," Sabrina cried out.

Jessica bolted up and rushed to her. Sabrina sat up in the bed with Teddy staring at her. Jessica sat on the bed and held out her arms. Sabrina dove into them without any hesitation. Teddy rubbed against them, as they embraced. She found herself humming the melody Brandon and Wendy shared with her.

The next morning Teddy noticed Jessica's face then

Sabrina's. Both of them stretched and got off the bed. Teddy danced on the floor then headed for the living room.

"Did he spend the night?" Sabrina asked in a low voice.

"I guess so," she answered back. "Let's get you and Teddy fed. Is Cheerios and milk okay?"

Sabrina nodded, so they walked into the kitchen. Jessica prepared Sabrina's breakfast while Sabrina did Teddy's.

"Good morning, Brandon," Sabrina said to him.

"Good morning, little one," he said back. "Did you sleep well?"

"Yes, after Mommy came in," Sabrina answered calmly. "She makes the bad man go away."

"Mommy?" he questioned her.

Sabrina pointed to Jessica. Jessica held out a bowl of cereal to her.

"Thank you, Mommy," Sabrina said, as she took it to the floor and sat next to Teddy.

"Cheerios, Brandon?" Jessica asked him politely.

"Uh... no, thanks, I should be going now," he answered back. "Do you have assignment yet?"

"I asked her not to give me assignment until we found Sabrina. But, oh gosh, will she remember we were to meet today at her office to discuss my career?"

"I guess, you'll have to go and find out," he answered, as he left the kitchen.

"Brandon wait," Sabrina called out to him.

He stopped at the door and looked back. She rushed up to hug him. He picked her up and held her tight in his arms. Jessica noticed a sparkle in his eyes, as he held her in his arms.

"Daddy material," she whispered to herself.

"Love you, princess," he said with a smile for her. "Bye, Jessica."

He had put Sabrina down and the door open. He bumped into Jennifer. Jennifer looked happy and her normal self again. Jennifer and Nathan stood there hand and hand with big smiles on their faces.

"Sorry, guys," Brandon said quickly, "Got to go."

"Bye," Jennifer said with a big smile. "We'll see you later then."

Brandon nodded. They walked in deeper into the apartment behind Sabrina. Sabrina went back into the kitchen.

"So you seemed in a better spirits now," Jessica commented with a return smile.

"Yes. What are you doing today?" Jennifer asked her now.

"I have a meeting with Beverly then from there I don't know. It depends if she has an assignment lined up since I put my career on hold until we found Sabrina. Why?"

"We're wondering if you could join us today," Jennifer answered, as she shuffled her feet happily.

"You two are up to something, Nat. You're being too quiet. What's wrong?"

"Damn, I told you about how I shouldn't have come," Nathan answered back quickly. "She knows me better than anyone in this whole world including you, babe."

"We got this crazy idea last night. After we talked

for hours after I got off work," Jennifer started to explain.

"We wanted someone to legally marry us."

"But you have started to plan a February wedding," Jessica pointed out.

"But that's not set in stone yet," Jennifer continued to snuffle her feet. "We wanted to do it today or tomorrow but prefer today if possible."

"And we want you, Sabrina and Brandon to be there with us," added Nathan.

"What about Ryan?" she asked him.

"I forgot about him, but he'll understand."

"No. You wait for your best man. When will he be here in New York?"

"He's here already. He drove with me and is asleep in motel outside of City. He and I had business yesterday. Remember?"

"Let him rest today; and we can discuss it all later. We have to meet Beverly."

"We can stay with her here," offered Jennifer.

"Uh..."

"I'm good with them, Mommy."

"Okay," Jessica replied, as she hugged and kissed her. "I'll call you when the meeting is over. I promise."

"Love you, Mommy."

"I love you, Sabrina," Jessica replied, as she rushed out the door.

She didn't want to explain to anyone yet that she planned to adopt Sabrina. The only person knew her secret about Sabrina's adoption was Brandon, and he didn't know the whole story yet. But she did plan on telling him soon.

She didn't mind Sabrina calling her Mommy. It

warmed her heart every time she heard it. Jessica wanted to get this meeting behind her now.

Having Sabrina living with her had changed her more now. Her apartment wasn't just a place she would crash at in between assignments now. She had someone to come home to.

Jennifer was right about New York, and she belonged here. This was home to her now. She smiled at that thought since she hadn't thought of it in that way ever. Jessica skipped down the hallway and out into the busy New York day.

She smiled, as she took it all in. She flagged a taxi and gave him directions to Beverly's office. She didn't mind the traffic or the noise, as she rode alone through the streets.

"Ms., we're here," said the cabbie.

She paid him and slipped out. She headed upstairs to Beverly's office. She opened the door and walked in. Then she stopped in her tracks.

"Jessica Hudson?" asked the policeman.

"Yes."

"I'm ordered to bring you and Ms. Rivers' downtown."

"Did I do anything wrong, officer?"

"No, ma'am, the detective will explain. Please I have an unmarked car waiting outside, ladies."

"I'm ready," Beverly said, as she stood at her closed door now. "It's no big deal, girlie. We didn't do anything wrong. It's about Jim or Clifford. Can't you at least tell us which one now?"

The officer didn't answer her. Jessica sat in the

backseat while Beverly sat up front with the officer in unmarked car. They traveled a short distance. When Jessica got out of the car, she was greeted by Ted. He was dressed in tan business suit and looked different somehow.

"Thanks, Officer Jameson, I'll take them from here," Ted said politely to him.

"Yes sir, Detective," Officer Jameson said, as he walked away.

"Detective?" both women asked together.

"I'll explain inside, ladies," Ted answered calmly.

They all walked into the police station. He directed them to a private office. They walked in and sat down. They faced him. Ted joined them after closing the door.

"Before we start, thank you for coming down here ladies today," Ted started to say. "Now I know, you're confused right about now, and I'll do my best to explain it all. It's going to be hard on all involved in this case."

A woman officer walked in with two Starbucks Grande cups. She placed one in front of Beverly, and the other was in front of Jessica. Then she sat at a distance from them.

"Thank you, Joyce," Ted said politely.

Joyce nodded. Then Ted focused on Beverly and Jessica.

"We've been watching the orphanage for awhile now," Ted continued on.

"Um sir, fourteen years to be exact, sir," Joyce said calmly.

"All right fourteen years, happy," Ted said, as he shot her a quick glance then back to them. "Kids were disappearing from there, and nobody seemed to notice it.

That's until you and Brandon did with Sabrina. We had been watching Claymore for a number of years. Then Jim entered the picture early in our investigation. But he was looking into her records, and we didn't know why. Claymore opened her confidential files to him for a price."

"Taylor, my son said had been there briefly," Beverly said calmly.

Jessica stared at her now in shock.

"Yes, he told me last night. He told me all about his rough life, too. I was shocked to hear it but glad he told me. He showed me his scar," Beverly said calmly.

"Did he..."

"Yes. And you were there for him, and I owe you a lot, Jessica."

"Ladies, can I continue here?" asked Ted.

"Sorry," they answered together.

"We didn't know why Jim was there, but in time he started to be suspicious. He was following Brandon around. We saw Taylor watching Jim when you entered with Sabrina," Ted said, as he cleared his throat. "Things were moving fast after that because Claymore took Sabrina to the airport alone."

"We caught up with her at the airport where she left Sabrina there," Joyce said, as she sat closer to them. "Jim approached her and offered to be her companion. Sabrina wasn't sure at first and may not even remember much of that day. But he said something to her that we don't know what it was. However, she went with him willingly. She was frightened, but we lost them in the crowd of people."

"That's when I decided to go undercover," said

Ted. "Brandon and I had been friends on and off for years. He doesn't know that I'm a police detective, but he'll know soon enough."

"I dug into Brandon's private life and made the connection between two men," said Joyce. "There was a model who died by suicide or accident in Paris, France."

"Rebecca," Beverly said calmly.

"Yes. Jim shifted his focus on you, Jessica and Brandon. He had Sabrina and wanted to make you both squirm. He had inside information, and we can't figure out from whom," added Ted. "Now Jim admitted to killing Jill Claymore, but he won't tell us who kept him a couple steps ahead of us."

"Why are we here?" Jessica asked with interest now.

"He asked to speak to you both. Plus we wanted you to know what was going on," answered Joyce.

"I'll go first," Jessica replied, as she stared at Beverly. "I think you'll want to talk to him longer than me. You have a lot of catching up to do."

Jessica got to her feet, and Joyce followed her into another room. Jim sat there and looked at his hands.

"Visitor," Joyce said to him. "She wanted to go first since you and the other have some catching up to do."

"Jessica Hudson," Jim said in a soft voice.

"Uh...Jim..."

"It's okay. Please sit," he said politely.

She sat across from him and clasped her hands in front of her. Joyce sat in a chair away from them.

"I was angry at Beverly and Brandon, and I took it out on you, Taylor and Sabrina. I'm sorry. When Rebecca died, I found a letter she wrote to Beverly, and I was shocked and angry at the same time. Rebecca was still lusted for Brandon, and she knew Beverly was pregnant," Jim explained calmly to her. "Rebecca said she lusted for Brandon's young body was not in love with him. I couldn't get my head on straight for awhile there. I did and still do love Beverly. When I started to look for our child, I didn't know it was a boy until I found a place Switzerland. It's where Beverly went to have Taylor and give him away."

Jim paused for a moment and collected his thoughts before he continued on. "I tracked him back to New York and the orphanage then lost him. Claymore strung me along about Taylor's whereabouts. She made me angry and laughed and said I just tortured my son. I was shocked by it. I killed her in full of rage. I plan on Beverly telling all this, too."

"What about who told you where we…"

"No can do, little lady," Jim interrupted her. "I'm sorry your Dad sexual abused you and hurt your brother. He should have died, not your Mom. She was sweet lady."

"You meet my Mom!" exclaimed Jessica.

"She was the one who told me about the Clayton mine," Jim said calmly.

"I'm so out of here," Jessica replied, as she started to head out of the room. "I want to go home now."

"I need you to hear me out, Ms. Hudson."

She stopped and stared at him. "Why?"

"I learned a lot about you from your Mom. I think you'll want to hear it."

She glared at him now and returned to her chair. Ted was at the open door, but Joyce closed the door and stood in front of it.

"Fine."

"I know how much she loved and cared about you. She was also very proud of you and your career. I saw her beam with so much pride that I wish I had taken a picture to share with you now," said Jim. "Her face lighted up when she talked about you, Jessica. A pride only a parent could have for their child. I wanted to know that feeling with my own son."

He paused for a moment again. Then Jim cleared his throat then looked at her before he continued again.

"I know, I was late in the game, but I had to at least try. But Claymore wasn't working with me about finding Taylor. I wanted my family more than ever. Why do you ask? I saw how sad your Mom got when she said you and her weren't close. It wasn't fake, Jessica. She had regrets with you, but I didn't press it. It was between you and her and not my place to prey."

"So you left her as a basket case. How did you know where she was?"

"No, she was already thinking of you when I found her there in Southwest Care Home. I had time to be through and the resources to check out things. But I didn't know you from Adam, but you were a part of Brandon's life. I taught him about fashion photography early in his life, and he blossomed after I left."

"Did you ever approach the bastard?"

"Your Dad no," Jim answered back. "But now he was something. I knew when I saw him at a distance something wasn't right about him. I was shocked to hear what he did. I didn't think he would kill. Heck, I didn't think

I could with my own two hands, either."

"I'm so out of here," Jessica replied back. "I've heard enough. It's Beverly's turn. I need a ride home. Please. I don't want to wait for her to be done."

Ted nodded.

"But you're not done, Jessica," said Joyce.

"What do you mean?" she asked her in anger.

"Jim," Joyce said to him.

"Oh yeah, you want to know what made me crazed over Rebecca lusted for Brandon. Why I wanted revenge?"

Joyce nodded.

"He was young and active. He could have any girl in the world, but why someone old enough to be his Mom lusted for his young body. She lusted for a boy that's a shot to my manhood. I thought I was a real ladies man. I had Beverly. Didn't I?"

"You're sick like the bastard," Jessica yelled at him. "I don't want to hear anymore of this. Take me home or I'm walking."

"Slow down Jessica," said Ted.

"No, enough is enough," snapped Jessica. "I'm not going be your whatever. I don't want any part of this. I'm going home now. I'm walking. Goodbye to all of you."

She shoved Ted aside and headed out the door. Beverly was on her feet.

"What's going on in there?" Beverly asked her.

"Ask them. I've had enough. Oh, did you have an assignment for me?"

"Working on it, girlie," answered Beverly.

"Make it happen, Beverly. I know you said the time off could affect my career, but I'm sure my proven track record should please any client."

"Good point, girlie," Beverly said with a smile.

"Good," she replied, as she marched off.

Jessica continued on out of the police station. She began to calm down. She flipped open her cell and scanned for Brandon's number but then decided not to call him. She decided to walk back to her apartment and come home to Sabrina. Sabrina made her smile.

Honk. Honk. She stared at the honk direction.

"Get in," snapped Ted.

"No."

"Get in, or I'll arrest you."

"You can't do that, Ted. I've done nothing wrong," she snapped back at him.

"Please, Jessica," he pleaded with her.

She stopped, so he stopped his car. He got out of his car and walked up to her.

"I'm sorry. I shouldn't have let it go that far. But I need to know how he was always ahead of us when we were trying to get Sabrina back. Don't you want to know, too?" he asked her back.

"Yes, but not at that cost; I didn't need to know he talked to Mom. But you're walking a very, very thin line with me right now, Ted. I was beginning to trust you and...."

"I know it isn't easy given what your Dad did you. I get it, Jessica. But we need to know before he goes to trial. Please, he might tell you."

"Have Beverly do it?"

"She's too emotional. You're detached from him. You don't know him like she does."

"She's the perfect one to get him to open up. She knows him."

"No can do, Jessica. Please."

"No, and that's final. Leave me alone, Ted."

"Very well, Jessica," Ted said, as he got back into his car. "But at least let me drive you home."

"Fine."

When she got home, she had a message from Beverly about an assignment, so she looked at Nathan and Jennifer. They gave her the heads up ahead, so she ignored the rest of the message except to call Brian. So she took the handheld phone into her room and got the information of what the assignment was about and the rest of the information from Brian.

Then she took them all out to dinner but not Mama's Pizza Shake. She wanted a nice place since they needed to discuss Nathan and Jenny's wedding plans. They wanted to convince them to put it off until February.

22

The next morning Jessica was called out of City for a day shoot. She did it, so she wouldn't have to face Beverly, and what Jim admitted to her. She placed a call into Jennifer and reminded them to look after Sabrina. They were going to take her to the zoo.

"Jessica, focus on me," said Brain. "Take five."

Jessica relaxed and drank some water. Brain walked up to her.

"What gives?" he asked her.

"I'm sorry, Bra," she answered calmly. "I have a lot on my mind."

"I can see that. We all heard about Jim. It must be very hard on Beverly. You know, she's been in love with him a very long time ago," Brain said, as he shook his head.

"They still love each other," Jessica commented but regretted saying it afterwards.

"Oh, you know more than most. Why did he kidnap that orphan? Tell me all the details," Brain asked with excitement.

"Can't, the cops want to keep it quiet until the trial. Sorry. Let's wrap this up. We only have an hour or two before we lose our light."

"You're the only model I know who knows what us photographers need and want without all the drama," Brain said with a small smile.

She leaned on the nearest tree and smiled back at him.

Brain snapped several shots at different angles. An hour passed, and Jessica was back in the City again. She, Sabrina, Jennifer and Nathan had meet at Mama's Pizza Shack for dinner. Sabrina was non-stop about the visit to the zoo. Nathan placed an oversized envelope next to Jessica.

"For you, Sis," he said with a smile back.

"What is it?" she asked with interest.

"Open it."

"Fine," she replied, as she saw Sabrina pointed to monkey in the cage.

"They're not professional quality like Brandon's but..."

"They're great, Nat. I wish I was there. Thank you so much," she replied, as she hugged him.

"Mommy, can we go back soon?" Sabrina asked her.

"Mommy?" asked Nathan.

"Let it go, Nat," she answered back. "For now, please."

He nodded. Sabrina leaned in and looked at the photos with Jessica. Wendy placed the large pizza and pasta on their table and left.

"It must be hard for her now," commented Jennifer.

"Why?" asked Nathan.

"Taylor is her nephew, and she didn't know it all these years. His dad...." Jennifer answered, as she looked at Sabrina.

"Grandma forgot the forks and plates," Sabrina said, as she glanced at the table.

"Give her time, Sweetie," Jessica whispered to her.

"I'll help," Sabrina said, as she crawled under the table and headed for the kitchen.

"She spends way too much time here," said Jennifer. "Can't you enroll her in school or something?"

"No, I'm not legally her Mom."

"But she calls you, Mommy," said Nathan.

"It's part of her therapy and the healing process," stated Jessica.

"Interesting," he said thoughtfully.

"How's Beverly dealing with fact Taylor being her long lost son?" asked Jennifer.

"Fine, I guess. They talked the other night, and he asked his question."

"What was it?"Jennifer asked her.

"Did she ever love him?"

"What did she say back?"

"Not sure really, I didn't press it since we were going to the police station. Then I did that photo shoot with Brain today. Thank you for in stepping and taking her for the day and put your plans on hold."

"Police station, you didn't tell us that fact last night. Why?" asked Nathan.

"They'll be calling us all in," Brandon answered, as he stood at their booth. "So keep your time free in the next couple days. Jessica, can I speak to you privately?"

"I got the plates. Grandma says, we can take forks from the salad bar," Sabrina said, as she held the plates.

"Maybe later, I'm really hungry. I haven't eaten all day," she answered politely to Brandon. "You should check on Mama."

"Fine," he said with a little irritation in his voice.

He walked towards the kitchen, after he touched Sabrina's head. She smiled at him. She always smiled at him ever since he taken her out of the mine.

"Let's get some forks, Brie," Nathan said to her.

Sabrina nodded. They headed for the salad bar together. Jessica took a slice of pizza and devoured it quickly by chewing fast.

"Cat got your tongue?" asked Jennifer.

"What?"

"Until Jim walked in that door, you and Brandon were closer than ever before," Jennifer answered back. "I noticed the glances and hand holding that you two were doing. Are you going let Jim destroy, what you two started to express for each other? Or are you two going to go your separate ways and pretend those feelings aren't real?"

"Not everybody is romantic or lovely dovey like you and Nathan. You two barely know each other and are going to get married," Jessica snapped back. "If you hadn't realized, a big bombshell was dumped here a couple nights ago? People are still in shock of the whole thing."

"But that shouldn't affect how you and Brandon feel about each other? Jess, do you love Brandon?"

"Yes. But I don't think he wants me for the long term," Jessica answered painfully. "He knows my past."

"Awesome."

"What? Did you hear me? He knows what happened in my past, but he gives no indication of anything that mattered to me as a little girl," Jessica replied with tears glide down her face now.

She bolted to the ladies' room and slammed the door behind her hard. She leaned against it and cried, as she slid down onto the tile. She buried her head between her knees and chest. Then she ignored the repeated knocks on the door.

She sent out a message loud and clear. She wanted to be alone with her own pain, loneliness and anything else that she let herself feel at this moment. Jessica wanted her Mom but remembered the bastard took her from her. It made Jessica cry longer and harder now.

Then Jessica felt a strong push against the door. But she dug in and pushed back with her legs and back. Whoever was behind the door was stronger since her legs began to buckle with the intense pressure.

"Go away," she yelled out loud.

"No," Nathan snapped back. "I'm not leaving, Chubby Bear. We're going to talk now."

She sprung up and jerked open the door. "Stop calling me that name. It's ancient history."

"Would you rather be called Piggy Wiggy?" he asked her back.

"Damn you," she answered, as she started to slam the door again when he caught it.

She stepped back and bolted to the sinks. Nathan was there too, and Brandon was not far behind.

"Stop the name calling," Brandon said to Nathan. "Can't you see it pains her to hear that name? Where the hell is your head at?"

"He doesn't know what he did to me! You're the first person outside my lawyer I've told," she answered with tears glide down her already puffy face.

"Who?" Nathan asked her. "Will one of you tell me who you're talking about here?"

"You want to know the ugly truth why I left home and haven't been back until now," Jessica answered back painfully.

"Jessica, don't say it unless you're ready to share it," warned Brandon.

"Yes, the bastard hurt me the worst way possible for a man could do to a girl and woman he confessed to love," she snapped back at Nathan. "Chew on that for awhile then maybe just maybe we can sit down and talk about it."

She darted by them both and marched out of the restaurant.

"Jess, stop please," Jennifer pleaded with her.

Jessica stopped and looked back. Jennifer struggled to catch her breath, as she walked up.

"You've been trying to tell him but couldn't bring yourself to say it," Jennifer said calmly. "You said he abused Nathan, and it got Nathan to share it with me. I was the second person Nathan admitted your Dad's abuse to. You were the first, but I've accepted him scars and all. Your brother is kind, understanding and loving just like you. That's why I love him so damn much. It bothered him not knowing why you left. Now you're back in his life, and question is still there."

"But not anymore, I told him the best why I know how. We're all confused by what Jim did. We don't know how to move forward either. Life's hard, and no path is clear cut or obstacle free. It's a mess. Look at Taylor's, Sabrina's and even yours," Jessica replied back thoughtfully.

"And yours and Brandon's too," Jennifer added to

the list. "I get it what you're saying here, and what you said or tried to say in the bathroom back there. I..."

"Jessie, I understand now," Nathan interrupted with tears in his eyes now. "You changed that summer because of what he did to you. You're right that he had no right to do that to you. But what I don't understand is..."

"Arnold was Mom's boyfriend before Dad. They got into a fight, and he stepped in. Arnold heard what he planned to do with Mom," she interrupted him.

"Did he rape her?" asked Nathan.

"I don't think so, but he intended to take away her virginity and planned to get her pregnant. He wanted no other boy or man to have her including Arnold. He never got over Mom all these years, so that's why I want Arnold to lay next to Mom after he's gone instead of the bastard."

"Yes. But..."

"The bastard planned on doing it with me onto into his old age. I had to leave California and him behind. The hardest part was leaving your and even Mom. But Mom knew."

"When? How?" Nathan asked quickly.

"The last attack before the one he killed her. She admitted it to me when I brought her the book."

Nathan stood there drained. Jessica felt drained, too, but she noticed Brandon approach them.

"You," she snapped back at him.

"I warned you," he said back. "You didn't have to until you were ready to."

"Go to hell! I trusted you, and this is how you pay me back for twelve years of loving and caring about you. Go to hell, Brandon!" she snapped back at him. "Don't say a damn word."

"But he filled in the blanks, Jessie," said Nathan.

She shot him a look and turned to walk away. Someone grabbed her arm softly. She glanced at the hand and looked up.

"What about Sabrina?" asked Jennifer?

"Drop her off when she's ready to come home. Teddy and I will be waiting," she answered politely. "But keep him away from me."

She shifted her eyes towards Brandon. Jennifer wanted to say something but decided against it. Jessica noticed the quiver in her lips, so Jessica walked to her apartment alone. She felt the fall's crispness in the air and changes slowly entering the City. This is home now not California.

Jessica paced her apartment and didn't find the classical music peaceful or relaxing like in the past. It seemed to agitate her more. She glanced in her room to the bed. Teddy managed to sleep through her bad mood. A knock was on her door now, and she bolted to answer it quickly.

Nathan had Sabrina in his arms asleep. He walked to Jessica's room when Jennifer stood in the open door. Jessica didn't know what to say to him much less Jenny. She walked deeper into her apartment and sensed Jenny was behind her.

"You forgot these," Jennifer said calmly.

"Thank you. Leave them on the..." Jessica replied, as she turned to face Jennifer. "What?"

"That was some bombshell you dropped on us out there on the street. But Brandon seemed to know about it since he calmly filled in the blanks," Jennifer answered calmly.

"It explains your feelings toward him," Nathan said in a low voice, as he walked into the room. "You got him to take those new meds without a struggle. Did he want..."

"Yes," Jessica interrupted him. "Now you know why I had to leave. Did you ever wonder why they never had a wedding photo like other parents we knew? According to Arnold..."

"Stop!" Nathan exclaimed in a harsh voice. "Sit down, Sis. This isn't going to be easy."

She stared at him and knew something was off. She gulped down some air, as she felt for her couch. "It's about Arnold. Isn't it?"

Nathan nodded. "He asked before I came out here to be buried next to Mom. I didn't know why, but what you said makes sense now. So Arnold was Mom's first love, so she didn't tell me the truth years ago when I asked her."

"That's what he told me," she replied, as she sank into the couch. "Could we bury him next to Mom? We can bury the bastard with his folks and sister."

Nathan nodded. He walked over to her now.

"I know you wanted to tell me everything, but he held you hostage with your body but most of all your heart. I saw you and Mom weren't close like a mother and daughter should be growing up. I didn't know why. I saw you trying, but Mom kept her distance. It had to hurt like hell," Nathan said, as he looked into her eyes now. "I know it too, Jessie. He ignored me and kept his distance from me like Mom did to you. So I began to build up a wall around my heart and soul and only let you and Mom in. Then you left me, and I wondered what I did to drive you away."

He had tears fall down his face now. She touched his face and felt the wetness on her own face now.

"You did nothing but love me, Nat. I had to go because of him. Don't you see?"

"I see it now but not then. When I saw you again, the floodgates busted open, and I was so overwhelmed with love and guilt," he answered back.

"Guilt or love?"

"Guilt over how I drove you away. Love for loving you, Jessie and was starting to find love for the first time in my life. It scared the crap out of me to love someone other than you and Mom," he answered, as he glanced over at Jennifer. "I heard you said you would marry for love. You broke those walls completely down, as we walked the streets looking for Sabrina." Then he turned back to Jessica. "You were breaking a little at a time, but you had your own walls, too. I could hear Brandon warning you about what Dad did to you. It's clear he's a man who knows about walls."

"Um... excuse me," Brandon said, as he stood in the doorway. "I've been trying to say this for awhile now. But Jessica, don't run away from me. I don't think I could stand another closed door. I have to say this before I lose this moment again."

Brandon walked into the room. Nathan got to his feet and pulled Jennifer closer to him. They stepped away from the couch since Brandon moved towards Jessica. She froze, as he knelt before her.

"When we met June 16, 1999, I didn't think I could feel my heart race again, but it did, Jessica. You were eighteen and nervous as hell on our first assignment together. Do you remember?" he asked her.

She nodded.

"I hated the contract my auntie had in place. I never preyed into your personal life because I couldn't stand another man kissing those lips of yours. I had a lot I mean a lot of cold showers these past twelve years." He paused for a moment then continued. "You don't know how many times I wanted to cross that damn line, Jessica."

"But you never did until...."

"Sabrina. She touched you in a way I didn't fully understand myself. But I got caught up in it too, and I wanted to tell you everything not just about Rebecca and Greece but being an orphan too," Brandon interrupted her. "Taking your hand that first time I knew, I had come home. What my heart knew was true? Love, as we peeled back the layers of our past, I knew I was falling on love with you."

"But you told Becky..."

"I regretted it after I said it. I should have told you right there I was falling in love with you. It's why I could say what he did to you wasn't your fault. You were telling me how you lost all that weight. You grieved for your Mom. I could hear it all and keep it in my heart if meant I had your trust. But what I wanted most of all is your love. You held me, as I revealed Greece. You got through when Mama hadn't. You have my heart if you want it, Jessica. I know I'm head over heels in love with you. That's what drove me to keep putting one foot in front of the other, as I walked out the Mojave Desert. The image of getting back to you the woman I love."

"I love you, Brandon," Jessica replied, as she touched his face.

He started to kiss her when she pulled her head back. He looked confused.

"I thought no man could love me knowing happened in my past with him. But you proved me wrong time and time again. You held me as I cried. You pushed me so high on that swing Nat was afraid I would die young. I couldn't do it to him because I know his love was real and true just like yours," she replied calmly. "It was the turning point in my life to another part of my life I wouldn't have explored if I hadn't promised not to die young to him. It would not have gotten me here sitting before you. Hearing you love me and knowing what got me to this point in my life. I do love you Brandon. You have the key to my heart."

She leaned in and kissed him. She felt the warmth of his lips on hers. She was back on the swing soaring higher and higher in the sky. Meow. She pulled away to see Teddy on the couch next to her. Sabrina giggled and joined them.

"Why don't you and Brandon adopt me?" We can be a family," said Sabrina.

"It's not that easy, little one," Brandon said to her with a smile. "There's lots of paperwork to be filled out and process."

"But you love each other and me and Teddy," Sabrina pointed out.

"Yes, Sweetie, we do love you and Teddy," Jessica replied calmly. "But..."

"Let's get some sleep and talk about this tomorrow," Brandon said with a smile.

"No, now," said Sabrina.

"Tomorrow, we, adults, need some rest and so do a little girl and her kitty. Teddy looks tired," said Nathan.

"For Teddy's sake," Sabrina said, as she picked him up. "We discuss it tomorrow."

Sabrina walked into Jessica's room and closed the door. Brandon laughed then Jessica and Jennifer and Nathan did, too.

"Mom would have loved her," said Nathan.

"Do you think so?" asked Jessica.

He nodded and kissed her on the forehead. He had Jennifer's hand in his. They left the apartment without another word. Brandon sat next to Jessica.

"I'm glad we cleared the air. No more secrets."

"I have a confession to make," she replied, as she looked down at their hands now joined together. "It might take our relationship to a whole new level you may not be ready for."

"Jessica, you're stalling."

"You met Susan, and I told you before she was a friend of Danni's. And we have been working on the adoption proceedings since she has been found. But I have to ask how you feel having her as part of the package."

"That's ...still great. You'll be a great Mom. She loves you and already calls you, Mommy. So she will be a part of your life and mine too," said Brandon. "It's that change I noticed in you after you two met. You had something within that was reaching for it. So how can I deny what you feel for her and stop it. You might lose yourself again, and I can't have that, Jessica, not again."

"So you're saying this okay with you in what I'm

doing," she replied back.

"Yes. Auntie Beverly was adopted, and Mama took me in. Why would this be a problem?" he asked, as he hugged her and rocked her. "You have to big, loving heart Jessica... uh Hudson."

"Marie is my middle name," she replied, as she gazed into his face.

"I love you, Jessica Marie Hudson," he said with a kiss on her lips gently. He nuzzled down near her left ear. She tensed up. "What?"

"Nothing."

"Jessica, didn't we say any secrets?"

"Did you notice..."

"Your birthmark. Yeah over eleven years ago when you pulled back your hair for that Glamour shoot. It's cute, but I won't lick it or anything like that. Maybe kiss it. But I rather have your lips locked with mine."

"Brandon," she replied, as she playfully slapped him on his chest. "We need to sleep now. You have the couch if you want to stay."

He nodded, as she got to her feet. She headed for her room. She winked at him. Brandon blew her a kiss. She walked deeper into her room. Sabrina was on the bed petting Teddy. She heard his purr, as she walked closer to them.

"You need to sleep, Sweetie."

"I know. I was waiting for you. You love Brandon, and Brandon loves you. Why don't you two get married like Jennifer and Uncle Nathan plan to do? Then you both can adopt me and Teddy."

"Sleep, we'll talk in the morning, so now in the

covers, young lady."

Sabrina snuggled into the covers, and Teddy moved closer to her. Jessica felt tired but also excited, too. She knew Brandon was on her couch and was in love with her. This thought made her smile.

"How do you know when you're in love or just a crush, Mom?" Nathan asked Stephanie.

"Well Sweetie, that's easy for girls to know, but I'm not sure about men and boys," Stephanie answered, as she handed him another sandwich. "How many is that now?"

"Four, Mom," he answered, as he looked into the ice chest, "One more just in case Jessie gets really hungry out there."

"Okay. Is there someone you're interested in Nathan?" asked Stephanie.

"Jenny. She's the same girl who followed me around the soccer field when we four then again at seven on our first communion," he answered back. "I've been thinking of asking her to the prom. But I don't know, Mom."

"If you only see you going as friends, you need to tell her that but don't lead her on. Honesty is the best when it comes to matter of the heart, Sweetie."

"Was Dad your first boyfriend and first love?"

"Uh...yes I suppose."

"I'm ready," Jessie replied, as she emerged from the hallway into the kitchen.

"I think we have enough, Mom. Thanks, Mom. Let's go, Chubby Bear," Nathan said, as he closed the ice chest.

Jessica wiped away the tears from her face and looked down at her hands, "Sorry, Nat, Sorry, Mom. I didn't give you a chance to explain," she whispered to herself.

"Why, Mom? I wanted to know so much, but you seem so distant to me back then."

A knock on her bedroom startled her. Brandon opened the door, and he peered in.

"I thought, I heard someone crying," he whispered in the darkness.

"Everything will be fine, Brandon. Please go back to sleep."

But she tracked his movement to her side of the bed. He knelt beside her and looked at her. The light of the moon casted a light on his face now.

"I love you, Jessica Marie," he whispered to her then kissed her.

"I know."

Then he walked out of the room. She touched her lips and cried silently. She didn't know what she had done right in her life to be this happy. She didn't want to take any of it for granted now.

She didn't know what her Mom thought about her life, but the poem was Stephanie's hope for her in the future. Maybe it was a good place to start with her new life with Sabrina and letting Brandon be a part of their lives, too.

She didn't know what the future held for them. She didn't want to think of how long their relationship would last. Somehow she remembered Wendy telling her about orphans, and how some were chatter boxes and same were closed up. Brandon was the second but for how long. They had discussed a lot of their past and didn't discuss a future just for the moment.

Maybe tomorrow would reveal something. She shook her head and wiped away her own tears. This would have to wait and ride itself out. Could she stand Brandon walking out of her life down the road? She didn't want to think about it now. She focused on the here and now.

She touched Sabrina's hair, as she laid there on the bed next to her. Teddy was fast asleep with his little paw in Sabrina's hand. He seemed happy with his little life. He had a little girl who adored him. Jessica also grew to care and even love the kitten. He opened an eye then the second one.

"Go to sleep, little guy," Jessica whispered to him.

Teddy began to purr again, as he closed his eyes again. She watched his little chest rise and fall and felt her eyelids getting heavier. She remembered a poem from her childhood. It went something like this:

DREAMS

Dreams aren't just for the rich and wicked.
But for all who dare to dream.
Because it's how we live for a better life.
I know your dreams come in the night.

Nobody sees them but you.
They're yours alone.
Unless you find your soul mate.
My dear mate for life.

How can two people share the same dream?
Easy to explain really.
We were meant to be together forever.
But do we share too soon or too late.

Is that the true question?

FOLLOW YOUR HEART

When is the right time?
Do we really truly know?
So many questions and so little time for answers.

That's what dreams cause.
So when you close your eyes dream of me.
Maybe I'll be in your dreams this night.
Or in the night to come in the future.

23

"Your honor, I don't want to waste the court's time and taxpayer's money on a lengthy trial. I kidnapped the orphan child named Sabrina, and she was an innocent victim of child endangerment. I take full responsibility for those actions. My only regret Sabrina will bear the scars of my actions of revenge on Brandon Morgan, Beverly Rivers and Jessica Hudson. I was angry at them all, but Jessica Hudson was and is another innocent victim of my anger towards Brandon for that I'm truly sorry to dig up painful memories of your personal life, Jessica." Jim addressed the court and stopped to catch his breath before he continued on.

"Furthermore, your honor, I openly admit to killing Jill Claymore with my own two hands. She taunted me but that was no excuse for me taking her life since she knew the whereabouts and who my son was that Beverly Rivers and had conceived. She kept saying she would give me his name and his whereabouts. Then she laughed in my face when she pointed out what I just did to my own flesh and blood Taylor. I saw what I did to him, so it made me very angry to do that kind of thing to him. I do regret it." He paused again to catch him breath.

"In conclusion, Becky didn't know I hacked into her computer and got access to her files or personal journals. It was how I was able to stay a step or two ahead of Brandon after he got involved with Sabrina's disappearance? I knew he would because he was an orphan himself. It's how I lured him in. Brad, his dad, told me years earlier that

Brandon wasn't his biological son, but he loved him very much because loving Wendy was the best thing in his life. I don't know why they never had a child of their own because we never discussed it. I know I have done wrong, your honor. I should be sentenced to life in prison without a possibility of parole. I took a life that I had no right taking. I'm also guilty on all the other accounts, too, your honor."

Jim placed his hands before him and stared at the judge now.

"Are you done, sir?" asked the judge.

"Yes, your honor," answered Jim.

"Then by the power invested in me from the State of New York, I find you James Barely guilty of all charges. I sentence you to the State of New York's Correctional Facility for life for the murder of Jill Claymore, kidnapping and child endangerment of a minor and illegal hacking into someone's personal computer for personal gain. This case is closed," the judge said, as his gavel hit the wood on his desk.

"No," cried out Beverly.

Jessica sat there with Sabrina on her lap. Brandon sat next to them. Taylor was next to him followed by Beverly then Wendy. Becky sat there stoned faced on other side of Wendy. Jessica glanced down at Beverly and saw tears in her eyes.

"James," Beverly cried out to him.

He turned to her and said, "I'll love you for the rest of my life. Taylor, I have no right to ask you this now after what I did to you. But I'm truly sorry, son. But I ask you to take care of your Mom. She must love us both very much to bring you into this world. I love you, too, Taylor."

Jim was led away by a guard out of the courtroom. Jessica motioned Sabrina up and took her little hand into hers. They walked out of the courtroom together. Becky walked with Wendy and Beverly. Taylor walked with Brandon behind everyone.

"That was unexpected," Ted said, as he walked up to Jessica and Sabrina. "We had..."

"Let's drop it, Ted," Jessica interrupted him. "Can't you see who's affected by it?"

Ted looked behind her then nodded. He walked away and met up with Joyce who stood by the main doors of the courthouse. Together, they walked out of building. Sabrina and Jessica stopped at the doors and waited.

Beverly stared at her and shook her head. Taylor walked closer and held out his hand to Beverly then pulled it back. But Beverly noticed his effort since her eyes weren't completely fixed on Jessica.

"Jim or James could be a loving man but also a funny man, too. It's two of the reasons I fell in love with him. But seeing and hearing him in the courtroom, it wasn't a man I knew and loved. I can't imagine James being angry and want revenge. Revenge he didn't explain in detail in the courtroom. But I know he does regret what he did to Sabrina and Taylor. That's the man I know and yes still love."

"But he asked Taylor to take care of you. I know, you and Taylor have been talking and ..."

"Find our way after sixteen years," interrupted Beverly. "But we're not getting through to each other. He still has some of his walls up, and I don't know how to reach him completely. He's very angry still."

"You said you didn't see or know of Jim's anger. Maybe you need to answer Taylor's one question he must have asked you already," replied Jessica.

"I know, I've been really avoiding it, but I guess it's worth a shot," Beverly said to her.

"Um... excuse me," Taylor said in hesitation. "Could I speak to you privately?"

Beverly nodded and followed Taylor. They walked out of the courthouse together. Sabrina took Brandon's hand into hers. She looked up and smiled at him.

"What are you thinking, little one?" he asked her.

"You and Jessica can adopt me," Sabrina answered thoughtfully. "I thought, I could settle for just Mommy, but now I want you to be part of our lives forever."

"No, this can't be happening. You said you and Jessica are only friends," Becky snapped back at Brandon. "Were you lying to me that day in your studio and in Paris?"

"No, I wasn't lying to you," Brandon answered calmly. "I had to sort out some things in past, and I didn't think I could be happy again."

"And you found it with her after knowing how I feel about you. You knew in Paris and here how I felt, but you wanted the pretty model. I'm out of here for good. I quit, Brandon. Goodbye," snapped Becky.

She marched out of the courthouse. Sabrina started to cry, so Jessica knelt before her to wipe away the tears.

"What's wrong, Sweetie?"

"Becky yelled at Daddy," Sabrina answered sadly. "She's never been mad at him before."

"Come here," Jessica replied, as she held out her arms for her to come to her.

Sabrina hugged her, and Jessica found herself humming to her. They walked out of the courthouse. Taylor and Beverly stared at each other.

"I'm taking her home," she told Brandon.

He nodded. He walked with Wendy now. He flagged for a taxi and gave the cabbie directions to Jessica's apartment and some money. Jessica held Sabrina in her lap. When they arrived at the apartment building, they walked hand and hand upstairs. Sabrina played with Teddy and was extremely quiet now. A soft knock was at her door now.

"Hi. How did it go?" asked Nathan.

"Jim admitted to the judge everything. He'll be spending the rest of his life behind bars," she whispered to him.

"She's quiet," Nathan said, as he walked in.

"Yes, Becky found out Brandon and I are together. She stormed out of the courthouse. I think it was too much for her to handle."

"What do you mean, Sis?" he asked with interest.

"Jim hacked into her personal computer and read her private journals. They revealed where Brandon was in the search for Sabrina. Plus Becky's true feelings for Brandon had been there, too. She feels betrayed by Jim, me and even Brandon. She yelled at Brandon in front of Sabrina."

"What a mess!"

"On top of it all, Sabrina wants Brandon and me to adopt her together as a couple."

"Oh crap!"

"Jessica, can we talk?" Brandon asked, as he stood behind Nathan now.

"I need to talk to Sabrina. I need to tell her what I've been working on since before she was found," she answered back, as she turned to look at Sabrina. "Sweetie, can I talk to you?"

Sabrina nodded. They walked over and sat down on the couch. Sabrina petted Teddy who jumped into her lap now. He purred loud.

"I've looked into and in the process of adoption," she explained carefully. "There are a lot of things to do before it could possibly happen. I'm doing my best."

"What if doesn't happen?" Sabrina asked her. "Taylor and I talked about being orphans and never finding homes. But he has Beverly now."

"You know we're going to keep a positive attitude and thinking to make you and me a family," Jessica answered confidently. "I want it, and you want it. So..."

"Uh...Mommy, do you believe in God?" Sabrina asked her.

"He created everything on the planet including us," Jessica answered back with a smile.

"Can we talk to him?"

"Uh...yes."

"Can I say something here?" asked Brandon.

"Of course."

Brandon focused on Sabrina now. She stared at him as she continued to pet Teddy. "God hears formal but also informal prayers. Mama told me that a long time ago. So he's waiting to hear your prayer anytime and anywhere," he said to her calmly.

"Say I tell God that I want you and Jessica to become my Mommy and Daddy. Is he hearing me now?" Sabrina asked him.

"Yes. But now understand he takes awhile to answer sometimes. But he's always choosing what's best for us, so it may not come out the way we want it to be," Brandon answered with a smile. "Do you understand me, little one?"

"So if I don't get adopted by Jessica as my Mommy then you and her can try adopting me as a couple," answered Sabrina.

"Let's leave it in his hands," replied Jessica.

"Yes, let's do that," said Brandon.

"Hey guys, I'm still here," said Nathan.

"Sorry Nat. I forgot you were there. Thanks for taking her to the zoo and everything else I might have overlooked."

"It's okay. So I might be her uncle if the paper work goes through," Nathan said to Jessica.

"Yes, they're doing background checks on all the people close to me, and how they will be a part of Sabrina's life," Jessica answered honestly. "I don't have any more secrets in my past. What about you guys?"

"Nada," answered Nathan.

"Nope, but I still need to talk to you about something," Brandon answered, as he stared at her now.

"Later," she replied back.

"Chubby Bear....Jessica whatever," Nathan stumbled to say.

"What's wrong?" she asked, as she focused on

Nathan.

"I faced him with what he did to me and Mom. They had him restrained to his bed. I told him what he did to me and Mom that we didn't deserve his abuse," Nathan answered quickly. "I think you should go back and confront him about

what he did to you, too. So you can move ahead, Sis."

"I agree," Brandon said, as he focused on her completely now.

"You both are insane," she replied, as she went to her window.

"Jennifer," Nathan called out to her. "Take them to your apartment please."

"Sabrina, bring Teddy with you. Let's go have some milk and cookies," Jennifer said, as she appeared at the doorway now.

Jessica glanced back at her. "It's okay, Sweetie. It's grown up stuff. Go with Teddy and Jenny."

Brandon took Teddy, and Sabrina took him back. She glanced over at Jessica. Jessica smiled. Jennifer, Sabrina and Teddy walked away. Jessica stared out the window again.

"Hadn't I had enough going back there for…"

"Sis," Nathan interrupted her calmly.

"Let me. Jessica, listen to me. You need closure with him. Nathan has and he will heal from it now," pointed out Brandon. "I wish I had told Brad that I still loved him. But I can't tell him that fact face to face, and you know why. My hot head got in the way, so I couldn't tell him. I needed to find my own way in life, and it wasn't following in his footsteps. I couldn't put it behind me and really move on until I told you. You helped me heal finally."He gulped hard as she stared at him now. She saw his face and Nathan's before he continued on. "I'm glad you told me. But now you need to face him. You need this behind if not just for yourself. There's a little girl who is counting on you being her real Mommy. But she needs a Mommy strong and healed within. Then we can address another issue."

"No more added pressure there," snapped Jessica. "Fine, I'll go back to California, but I'm doing it for Sabrina. Let's make it clear now. I'll do anything for her because Mom wasn't truly there for me. But I won't hide my past from her either like Mom did for decades. I won't let Sabrina's confidence or anything else be second guessed by anyone in this entire world. Do you understand me, gentleman?" She faced them now. They both nodded. "Good. Can you and Jennifer take care of her while I go back there?"

"Sure, Sis," Nathan answered back a little surprised.

"I'm going with you. We'll go in my plane," said Brandon.

"Fine, I'll tell Sabrina that we're going out of town for a few days. Book your flight plan and whatever else you have to do. I'm going to see Sabrina and Teddy. Please excuse me."

Jessica left the apartment and headed for Jennifer's. She knocked on the door, and Sabrina opened it. Teddy was at her side like always.

"Oh, come in," Jennifer said, as she walked by the

open door. "What's up?"

Jessica followed Sabrina and Teddy into the crowded apartment. She noticed boxes everywhere.

"Moving," she asked her.

"No. They're Nathan's files on his patients in California. The movers brought them here instead of the doctor who took over their cases. You didn't answer me. What's up?"

"Brandon and I are going out of town for a few days," she answered, as she stared at Sabrina. "But we'll be back, Sabrina. I promise you. I love you, Sweetie."

"I love you, Mommy," Sabrina said, as she hugged Jessica's legs.

"Where to?" asked Jennifer.

"California," Jessica answered honestly. "We have or I have some unfinished business there."

Jennifer moved another box, "With him."

She nodded, as she picked up Sabrina. "I'm going to miss you and Teddy so much. But remember this you're loved always."

They hugged each other tight then laughed. Meow. They looked down at him then hugged him, too.

"We have one stop before we leave town," Brandon said, as he stood at the open door with Nathan.

"Those boxes need to go back," said Nathan. "Do you mind?"

"Not at all," Brandon answered with a small smile. "But this isn't what I was referring to."

"Yeah, I know. Hold on a second," Nathan said, as he headed for Jennifer's spare room.

"What's up?" asked Jennifer.

"You two and him get your best clothes on," Brandon answered, as he stared at Jessica, Sabrina and Teddy now.

"Hold these," Nathan said, as he held a box out to Brandon.

"Our rings?"

"This our day now go get changed. Brandon arranged for a judge to marry us in her chambers in a couple hours. Go," Nathan answered, as he slapped her butt.

"Jess, it's happening today," Jennifer said with excitement.

"Go change. Let's go, Sabrina. Teddy," Jessica replied back. "Give us fifteen."

"Sounds good," Brandon said with a big smile now.

"Oh, crap. Where's my suit?" asked Nathan.

"Coat closet, babe," Jennifer answered from her bedroom.

"I'll have some more calls to make," Brandon said, as Jessica, Sabrina and Teddy passed him.

Jessica flew into her bedroom to her closet. Sabrina was behind her with Teddy.

"Why not this?" asked Sabrina.

"Uh...looks good," she answered in hesitation.

"Yours looks still good," Sabrina said, as she looked at her.

Jessica slipped out of her dress and into a green one quickly. She stepped into her low heel black pumps before she headed for the front door. Then she darted back into the bathroom for two hair bands and was back at her door again. Sabrina stood there with Teddy in her arms.

"I'll put this on you on the way over," she replied, as she motioned her outside the door.

Sabrina nodded. Brandon picked up Sabrina and Teddy in the hallway. Jessica closed and locked her door. Jennifer had her eyes closed.

"What's wrong?" Jessica asked her.

"I don't want to see Nathan, yet."

"He's in the limo front seat," answered Brandon. "Yes, I called the mansion earlier. I'll be changing into a dress shirt and tie also coat. Let's go ladies."

Jennifer opened her eyes, and Jessica took her hand. They rushed downstairs to the waiting limo. Brandon opened the backdoor and shielded Jennifer from Nathan's eye. He stared at Jessica and looked nervous as hell now. They got into the back, and Jessica put a hair band in Sabrina's hair.

"I don't have anything blue," Jennifer cried out.

"Here," Jessica replied calmly. "I figured you wanted something traditional. I'll put yours in after hers."

"Thanks Jess."

"No problem. We're done, Sweetie. There's a ribbon in my purse for Teddy," Jessica replied with a big smile now. "Next."

Brandon slipped off his polo shirt and put on his white dress shirt. She noticed his deep, rich brown tan that she hadn't seen since Spain. She shook her head and proceeded to put the finishing touches on Jennifer's hair.

"We're here," Brandon said to them. "Teddy. Sabrina, come with me. Nathan and I are going to carry you. It's faster that way. Nathan won't have time to look at his bride who looks stunning by the way."

"Hey..."said Nathan.

"Take Teddy and move, man. I've got Sabrina. March ahead and don't look back," ordered Brandon.

"This is a side of him I haven't seen before," Jessica replied, as she got out and helped Jennifer in her off white dress with some lace at the collar.

"Stick with him, Jess. I'm sure there's more to come," Jennifer said with a big smile. "I'm getting married today, Jess."

Jessica didn't remember much of the ceremony since she stared at Brandon through most of the service. Now Nathan and Jennifer were married, and she and Brandon were on his plane. She glanced out the window now as she felt someone take her hand.

"Easy, Jessica," Brandon whispered, as he stared at her now.

"Who..."

"I do have a real pilot fly sometimes," he interrupted her. "I didn't want to leave your side for a second. I know this is going to be hard and painful, but I'm here for you always."

"But..."

"Close your eyes. Sabrina and Teddy are fine. I called them. We'll be there in a few hours."

She closed her eyes and rested her head on his shoulder. He hummed a light unrecognizable tune to her. She fell into a deep sleep as he held her hand in his. It had been several hours later, and Jessica sat in the care home. They wheeled Arnold out.

"Hi, baby doll," he said to her, as the orderly and

he got closer.

"Hi, Arnold," she replied, as she got up to kiss him on the cheek. "How are you?"

"Can't complain," he answered back. "You look beautiful. What's the occasion?"

"My best friend and twin brother Nathan got married earlier today in New York," she answered with a smile.

"Good for him. When's yours, Honey?"

"I don't think so."

"But that's what your Mom wanted for you. She loved you and Nathan so much. She knew he was unfaithful to her but didn't know with whom. Then she found out, and it hurt her deeply. But she didn't blame the other person but him that was odd for me understand."

"Did she tell you who?" Jessica asked, as she sat up straighter.

"No, she took it with her. Why are you here?"

"To see him one final time."

"He's been in and out of it since the last time you were here last week. So you won't be coming back to see me either?"

"No, I'll make an effort to see you as often as I can," she answered with a bright smile. "You knew, cared and loved my nom, so you're a big part of my life now."

Arnold smiled back. "You have her smile, you know."

"They're ready, Jessica," Brandon said, as he walked up. "Hi, Arnold, do you want to play chess or checkers today?"

"Do I know how to play them, sonny?" Arnold

asked, as he looked up at Brandon.

"We'll give one of them a try then if that one doesn't work we try the other. Okay?" Brandon answered back, as he winked at Jessica. "I'll be here when you're done."

She got up and kissed Arnold and Brandon on their cheeks before she walked down to his room. She felt her stomach flip and flop and a lump in her throat as she pushed open the door. They had restrained him, as she approached the bed.

"Uh…" she replied in hesitation.

Dillon smiled at her. "Hi, Piggy Wiggy, let's do it here. Nobody's watching us. We've missed you."

"No more! It should have never have happened in the first place. Mom knew about it because you told her as you beat her up at the house. You killed her here. Why? Why, bastard?" she asked, as she stepped back to the door.

"I didn't kill her," Dillon answered back. "I went to see her, and she wanted him. I…"

"Your friend, she could have done fine without you. She had hopes and dreams too, but you took her away from Arnold who loved her with his whole heart and soul. Tell the truth for once in your damn life. You intended to get her pregnant so no man but you could have her. But you didn't stop there. Did you, bastard?" Jessica asked in anger.

"What's going on here?" a woman dressed in a white uniform asked, as she stood at the door.

"Get the hell out of here!" Jessica exclaimed, as she turned to face her. "Don't make me say it again."

The nurse eased herself out the door, and Jessica stared at Dillon now.

"She wanted Arnold. I couldn't take her being still in love with him after all these years. I had to screw her, so she would remember our sex life wasn't the best but good no less. You are the best screw ever. I couldn't get enough of you, Piggy Wiggy. No other man will want you the way we do. I truly love..." Dillon said with tears in his eyes now.

"No. You're wrong about that. Fathers and daughters don't do what we did. You disgust me. I questioned it then that's why I left here over twelve years ago. Somewhere deep inside me I knew it was wrong, and you weren't going to stop. So I left, but Mom and Nathan suffered because of it. You're animal not a man. I never want to see you ever again." She caught her breath and pressed on. "I've fallen in love, and we haven't done it yet. I don't know where this relationship will lead, but I'm going to ride it out for however long it lasts. Anything is better than what you did to me, and the way I cut myself off from people knowing the real Jessie Hudson behind the professional model Jessica Hudson. We're done forever. But why did you kill her?"

"She wouldn't stop saying his name, as I got inside. I wanted her to realize it was me releasing in her not him. But she wouldn't let it go, so I killed her. I know I released two maybe three times before she died."

"You're sick, Dillon. You're going to rot in hell," she replied, as she walked out of his room.

Jessica began to shake but found Brandon alone. She ran to him, and he held out his arms. He held her close to him. She could feel his heart beat against her cheek.

"You're safe now," he whispered to her.

"Where's Arnold?"

"Hush, he was taken back to his room. He's slipping away from us," he whispered softly.

"I faced him with what he did to me. I asked him why he killed her. She thought of Arnold," she replied, as she cried. "He was still on her mind after all these years."

"I'm sorry, Jessica."

"Can we tell them to contact us back in New York about Arnold's status?"

"Yes. We can do anything you want. It's okay with me. I'm here for you like I said I would."

"I know, and thank you."

"Anytime," Brandon said calmly. "Do you want a civil or traditional ceremony?"

"What?" she asked a little confused, as she gazed up at his face.

"Will you marry me, Jessica?"

"Are you sure?"

He nodded.

"Yes," she answered with a small smile. "And traditional, I think Mom would have wanted it for me."

"Then that's what we will have, my love. Let's go home and plan the wedding of your dreams. I don't know if we'll have the half dozen kids and life you wanted, but I do. I want to make you happy Jessica for the rest of your life," Brandon said, as he gazed deep into her eyes. "You gave me hope again when I thought I lost it forever."

"And you gave me a future that I thought slipped away from me forever. Thank you. I love you, Brandon Foster."

They left the care home after giving their information to contact them about Arnold and headed back to New York and their life there. Jessica returned to the place she called home.

Epilogue

It had been over two years since things spun out of control for Jessica Hudson. But it all brought her to this point in her life, and she couldn't be happier. She stared out on the back Terrance to see Sabrina.

Sabrina was seven now and well-adjusted since her kidnapping. She had stopped screaming out for Jessica within days of their 'I dos' meaning Brandon and Jessica's. It was four days into the New Year. Two days later it was official Sabrina would be theirs forever.

Taylor was eighteen and enrolled in a culinary school to be a chef and was truly happy to have Beverly as his Mom. In the past two years, they managed to make up for the lost sixteen years that they weren't together.

Beverly smiled and laughed more when people saw her and Taylor together. He was the center of her world despite her career was still thieving. But Jessica wondered what was in the back of Beverly's mind since she visited Jim in prison four sometime five days out of the each month.

Brandon convinced Mama or Wendy to move back to the mansion to help raise Sabrina. He too had seemed to be healing from his past with Rebecca and Brad. Jessica noticed a few white hairs at Brandon's temples. But she didn't fuse over them. His happiness was all that mattered to her now.

"Jessie," Wendy whispered to her.

"Uh Mama," she replied, as she smiled at her

mother-in-law.

"You seem even happier since Steven was born," Wendy said with a smile.

"Stevie is wonderful and so is my life since I fell in love with your son, Mama."

"You two had twelve years to let that love grow and didn't realize it had. Brandon seems so at peace now and so have you, Jessie. I'm so glad you have allowed us who are close to you to be less formal now. So we don't have to say it without you being on edge. And he cradles Steven in his arms so naturally just like he was in mine. But I often wonder how you two arrived with that name for Steven."

"Steven is the male version of Stephanie, and Mom's first love was Arnold. She never admitted it to Nathan when we were teenagers. But Arnold told me the truth, and I don't hold it against Mom. So I decided I wanted to honor them both," she explained very confidently.

"Do you think she's at peace now?" asked Wendy.

"Yes finally. Arnold had asked to be buried next to her. I honored his wishes since he truly loved her."

"What about..."

"Him. We buried him with his parents and sister," Jessie interrupted her.

"You better go out there with that video camera. They only do that a short time then it's gone forever, Jessie," Wendy said, as she touched her arm.

Jessie stepped out onto the Terrance now. Her eyes focused on them and only them now.

"Hey, Stevie, Mommy's coming with the camera

again," Sabrina said to a little boy Brandon supported with his hands connecting to each other between his legs.

"Ma Ma," Stevie said with a big smile, as she held the camera closer to her eye.

"Hi, baby," she replied with a big smile, too.

Teddy rubbed against Stevie and Brandon. They all laughed as he looked back at the camera and meowed.

"Where's the big birthday boy?" Nathan asked, as he stepped onto the Terrance, too.

Brandon released his little hands, as Stevie waddled over to Nathan. Teddy and Sabrina followed close behind him. So Jessie focused on them all now.

"Don't get me in that shot," warned Jennifer.

Stephanie walked up and hugged Stevie, as he fell on his little butt. He stared at everyone before he laughed, so everyone laughed with him. Jenny had become self-conscious of how she looked after Stephanie was born. Jenny was a manager of a Starbucks now but also a wife and Mom and knew image was everything at work.

Jessie shut the camera off and stood tall again. Brandon stood beside her with a big smile on his face, too. But before they could exchange words Bridget, Stanley and their children arrived for the big celebration.

"How's the shuttle business?" Brandon asked Stanley.

"Growing each day, thanks for the backing," Stanley answered, as they shook hands.

"I'm glad we moved to New York," Bridget said to Jessie. "It gives you two a chanced to be with your godson."

"Yes, it's nice," replied Jessie.

"Where are Ted and Joyce?" Bridget asked her.

"They'll be here along with Ryan than most of us," she answered, as she smiled at her.

"Ah, the single life," commented Brandon.

"Do you miss it, my love?" Jessie asked, as she gazed up at him.

"No. This is the life for to grow old with you at my side forever," Brandon answered, as he kissed her.

"Well put, man," Ted said with a smile.

"Good to see you and Joyce. Are you two still dating?" asked Bridget.

"Two weeks ago in a civil ceremony at the courthouse. Don't you remember the surprise wedding we invited you all to?" asked Ted.

"That's right I remember now," Bridget answered now with a nod of her head.

"Where are Danni and Susan?" Joyce asked with a big friendly smile.

"They'll be here," answered Jessie. "Oh there, they are with Mama now. Excuse me."

She walked over and hugged them both. Danni held out a card.

"For the birthday, boy," Danni said with a bright smile. "I figured you know what's best of your son?"

"Thank you, Danni," she replied back. "I'm glad you two came."

"Wouldn't miss it for the world," Susan said, as she looked at Sabrina. "She's really happy now. Isn't she?"

"Yes, she seems to be and loves having a little brother," Jessie answered, as she stared her with Stevie and the other children.

"Did you plan to have children, Jessie?" asked Danni.

"Half dozen if I recall correctly, she wanted them to beat me up," answered Nathan. "But you have at least one biological and one adopted, Sis. You deserve your happiness after what you went through with him."

"So do you, Nat," she replied with a smile for him.

"Thanks, Sis," he said with a gleam in his eye now. "You're going to be an aunt again."

"Oh that wonderful," she replied, as she hugged him.

"Jenny has mixed feeling about it," he added calmly. "Whatever happened to Becky who was his assistant?"

"No one knows after Jim's trial. She seemed to vanish, but Brandon seems to think she needs time to sort out her feelings for him. Plus she got the blow of being the leak. But I hope someday she will be back again in our lives. She was good to me during my modeling career. I hope I can tell her that I don't blame her for how it all came about with Jim."

"That's the loving and caring sister I remember before things changed. I love you, Jessie," he said, as he kissed her on the forehead. "So what's to eat, Sis?"

"It's in Taylor's hands. He asked Brandon to pay the bills as they came in while he planned it all between school and working at Mama's Pizza Shack. But Brandon made only one request."

"What was that?" Susan asked with curiosity.

"Some hand held food for the most part since we have a kid's birthday party here."

"Good thinking," Susan said with a smile.

Beverly stood at a distance and gazed at Taylor. Jessie noticed her at Helen approached her. They exchanged words now. People started to gather up into small groups. They watched Taylor start to place trays on the two long tables but didn't approach. He noticed them all and smiled, as he headed back to work but stopped for second first.

"Come on everyone," Taylor called out in a loud but confident voice.

So they slowly walked up to the tables. Brandon picked up Sabrina who held Teddy. So Jessie picked Stevie who tugged at her long, brown hair. She had dyed it back to its original color when she and Brandon got married.

"What do we have all here?" Brandon asked him.

"Well here we have Mac and cheese which is made with three different kinds of cheese by the way," Taylor started to explain. "Feta cheese and Canadian beacon on whole wheat pizza dough over there. Three cheeses triangles and cheese and spinach baked in filo. Then we have tomatoes, Greek olives, cucumbers and red onions as a salad topped with Feta cheese and a light olive oil. Then the kabobs have chicken and lamb with no fat on the meat with vegs and red and green bell peppers with hums sauce on the side. Original and garlic flavors in the bowls beside the kabobs for you to dip the meat and vegs in. Next is sautéed in olive oil fresh vegetables and finally Greek French fries with garlic, parsley and Feta cheese. So enjoy everyone."

"Wow!" Brandon exclaimed in amazement.

"Why the Greek theme mostly, Taylor?" asked

Wendy.

"I got the DNA tests on Brandon's genetic make-up. Thanks for the help Ted and Joyce couldn't have done it without your help," he answered calmly and confidently. "He has Greek and French in him. Nathan told me of your Mom's background being Spanish, French-Canadian and Greek, Jessie. So then I added a few dishes of you and Nathan's past Mac and cheese and homemade pizza. I wanted to surround Steven with his heritage, and who he will be someday. This is your legacy to your son Jessie and Brandon. He will lead his generation from working class America to blue collar America with pride and not be ashamed of where he came from because you see, we all have roots to whom we are, and who we can be."

Jessie allowed the tears flow freely down her face now. She started towards him with Stevie still in her arms. But he held out his hand to her, so she stopped within inches of him.

"I'm not done," he said, as he clapped his hands.

A cart rolled out with a cake on it. The two servants who helped him stepped away, as he encouraged her forward. Jessie glanced down to see colorful roses on the edges and in the center in royal blue icing: **Steven Arnold**.

"That's your name, Stevie," she whispered to him.

Stevie squealed in delight as he leaned towards the cake. But she held onto him firmly.

"It's chocolate and white cake layered thinly with grape jelly in between since our birthday boy loves grape so much."

Taylor smiled at Jessie now. Brandon was at her side again but Sabrina stood next to him with Teddy in her arms. Brandon took their son from her arms, so Jessie rushed up and hugged him tightly. He squeezed her back.

"But I still have one more thing," he whispered into her ear.

She pulled back and stared at him. "No more." She started to protest. "My heart can't take..."

"It's my gift to Stevie, but later when it's dark out. But this is for you, Jessie now. Open it," he said calmly.

"No not now but later. After Stevie's in bed and the party is over. This is his day not mine."

"Very well, but we will make time for this," he said seriously.

"I promise."

Music started to play now. Everyone started to enjoy the food and company. Jenny even allowed a few pictures be taken of her with Stevie, Nathan, Brandon and Jessie but also Sabrina and Teddy because they were all family. People danced, laughed and played like kids again. As the sun faded and a colorful sunset formed in the distance, jackets, sweaters and blankets appeared out of nowhere. The cool, crisp air made Jessie headed inside with Stevie.

She slipped him into his pjs and a sweatshirt that had sea lion's head on it. She smiled. It was a gift from Taylor after he and Beverly traveled out to California a month ago. They used it as a way of sealing their bond even stronger as Mom and son. Jessie slipped on a flannel shirt over her navy blue dress that she wore all day. Stevie smiled from his crib.

"It's Daddy's," she replied, as she smiled at him. "Let's go find Daddy and Brie."

Stevie giggled, as she picked him up again. They walked back onto the Terrance which had colorful lights everywhere. His eyes danced with delight, excitement and a squeal.

"Here's the man of the hour or should I say day," Brandon said, as he walked up to them. "I love you both so very much."

"We know. Where's Brie?"

"Sleeping on the lounge chair by Nathan, Jenny and Stephanie."

"Jenny's pregnant again," she whispered to him. "How do you feel about that, my love?"

"I'm okay with it. We adopted Sabrina, and we were blessed to have Steven. If we want more, we can ask Susan to help us adopted one legally. Otherwise, I'm happy with our life together. Are you?"

"Yes very much so, my love. I'm very..."

"Ladies and gentleman and for all the kids here, this is my gift to you, Steven Arnold," Taylor announced in a clear, loud voice.

Fireworks filled the fall sky. Each one more colorful than the one before, Stevie pointed to them as they spread out across the sky. Taylor walked over to them with a big smile.

"What do you give a little guy who can have anything he wants?" he asked them.

"Without the silver spoon dangling out of his mouth," Jessie answered with a small not serious smile.

"I remember you saying that about me once long ago," commented Brandon. "But Mama never did that with me, I'm afraid. She kept me grounded my whole life despite I wanted to free of her and Brad as I hit my teens."

"Are you saying you're getting old?" asked Taylor.

"No just remembering our history," Brandon answered with a smile.

"They're so beautiful," replied Jessie. "He seems to be really enjoying them."

"It seems so," said Taylor, "Time for the last ones."

Colors filled the sky with a Greek, Spain, French and Canadian but lastly an American flags. They disappeared as quickly as they arrived. Taylor looked back at Brandon and Jessie.

"That was beautiful, Taylor," replied Jessie.

"We have some unfinished business, Jessie," he said to her.

"I'll take him to bed then. I'll be back for Sabrina," Brandon said, as he took Stevie.

They walked into the house. Friends and family slowly followed him to their rooms. Yes, they were house guests because Jessie didn't want anyone driving into the City after eight. The mansion had twelve bedrooms in all, so there was plenty of room. Eight rooms were vacant most of the time.

"Jessie," Taylor said, as he held out the box again.

"All right, a promise is a promise," she replied, as she took it from him.

She opened it and her jaw dropped in shock. She glanced at it and struggled to hold onto the box. He guided her to a chair.

"It's stunning," she replied, as she found the words to say finally.

"It's your Mom's birthstone and you and Nathan's

on each side followed by Brandon's, Sabrina's, Jennifer's, Stephanie's and their unborn child's. Perfect circle since she's the root of your and Nathan being here," he explained with a confident smile.

"Why?" she asked, as she looked up at him.

"You took me as I was when I told you about my life. You were my bright spot of hope not to say Wendy and Jennifer and even Brandon, but you were and are a true friend. I'm sure they all questioned you what my question was for my Mom. But you held it dear to your heart and very soul. So your light was brighter than all three of them combined. So I wanted to give you something special this night of all nights that I could pick from in my life since you entered my life."

"Again why?" she asked confused.

"I told you about my life not being so pretty on the streets. I had just rescued you from Clifford."

"I remember now but enough said. Thank you. Will you put it on me?"

He nodded and lifted it out of the box and placed it on her left wrist. Then he stepped back. She dropped the box and hugged him.

"I love you, Taylor always and forever," she whispered into his right ear, "Don't ever forget that, young man."

"I won't," he said, as he stared at her when they stood face to face now.

"Excuse me, Taylor," Brandon said politely.

Taylor nodded and walked by him. Brandon took hold of his arm. They exchanged looks.

"Thanks for everything today. It was great."

"It was my pleasure. Do you remember that island in Greece?"

"Can you be more specific?"

"Krete, I was able to link it to you. I thought you should know. Goodnight, Jessie, Brandon," he said, as he continued his walk.

Brandon had released his hold, and they watched him picked up Sabrina. Teddy followed them into the house. So Brandon walked up closer to her and led her to front part of the house now without a word exchanged. Jessie enjoyed walking with him. It was their time a lone time. But tonight he seemed to be in very much deep thought than passed nights. She noticed the look was different.

"Jessie," he said, as they headed down the long driveway.

"Yes, my love."

"You and I have traveled an interesting life to say in the least. Right?" he asked, as he turned to her.

She nodded and still focused on him.

"It has been a wild ride that led us here. I came back here to raise my or our children. I could do it with you at my side. I've given a lot of thought of what Taylor said today. I don't want to tell our children to go to college and follow their grandfather's footsteps. Heck, I didn't, and he wasn't even my real father. But I did love and care about him like he did about me. You were right about that. But our kids must find their own path like I did and you did, too. Do you regret leaving the modeling industry to marry me? Wait don't answer that just yet. Let me finish. Does any of what I'm saying make sense to you?"

"No, and it does make sense to me, my love."

They reached the main gates and looked at the Oak tree. He walked over and touched it.

"Remembering Rebecca?" she asked him.

"No. I wanted to take you in my arms that day we dropped off the ransom and kiss you like no other man had before."

"But you didn't."

"You walked away in your own thoughts, so I backed away despite I wanted to know all aspects of your life."

"I was startled when I touched the Iron gates. I saw Mama, a man and a small boy when Jenny and I came out here before you brought me here. I didn't know it was you, Brad and Mama at the time. I was confused," replied Jessica. "I walked away because you were also in your own thoughts that day, too. I didn't want to press you to share it."

"We have company," he said in a calm voice.

"Uh..."

A dark figure stopped closer to them now. Jessie saw a thin shape appeared closer to Brandon then her.

"Hi, guys," the female voice said to them.

"Becky?" Jessie asked a little stunned.

"Yes. It has been awhile," Becky answered calmly.

"How are you?" asked Brandon.

"Fine, you know, I had to leave back then. It was hard to see you two together as a couple. Then how Jim kept one or two steps ahead of you in finding Sabrina because of my computer I wish I hadn't..."

"Listen you didn't know he would get access to

your computer journals. You thought they were private and safe from anyone's eyes but your own. I don't hold it against you," interrupted Jessie. "I've missed you being my friend. I meant it when I said we were friends. It still stands now. Are you coming back here to stay?"

"I don't know yet, but I had to see you both alone and give you this," Becky answered, as she held out a package.

Brandon took it and passed it onto Jessie. Where had she opened it to find a picture frame, so she stepped into the moonlight to have a better look at the photo in there? It was the three of them in Spain. She smiled, as it and held it out to Brandon. He looked at it and smiled, too.

"We were happy at the end of that assignment. We vowed to be friends forever no matter where our careers took us," Brandon said thoughtfully. "Thank you, Becky."

"Yes, thank you. It still stands you know friendship forever."

"It was the first time with your own camera on a tripod," Brandon recalled, as he blurted it out.

"Yes, but I hardly ever picked it up after that. I was too busy admiring your skill as a photographer. You were and are so much better than me," said Becky. "I couldn't compare."

"Don't talk like that," said Jessie. "Remember you helped me in Paris. I knew nothing about photography, but you got me hooked."

"What do you mean?" asked Becky.

"She takes a lot of the movies and stills at the gatherings like today instead of me," answered Brandon. "She's gotten really good since Steven was born."

"Steven?" asked Becky. "Don't answer that."

"Becky, please let us know where you are when you're ready," Brandon said seriously to her.

"I'll think about it," Becky said in a faint voice before she walked away from them.

Silence of their voices was the order of the night now. The only sound was of the light breeze would remind them that they were in the fall time of year. She knew Brandon was in his own thoughts now about Becky. They had known each other before they met. Now Becky came and went again, and she didn't tell them whether she would be back in their lives.

"We have our closure now, I guess," Jessie replied thoughtfully.

"I guess so," he said thoughtfully, too. "But we are happy. Right, Jessie?"

"Yes very happy, my love. I want her to be happy someday, too."

"That's nice of you to say," he said, as he kissed her.

She gazed deep into his eyes and smiled. She touched his hair lightly.

"What?"

"I was remembering what Mama has always said the heart knows what it wants and needs and follow your heart. I said once she was a wise woman back then to my Mom. She agreed. I still think she is. I only wish I knew what my Mom thought when it came to matters of the heart."

"You still have the black book with the poem she wrote the day you and Nathan were born. Is there more?"

"I don't know. It's in our library with all my other books I read in recent months. I never thought of looking through it."

"Maybe you should," he said with a smile. "You know I love you, Jessie."

"I know."

They held each other close then walked up to the mansion hand in hand.

FOLLOW YOUR HEART

www.ingramcontent.com/pod-product-compliance
Lightning Source LLC
Chambersburg PA
CBHW070806030726
47504CB00003B/715